Heidi Stephens has spent her career working in advertising and marketing; some of her early writing work includes instruction manuals for vacuum cleaners, saucepans and sex toys. Since 2008 she has also freelanced as a journalist and, on autumnal weekend evenings, can be found liveblogging *Strictly Come Dancing* for *The Guardian*. Her debut novel, *Two Metres From You*, won the 2022 Katie Fforde Debut Romantic Novel Award. She lives in Wiltshire with her partner and her Labrador, Mabel.

By Heidi Stephens

Two Metres From You
Never Gonna Happen
The Only Way Is Up
Game, Set, Match

HEIDI STEPHENS

GAME, SET, MATCH

ACCENT

First published in 2023 by Headline Accent
An imprint of HEADLINE PUBLISHING GROUP

1

Cataloguing in Publication Data is available from the British Library

ISBN 978 1 4722 9358 9

Typeset in 11.6/15pt Bembo Std by Jouve (UK), Milton Keynes

Printed and bound in Great Britain by Clays Ltd, Elcograf S.p.A.

HEADLINE PUBLISHING GROUP
An Hachette UK Company
Carmelite House
50 Victoria Embankment
London EC4Y 0DZ

www.headline.co.uk
www.hachette.co.uk

To my fellow TITS ladies – thanks for
all the tennis and good times

PART ONE

First Set

CHAPTER ONE

'We need to talk,' said Hannah, pulling the pin out of each word and tossing it over the furniture like a tiny grenade. She hovered in the doorway between the lounge and the kitchen, wondering if any phrase in the English language was a bigger red flag for impending doom. Nothing good ever followed *we need to talk*.

Hannah waited for the explosion to go off, staring at the back of Graham's head on the teal sofa. There was no indication that he'd felt the impact, or in fact that he'd heard her speak at all. His gaze remained firmly fixed on the rugby match playing on TV, and the only sign that he wasn't dead was a brief lifting of his right arm in a half-hearted wave.

Her gaze shifted to his feet on the coffee table, and the big toe protruding through a hole in one of his socks. A wave of annoyance washed over her – he was thirty-two years old, for goodness' sake. Why couldn't he sew it up, or better yet, buy a new pair? Presumably he was waiting for her to do it, and after fourteen years of compensating for his abundant flaws, it felt like the sock that broke the camel's back.

'Hey, Han,' he said airily, still not turning to look at her. 'I saw you got some chicken out for dinner – was I supposed to do something with that?'

'We talked about it yesterday,' said Hannah through gritted teeth. 'You were going to make a curry.'

'Yeah, that's not happening,' said Graham. 'Oh, come on, that was obviously a knock-on. This referee is either blind or stupid.'

'So what are you making instead?' Hannah didn't actually want dinner with Graham; right now the thought of watching him eat made her feel sick. But that wasn't the point.

'We can still have a curry, I'll just get it Deliverooed.'

'We had takeaway pizza on Tuesday. You were supposed to cook then, too.'

Reluctantly, Graham dragged his eyes away from the TV and glanced round to offer a hard stare. 'Han, don't nag, OK? I want to watch this, and then I want to eat. If you want to cook, feel free. But if it's my turn to do dinner you don't get to decide where it comes from.'

Graham's attention drifted back to the thirty men trampling through her collapsed scrum of a marriage. Hannah looked at the protruding toe again, pink and shiny like a newborn vole. His toenails needed cutting.

'I don't want to be married to you any more.' She waited nervously, not entirely sure whether she'd said those words out loud, or just in her head.

'Sure,' Graham replied absently, raking at his neck with his fingernails. 'Come on, are you BLIND? That was obviously a high tackle.'

'Great, so let's agree to get divorced as soon as possible.' OK, that was definitely out loud. The grenades clearly hadn't worked, so she imagined the words bobbing across the room like helium balloons, then bonking him repeatedly on the head.

Graham vented his frustration at the TV in a series of

4

incoherent noises, then finally turned to face her. 'This is the worst match I've ever watched. What did you say?'

Hannah held his gaze, still leaning against the doorframe. 'I said I don't want to be married to you any more, and we should get divorced as soon as possible.'

'What the . . .?' The colour drained from Graham's face. 'Where did that come from?' He reached out for the remote and finally silenced the TV, almost falling over in his haste to stand up. He hurried around the end of the sofa and made a move towards her, then changed his mind, like she might have lethal objects hidden about her person. 'Are you serious?'

'Yes,' said Hannah, swallowing hard to stop her voice from wavering. 'You're cheating on me, for starters, so clearly you don't love me. But aside from that, I don't love you either. So yes, Graham, I'm entirely serious.'

His face turned from ghostly white to bright red, like he'd pulsed it in a blender. 'What . . .? How . . .? I don't . . .'

'You've been sleeping with Lucy from your office for six months,' said Hannah, her jaw clenched. 'She called me earlier to tell me she's now four months pregnant and apparently you're being awful about it.'

'I . . .' spluttered Graham, who was now visibly sweating. 'Lucy's not very stable, she's . . .'

Hannah held up a hand to silence him. 'She gave me dates and times and forwarded me text messages.' She furiously blinked away the tears as she thought about the texts Lucy had sent her; some featuring endearments Graham had once used for her, and others that were considerably more . . . colourful. The kind of words that she couldn't even say in her head without fear of being struck by lightning.

Graham retreated behind the sofa, rubbing his hands

across his face. 'Look, Han,' he said, panic bubbling in his voice. 'I know it looks bad, but it's not what you think.'

Hannah gave a hollow laugh, tucking her hands under her armpits to hide the shaking. She needed to get out of here. 'I mean, I'm pretty sure it's exactly what I think. So I'm going to Sainsbury's to get myself something for dinner, and I'd like you to be packed and gone by the time I get back.'

'But—' Hannah turned to leave, her heart pounding in her ears and bile rising in her throat. 'Hannah!' he called one last time, but he didn't follow.

'Are you OK?' said a man's voice, his hand reaching out to gently touch Hannah's arm. She jumped and looked up. He was only in his early twenties, not much older than her brother Luke. Wearing a Sainsbury's maroon and orange jacket with a badge that said 'Mo'.

'Sorry?' Hannah looked around, momentarily blinded by the supermarket lighting.

'You've been staring at that broccoli for ages,' said Mo. 'And you're squashing that avocado into guacamole.'

'Really?' Hannah's laugh sounded a little manic, her curls bobbing into her eyes as she frantically shook her head to dislodge the buzzing in her ears.

'Yeah. I just wanted to make sure you were OK.'

Hannah forced a smile. 'Sorry. I was miles away. I'm fine.'

Mo nodded, looking a bit disappointed. Hannah wondered if he'd just got his Mental Health First Aid certificate and was primed to deal with his first woman having a nervous breakdown in Aisle Two.

Throwing the broccoli and the mashed avocado into her basket, she hurried off, suddenly conscious that her tennis skirt barely covered her backside. She'd been ready for her 6 p.m. tennis lesson when Lucy had called, but she hadn't gone, obviously. Instead she'd sat in her car for an hour, taking deep breaths and planning how to deal with Graham.

Hannah chucked some prawns in too, the cold from the supermarket fridges giving her goosebumps. She'd grown up in a household where modesty was paramount, and every inch of exposed skin was noted and discussed at length. Her parents had both been members of a fringe church, one of the more ardently evangelical ones, and for a long time church people were the extent of her friends and family.

Graham's family had been members of the church too, and the two of them had grown up catching each other's eye at prayer meetings and interminable sermons, more out of a mutual desperation than any real attraction. They'd married when they were eighteen, an unspoken pact to save each other from a suffocating lifestyle that neither of them had the disposition for. Hannah had too much passion and spirit for a life of fervent worship, and Graham not nearly enough. It was a terrible reason to get married, and fourteen years later Hannah could only marvel that they'd dragged it out for so long.

Right now she felt surprisingly calm, like she'd disconnected herself from everything and was floating above the chaos in a world where her only priority was selecting the first meal of the rest of her life. She looked at the basket – sugar snap peas, mushrooms, broccoli, avocado, baby sweetcorn, prawns. Not the most celebratory of meals, maybe, but also everything that Graham either hated or was allergic to. But that was fine, because this was a dinner that she definitely wasn't going to be sharing.

★

Graham's Audi was still in the driveway when she got back, which was no great surprise to Hannah. He might specialise in wills and mortgage conveyancing rather than having his day in court, but he was still a lawyer and could talk a good game when the occasion demanded it. Presumably he'd spent the last forty minutes polishing his defence.

'You're still here,' she observed, dumping her bag for life on the kitchen counter.

'I know, but we need to talk about this,' said Graham, filling the doorway with his big frame. He'd played rugby at university, spurning offers of beer-fuelled sessions with the team in favour of returning home to dinner cooked by his teenage wife. Hannah noticed that he'd changed out of his joggers into jeans, a clean shirt and a pair of socks that were hole-free. He was handsome in a scruffy, bear-like way, and as a teenager she'd convinced herself that escape was the primary objective, and love and physical attraction would come later. It had never happened, but she'd tried her best to make it work anyway.

'Lucy doesn't mean anything to me,' he said beseechingly, launching into his pre-prepared speech. 'It was just a stupid fling, the stress of work. I'm not even sure it's my baby. We can work it out.'

Hannah set her face to *implacable*. 'No, we can't. The thing is, Graham, I'm not really asking for a divorce because you got Lucy pregnant. I'm asking for a divorce because when I heard you'd got Lucy pregnant, I realised I didn't care.'

Graham said nothing for a moment, his mouth hanging open and his eyes boggling as he searched for loopholes in this damning response. 'OK, wow,' he gasped, holding up the palms of his hands and backing away. 'That's an awful thing to say.'

'I know, but it's the truth.'

Graham took a deep breath, then regrouped and changed tack. 'Look, Lucy was just a moment of madness. It only happened because you . . .'

Hannah held up her hand. 'Don't, Graham. Please don't try to find a way to make this my fault. I've tried, OK? I've really, really tried. But you won't grow up.'

'What does that mean?'

'It means that despite my best efforts, this marriage is dead. You don't respect me, you won't cook unless you're trying to impress people, you don't clean, you have no concept of laundry.'

Graham rolled his eyes. 'Really? This again? You want a divorce because I don't remember to turn on the washing machine?'

'No,' said Hannah calmly. 'Let's be clear about one thing. I want a divorce because another woman is now carrying *your* child.'

'Then why are we talking about laundry?'

'Because you're still a teenager, Graham. And you're never going to change. Even without the whole Lucy thing, we've both been miserable for years. I'm not your mother, so I'm done. Go and live with Lucy, have your baby. She can wash your pants.' She kept her voice strong and reminded herself to breathe, determined not to show Graham any cracks in her armour. Right now she had the upper hand, but the minute she crumpled he'd seize the advantage.

'But I don't want to live with Lucy; I want to live with

you.' His voice took on a wheedling tone, like this was in some way endearing.

'Well, that option is no longer available.' She swallowed her natural inclination to add *I'm sorry*, because it was the one thing she definitely wasn't right now.

'We've been married for fourteen years. You can't just *leave*.'

'You're right. I'm not leaving,' said Hannah, shaking her head. 'You are, because this is MY house.'

Graham pursed his lips and folded his arms. 'I'm not going. Not until you give me a chance to explain.'

Hannah smiled thinly and put her hands on her hips. 'Graham, please don't make me call your mother and tell her she's finally got a grandchild on the way.'

His eyes bulged. 'You wouldn't.'

Hannah tilted her head and held his gaze, wondering how she'd stood in front of a fire-and-brimstone pastor and promised to love, honour and obey this man for ever. 'Believe me, I definitely would.'

'She'll lose her mind,' he said desperately. 'Nobody gets divorced in our family.'

'Well, think of yourself as a trailblazer. And don't lie to her about what you've done; you'll only make it worse when she finds out.'

'I can't tell her,' he croaked, clearly on the verge of tears. 'She'll be devastated.'

Hannah looked away, determined not to feel sorry for him. 'Maybe you should have thought about that before you had an affair with your assistant.'

Graham covered his face with his huge hands and started to sob, the last remaining defence of the cornered and

10

desperate. 'I'm so sorry, Hannah.' He rubbed his eyes like a little boy. 'Please don't do this.'

Hannah walked towards him, then gently rested her hand on his arm, suddenly aware that this was probably the last time she would ever touch him. 'Come on. Be honest with yourself, and with me. This marriage isn't working, and it hasn't been for a long time. Do you really want to spend the rest of your life like this?'

Graham looked up, his eyes filled with tears and confusion. He gave Hannah a long, searching look, and it felt like the most powerful moment of mutual understanding they'd shared in years. He closed his eyes briefly as he shook his head, then opened his arms to invite Hannah in for a hug. She paused for a second, then moved into them. She could give him this one final moment, but then they were both on their own.

CHAPTER TWO

'This isn't working.' Rob let go of the suitcase lid, prompting it to spring open like a jack-in-the-box. The stack of shorts and polo shirts inside slumped sideways and fell onto the bed, ruining all his careful folding.

'You're trying to squash too much stuff in,' said Nina with an eye roll, scrambling onto the pillow so she could shove the T-shirts back in, push the lid down and hold it in place with her pert backside. 'Why don't you just take another bag?'

'Because it's an extra seventy quid,' Rob said grumpily.

'You could take me,' she added sweetly, bouncing up and down on the lid while Rob wrestled with the zip. She opened her legs to spread the weight and jiggled her boobs in his face, and he momentarily wondered if she was doing it on purpose. 'Then I could bring some of your stuff in my bag. I'd only need a bikini. And my hair straighteners.'

'Not great timing for that suggestion,' laughed Rob. 'My plane leaves in three and a half hours.'

Nina pouted prettily, still sitting on the hard shell of Rob's suitcase, her knees now together with her feet splayed like she was about to kick into a Charleston swivel.

'I could come over to Spain when I'm done with uni in May, though. Maybe you could teach me to play tennis.'

Rob smiled, realising this was a joke. Nina hated tennis;

in fact, she hated anything that made her sweaty in public. In private was a whole other matter, however. 'I don't think that would work,' he said.

'I just can't believe you're not going to miss me.' She was trying to play it cool, but Rob could hear the neediness in her voice.

'Of course I'm going to miss you. But we always knew this was coming.'

'I know,' she said quietly. 'But I thought you might change your mind. You know, because of me. Well, us.'

Rob looked at her carefully, trying to gauge if she was still joking. Her lip gave a tell-tale wobble and he realised she was about to cry. *Oh, shit.*

'Nina, I . . .' He was suddenly aware that he was way out of his depth. They'd been casually dating for less than two months; a slippery Valentine's Day encounter on some ice outside Bath Abbey that had moved from a coffee to an exchange of numbers, then drinks, then mini golf, then a great deal of intense and mutually satisfying sex, all in the space of forty-eight hours. He'd thought they were on the same page – just a fling, no pressure, no commitment, feel free to see other people. Apparently not.

'It's fine,' she said, clambering off the suitcase and pulling the cuffs of her jumper down over her fists. It was a reminder of how young she was; only twenty-one, inclined to retreat to childhood in moments of stress. Losing herself inside her clothes, curling her hair round her finger, chewing the knuckle of her thumb until it bled.

'I'm sorry,' said Rob gently, looking her firmly in the eye. 'I've had a great time, but I thought you were cool with this.'

Nina gazed up at him with her big green eyes, pressing

her fists together under her chin like she was auditioning for the part of adorable, picture-perfect girlfriend. 'I was,' she said breathily. 'But now you're actually going I've realised that I really love you.'

Oh Jesus, thought Rob, realising that this whole situation was rapidly spiralling out of his control. He needed to be kind, obviously, but also very clear on where they stood. 'I can't . . .' he said. 'That isn't what we talked about.'

'I know.' Nina reached out to take his big hand in her tiny one. 'I just need you to know how I feel, before you leave.'

Rob nodded slowly, unable to shake the feeling that something wasn't quite right. He reminded himself that Nina was studying for a BA in Acting at university and absolutely LIVED for this kind of *Love Island* drama. He suspected that this wasn't an impromptu declaration; this was a scene she'd played out in her own head over many hours, an opportunity for Nina Taylor to star in her own Richard Curtis romcom. A Valentine's Day meet-cute on an icy pavement, a whirlwind romance, tell the boy you love him just as he's about to get on the plane, passionate kiss, camera zooms out as it takes off into the sunset without him. The End.

'I'm really sorry,' he said helplessly. 'The last couple of months have been really fun, but I'm going to Spain.'

'What?' said Nina, snapping from 'tearful' into 'outraged' like she'd just screwed on a different head. 'Are you fucking kidding me?'

Rob turned his palms upwards in surrender. 'Nina, this was always the plan. We've had a great time, but you and I were never a big thing. You said the same.'

'I've just told you I love you,' she shrieked.

'I know,' said Rob, determined to stay reasonable and not give her further ammunition. 'But I don't feel the same way. I'm really sorry.'

'I can't believe you would do this to me,' she gasped, her hand clutching imaginary pearls.

'Why have you waited until now to tell me this?' he asked, trying to keep the edge out of his voice. 'What did you expect me to do? Give up a job I've been lining up for the past year?'

Nina flicked her hair dramatically and shrugged on her silver padded jacket, then turned in the doorway to deliver her final line. 'This isn't what I wanted, but maybe it's for the best.' She looked him up and down like he'd just trodden on a kitten. 'I know exactly who you are now and I hope you find someone who makes you happy.' Her voice cracked on the final word, suggesting she hoped nothing of the sort. Rob didn't move as he listened to her stomp down the stairs from his flat, then slam the heavy front door behind her.

What the fuck just happened? He'd imagined a final hug, then wishing each other all the best and promising to stay in touch but not really intending to. How did that suddenly turn into an episode of *Hollyoaks*?

He took deep breaths and tried to unscramble his brain, until a car beeped in the road outside; his mum and dad, who'd offered to take him to the airport. Rob dragged up the sash window and held up his fingers to indicate two minutes, then did a final check in each room to make sure he hadn't forgotten anything. His parents owned the flat, and they'd found a tenant for the next six months. A van was coming to shift all his boxes to his parents' garage later, then cleaners would be arriving tomorrow to de-fumigate the

15

place. A flutter of excitement bloomed in the pit of his stomach as he hauled the suitcase off the bed and grabbed his rucksack and tennis bag.

'Got everything, son?' Guy Baxter was very much a man's man, prone to hale-and-hearty arm slapping from years of forging important connections on the golf course. Even though Rob was now twenty-eight, Guy still talked to his son like he was ten years old and had just led his prep school team to cricket glory for the first time.

'He doesn't need much, do you, darling?' said Rob's mum, in the indulgent style of a mother dealing with her youngest child and only son. Kate Baxter had lost none of the beauty that had led to some uncomfortable conversations at school between Rob and his classmates, who occasionally forgot that the English teacher they deployed as fantasy wank-fodder was Rob's mum. He suspected she'd had some subtle work done – about five years ago she'd disappeared to a 'literary retreat' for the whole of the school summer holidays and come back looking like a poem by John Keats. She was now retired and from the neck upwards could pass for about forty on a bad day.

'Just the one suitcase.' Rob lifted it into the boot of his dad's Lexus, throwing his tennis bag in with it. 'The club provides all my coaching gear.'

'You get in the front, darling,' said Kate, opening the door to take the back seat behind Guy, as she had for forty years. They had met at university and married straight after graduation, after which Kate had taught English at an independent school in Bath and raised their three children with the help of an au pair while Guy built and grew a very successful haulage business. They were one of those families that everyone's heard about but nobody's ever met – big house, happy marriage, healthy retirement fund, not even a whiff of a child with a meth habit or a grandchild who shop-lifts for attention.

'It's fine, I'll sit in the back,' said Rob, marvelling that marriages like his parents' still existed. He couldn't think of a single one of his friends whose parents were still together; most of them were either miserable divorcees or on third marriages to partners younger than their kids.

'So, we won't see you for six months,' said Guy, shaking his head. None of the Baxters had strayed too far – one of Rob's sisters lived in Cheltenham, and the other in Chew Magna, only a few miles from Bristol Airport. His parents were stopping there for lunch after dropping him off.

'Not unless you fancy a trip to Spain,' said Rob mildly. 'It's a nice resort, not far from Marbella. Mum can lie by the pool while I teach you how to play tennis.'

Guy laughed heartily but didn't argue. It had been many years since he'd been able to give his son a run for his money on the tennis court. 'And you've got a job lined up for when you get back?'

'Yeah,' said Rob, trying not to roll his eyes. 'Head Coach for the under eighteens at the Uni tennis academy, starting in October. An actual proper job, with salary and benefits and everything.'

'We're very proud of you,' said Kate, glancing at her husband. 'Aren't we, Guy?'

'Of course,' said Guy, although he didn't look it. The Baxters had a rich history of high achievement in proper, professional jobs – Rob's eldest sister was a GP, and the

17

younger was the VP of European Sales for a US software firm. As far as Guy was concerned, tennis coaches were in the same bracket as ski instructors and yoga teachers. Lay-about jobs for itinerant wasters.

'Maybe we'll pop over for a few days,' said Kate. 'After we get back from Bermuda.'

Rob smiled, conscious that only a mother's love would get his parents on a budget flight to Malaga after ten days in a private villa in Bermuda.

'Did you say your farewells to the girl?' Guy asked. 'What was her name?'

'Nina,' said Rob. 'She told me she loved me, then slammed the door on her way out when I didn't return the favour.'

'Oh, poor thing.' Kate pressed her hand to her chest.

'Still breaking hearts, then,' chuckled Guy.

'I actually considered it as a career.' Rob gave a wry smile. 'But I've decided tennis is more my thing.'

'We just want you to be happy,' said Kate. 'Settled down, you know.'

'Bollocks,' said Guy, swerving to avoid a driver in the wrong lane on the roundabout. 'He's too young to settle down, he's only twenty-eight.'

'We had a mortgage and two daughters by the time we were twenty-eight,' Kate retorted, mildly affronted.

'Yeah, but he's never met a woman like you,' said Guy, turning to look at his wife. 'He's never been knocked side-ways by love.'

'You'll be knocked sideways if you don't keep your eyes on the road,' laughed Kate. Rob watched his father reach over and take his mother's hand, endlessly fascinated by the spark between them that had burned for nearly forty years.

How was that even a thing? He'd had plenty of girlfriends, but they'd all been casual flings and none of them had even come close to knocking him sideways. Maybe he'd never met the right woman, or maybe he wasn't a sideways-knocking kind of guy. Or maybe his parents were just one of a kind. Either way, they needed to get a room.

He looked out of the car window as Bath's famous Georgian townhouses faded into Victorian terraces, excitement fizzing in his stomach. He'd been coaching tennis for years, but always as a side job alongside studying and bar work, not as a way to make a living. But for the next six months he'd be working full time at a luxury tennis resort in Spain, and then he'd be starting his dream job right here in his home city. Everything he'd worked towards was waiting for him at the end of a two-and-a-half-hour flight, and being knocked sideways by a woman was definitely not on the list. He made a silent vow as he glimpsed the first sign for Bristol Airport. No women, no stress, no drama. Just tennis.

CHAPTER THREE

The doorbell rang as Hannah was wrestling brown packing tape onto a cardboard box – Graham's collection of vintage Star Wars books and figurines, bought from various car boot sales and toy fairs during one of his hobby crises. Every few years he would get in an insecure huff about how much time Hannah spent playing tennis and announce he was taking up indoor climbing, or fencing, or cultivating his collection of overpriced Han Solo tat. He'd been round to clear out most of his belongings while Hannah had been at work earlier, but this stuff had been tucked at the back of a wardrobe and he'd clearly forgotten about it. Hannah briefly considered taking it all to a charity shop, but maybe she needed to build up to that level of petty vengeance.

So her first thought when she heard the doorbell was that Graham had come back for his Wookie toys, but the reality was FAR worse. Hannah opened the front door to a two-pronged mum attack – Graham's mother Ruth, and her own mother Elena. They were both dressed for some kind of Friday worshipful gathering – Ruth in a hairy tweed two-piece, and her mum in a horrible yellow shift dress with huge batwing sleeves that made her look like Big Bird from *Sesame Street*. Elena forced a weak smile that was more like a grimace, but Ruth's mouth was pinched into the tightest of cat's bums.

'Can we come in?' asked Ruth.

'We're just on the way to prayer group,' added Elena, already flapping her way into the hall. They'd both left the evangelical church for good not long after Hannah got married, when rumours were circling about various shady/illegal/perverted practices happening in the parent church in the US. They'd shopped around every denomination of Christianity in Woking and Guildford over the course of a couple of years – Methodists, Baptists, even a brief foray into Catholicism, before settling on the local parish church of St Paul because it was the warmest in winter and had a twinkly-eyed priest. Elena also earned bonus Jesus points by attending a weekly service at the Orthodox church in town; apparently the incense and chanting reminded her of her Greek childhood.

Hannah held the door open as they passed, suppressing a sigh. Facing these two together was like being the disappointing meat in a judgement sandwich. She'd stopped being scared of them a long time ago, but it was hard not to feel like she was still a child with unruly curls and a grubby face who was about to get a serious telling-off.

'What can I do for you?' she asked, leading them into the kitchen. She didn't put the kettle on, since that would indicate the two mothers were welcome, which they were very much not.

'You know why we're here,' said Ruth smoothly. 'Graham is very upset.' She glanced at the box waiting by the back door, then fanned her eyes with her hand to stop herself crying.

Hannah raised her eyebrows. 'What did he tell you?'

'He said that there was some nonsense with a girl at work,

a big misunderstanding,' said Ruth. She put her handbag on the kitchen counter, but not before she'd run her finger along it to check for grease, which made Hannah press her lips together and breathe through her nose. 'And apparently you've blown it out of all proportion and told him to leave.'

'Surely things can't be that bad, my dear,' said Elena. Even though she'd left Crete over forty years ago, she'd retained a trace of an accent and occasionally went off in a torrent of Greek when she was upset about something – Hannah's brother Luke described it as 'Mum's gone full Heraklion'. She'd gifted Hannah her dark curls and olive skin, plus a little of her own mother's fiery spirit; Hannah's 'yia-yia', who had lived with them until she'd died when Hannah was twelve.

'I've blown it out of proportion? Is that what he said?' Hannah glared at the box by the door, mentally impaling Luke Skywalker on his own lightsaber. 'He didn't mention anything else?'

'That's all,' said Ruth. 'I told him to give you some space to calm down and you'd see things more clearly.'

Hannah folded her arms and fixed her mother-in-law with a steely glare. 'I can see very clearly, thank you, Ruth.'

'Don't be sarcastic,' said Elena, wagging her finger. 'It's not becoming for a woman. You know we love you both.'

Hannah ignored her. 'Does Graham know you're here?'

'No,' said Ruth. 'He wanted to come to prayer group with us and ask the Lord for forgiveness for his sins, but I persuaded him to stay at home.'

So Graham had gone home to his mother and was pretending to be a good Christian in exchange for her support. Hannah could smell the desperation from here.

'OK,' she said, trying to keep it light and friendly even though her teeth were silently grinding. 'I'm listening. What would you both like to say?'

'We want you to reconsider,' said Elena. 'Don't make the mistake I made and throw everything away.'

'Well, I'm not making Graham leave the country, so I guess that's something.' It was a cheap dig, but Hannah couldn't help it. When she was fifteen her father had cheated on her mother, which had created huge drama within the church community. Hannah still didn't know the whole story, but he'd moved abroad shortly afterwards and had never come back. Elena had banned any mention of his name ever since.

'Graham made a mistake,' said Ruth, resting her hand on Elena's arm in silent support. 'You've been married too long to throw it all away because his eye wandered a little. That's just men.'

'OK, two things,' said Hannah sternly. 'Firstly, I'm not thinking about the years I'm throwing away – they're already gone. I'm thinking about the years ahead, which I no longer have to spend being a surrogate mother to your son.'

'What's that supposed to mean?' said Ruth, her eyes boggling in outrage.

'It means not cooking for him, cleaning up after him, buying all his family's Christmas presents, noticing when his socks have holes and buying him new ones. He's thirty-two, Ruth. When we got married I thought he'd grow up, but it's never happened.'

'You have an easy life compared to most,' scoffed Ruth. 'No children to look after.'

'Thank you for the reminder,' said Hannah. Her barren

23

status had been a source of much crying and prayers since the early days of their marriage, but secretly she'd been relieved when the years of trying were declared a waste of time. She'd never been particularly maternal, and it was clear she'd get no help from Graham.

'You're right, I don't have children,' she continued. 'Apart from Graham. And there's nothing you can say that will make me take him back.'

'He's just like his father,' said Ruth. 'Richard doesn't lift a finger either, but that's hardly reason to give up on your marriage.' She looked at Hannah beseechingly, then turned to Elena as if to invite her to pitch in.

Elena shrugged. 'You both earn good money. Get a cleaner, and keep your husband.'

'I said there were two things,' said Hannah, furious with Graham that he'd been too much of a coward to tell his mother about Lucy. She paused, taking mental bets on what the reaction would be. Her own mother would be horrified, obviously, but Ruth could go either way. A grandchild was a grandchild, after all.

'What's the other thing?' asked Ruth, a note of trepidation in her voice.

'Graham mentioned there'd been a woman at work,' Hannah said. 'I think you called it "some nonsense".'

'Yes, he told me,' said Ruth. 'He told me her name, but I've forgotten.'

'Her name is Lucy. Did he tell you she's pregnant?'

Both women gasped. 'What?' shrieked Ruth, as Elena clamped her hands over her mouth.

'She's pregnant. With Graham's baby.'

'Is she keeping it?' squealed Ruth, prompting a whiplash

head swivel from Elena. Having arrived very much on the same page, they were about to part company in the most dramatic fashion.

'I believe so,' said Hannah. 'I think she's four months along already.'

'Graham's going to be a father,' Ruth whispered to the light on the kitchen ceiling. *And there it is*, thought Hannah.

'You're happy about this?' spat Elena, taking a step away from Ruth and towards Hannah.

'No, of course not,' said Ruth, blushing to the roots of her salt-and-pepper hair. 'These are grave sins, and not how things should be. But none of this is the child's fault.' Her eyes darted from side to side as she frantically weighed up whether adultery ranked higher on the sin scale than abortion. Lucy's willingness to avoid the latter would almost certainly cancel out the former, particularly if Graham secured a quickie divorce from Hannah and married her. Ruth's eyes misted over, and Hannah could see her mentally knitting booties.

'I think that's enough breaking news for one day, don't you?' Hannah said. Elena nodded and patted her daughter's arm in solidarity, throwing Ruth a furious glare as she gathered up her handbag.

'I'm sorry things between you and Graham have ended this way,' said Ruth piously. 'But I can see there's no way back now, and I'm afraid you must take some of the blame.'

Hannah gave a hollow laugh. 'Thank you for your sympathies, Ruth, but I regret to inform you that I'm taking absolutely none of the blame.' She held open the front door as the two women left, Elena turning to give her daughter a watery smile and blowing a kiss. Hannah watched them walk up the street, neither of them speaking and spaced as far apart as the pavement would allow without one of them falling into the path of a Waitrose delivery van. Their long friendship had weathered many storms, but this one might just finish it off.

She went back to the kitchen and looked at the box by the back door, then thought about the pile of old books and clothes she'd found in the loft. All of that could go to the charity shop; Graham wouldn't miss any of it. She was fed up with putting him first, and right now all she wanted to do was play tennis.

Hannah smacked the ball over the net, then re-set her stance: legs wide apart, feet planted, knees soft. There was a pleasing, pulsating rhythm to the game, and when Hannah was playing tennis, it was as though she developed a tunnel vision that blocked out everything beyond the boundaries of the court. It was just her, the white lines and the fuzzy yellow ball.

'Are you OK?' asked Noah, ambling over with a furrowed brow as Hannah took a break to swig out of her sports bottle, breathing heavily. He was the club's newest coach; only twenty-six and wearing a hoodie with 'Ask Noah to knock you up' emblazoned on the back. As monogrammed tennis gear went, it wasn't exactly giving Roger Federer a run for his money in the style stakes.

'I'm fine,' said Hannah, realising she was gripping the net post so hard her knuckles had gone white. 'Why do you ask?'

Noah shrugged. 'I don't know, you just seem a bit . . . tense.'

Hannah gave him a weak smile. 'I'm always tense. Ask anyone.'

Noah laughed. 'You had enough?'

'No,' she replied a little too quickly. 'I'm fine, just a lot going on right now. This is helping, so let's keep going.'

'OK,' said Noah, spinning his racquet in his hand as he loped back to the baseline. 'Let's step it up another gear.'

'Hannah, have you got a minute?' shouted a female voice. Hannah looked up, surprised to see three of the Bitches of Westwick ambling towards her. She wouldn't call them that to their faces, obviously.

'If you're quick,' she said, aware that she sounded a bit snippy. This week's events aside, these women never brought out the best in her. They weren't mean or snobby; they just reminded her of the girls at school who smirked at her unfashionable clothes and weird family. In fact, all of them *had* gone to her school, but they were a few years older and would never have noticed someone like her. They also always travelled in a pack, like those prowling hyenas in *The Lion King*. Usually four of them, but Carla was missing this evening.

'It will only take a sec,' said Jess, the tallest and most athletic of the three. She was wearing a white vest and a matching neon-pink Lululemon tennis skirt that showcased a thigh gap you could drive a BMW through. Gaynor and Trish were less perfectly co-ordinated, but still unfeasibly gorgeous and well put-together. In comparison, Hannah's tennis skirt had seen better days, and her dark, curly hair was pushed back from her make-up-free face with a stretchy bandana, bought for three pounds from a church fete a decade ago.

27

'O . . . K . . .' said Hannah, trying to hide her scepticism whilst silently reminding herself that she could beat every one of these women on the tennis court. 'What can I do for you?'

'Well, hopefully it will be the other way round, actually,' said Jess. She had one of those sing-song cheerful voices that made her sound like a kids' TV presenter. 'Can you meet us for a drink after?'

'Who's us?'

'Me, Gaynor, Trish. We've got a proposition for you.' Trish nodded in agreement, dragging her attention away from Noah, who was squatting down in very tight white shorts as he re-tied his shoelace.

'What kind of proposition?'

Jess gave a tinkly laugh. 'That would be telling.'

Hannah sighed. 'Is it tennis-related?' She wasn't sure she could handle any more revelations about Graham. For all she knew he'd been having sex with his PA, his dry cleaner and half the Woking Women's Institute.

'Yes, absolutely,' said Jess. 'Nothing bad, I promise.'

'Fine,' Hannah said resignedly, rationalising that she had absolutely nothing to go home to.

'We can go for a wine at the Black Stag,' said Jess, nodding towards the pub that backed onto the courts. 'Or a coffee, if you like.' Hannah was known for not being a drinker; another old family habit that died hard, like sensible knickers and not swearing.

'I'll be half an hour,' she said, hating herself for being a tiny bit curious. She watched them whisper to each other as they sashayed towards the clubhouse, Jess's racquet bag bouncing in time to her chestnut ponytail as men on adjacent courts took a moment to towel off so they could track their progress with slack jaws and hungry eyes. Hannah had no idea what the Bitches of Westwick could possibly want with her, but there wasn't room in her brain to think about it right now.

'Ready?' said Noah.

'Yeah.' Hannah straightened her bandana, then headed back to the baseline.

CHAPTER FOUR

'So listen, here's the thing,' said Jess, who was clearly leading the ambush. Even though it was April, there was a bitter wind that firmly belonged in January, so they had bagged the table in the bay window by the wood burner before the Friday-night rush started in the Black Stag. 'We were just—'

'Drinks,' said the barman, cutting across Jess as he placed an ice bucket containing a bottle of Pinot Grigio and four glasses on the table. He unscrewed the cap and poured an inch of it into each glass, while Jess impatiently drummed her fingernails on the arm of her chair. Her hair and make-up were immaculate, even after an hour of tennis drills. Did the woman never sweat?

'As I was saying,' she said once the barman had retreated to eavesdrop from behind the bar. 'We were wondering if you'd like to come on a girls' tennis holiday with us.'

'Who's we?'

'The three of us.' Jess looked between Gaynor and Trish, who were flanking Hannah on either side. 'We're looking for a fourth.'

'What happened to Carla?'

'Can I say?' Jess directed her question at the other two. They both shrugged.

'She's just found out she's expecting twins,' said Jess. 'But that's not common knowledge, so don't tell anyone. She's pushing forty so it's kind of a big deal.'

'IVF,' mouthed Trish, like Carla only had herself to blame.

Hannah nodded. 'Right. So why are you asking me?'

'What do you mean?' replied Jess.

Hannah cleared her throat. 'Well, it's not like we're all the best of friends or anything.'

Jess looked at Gaynor, who smiled weakly and gamely picked up the baton. 'Right, but we're not NOT friends. We play tennis together all the time.'

Hannah laughed. 'Gaynor, I've been a member at Westwick since I was eight years old. We've played ladies' doubles together for a decade, we've spent hundreds of hours at the club, and this is the first time any of you have ever asked me out for a drink.'

They looked at each other awkwardly, until Trish continued, 'Yeah, OK. Look, it's not that we don't *like* you or anything, it's just that we're all quite . . .' She looked helplessly at the others for an appropriate adjective.

'. . . different?' concluded Gaynor, though it sounded more like a question. 'Like, you've never done much of the social stuff at the club, we don't see you on the school run. You don't really drink. We haven't had the chance to get to know you, I guess.'

'Do you still do the church thing?' asked Trish.

'No,' said Hannah. 'And I do drink, sometimes.' She held up her wine glass. 'I'm working a late shift tomorrow, so I don't have to get up early.'

'Where is it you work again?' Gaynor asked.

'I'm office manager at Upton Country Club,' Hannah said.

'Oh yeah, I think I've seen you there,' said Gaynor, like she was a regular. Hannah knew for a fact that she'd visited occasionally as a guest of her sister-in-law but wasn't a member herself. 'Do you get free treatments in the spa?'

Hannah shrugged. 'I get a fifty per cent discount, but I don't tend to use it.'

Trish perked up. 'Can we use it?'

'No. Tell me about this tennis holiday.'

Gaynor smiled and pressed her hands together in excitement. 'We've been loads of times. It's at this place called Club Colina, it's a five-star tennis resort in the hills above Marbella.'

'I wonder why it's called Colina?' mused Trish. 'Maybe it's owned by a guy called Colin.'

'*Colina* is Spanish for hill,' said Hannah, trying not to roll her eyes.

'I knew that,' said Trish quietly.

'Anyway,' continued Gaynor. 'It's, like, five hours of tennis every day, for six days. Drills, bootcamp, one-to-one coaching. There's a pool and a spa and really nice bars and stuff. It's amazing.'

'And you guys go every year?' Hannah had noticed the four women disappearing from training every now and then but had never considered where they might go.

'Most years,' said Jess. 'We've taken a few off to have kids and stuff. Our husbands trade us a boys' golfing trip in September.'

'My mum and sister look after my kids,' said Trish. 'I'm single.'

'And you're married, right?' Jess asked Hannah.

'Actually, I'm separated.' Hannah hesitated slightly, feeling the word take shape in her mouth for the first time. It tasted strange but somewhat sweet, like a cocktail she'd never tried before.

'Oh wow, I'm really sorry,' said Jess, her eyes widening.

'Don't be,' said Hannah quickly. 'I'm not. So no Carla, which means you're one short.'

Jess nodded. 'Yeah. And if we don't have four, there's a chance the coaches will lump us with a spare. Somebody on holiday on their own.'

Hannah sucked air through her teeth. 'That's risky.'

'Exactly,' said Jess. 'And I don't want to blow our own trumpet or anything, but we don't want someone who isn't up to our standard. Last time we went, there was this group of guys who had seven in their group, someone dropped out at the last minute. The coaches subbed in this random who could barely hit a ball.'

'So you want me for my tennis rather than my party life-style?' Hannah asked with a playful smile.

Jess laughed. 'Yeah, but it will be really fun too. Gorgeous hotel, some fun nights out. And the tennis is amazing. We all get loads out of it.'

Hannah gave it some thought while Gaynor topped up her glass. Five hours of tennis every day in the Spanish sunshine, a long way away from this Graham-infested town. It was tempting. She couldn't remember the last time she'd had a proper break from work. She and Graham rarely had the chance to go away in the summer because of her duties as ladies' tennis captain, and Graham didn't like flying. The idea of spending a week in the sunshine, playing tennis – actually it was more than tempting.

Her mind whirred as she thought about taking a season

off from her tennis captaincy, maybe extending her trip and making use of the month-long sabbatical she was owed from work. Perhaps she could even visit her dad, who she hadn't seen for three years and who only lived a couple of hours from Marbella. Maybe it would be a good way to draw a line under the first set of her life, then start the second with a dramatic change of scenery.

'What do you think?' asked Jess, snapping her out of her reverie.

'When is it?' Hannah asked.

'Well, that's the thing,' said Jess, looking a little awkward. 'It's in three weeks. We fly on the first of May.'

'Oh wow, you really are desperate. How much?'

'About two grand. So it's not cheap, obviously. But that's all inclusive. Flights, food, drinks, coaching, everything.'

'Do I have to share a room?' Hannah looked around at the three women, wondering which one she'd rather share with. Trish, probably, because she wouldn't spend the whole time moaning about her husband. But she also looked like she might have a tendency towards drunk, ugly crying. Tough choice.

'Absolutely not.' Jess looked horrified. 'We all have our own room. God, could you imagine sharing?' The three women laughed at the unimaginability of sleeping in close proximity to another adult human.

'Can I think about it?' Hannah asked, not wanting to look too keen or desperate. 'I don't know if I can get time off work at such short notice.'

'Yeah, of course,' said Jess, digging her phone out of her bag. 'Why don't you give me your email and I'll send you all the details?'

★

34

Hannah's brother Luke was waiting on the doorstep when she got home, leaning against the door and tapping on his phone, his shaggy curls falling around his face in two curtains. He was eighteen and a final gift from the heavens after many painful years of failed pregnancies, but one year later their parents' marriage broke up and their dad left the country for good. Hannah had been fifteen, but Luke didn't even have a memory of him.

'Where've you been?' He stood up. 'I've been waiting ages.'

'I went out after training. Sorry, left my phone in my tennis bag.'

'Are you OK? Where's Graham? I rang the doorbell but nobody answered, so I rang Mum to ask if you were both away and she did that thing where her voice goes all high-pitched and she starts banging on about the weather.'

Hannah sighed, unlocking the door. 'Come in,' she said, kicking off her tennis shoes and dumping her bag at the bottom of the stairs. She headed into the kitchen, a wave of tired sadness washing over her as she took a deep breath and turned back to face Luke. 'Graham's gone.'

'Gone where?' asked Luke, helping himself to a Coke Zero from the fridge.

'Gone gone.' There was no point beating around the bush with Luke; he was eighteen and only dealt in facts and logic. 'We've split up.'

'Shut up. You haven't.'

'We definitely have. Yesterday, actually.' Had it really been only twenty-four hours since she'd come home to call time on her marriage? It felt like a lifetime.

Luke popped the tab on the can and took a swig, then

covered his mouth with the back of his hand as he burped. 'Wow, that's huge. What happened?'

Hannah shrugged. 'Things have been bad for ages. But he's also been having an affair, so that finished it off.'

Luke looked away shiftily, prompting Hannah to bear down on him with a narrow-eyed glare.

'Wait, did you *know*?'

'I've, like, *heard rumours*,' he said, blushing a little. 'But I didn't know for sure. I'm really sorry.'

'What kind of rumours?'

'Well, just about him and Sonia. I don't know if . . .'

'Wait, what?' Hannah held up her hands. 'Estate agent Sonia?' She shook her head, trying to rearrange the puzzle pieces in her head so this all made sense.

'Yeah,' said Luke. 'I heard it had been going on for a while.'

'Heard it from who?'

Luke shrugged. 'I don't know, it's a small town, Han. I think it was a guy who runs the barbers by the chip shop. Or maybe his brother.'

Hannah shook her head and pressed the heels of her hands into her eyes. 'Graham does Sonia's conveyancing.'

'Not all he was doing, by the sounds of it,' said Luke, opening the fridge again in search of food. 'But you knew, right?'

'I knew about someone, but it wasn't Sonia.'

'Oh wow. Is it Mel?'

Hannah raised her hands in frustration. 'Who's Mel?'

'I don't know,' said Luke, breaking the corner off a slab of cheese and putting the clingfilm back. 'I just heard about Graham and a woman called Mel, from the guy in the Co-Op. I think she's moved away now, though.'

Hannah threw her hands up in frustration. 'OK, so why didn't you tell me about any of this?'

Luke looked away guiltily. 'I asked Mum if I should, and she made me promise not to. She said there was no proof, and it was a sin to gossip.'

Hannah took deep breaths through her nose, her fists clenched. 'And adultery is fine, is it?'

Luke shrugged helplessly. 'You know what she's like, she made me SWEAR. She said it was between you and Graham.'

'And Sonia, and Mel and Lucy, apparently.'

'Who's Lucy?'

'Never mind.'

Luke gasped excitedly. 'Wait. If Graham's gone, can I move in here?'

'What? No.'

'I need to get out of Mum's. She's doing my head in.'

'Then move out. Rent somewhere. You've got a job.'

'I can't.' Luke put a slice of bread in the toaster and started opening cupboards in search of something to put on it. His hand wavered between peanut butter and raspberry jam, then skipped to the Nutella. 'If I rent my own place she'll be round every five minutes to check if Dan and I are, like, a thing.'

'Do you want dinner?' Hannah asked, fishing the bread back out of the toaster. 'I have actual food.'

'Yeah, please. I'm starving.'

Hannah opened the fridge and started pulling out the ingredients for a stir fry. 'And ARE you and Dan a thing?' Dan was a friend Luke had made at college, who'd been a hovering presence in her brother's life for the past year. He was quiet and shy – Hannah wasn't sure she'd ever heard him speak more than three words.

Luke was still for a moment, his hands flat on the kitchen counter and his head bowed. 'Yeah. I think so.'

Hannah put down all the cooking ingredients and gathered her brother into a hug. 'Good for you,' she said quietly.

'Really?' Luke whispered.

'Of course.' Hannah let him go and turned back to the chopping board.

'No big-sister wisdom?'

Hannah laughed and put the knife down. 'Lu, I got married at eighteen, and look how that turned out. I'm happy that you've met someone you like; I don't care if it's Danielle or Dan or Dan formerly known as Danielle.' Hannah had been practising that line since she'd first realised there was more than just friendship between Luke and Dan, waiting for the time when her brother was ready to tell her. It felt important to say the right thing at a moment like that.

Tears welled up in Luke's eyes, but he brushed them away with the heel of his hand. 'Thanks, Han. You're the best.'

'Just be gentle with Mum when you tell her, OK?'

'I will.' Luke blew out a huge sigh. 'She's gonna go full Heraklion, so might save that for another day.'

Hannah nodded and kept chopping as Luke dug the wok out of the cupboard. She had taught her little brother to cook in this kitchen, on evenings when he needed a break from their mum and Graham was working or watching rugby. They'd put some music on, pick a recipe and make it together.

'Wow, so you're single now,' said Luke with a grin. 'What are you going to do?'

She thought about it for a moment as she chopped spring onions into tiny slices. 'I'm going to spend some time with myself,' she said.

'Are you going to join a dating site? Like, have you ever dated anyone apart from Graham?'

'The answer to both those questions is no.'

'You should probably join Tinder or something,' teased Luke, nudging her with his elbow. 'Do some hook-ups, make up for lost time.'

'Yeah, that definitely isn't going to happen, I'm having some time out. And what do you know about hook-ups?'

'Nothing,' Luke said quickly. 'Do you have to sell this place now and give Graham his share?'

'No. This is my house, I paid for it.'

'Really? With what?'

'With the inheritance I got when yia-yia died. It was in trust until I was eighteen, and then I used it as a deposit on this place so Graham and I could get married.'

'Really? Didn't he even pay the mortgage?'

'No, I paid it. Graham never earned much at first; he was either training or trying to get his practice off the ground. He helped out with the bills and stuff, but I finished paying off the mortgage a couple of years ago. It's all mine.'

'Shit, I can't believe yia-yia dying got you a house. Why didn't I get anything?'

'Don't swear,' said Hannah. 'You hadn't even been born yet. Tough luck.'

'OK, but now you've got the chance to make it up to me, by letting me move in.'

Hannah smiled and shook her head. 'I'll think about it.'

'Come on, please. I need to get out of Mum's.'

'I said I'll think about it. But in the meantime, I might be going away soon, so you can house-sit.'

'How long for?'

'I'm not sure, maybe three or four weeks. I need to talk to work about it, so I'll let you know next week.'

'Can Dan stay over? If I'm living here for a bit?' He looked at her hopefully, and Hannah had to remind herself that he wasn't a little boy any more.

'Yes, but if Mum asks, you need to promise me you won't lie to her. If you want to be treated like an adult, you need to start taking responsibility.'

Luke looked at his feet and took a deep breath. 'Yeah, fair enough. Where are you going?'

'Spain.' Hannah glanced up at him with the briefest pause. 'So I might go and see Dad.'

'Really?' said Luke, his eyes wide. 'Again?'

Hannah gave him a look. 'It's been three years, Luke. You don't have to come, but the offer is always there.'

'I definitely don't want to see him,' said Luke, chewing on the end of his little finger like he used to when he was a toddler and feeling anxious.

'You can't punish him for ever, Lu. Sometimes marriages don't work out and people move on.' She gestured towards the formal photo of her and Graham on the chest of drawers by the dining table, both looking like children playing wedding dress-up.

'He didn't move on, he moved AWAY,' said Luke. 'He left the fucking country when I was, like, a year old.'

'I know, but you still don't need to swear about it,' Hannah said gently. 'He's your dad. Are you really going to shut him out of your life for ever?'

'I don't know,' said Luke. 'Maybe.'

'For ever's a long time. And if there's one thing that this week has taught me, it's that everyone makes mistakes.'

'Yeah. But some are more forgivable than others. So is that why you're going to Spain? To see Dad?'

'No.' Hannah felt a bubble of excitement in the pit of her stomach. 'If I can get the time off work, I'm going to play tennis.'

CHAPTER FIVE

Rob hadn't been entirely sure what to expect from Club Colina, but he left the UK in heavy rain and gale force winds and arrived in Spain on a warm April evening, and that felt like a good start. It had been dark when he arrived at the resort, with just enough time to grab a sandwich from the café and unpack his bag before bed. His room was halfway down a quiet corridor on the first floor of the hotel, which he supposed was where all the staff slept. It was small but still had a double bed and a tiny en-suite bathroom, and he didn't have to share it with anyone. An apartment would have been nicer, but he didn't want to waste the money. He could definitely make this feel like home for six months.

When he woke up early on Saturday morning he could hear other people talking and lugging suitcases down the corridor over the hum of the air conditioning, but he didn't go out to say hello. It felt a bit like the first day at uni, although on that occasion he'd propped open the door to his room in halls with a case of beer and invited his fellow first years to help themselves in exchange for some introductory chat. This seemed different, somehow – partly because he was ten years older, but also because he felt like the new boy at a school that everyone else had been going to for years.

He showered and dressed quickly, then grabbed a pastry and a coffee from the restaurant and headed out for a walk.

It felt glorious to wander around with nothing more than joggers and a T-shirt and sunglasses on, wandering the streets of smart villas that formed terrace-like rings down from the Club hotel and tennis centre at the top of the hill. It was quiet at this time of day, just a few runners out pounding the pavements and workers emptying bins in Club Colina golf carts. He strolled around for a couple of hours, discovering small clusters of apartments, giant villas with private pools shaped like kidneys, little communities of shops and restaurants and bars tucked away down narrow alleyways that disappeared into the hillside. The whole place had an air of calm and exclusivity, like even the birds had been told to keep it down so as not to disturb the residents.

Rob saved the tennis centre for last, having only seen it in photos on the Club Colina website. Sixteen pristine courts laid out in four rows – eight umber-coloured clay courts, four blue hard courts and four green AstroTurf, all landscaped with flowering shrubs and palm trees. Overlooking it all was a smart clubhouse and café, with not a flake of paint or a pebble out of place. Rob had grown up dreaming of playing tennis in places like this – he couldn't wait to get started.

He dug out his phone and took a selfie from the terrace above the courts, then added it to the family WhatsApp group. He didn't write a message; hopefully his excited grin and the clear blue sky would tell them everything they needed to know.

'There are rules,' said Mark, the Head of Tennis at Club Colina. He was dressed in the Club coaching gear – a white polo shirt with a royal blue stripe across the chest and matching blue shorts, from which protruded the brownest legs Rob had ever seen on a white man. Surely that must be out of a bottle? 'I'm only going to explain them to you once, and then I'm going to give you a piece of paper with them written down, so you've got no excuse.'

'What's wrong with him?' whispered Aaron to Rob. 'Why is he talking to us like we're five or something?'

'Ssh,' said Rob with a grin. 'I'm actually listening.'

'Rule number one,' said Mark. 'You wear your Club Colina kit all the time when you're in the resort. Most of the people on this hill are staying outside the hotel in apartments and villas, so you handsome fuckers are the best advert we've got for private lessons.'

Rob glanced around the hotel breakfast area, which was currently serving as a meeting room. There were six coaches in total, plus Mark. Three of the coaches, Chris, Jonno and Olly, had done seasons here before and were standing together by the coffee machine, looking bored. Rob and the two others, Aaron and Nick, were all new. All men, no women. Rob wondered if that was just coincidence, or some kind of unspoken hiring policy. But he had to admit that they were, without exception, handsome fuckers.

'Having said that,' Mark continued, 'if you're getting hammered in Marbella on your day off, do NOT be wearing your Club Colina kit. Keep it clean, change it often. If you look like you've slept in a hedge or you stink, I will fire you. Is that clear?'

Everyone nodded and mumbled assent, so Mark carried on. 'Rule number two,' he said, holding up two fingers in a peace sign. 'You are on court by eight thirty every day to prep for warm-up drills, which start at nine. Lunch is at twelve on the terrace, and coaching ends at three, unless you have private lessons. ALL of you are expected to accept bookings for private lessons, which are open to anyone, guest or not. You get to keep half the earnings plus any tips.'

'I've heard that's worth having,' whispered Aaron. 'Lessons are, like, sixty euros an hour. Couple of hours a day, six days a week, plus tips. You could bank an extra three or four hundred a week.'

'Eight-thirty start,' said Mark, glaring at Aaron. 'If you are late, I will fire you. Rule number three: Saturdays are changeover day, and also your day off. Fuck off and do whatever you like, but do NOT be hungover on Sunday or I will fire you. Likewise, do not fuck off on Friday night, because we do an end-of-week party and prizegiving for the guests in the hotel bar and you are expected to be here, on your best behaviour.'

'If we're not, do you think he'll fire us?' muttered Nick, making Rob snort with laughter.

'And finally, do not, under any circumstances, shag the hotel guests. Do not flirt with them, do not finger them, do not exchange any kind of body fluids. If you do, you're on the first flight home. No exceptions.'

Chris leaned over behind Rob, Nick and Aaron. 'He's so full of shit,' he whispered. 'I know of at least three guests he's shagged over the past couple of years.'

'Really?' said Rob.

'Yeah,' said Chris. 'But he's in charge, so he can do whatever he likes.'

'Those are the rules,' said Mark. 'I'm going to give you a copy, so study them hard. First guests arrive this afternoon, so feel free to check out the courts and have a hit amongst yourselves, get acclimatised. Don't get sunburned, I'm not your fucking mum. Nick doesn't need to worry, obviously.' He grinned at Nick, who was black, and was gifted with a stony glare in return. 'Stay out of the way while the guests are checking in, and I'll see you all at eight thirty on court tomorrow.' Mark forced a smile as he handed out sheets of A4, then left the room like he'd just ordered an air strike on some insurgent nation and had to get to the situation room.

'Right, who fancies a beer?' asked Olly, screwing his sheet of paper into a ball and tossing it over his shoulder into a tray of coffee mugs. He had a braying, public school drawl and an elongated head with the squarest jaw Rob had ever seen, like a human coffin.

'Me,' said Aaron, thrusting his hand in the air and immediately outing himself as the kid who was most likely to have his head flushed down a toilet before lunch.

'I might go and hit some balls,' muttered Rob, who wanted a clear head for tomorrow.

'Don't be a twat on your first day,' said Olly, cuffing him round the head. 'You can start tomorrow.'

Rob glanced at Nick, who shrugged. 'Fine,' he said, trudging out after the others and wondering which one of these pricks was going to use the word 'banter' first.

Olly led the other coaches to a place a little further down the hill, where they wouldn't be spotted by arriving guests doing a tour of the hotel. It was a sports bar with a chessboard-tiled floor and a Premiership football match on the TV, with seating outside on wipe-clean sofas and glass tables.

'Estrellas all round,' yelled Olly to the barman, draping his arm along the back of the sofa with one foot propped up on the opposite knee. It was an alpha male power stance that took up half the sofa. 'So, new boys,' he said. 'How are you feeling about your first day at Club Colina?'

'Fine,' said Nick. 'I've done coaching seasons before, just not here.'

'Same,' said Aaron. 'I did La Manga last year.'

Olly nodded slowly. 'Nice. You?' He looked at Rob, who shook his head.

'Just in the UK.'

'Excellent, a proper Colina virgin. How old are you?'

'I'm twenty-eight,' said Rob with a steely glare, 'so perhaps you could stop talking to me like it's my first day at prep school.'

'Ooh, a fellow private schoolboy,' said Olly. 'I won't ask where – doubt it's anywhere interesting. What about you two?' He nodded at Aaron and Nick.

'Nope,' said Aaron. 'Local comp, mopped floors at David Lloyd on the weekends to pay for lessons.'

Nick shrugged. 'Yeah, Eton. My father is a Nigerian prince.'

'Really?' said Chris, his eyes boggling.

'No,' said Nick. 'I'm from Croydon. Fuck off.'

Rob laughed as he took his beer from the barman's tray and decided that Nick was his kind of guy. Aaron was naive but harmless and Chris seemed pretty cool; Jonno hadn't said a word yet, so the jury was still out on him. Olly was an arrogant dick, but he'd dealt with his type plenty of times before.

'So, who knows about Club Colina Bingo?' said Olly, rubbing his hands together as the tray of beers arrived.

'I fucking love this time of year,' said Chris, lighting a cigarette and turning his face into the sun. 'Beats the shit out of Manchester.'

'Anyone?' asked Olly. Rob, Nick and Aaron all shrugged and shook their heads.

'It's a game we play every year,' said Olly.

'A stupid game, if I may voice my opinion,' Jonno interrupted, revealing a very strong Welsh accent. 'Just so you're all clear on where I stand on this matter.'

'Fuck off, you tedious wanker,' said Olly. 'Jonno has no sense of humour, and he's very bad at this game.'

'What are the rules?' asked Aaron. He looked like the youngest of the group, maybe twenty-three or twenty-four. He was clearly desperate to fit in, and Rob wondered how many devious ways Olly would find to exploit that.

'We each put one hundred euros in the pot,' said Olly. 'So that's six hundred in total.'

'Hark at Carol Vorderman,' muttered Chris.

'There are six types of women on the bingo card that you have to hook up with,' continued Olly, his full lips curled into a sneer. 'Whoever ticks all six off first wins the pot.'

'But how would anyone know?' asked Aaron, his brow furrowed in confusion. 'Where's the proof?'

'It has to be done in public,' said Olly. 'You don't have to shag them, although obviously you can if you like. Just pull them, you know. A kiss with tongues and a cheeky arse fondle, that kind of thing. It just has to be witnessed by at least two of us.'

'Jesus,' said Rob. 'What are you? Fourteen?'

Olly shrugged. 'It's just a bit of fun, my friend. A way to pass the long summer evenings.'

'What are the categories?' Aaron asked eagerly.

Olly folded his arms and smiled. 'First up, a woman older than your mum.'

'I hate this one,' said Chris. 'I'm thirty and the youngest of four. My mum is, like, nearly seventy.'

Olly laughed. 'Tough luck, my friend. Second category is an easy one. Fake boobs.'

'This is usually the only one I ever score,' said Jonno mournfully.

'Number three, a woman who weighs more than you do.'

'OK, this is just offensive,' said Rob.

'Like you didn't spend your teenage years wanking off to Serena Williams like the rest of us,' snarked Olly, prompting a reluctant snort of laughter from Nick.

'Next up,' Olly continued, 'a woman who's still wearing tennis gear when you pull her.'

'This one's deceptively difficult,' said Chris, wafting his cigarette. 'Means a daytime pull, which is much harder.'

'Number five,' said Olly, holding up his hand with his fingers splayed. 'A married woman.'

'What if she's separated?' asked Aaron. Rob shook his head and sipped his beer, wondering why the little keener wasn't taking notes.

'Doesn't count,' said Olly. 'She has to be wearing the ring when her hand is down your pants.'

'What's the last one?' Nick asked. Rob couldn't tell if he was genuinely up for this stupid game, or just pretending to play along to avoid singling himself out. Probably not a bad strategy, to be fair.

'The ultimate challenge,' said Olly, his eyes twinkling. 'A guest at the hotel.' Chris chuckled gleefully, while Jonno rolled his eyes.

'Woah,' said Aaron. 'I thought that would get us fired?'

'That, my friend, is the challenge,' said Olly, one eyebrow

49

raised. 'You have to do it, have witnesses, but not get caught by Mark.'

'Ah fuck, man,' said Nick, shaking his head.

'Guys, I'm not interested,' Rob said, wafting Olly away dismissively.

Olly observed him coolly. 'Girls not your thing? That's not a problem, you can do the guy version.'

'We had a gay guy here last year,' said Chris. 'He totally smashed it, took all our cash. We swapped fake tits for fake tan.'

'No, I'm not gay,' Rob said, trying to laugh this whole thing off. 'I'm just not cool with treating women like boxes on a checklist. Not my thing, sorry.'

'Gentlemen, we have ourselves a feminist,' said Olly, sweeping his arm in Rob's direction.

'Fine, if you like.' Rob shrugged. 'You guys do what you want, but I'm out.'

Olly shook his head. 'Thank you so much for your permission to enjoy ourselves, Reverend Rob. Who's in?' Chris and Aaron raised their hands immediately, followed more reluctantly by Jonno. Nick glanced apologetically at Rob, then raised his hand. Rob shook his head and looked away, wondering if he hadn't just made life difficult for himself. *Oh well, too late now.*

'Who wants another beer?' asked Chris.

'Me,' said Olly, standing up and stretching lavishly, revealing a washboard stomach and Armani boxer shorts. 'One more round, *garçon*, and let another season of tennis, totty and top banter begin.'

Oh God, thought Rob. *What have I done?*

CHAPTER SIX

'Are you OK?' asked Sam, the only other person manning the front desk. Upton was an exclusive members–only country club about six miles from Guildford, complete with golf course, spa, stables and restaurant. It also had four beautiful tennis courts set in acres of Surrey countryside, but Hannah was only allowed to play on them by invitation, which only ever happened when Upton Ladies needed a secret weapon. Her official job title was Office Manager, but that covered a multitude of sins from managing IT and recruitment to ordering toilet rolls and working on reception.

'I'm absolutely fine,' she lied, forcing a smile. In truth, she was waiting for Janice, Upton's General Manager, to arrive so she could tackle her over the minor matter of her sabbatical. Until that was done, she couldn't say yes to the tennis trip.

'I love Sunday afternoons when it's pissing with rain,' said Sam. The golf course and tennis courts were empty because of the weather, and the spa closed at 2 p.m. on a Sunday so they could scrub down the sauna and filter all the fake tan out of the jacuzzi. All of which meant that the only members in the building were in the gym or lingering over Sunday lunch in the restaurant. A perfect opportunity to make a head start on summer staffing admin, not that this would be Sam's idea of a good time.

'Have you ever considered coral lipstick?' he asked casually, examining Hannah's face with a critical eye. 'It would look amazing with your skin tone.' Sam had previously worked in the MAC store in Guildford before deciding to take his customer service career in a different direction. Despite his lack of experience, jet-black hair shaved into an undercut and multiple piercings, Hannah had taken a chance on him. Mostly because he gave off good energy, but also because he looked nothing like the kind of person you'd expect to be manning the front desk of an exclusive country club. He'd turned out to be the best hire she'd ever made.

'I've never really considered any shade of lipstick,' she said, shuffling through a pile of membership applications. 'I just use lip balm.'

'Such a waste on a face like yours,' said Sam. Usually Hannah would brush off this kind of compliment, but she forced herself to engage. If she was going to get her act together for the next stage of her life, someone like Sam might be able to help her.

'What would you do if you were me?' she asked. 'If I wanted to update my look but still be Hannah, where would you start?'

'OK, wow, this is HUGE,' said Sam, holding his palms up.

Hannah rolled her eyes. 'This isn't huge, Sam. It's just a casual enquiry.'

Sam analysed her for a minute, taking in every inch from her curly hair to her sensible shoes, making her feel weirdly naked and vulnerable. 'Can I think about it? Do you a mood board? I don't want to say the first thing that comes into my head.'

'Sure. Take your time.'

'Will you actually let me see it through?' he asked excitedly. 'Take you shopping, get your hair cut, show you some make-up tips?'

'Maybe,' said Hannah. 'But only if you promise to keep it simple. I don't want some kind of extreme makeover, I'm not a doll. And you can't tell anyone.'

'Ooh, a secret project,' said Sam, clapping his hands. 'My favourite kind.'

'Well, we'll see.'

'Can I ask what's brought this on?'

Hannah looked at the genuine concern and affection on Sam's face and wondered if she should tell him. Sam wasn't a gossip, and he'd get a huge kick out of the Graham saga.

'One episode at a time, I think,' she said with a smile. 'Like TV shows in the old days.'

'Oh, come on,' pouted Sam. 'Let me binge the box set.'

Hannah shook her head. 'That wouldn't be any fun, so let's check the May staffing rotas instead.'

'Ugh,' said Sam in disgust, but he already had the file off the shelf.

'Hello, you two,' said Janice cheerfully, her heels clacking on the marbled floor. She and her husband Roger ran Upton Country Club on behalf of some foreign investors, and most of the staff assumed it was a front for money laundering; the place was always undergoing renovation or expansion and seemed to have an unlimited amount of cash.

Sam and Hannah both smiled, glad they'd been caught looking busy. In Janice's world there was never time to sit around doing nothing.

'I got your message,' she said to Hannah. 'Come on through.'

She disappeared into the back office without breaking her stride, so Hannah wiped her clammy hands on her skirt and followed, ignoring Sam's questioning look.

'I wanted to talk to you about my ten-year sabbatical,' said Hannah, once she was settled opposite Janice and it was clear that there would be no casual chit-chat. 'It's booked in for August.'

Janice sighed. 'I know we owe you, but that's an awful time for you to be away.' She was a good boss and paid her staff well, but she had an air of being permanently stressed and overburdened.

'I know. So I was wondering how you felt about May instead.'

'What, this May? That's two weeks away.'

Hannah nodded. 'I know it's short notice, but it would mean I could work the whole summer.'

Janice's eyes widened. 'You'll do the whole of July and August? Full time, no holidays?'

'Yes,' said Hannah, before pulling out her trump card. 'I'll even supervise junior tennis if you can't find anyone else.'

'Really?' gasped Janice. Upton ran a very expensive school holiday club for members' children, including tennis coaching for spoiled brats who would much rather be in the pool or playing video games. It was a nightmare assignment that Hannah had only previously agreed to do in exchange for danger money.

'Yes,' she said, praying that there'd be an apocalypse before July. Maybe a meteor, or an alien invasion, or the Rapture. Anything that would get her off the hook.

'Well, in that case,' said Janice thoughtfully, 'have a lovely sabbatical. My daughter Steph has reception experience and isn't working right now, so she might be interested in covering for you.'

'Great,' said Hannah, feeling a buzz of excitement for the first time in what felt like months. 'If she pops in next week I'll talk her through everything.'

'You're amazing,' said Janice. 'Where are you going?'

'On holiday. On my own. Well, with some friends first, and then a solo road trip.'

'Wow.' Janice gave Hannah an appraising look. 'Don't take this the wrong way, but that doesn't sound very much like you.'

Hannah shrugged and smiled. 'Well, I'm trying something new.'

Janice looked slightly disconcerted. 'You ARE going to come back, aren't you? You're not going to fly off to Thailand, take a load of mushrooms and have some kind of spiritual awakening?'

'I promise, Janice,' laughed Hannah. 'Whatever happens on my sabbatical I will not take mushrooms, and I will definitely come back.'

Janice gave her a motherly smile. 'Well then. Let's get back to work, shall we?'

'What are you doing next Friday?' Hannah asked, once Janice had clacked off to deal with a complaint about the lack of vegan options in the restaurant.

'No big plans,' Sam replied. 'We're both off in the afternoon, Janice is covering. Why do you ask?'

Hannah took a deep breath, the fizz of excitement now spreading from her chest to her belly. 'Just carrying on from our conversation earlier, I was wondering if you'd take me shopping.'

'Shit, really?'

'Yeah. Clothes, shoes, make-up, the lot. Maybe give me some ideas on a haircut. I'm going on a girls' holiday.'

'Are you kidding?' said Sam. 'Oh my God, I LIVE for this kind of stuff. Wait, I saw this collection the other day that would be perfect for you.' He craned his neck to check nobody was coming down the ornate staircase that led to the dining room, then grabbed his phone and tapped furiously until he found what he was looking for. 'Here, what do you think?'

Hannah looked as Sam scrolled through an eye-watering montage of outfits in white, turquoise, red, orange and yellow. Maybe this was a bad idea.

'Fire colours,' said Sam. 'You have a fabulous body and gorgeous colouring, so – with respect, hun – you really need to dump the black and navy and fucking BEIGE.'

'My mum has a horrible dress in that shade of yellow,' she said doubtfully, thinking of Elena's Big Bird outfit from Friday.

'Right, but is it the yellow that's horrible, or the dress?'

Hannah thought about it for a moment. 'Definitely the dress.'

'Exactly,' said Sam triumphantly. 'And anyway, colour is only part of the solution. You need pieces that complement your shape, show off your legs and make you look cute and sexy.'

Hannah swallowed nervously and looked around for lurking guests. 'Sam, I definitely can't do sexy. And this whole thing isn't about attracting men or anything. I just want to feel . . . different. I will never relax if my bum or my boobs are on show.'

Sam wafted his hand dismissively. 'Fine, no titties. What about swimwear? Is a bikini OK, or do you need some kind of shroud?'

Hannah pulled a snarky face. 'A bikini is fine. Just one of the sporty ones with a crop top and proper pants, not three lace triangles and some dental floss.'

'Totally,' said Sam happily. 'I'm thinking Baby Spice rather than Ginger Spice.'

'Yes, but also age appropriate. I'm thirty-two.'

'Understood. But just to be clear, we're leaving Sporty Spice behind, right?'

Hannah sighed heavily. 'Do we have to?'

Sam reached over and touched her arm. 'Hey, of course not,' he said softly. 'It's your body, you can wear whatever you like. I'm not saying you should throw out all the sports-wear, it's a big part of who you are. I'm just suggesting broadening your horizons a little, having some fun. If it doesn't feel right, we won't buy it. No pressure, I promise.'

Hannah nodded, feeling a wave of affection for her friend. She took a deep breath and pressed her lips together with determination. 'OK. Let's do it.'

CHAPTER SEVEN

'Holy SHIT,' gasped Gaynor, boggling at Hannah as she walked into the bar. 'What happened to you?'

'What do you mean?' said Hannah innocently. She hadn't been able to resist wearing one of her new outfits, a pair of cropped jeans with cute silver sneakers and a coral-pink jumper with a wide neck and thin straps to stop it falling off her shoulders. She was still wearing the make-up from the lesson she'd had at the MAC store earlier, and the hair stylist had worked some magic on the shape of her hair at the back, which took the weight out of her natural curls and gave it back its bounce. He'd added a few blonde highlights too, which sparkled under the twinkling lights in the bar.

'You look incredible,' said Jess, turning to Trish, who was at the bar. 'Trish, come and look at Hannah.'

Trish walked back to their table, her eyes widening. 'Oh my fucking GOD. What the hell happened? You look SPECTACULAR.'

Hannah blushed. 'Thanks, guys. Did I really look that bad before?'

'Of course not,' laughed Gaynor, twiddling her finger to prompt Hannah to give them a twirl. 'But we always said you needed a little makeover. Why didn't you ask one of us to come with you?'

'I had help,' said Hannah, 'from my friend Sam. He's really into fashion.'

'Does he charge?' asked Jess. 'I'd totally hire him.'

'Yes,' said Hannah quickly.

Trish returned to the bar and came back a minute later, manoeuvring her way through the crowd with a tray of drinks.

'I've just ordered a round of Pornstar Martinis. Do you want one?'

Hannah nodded, having no idea if she wanted one or not. She felt a bit giddy, if she was honest. On the way home she'd stopped at a homewares store and bought the first full-length mirror she'd ever owned. She'd lugged it up the stairs to her bedroom and tried on all her new outfits again, feeling more excited than she had in ages. Sam was right – it HAD been fun, and she could feel good about herself in something other than leggings and tennis skirts.

'So are you coming?' asked Jess excitedly, as they found their way to a table by the window. 'Please tell me you haven't gone to all this trouble just to blow us out.'

'I'm coming,' said Hannah, prompting happy whoops from Jess and Gaynor. 'But let's wait for Trish to get back, because I have some conditions.'

'Uh oh,' said Gaynor.

'I can't believe what a difference your haircut has made,' said Jess, leaning round to look at the back. 'It's totally changed the shape of your face.'

'I'm really pleased,' said Hannah. 'I can't stop touching it.'

'I'm SO jealous,' said Trish, arriving with another orange drink and a shot of prosecco. 'You've had a movie makeover day. I bet it was really fun.'

'To Club Colina,' said Jess, tipping the shot of prosecco into the glass and holding it up. Hannah followed suit and did a round of cheers-ing, then took a sip, feeling uncharacteristically happy. The drink tasted sweet and foamy and not remotely like booze, which was always a worry.

'Hannah's coming with us,' Jess told Trish. 'But she has conditions.'

Trish pulled a face. 'Eek. Come on then, let's hear them.'

'OK,' said Hannah, putting her drink back on the table and looking round at the three women. 'First of all, I'm not going to be the group mother. You can do whatever you like, obviously, but I'm not going to clean up after all your mess, physical or emotional.'

'Wow, that's a brutal start,' said Gaynor.

'But point totally taken,' said Jess, waving her hand for Hannah to continue. 'Carry on.'

'If I don't want to go out drinking or partying, you're not allowed to give me a hard time about it.'

'Absolutely. You can also do whatever you like, no judgement.'

'I can't just drink booze and eat junk for a week. I need proper food, or I'll feel awful and play bad tennis.'

'That's easy. The food there is great and Gaynor's vegan, so we can't just eat any old shite.'

'Although churros are technically vegan,' Gaynor chimed in. 'Everyone forgets that.'

'Great. Also we play tennis, every day. I'm not going to sit around while you all nurse massive hangovers.'

Jess nodded firmly. 'Totally. That's actually one of our own rules. We've never missed a coaching session, I promise.'

'Perfect,' said Hannah. 'And finally, you have to support

me. I've never done this kind of thing before, so it's a really big deal for me.'

Gaynor moved to interrupt, but Jess put her hand on her arm. 'No, this is important,' she said softly, gesturing to Hannah to continue. 'Let her finish.'

'I can only be myself, and that's not always . . . conventional, I guess. But if you're all willing to have my back, I'd love to come.'

Jess, Gaynor and Trish all looked at each other and nodded, their faces breaking into huge grins. 'It's a deal,' said Jess, holding out her hand for Hannah to shake.

Hannah waited by the taxi rank across the road from the bar, in a warm and fuzzy state that denoted slightly drunk but not plastered. She'd had a fun night, but now she was ready for her bed. She'd bought some cute holiday pyjamas, so maybe she'd give them a whirl.

'Hannah?' said a male voice. She turned to see Graham coming out of the tiny Italian restaurant where they used to go on date nights, before date nights became three times a year, and then birthdays only. He was wearing old jeans and a green check shirt she'd bought him for his thirtieth birthday, a black bomber jacket slung over his arm. The colour of the shirt still matched his eyes, but it had fitted better a couple of years ago. Now the buttons strained over his broad chest.

'Oh, hi.' Hannah forced a smile, refusing to let a chance encounter with Graham spoil her happy mood. It was a small town, and they couldn't avoid each other for ever.

'What are you doing here?' His eyes widened as he took in her new look.

'I'm waiting for a taxi,' she said, pointing out the obvious. 'I've just been out with some friends.'

'What friends? Why are you all dressed up?' His eyes narrowed with suspicion. 'Have you been on a date?'

'No, Graham.' Hannah bridled at the disbelief and surprise in his voice. 'And even if I had, it wouldn't be any of your business.'

Now it was Graham's turn to bristle with annoyance. 'You're still my wife.'

'On paper, maybe,' said Hannah mildly. 'In reality . . . not so much.' Three Pornstar Martinis had made her a bit sassy, apparently, or maybe that was the new clothes.

'You've had your hair done,' he said, his tone now slightly accusatory. 'And you're wearing make-up.'

Hannah resisted the urge to roll her eyes, instead giving him a curious smile which she knew would infuriate him more. 'Why are you telling me things I already know? What are you doing here, anyway?'

'Oh, I . . .' Graham muttered, his voice trailing off as a woman in her mid-twenties appeared from the restaurant and walked towards them, wearing a pale pink dress that fitted closely to the gentle swell of her belly. She wrestled an arm into a denim jacket, shifting her handbag from one shoulder to the other so she could get the other arm in.

'Sorry,' she said breathlessly. 'Some woman was in the loo chatting on her phone, I had to bang on the door.' She noticed Hannah for the first time, then looked from her to Graham, then back again.

'Hi, you must be Lucy.'

Lucy looked at Hannah blankly.

'I'm Hannah.'

Graham cleared his throat and smoothed his hand over his hair, looking like he wished the pavement would open up and swallow him whole.

'Oh, wow,' said Lucy, looking frantically at Graham for support and finding him looking the other way, his hands now buried in his pockets. 'I'm . . . you're . . . it's nice to meet you.'

'You too,' said Hannah as a taxi pulled into the rank. 'Have a great evening.'

She opened the rear door and climbed in, but not before she heard Lucy hiss, 'You said I was much prettier than her, but she's gorgeous. Why would you lie?' Graham's evening was about to go rapidly downhill.

Hannah wiped her clammy hands on her jeans and took deep breaths. There was nothing she could do about Graham; he'd made his choices, and now he was going to have to live with the consequences. But for Hannah, it felt like the rest of her life was laid out in front of her for the taking, and it was terrifying and exciting in equal measure.

She wound down the window and let the fresh April air blow on her face, mussing her hair and making her eyes water. *I don't care*, she thought. *First game, second set. Players are ready.*

PART TWO

Match Point

CHAPTER EIGHT

Two Weeks Later

'Fucking hell, this is definitely my happy place.' Gaynor was stretched out and face down on a sun lounger with a Marian Keyes paperback dangling in her hand. 'No husband and no kids for a whole week.' She was wearing a yellow bikini that showed off her tan, which had been applied hastily from a bottle if the brown streaks on the back of her thighs were anything to go by.

'I know,' sighed Jess, 'this is the best week of my year. I already don't want it to end, and we haven't even started yet. Trish, you OK?'

Trish gave a small snore, her mouth hanging open. Their flight from Gatwick had left at 7 a.m., so they'd all been up at the crack of dawn. Much as Hannah couldn't wait to get on the tennis court tomorrow, it was nice to lie in the sun and doze with nowhere else to be.

'Where are we going tonight?' asked Gaynor.

'It's Saturday night,' said Jess, not even opening her eyes. 'Dinner in the hotel at eight, then we're off out to Marbella. I've got a taxi picking us up at nine thirty.'

Gaynor yawned and turned her head to Hannah. 'Jess is our organiser,' she said. 'Every girls' trip needs one. We go wherever she says.'

'Fine by me.' Hannah sat up and adjusted the straps on her

new bikini. 'It's what I do for a living, so I'm very happy to have a week off.'

'Are you sure?' asked Jess, suddenly alert. 'You can take over if you want.'

Hannah smiled and said nothing, feeling like she was starting to get a handle on each of these three women. She'd had a few catch-ups with them over the past couple of weeks, mostly drinks in the pub after training so they could make plans. Jess was the mother figure of the three, and whilst she moaned about taking responsibility for bookings and taxis and calculating the four-way split of the bill, it was clear she actually revelled in how essential she was to the smooth running of this trip. Gaynor was happy to go with the flow as long as she had booze and good company along the way – based on what Hannah had seen so far, Gaynor was likely to be the last one standing, probably on a bar lip-synching to Beyoncé, using an empty wine bottle as a microphone. Trish was the unpredictable one, prone to pouty sulking if things weren't going her way – Hannah had seen that side to her on the tennis court plenty of times. Everyone smoothed the path for Trish because she was adorable and funny, and you couldn't help but love her. Hannah hadn't quite worked out yet if that was natural charm or pure manipulation, so was on her guard as far as Trish was concerned.

She stood up and stretched, relishing the warmth of the stone tiles underfoot as she walked to the wide steps at the shallow end of the large, glistening pool. Her new bikini fitted perfectly, with a pink and orange crop top that was pretty much exactly like a sports bra, paired with matching bikini pants that covered most of her bum. There were a dozen or so other loungers occupied round the pool, mostly couples or other women; the hotel didn't cater for children. Nobody was paying her any attention; they were all just happy to be on holiday away from the spring rain in the UK.

'You have such an amazing body,' muttered Gaynor, following her to the water. 'Mine used to look like yours before I pushed out two kids.'

'Same,' said Jess, joining them both. 'Now I've got stretch marks and a fanny like a string bag.' They all sat on the warm step with their feet in the water, sunglasses on and their faces tilted towards the sun. 'You have nice feet too,' she added, looking at Hannah's freshly painted pink toes dabbling in the water. 'Mine have been trashed by killer heels.'

'I've never worn heels,' said Hannah with a smile. 'My friend Sam persuaded me to buy some, just low ones, but I'm still not sure I can walk in them.'

'You've never worn heels?' exclaimed Gaynor. 'Not even on your wedding day?'

'No,' said Hannah. 'I wore ballet flats.'

'All right, Jane Austen,' Gaynor snorted. 'What else is frowned upon in that church of yours?'

Hannah scowled and shook her head. 'It's not *my* church, hasn't been for a long time.'

'OK, but growing up,' pressed Gaynor, her eyes glittering. 'What weren't you allowed to do?'

'There was an actual list of forbidden things,' replied Hannah with an awkward smile, holding out her hand so she could tick them off on her fingers. 'Let's see. Tight or revealing clothing, tattoos, piercings, alcohol, smoking, drugs, swearing, make-up, sex before marriage. Oh, and masturbation.'

'What, no wanking?' said Jess, her eyes boggling. 'Including the men?'

'Hold on, I'm coming,' said Trish, shaking herself out of her nap and hauling herself off her sun lounger. 'Don't you dare have this conversation without me.' She hurried over and joined the other three on the wide steps, their feet cooling in the shallows. The late-afternoon sun made Hannah's skin tingle.

'I think masturbation was fine for the men. But it was considered sinful for women.'

'Typical,' said Jess.

'Fuck, have you seen the view?' gasped Trish, grabbing Hannah's arm as a group of men strolled down the side of the pool towards them. They moved in one fluid group, like cheetahs filmed in slow-motion on a wildlife documentary.

'That's the coaching team,' said Jess. 'I recognise a couple of them from last time.'

'I swear to God they get younger every year,' muttered Gaynor. 'Do you think being insanely hot is part of the job description?' She raised her hand as the man at the front of the group smiled in greeting, before turning into the glass doors to the hotel. 'What was his name? Olly, I think.'

'One of them's Olly and one of them's Chris,' said Jess. 'But I can't remember which one is which. The blonde guy Jonno, he coached us when we were last here. Welsh.'

'Sorry, can we please take a moment to acknowledge the tall guy with the dark hair at the back?' said Trish. 'I'm pretty sure he's new.'

'Can you guys hear yourselves?' laughed Hannah, who had struggled to take her eyes off the tall guy too, not that she was going to mention it. He wore a baseball cap and sunglasses so she couldn't see much of his face, but everything from the neck down was pretty impressive. 'You're practically drooling.'

'She's right,' said Trish gloomily, dragging herself away from the parade of superior manhood as they disappeared into the hotel. 'Let's get back to Hannah and her weird rules. No wanking or booze or piercings or tight clothes? You've left all that behind though, right?'

Hannah nodded. 'Pretty much. I've got pierced ears, and I drink sometimes. Love a bit of Lycra for sport, which was never OK when I was a teenager.'

'So how do you feel about sex before marriage now?' asked Trish.

'Fine,' said Hannah with a shrug. 'I definitely wouldn't get married again without it, anyway.'

'So what else has stuck?' asked Jess. 'Anything you still won't do?'

Hannah thought about it for a moment. 'I never swear.'

Gaynor laughed. 'Shit, I say "fuck" about a hundred times a day.'

'I've noticed,' said Hannah wryly. 'Look, I'm not a puritan or anything. It was just forbidden for the first eighteen years of my life, so I guess I've never got into the habit.'

'Sorry to rewind a bit,' said Trish. 'But I still have more questions about the sex before marriage thing.'

Hannah smiled and raised her eyebrows, surprised at how relaxed she felt in the company of these women. 'Go on.'

'You got married at eighteen, right?' said Trish. 'Does that mean your ex-husband, what's his name?'

'Graham.'

'Exactly. Does that mean Graham is the only man you've ever shagged?'

Hannah nodded. 'Yep.'

'And he was shit in bed?'

'I have no idea,' said Hannah. 'I've got nothing to compare it to, I've never even kissed anyone else. But if that's as good as it gets, I want a refund.'

'Fuuuuck,' said Gaynor, splashing her feet with excitement. 'This is HUGE. We need to get you back on that horse, and this is the perfect place.' She held her hands up, her fingers splayed for added drama. 'This holiday is going to be your journey of self-discovery.'

Hannah laughed. 'Sorry, but that's not my plan. I promised myself this trip would be about making time for myself, and I'm definitely not interested in men right now.'

'Not even a hot tennis coach?' asked Jess. 'If he was a total gentleman and wore a condom and everything?'

'Nope,' said Hannah, shaking her head firmly. 'And anyway, I'm not a casual sex kind of person. I wouldn't even know where to start.'

Gaynor grinned. 'It's easy. Since you and Trish are the two singles in our group, we start by making sure you both go out tonight looking a million fucking dollars.'

'I'm totally down with that,' said Trish.

'Can't we look a million dollars too?' asked Jess, her face mutinous.

'Course,' laughed Gaynor. 'We're just the boring marrieds who only get to watch.'

'That's fine,' Jess shrugged. 'We get to live vicariously through these two without the effort of taking our knickers off.'

'Oh God, we're old,' muttered Gaynor, sliding into the pool and turning to face the others. 'Do you think I can still do a handstand?'

CHAPTER NINE

By midnight Hannah was three mojitos down and ready to call it a night. Her toes felt squashed, her heels were rubbing and the balls of her feet were throbbing in the silver kitten-heeled slingbacks Sam had talked her into. She'd had an amazing night of cocktails and dancing, but she was also a bit drunk and more than a bit tired – all she wanted was a taxi home, a shower to freshen up, then her bed.

'One more,' said Gaynor, holding up her empty glass. 'It's my round. Pleeeeeease.'

Hannah rolled her eyes and nodded, not wanting to be the one who bailed out early on their first night. Her feet would be back in trainers tomorrow, and she'd never have to wear these stupid shoes again. 'I'll get them,' she said, sliding Gaynor's debit card into the pocket of her skirt. Getting the drinks meant she could order a virgin mojito and none of the others would be any the wiser. The other women whooped enthusiastically as Dua Lipa's 'Physical' started to play, heading back to the dancefloor as Hannah weaved her way to the bar. It was only two deep, so hopefully she wouldn't have to wait long.

Hannah was squatting down to adjust one of the rubbing straps on her left shoe when the man in front of her finished paying and turned around. He tripped straight over her crouching form, tipping what felt like several gallons of beer over her head and down her front before toppling sideways into a pillar. 'Oh SHIT,' he yelled, turning back as Hannah stood up, her eyes wide with shock.

'I . . .' gasped Hannah, looking down at her white silk top, which was now soaked to the point of being entirely transparent. She wasn't wearing a bra, and it now looked like she'd wrapped her boobs in clingfilm. She quickly crossed her arms over her chest and frantically searched for an appropriate response in a world with no swear words.

'Oh my God, I'm SO sorry,' said the man, clearly looking for a way to make this situation better without actually touching her, and coming up with nothing. 'I really didn't see you there.'

'I was fixing my shoe,' Hannah said pointlessly, cold lager now dripping from her hair and running down her cheeks into her mouth. 'I'll just go to the loo.' She rushed off, arms still clamped over her boobs and droplets of beer now spinning off in all directions.

'Emergency,' she squeaked, pushing past the queue of women outside the toilets and heading straight for the sinks.

'Holy shit, what happened to you?' said a blonde in a tiny black skirt and a hot pink boob tube, eight inches of mahogany-tanned abs on display in between. She popped her lipstick back in her bag and handed Hannah a stack of paper towels.

'Some guy just tipped his beer on me,' said Hannah, dabbing at her face as her hair dripped into the sink. 'It was an accident, but I'm soaked.'

'Shitting fuck,' said the woman, taking in Hannah's transparent top and extremely visible nipples. 'Do you want my emergency T-shirt?' She rummaged in her handbag and pulled out a drawstring bag, like the kind of thing Hannah used to put her swimming stuff in for school.

'Why do you have an emergency T-shirt?' asked Hannah with a confused smile, as the woman handed her a cropped white top with a sequinned rainbow on it.

'If I score later, it means I don't have to do the walk of shame tomorrow dressed like this. I've got a floaty skirt too, and some flip-flops. Do you need either of them?'

'No, this is perfect,' said Hannah, turning back to face the sink and quickly whipping off her wet top, using the remaining dry section to towel off her dripping chest. She pulled the T-shirt over her head, figuring that everyone in this toilet had already seen her nipples and now probably wasn't the time to be shy about it. 'How can I get it back to you?'

'Don't worry about it,' said the woman, wafting her away. 'We girls gotta help each other out, right? Just carry an emergency T-shirt from now on; pass on the love.'

'I will, thank you SO much,' said Hannah, giving her a quick hug and hurrying back to the bar. The smell of beer in her hair was making her feel sick, so she bypassed the queue for drinks and headed straight outside, plonking herself down on a bench and pulling off her stupid shoes. The feeling of cool air and unrestricted freedom on her crushed feet felt blissful.

'Oh, thank God, there you are,' said a voice. The man with the beer was back, this time holding two bar towels and a Bulldog Gin promotional T-shirt, still in its plastic bag. 'I begged these from the bar staff, thought they might help.'

'I'm fine,' said Hannah. 'A woman in the loos helped me out.'

The man sighed heavily and dropped the towels and

T-shirt on the bench. 'I'm really sorry. Can I sit down for a minute?'

Hannah nodded, looking at him properly for the first time as he plonked himself down next to her. Maybe a few years younger than her, but insanely good-looking. Tall, dark hair, wearing a turquoise polo shirt with jeans and black canvas skate shoes, the sleeves of the polo stretched around his tanned, muscular arms. He looked vaguely familiar, but right now she couldn't place him.

'Are you going to stab me with those?' he asked, gesturing to the heels she was holding by their ridiculous, skin-rubbing straps.

Hannah couldn't help but laugh, which prompted his features to soften into a smile. He wasn't just handsome, he was gorgeous, and for a second she felt like her lungs had stopped working.

'No,' she said, pulling herself together. 'They're new, and they're agony. I'd rather go barefoot.'

The man smiled and shook his head. 'Women have a rough deal. I just switch out of one pair of trainers into another.'

'I'm definitely in trainers from tomorrow. I don't care if it's a night out.'

'At least I didn't wreck your skirt.' Hannah looked down, hyper-aware that this guy was totally checking her out. Flirting was wildly out of her comfort zone, but the feeling of being noticed was new and not entirely unpleasant.

'It has pockets.' She glanced at him, expecting him to look thoroughly bored by this lame revelation. But his eyes never left hers, and the small smile on his lips made her wonder whether he was a bit dazzled, or just a bit drunk.

76

'I'm Rob,' he said, holding out his hand. 'Sorry for dumping my beer on you.'

'Hannah,' she replied, feeling herself blush as his warm, strong hand enclosed hers. She was suddenly aware of how close he was, and how great he looked, and how she had ratty, beer-soaked hair and a very tight rainbow T-shirt that didn't even cover her midriff. 'Sorry for knocking you sideways.'

He blinked twice, a startled expression on his face that Hannah couldn't quite read. Then he shook his head slightly, as if his attention had drifted for a moment, and smiled. 'Are you here on your own?' It sounded like an invitation, a precursor to 'Can I have your number?' and Hannah wondered for a reckless second if she would give it to him. *Where have I seen him before?*

'No, my girlfriends are inside,' she said. 'You?'

'I left mine in another bar,' said Rob. 'They're work colleagues rather than mates, and sometimes they do my head in.'

'Oh wow,' said Hannah. 'So do you—?'

'She's HERE,' said Trish's voice, calling to the others as she wobbled in Hannah's direction in vertiginous heels. 'Come on, we're going. Some guy is hitting on Gay and he's a total creep. Jess is getting us a taxi.' She glanced at Rob appreciatively, her slightly crossed eyes widening. 'Oh HELLO. I'm Trish, who are you?'

'We're going,' said Hannah quickly, worried that Trish might keel over and take Rob out for the second time this evening.

'TAXI,' shouted Jess from the side of the road. Gaynor was already climbing into the back, so Trish grabbed Hannah's hand and started to yank her over. Hannah winced as her bare feet caught on some loose stones on the pavement.

'Where are you staying?' shouted Rob, but Hannah was already being bundled into the cab, Trish following close behind.

'Who was that?' asked Jess, turning around in the front seat as the taxi pulled away. Hannah leaned forward to look out of the window, where Rob was watching them drive away, his hand raised in a half-wave. 'And why do you stink of beer?'

'Yeah, what happened to you?' asked Gaynor. 'You went to get drinks, then disappeared.'

'Is that a different T-shirt?' asked Trish.

Hannah felt suddenly hot and dizzy, trying to process her encounter with Rob and field this barrage of questions. Half an hour ago she'd have given anything to be in this taxi on her way to her bed, but now she only wanted to be back on the bench, telling Rob her skirt had pockets and seeing him smile at her like that.

Stop it, she told herself. *He's just a hot guy trying to get you into bed, you'll never see him again.*

'Oh God, tennis tomorrow,' slurred Trish. 'I'm going to be hanging.'

I'm in Spain, thought Hannah happily, reluctantly pushing Rob from her mind. *I've got five hours of tennis tomorrow, I've got a month off work, and Graham and Lucy are hundreds of miles away.* She pulled out her phone and held it up for a group selfie, then quickly WhatsApped it to Sam with the message *Drunk and happy. Heels going back in my suitcase, I'm all about the sparkly trainers from now on. Love you x*

'That was such a fun night,' said Gaynor, yawning lavishly. 'But I need my bed.'

Hannah's phone buzzed – a reply from Sam. *You look entirely fabulous. Knock them all out tomorrow xxx*

Or sideways, thought Hannah, already thinking about how great a shower and clean sheets were going to feel.

CHAPTER TEN

Hannah half-jogged towards the tennis centre, her racquet bag slung over her shoulder and her hair squashed under a white visor. She'd gone to bed with it wet last night, and this morning she'd woken up looking like Marge Simpson. If she'd known the rest of the group would be so unbothered about being late, she'd have taken the time to style it properly instead of just flattening it down and hoping for the best.

Jess had told her to go ahead in the end, sensing Hannah's frustration at the prospect of being late for their first coaching session, and promising to herd the others out the door within five minutes. So now it was just Hannah hurrying down the steps to court number eight, where their coach was busy laying out a basket of balls at each corner of the court. He turned towards her, and they both froze in silent shock.

'Oh, wow,' said Rob. He laughed nervously, then covered his mouth with his hand and looked up at her.

'OH,' exclaimed Hannah, as her brain connected the dots. She'd fallen asleep thinking about Rob last night, and now here he was, in Club Colina. 'Are you our coach?' She noted that her palms felt suddenly sweaty, even though it was only 9 a.m.

Rob nodded, looking flustered. 'Yeah, I guess I am. I hope that's OK?'

'Of course,' said Hannah, not entirely sure if it was OK or not. Her memory of last night was admittedly hazy and this was hardly her field of expertise, but it had definitely felt like there had been some kind of . . . *something* in the air between her and Rob, however brief. Her delight at seeing him again was tempered by the discovery that he was a tennis coach, and therefore almost certainly a total player when it came to women.

'Wow, this is so weird,' said Rob, rubbing his stubbly jaw. 'Did you get back OK?' The question was weak, all his confidence from last night suddenly gone.

'Yeah,' said Hannah, wondering if he'd realised she wasn't all that special without the beer goggles. The thought made her squirm with embarrassment. 'It was fine.'

'That's good,' said Rob. Neither of them said anything more, until the noise of Jess, Gaynor and Trish jogging onto the court gave them a welcome reprieve.

'Sorry we're late,' said Jess. 'I'm Jess.'

Rob regained his enthusiasm and shook her hand, then introduced himself to the other women. Hannah watched Trish carefully to see if she'd make the connection with the man she'd briefly met last night, but there wasn't even a flicker of recognition. No great surprise, considering Trish's eyes had been looking in different directions at the time.

'Nice play, Jess,' said Rob, giving her a clap as she finished off the point with a blistering forehand that had practically landed on Trish's feet. They'd already done a warm-up and a drills session, and now Rob was watching their match play to identify their individual weaknesses. Hannah crouched over, ready to receive Jess's next serve, trying not to feel self-conscious under his appraising gaze. He might not be interested in her as a woman, but surely he'd appreciate her as a tennis player? As long as she held her focus and didn't get distracted, anyway, which was already lining up to be a huge potential weakness. Why did he have to be so good-looking? And why was she sweating so much? It wasn't even that hot.

'Sorry, everyone,' shouted Jess, snapping Hannah back into the real world. 'I've broken a string.'

Rob glanced at his watch. 'We'll take a break. You can drop that one off at the clubhouse and get it re-strung.'

'Thanks,' said Jess. 'There's no hurry, I've got a spare.'

'Let's have lunch,' he called to the others. They all wandered over, breathing heavily from the exertion. Hannah bent down to grab a water bottle from her bag, turning to face him so she didn't give him a prime view of her backside in a pink and white tennis skirt.

'Where are we going tonight?' asked Gaynor, idly checking her phone for messages.

'The Luna Lounge,' said Jess. 'It's happy hour until ten, two for one on cocktails. I've booked us a table by the window from nine, so let's do dinner at seven thirty in the hotel.'

'This your first season here?' Trish asked Rob, sidling over to him. She pulled the band out of her ponytail and shook her hair free, which reminded Hannah of those birds that flash their plumage as part of a mating dance. Of course Trish would make a play for Rob – she was single and he was gorgeous. The question was, how would Rob respond? Hannah had only spent twenty minutes in his company and absolutely wasn't interested in a holiday fling, but the thought of Rob and Trish hooking up still made her a bit itchy. It was an unfamiliar feeling, and she didn't like it one bit.

'Yeah,' said Rob. 'How long have you ladies been coming?'

'This is our fifth time, but that's been spread over, like, a decade. We've had to take breaks for babies and Covid and stuff.'

'Hannah, I love that tennis skirt,' said Gaynor.

Hannah returned a shy smile. 'Thanks, it's new. Everything I brought on this holiday is new.'

'Hannah had a big makeover before this trip,' explained Trish, grinning at Rob. 'You wouldn't have recognised her a month ago, honestly.'

'I don't think Rob needs to know that,' said Hannah quickly, blushing under Rob's curious gaze.

'I've actually got a pretty good memory for faces,' he said with a shrug. 'You meet so many people doing this job, then one night you see them in a bar and they look completely different. So I have to pay attention.'

Hannah turned away to hide her smile, wondering if the penny would drop for Trish. There was no reason why Jess and Gaynor would make the connection from last night – Rob had just been a distant blur from a moving taxi – but Trish had practically sat on his lap.

'Yeah, I'm good at that too,' said Trish, giving him a megawatt smile. Rob caught Hannah's eye and his mouth twitched, and it felt for the briefest moment like they were back on that bench in Marbella again.

CHAPTER ELEVEN

Rob took the steps up to the terrace two at a time, leaving the women to grab food and drinks while he went to the bathroom in the clubhouse. He locked the door to the cubicle and sat on the closed lid, taking deep breaths and trying to make sense of the chaotic thoughts in his head.

First, the insane coincidence that the woman he'd met in Marbella last night was not only a guest at the hotel, but also part of the group he was coaching this week. He hadn't even planned to BE in that bar – he'd left the rest of the coaches circling a group of much older women in pursuit of a bingo win, and picked the first place that looked half-decent.

And God, her tennis. Mark had told him this would be the strongest group of female players he'd work with all season, and he wasn't kidding. Gaynor tended to lose focus at the net and Trish could generate more power in her backhand, but Jess was a solid all-rounder and they made an impressive team. But Hannah . . . well, she was definitely the star of this particular show.

Watching her this morning had taken his breath away. Strong shoulders, feet firmly planted, absolute focus on the ball. And that olive skin and gorgeous curly hair, never mind those legs . . . yet she clearly had absolutely no idea how well she played and how great she looked. The other three were hyper self-aware, but Hannah lit up the court without even trying. He hadn't been able to stop looking at her, in the same way he hadn't been able to stop looking at her in Marbella last night. Maybe he'd just had too much sun, or he'd gone too long without sex.

If he was honest, he'd gone to bed thinking about Hannah. He'd kicked himself for not getting her number – even though he'd vowed not to even look at women until he got back to the UK, there was something about her that had tested his resolve.

Rob dropped his head into his hands and rubbed his eyes. How could she be a guest at the hotel? Somehow that felt SO much worse than never seeing her again. Now he had to spend hours of every day with her, knowing that she was strictly off limits.

There's nothing you can do about it, and sitting in this toilet cubicle isn't helping, he told himself. He took a deep breath and headed out, only to discover Head Coach Mark using one of the urinals.

'Hey, Rob, you OK?' he asked.

'Fine,' said Rob, pointlessly washing his hands so Mark didn't think he had poor hygiene standards.

'How are you finding your group?' asked Mark, zipping himself up and following Rob out without going anywhere near the sink.

'They're great,' said Rob, conscious to avoid getting too friendly with Mark. He'd already drawn attention to himself by refusing to board Olly's Club Colina Banter Bus, and he definitely didn't want the others to think he was part of Mark's crew.

'I'm going to keep you on the next lot of Gloss Mums, I think,' Mark said thoughtfully. He had names for all the different groups of women who booked into Club Colina – the Gloss Mums were well-to-do women in their thirties and forties who had escaped from their families for a week and made the most of every single minute. The Menos were the women in their fifties who worried that the humidity might unstick their HRT patches, and the Lady Greys were the over-sixties. There were sub-categories of all three groups – Essex Gloss Mums, Loaded Lady Greys, Divorced Menos. Rob found the whole business gross and sexist, particularly as Mark didn't seem to have similar labels for the men. But Mark ran the show, and he was nothing but respectful when the guests could hear him. Much as it wound him up, Rob was learning to pick his battles.

'Why me?' he asked. He'd assumed that old hands like Olly and Chris and Jonno would get the best female players, and he and Nick and Aaron would get whoever was left.

'Because you're a great coach, and you don't get distracted,' said Mark. 'I see all the women chatting you up, trying to get you into the holiday fuck zone. Been there, done that, believe me.' His eyes glazed over with hazy nostalgia, like he was mentally re-living past glories. Rob said nothing, keen to avoid hearing about the notches on Mark's Club Colina bedpost. 'But you've got your eye on the ball. That's what I need here.'

Rob sighed internally, knowing this was just going to be another black mark against him on Olly's score sheet. He wondered if Mark knew about Club Colina Bingo, and that Rob had opted out.

'Got a few more good groups coming up in the next few weeks,' continued Mark, flipping through the pages on his clipboard. 'Great bunch of Gloss Mums from Kent first week in June, they've been a few times. First division district league players, almost as good as your Surrey lot. All pretty easy on the eye, too.'

'Shouldn't one of the more experienced coaches take them?' Rob had decided he'd rather coach men or floss-haired pensioners for the rest of the season, just to free himself from this relentless parade of hot women.

'Who do I have to shag to get some lunch around here?' bellowed Olly, bouncing up the steps to the clubhouse terrace two at a time. 'All right, Reverend,' he said to Rob with a sneer, shoving him on the shoulder as he passed. 'Good to see you getting cosy with management.' He barged his way through the loitering players to the lunch table, not noticing or caring when he elbowed a plastic cup of water out of one woman's hand and soaked her trainers.

'No,' said Mark, narrowing his eyes as he watched Olly take a sandwich off the tray, poke the filling with his finger and lick it, then pull a face and put it back. 'Whenever we have really great female players, I'd definitely like you to coach them.'

Once Rob had finished his lunch, every bite of which tasted like dust, he headed over to the coaches' table. It was on the edge of the terrace away from the guests, which meant they could talk business and scheduling during the breaks without being interrupted. 'How's your morning been?' he asked Nick.

'Good,' said Nick. 'Big mixed group of Greys from Kent. Decent players, nobody's killed each other yet.'

'I see you got the Surrey MILFs,' drawled Olly, wandering over with a huge slab of cake in his hand. 'You really are wanking Mark off, aren't you?' He chewed with his mouth open, his square jaw working away like a grazing cow.

Rob ignored him, watching Aaron scurry across the terrace towards them. 'Where are we going tonight?' he asked, obviously desperate not to be left out. 'I need a beer. I've got four Alpha Wankers from Windsor who've got four-hundred-quid racquets and don't know which end to hold.' In the absence of any official shorthand descriptors for the male groups, Aaron had been making up his own, and Rob had to admit that Alpha Wankers was a great fit.

'We should go to Marbella again,' said Olly, casting his eye over the women on the terrace and settling on Gaynor, who was squatting down to re-tie her laces. 'Maybe later in the week, when this lot start warming up.'

'How about the Luna Lounge?' said Rob, remembering Jess's plans. He only realised he'd said it out loud when it was too late, instantly kicking himself for his stupid lack of discipline. 'Um, I haven't been there yet, and I've read some good reviews.'

Olly raised his eyebrows. 'Well, if TripAdvisor here says we should go to the Luna Lounge, I'm not going to argue. Are you planning to go to bed early again?'

Rob smiled, desperately wanting to punch Olly in his giant bovine face, but deciding he wasn't worth getting fired over. 'I never leave before I've bought a round, which is all that matters.'

'That's actually true,' drawled Olly as Jonno joined them. 'Luna Lounge tonight, mate. Reverend Rob is getting his wallet out.'

'Will there be women?' asked Aaron. 'I need to tick off

some more bingo wins; I've only got one so far and it's stressing me out.'

'There's always women in the Luna Lounge,' said Olly with a wolfish grin. 'Why don't you introduce us to your group, Rob? I'd quite like to tick off hotel resident sooner rather than later, and they seem like a good bet.'

'I bet they're all married too,' said Aaron. 'Olly, can I tick off more than one box? Like if she's married, a hotel guest and has fake tits, can I claim all three?'

'No.' Olly looked at Aaron in disgust. 'You can only tick off one category at a time. Unless you manage a threesome.'

'Jesus,' said Rob, shaking his head.

'You ever done that?' asked Nick, his dark eyes glittering.

'Yeah,' said Olly, looking a bit misty-eyed as he polished off his cake. 'Mother and daughter. Ticked off older than my mum and weighs more than me in one night.'

'So what do you reckon?' asked Aaron, nodding towards Gaynor and Jess, who were deep in conversation. 'Would you chalk up one of those against hotel guest, or married?'

'Hotel guest is much harder than married,' said Chris, leaning back to check out the group. 'I reckon the one with the curly hair. Great legs. I wonder what time they open?'

Rob took deep breaths as he followed Chris's line of sight towards Hannah, the only one of the group with curly hair. 'I think she's gay,' he said quickly. 'I'm pretty sure I heard her mention a girlfriend earlier.'

'Is that on the bingo?' Aaron asked. 'Could I swap that for older than my mum?'

'Not a chance,' said Olly. 'Although aren't you, like, twelve?

I bet your mum isn't a day over fifty. Rob, call them over to say hello.'

'Do we have to?' Rob protested. 'It's their lunch break, and I'm not throwing my players into your fucking *Hunger Games* arena.'

'You're not playing, what do you care?' said Olly, a note of challenge creeping into his voice. 'I tell you what, why don't you invite them to the Luna Lounge tonight?'

'You can chat to the gay one,' said Chris. 'Leave the rest of them to us.'

Rob hesitated, conscious that he'd just inadvertently given himself a way to talk to Hannah without looking like he was chatting her up. It was powerfully tempting, even though what remaining common sense he had was telling him to stay well away.

'Fine,' he said. 'But you'd better behave yourselves; I've got to coach these women all week.'

'You poor baby,' said Olly, his voice dripping with sarcasm. 'You get to coach a group of really fit women, and all you had to do was suck Mark's tiny dick. Must be terrible.'

Rob sighed heavily and stood up, giving Olly the benefit of his full height. He leaned over to whisper gently in his ear. 'You know why Mark doesn't let you coach the top groups, Olly? Because you're a prick and nobody likes you, and also you smell fucking awful. I just thought you should know.' He walked towards the bar, smiling as he glanced back to see Olly surreptitiously scratching his armpit, then sniffing his fingers.

Hannah was between him and the bar, so he breathed in as hard as he could to avoid touching her as he edged past. He caught a whiff of her sun cream and some kind of fruity shampoo, and clenched his fists to control the urge to stroke the warm, smooth skin of her shoulders. By the time he grabbed a drink and moved to the far side of the terrace, he felt hot and anxious, like he was hyperventilating or something. He stood with his back to the crowd of players and coaches, taking deep breaths until he felt more normal. Whatever it was about Hannah that was making him unsettled, he definitely needed to get it under control.

CHAPTER TWELVE

The Luna Lounge was a small, dimly lit cocktail bar half a mile down the steep hill from the hotel – an easy walk down hundreds of steps that weaved between villas and apartments, then a thigh-burning workout or a taxi back up. They'd all decided to worry about that later, and in the meantime were relaxing at a table by the window overlooking the twinkling lights of Andalusia. Hannah liked it; it was less chaotic than the bar in Marbella last night, and the crowd was definitely less drunk. A band was warming up in the corner, after which a DJ would take over until the bar closed at four.

'Isn't that the coaching team?' said Gaynor, narrowing her eyes as the group of men pushed through the doors and towards the bar.

'Looks like it,' said Hannah, noisily sucking the dregs of her cocktail through the straw.

'How are they all so hot?' mused Jess. 'Like, what comes first? Do they become tennis coaches *because* they're hot, or does being genetically hot make them want to be tennis coaches?'

'Ski instructors are the same,' mused Gaynor. 'Never met one I wouldn't fuck.'

Hannah observed the group with the rest of them, using it as an excuse to watch Rob snake through the crowd. She'd spotted him about five seconds before Gaynor, because she'd been surreptitiously glancing at the door since they'd first arrived, wondering if he'd heard their conversation earlier about which bar they were going to. And now he was here, and she had no idea what, if anything, that signified, or why she even cared. He was off limits along with all other men, but there was something about Rob that kept creeping into her thoughts. Part of it was physical, obviously – he was insanely good-looking and the complete opposite of Graham – but there was something else that she couldn't put her finger on. It was just a feeling she got when he looked at her, and she'd caught him looking several times.

She wiped her sweaty hands on her yellow dress – another Sam-inspired purchase with puffed sleeves and a cute skater skirt that fell to mid-thigh. She'd teamed it with a pair of silver trainers and asked Trish to pin her hair up into a pile of curls.

'Gay, wave them over,' said Trish, digging a lip gloss out of her bag and hastily applying it with the tiny stick. Hannah saw Rob survey the crowd, his eyes locking onto hers for a fraction of a second before he returned Gaynor's wave. He leaned over to the other coaches and said something, then they all looked over and smiled.

'I think we've got company incoming,' said Jess.

'Could be worse,' replied Trish, draining her glass. 'Remember those awful golfers from Birmingham last time?'

'Didn't one of them drop a lit fag in Jess's handbag?' said Gaynor.

'Mmm,' said Jess. 'Set fire to a box of tampons. I grabbed it and tried to throw it out the window, but instead scattered twenty-four flaming Tampax across the bar. Everyone was screaming.'

The six coaches made their way through the crowd, leaving one of them behind at the bar to order drinks.

'Rob, can you introduce us to these beautiful ladies?' said Olly.

'Of course,' said Rob, raising his eyes ever so slightly. 'This is Gaynor and Jess and Trish and Hannah. And these are my fellow coaches – Olly, Chris, Nick and Jonno. Aaron's getting the drinks in.'

'Nice to meet you,' said Olly, grinning like a politician at a community barbecue. 'We've been admiring you from afar but it's gratifying to see you're equally as lovely close up.'

Hannah snorted with laughter and caught Rob's eye. He mouthed the word 'sorry' and rolled his eyes.

'So what brings you to this little bit of Spanish paradise?' said Olly. 'Your first time at Club Colina?'

Gaynor sighed and put her glass down, giving Olly a hard stare. 'No, Olly, it's not our first time. We were here a few years ago, with our friend Carla.' She smiled, waiting for the penny to drop, but he looked blank. 'Surely you remember Carla? You tried to fondle her tits so you could tick off the "married" box on your pathetic bingo card.'

'Oh shit,' laughed Chris as the colour drained from Olly's face. 'I remember that. Wasn't she a black belt in judo or something?'

'Taekwondo,' said Gaynor.

'She had him in a headlock,' Jonno told Rob and Nick. 'It was fucking epic.'

'We all weigh less than you,' said Jess, munching an olive off a cocktail stick. 'Two of us are happily married, none of us have fake tits, and none of us are old enough to be your mother. Bad luck.'

'For the record, can I just say that I actively object to this game,' said Rob, putting his hand up.

'Pat on the head for you,' said Jess witheringly. She tilted her head at Olly. 'So are you going to buy us a drink, or have we pissed on your bonfire?'

'I'm actually semi-hard right now,' said Olly with a wolfish grin. 'What are you all having?'

'So tell me more about this bingo,' said Hannah, shifting her weight onto one hip and pointing her left foot down, the knee bent. When Gaynor stood like this it looked cute and sassy and drew attention to her slim ankles, but now Hannah was wondering if she just looked like a flamingo. Rob was both far too close and not nearly close enough, and Hannah had no idea what she was doing. In her head this felt like a good opportunity to try chatting to a man, ahead of a time in the future when she might actually want to indicate her openness to a date. It felt a long way off, but there was no harm in getting some practice in. And Rob was as good a man as any. *Oh, who are you kidding, Hannah?*

'It's a stupid game the coaches play,' Rob said dismissively, glancing at Olly and Nick, who had wriggled their way onto the table and were wheeling out all their best lines. Chris, Aaron and Jonno had all dispersed to pursue easier targets.

'Is that why you came out to find me last night?' she asked. 'So you could tick me off the list?'

'What? No!' Rob exclaimed. 'I wasn't lying when I said I'd opted out. It's really not my thing.'

'Preying on women?' asked Hannah, a ghost of a smile on her lips. 'Or women generally?'

Rob shook his head and smiled. 'I definitely like women,

but that kind of thing is not my style. I've got two sisters; I'd beat the shit out of anyone who treated them like that.'

'And a girlfriend? Have you got one of those too?' She immediately wished she could take back such an obviously leading question. Presumably there were ways to talk to really hot men without sounding like she was awkwardly flirting, but apparently she'd missed that memo.

'No,' said Rob, meeting her questioning gaze. 'I was seeing someone, but we broke up before I came over here. So I'm off relationships for a while. Taking a break from women.'

Hannah blushed and looked at her feet, dying a little at the obvious rejection.

'What about you?' asked Rob.

'I've also just split up with someone,' said Hannah quickly, subconsciously rubbing the space on her finger where her wedding band used to be. 'But he was my husband, and we were married a long time.'

'I'm sorry,' said Rob.

'Don't be, I'm not. Anyway, what I mean is I'm taking a break too. A long one. Definitely not interested in a rebound fling.'

'Are you always this direct?' laughed Rob. 'I wasn't suggesting . . .'

'No, I didn't mean that,' she said, blushing and kicking herself again. 'I didn't think you were . . . I just meant I wasn't planning to be part of their bingo game.'

Rob nodded, looking at her curiously. 'You're off the hook anyway, I told them you were gay.'

Hannah let out a barking laugh, her eyes widening. 'Why would you do that?'

Rob shuffled his feet and buried his hands in his pockets.

'I don't know, they were making comments and it felt wrong, so I took you out of the game. I shouldn't have done it, which is why I thought I'd confess.'

'Why only me, though? You could have saved us all.'

'I don't know,' Rob mumbled. 'It just seemed like a good idea at the time.'

Hannah said nothing for a moment, looking at his full lips and feeling a little breathless as she wondered what it might be like to kiss him. Graham had been a wet, probing kisser, like he was doing a full survey on the inside of her mouth with his tongue. It never looked like that in movies; surely there was a better way? Rob caught her eye, and for a moment it was like he could read her thoughts. She needed to get out of here, and fast.

'I'm going swimming,' she said.

Rob laughed awkwardly. 'What, now?'

Hannah shrugged. 'Why not? It's hot, and I'm ready to call it a night. I usually do some lengths in the hotel pool and I haven't done any today.'

'Usually? You only got here yesterday.'

Hannah blushed. 'Well, today is my second day, so it's officially a habit.'

Rob shook his head and laughed. 'You're crazy.'

'Yeah, maybe.' She tried to keep her voice breezy, but she could hear the panic creeping in. 'I'm just going to pop to the loo first,' she said, making her escape before she made things worse.

Sitting on the closed toilet lid with her head in her hands, she felt hot and breathless, with a strange, wriggly feeling in her stomach. The best thing she could do now was say her goodbyes and get out of there as quickly as possible.

She flushed the toilet for no reason and washed her hands, patting her sweaty face with a paper towel before heading back to the group. Rob was back at the table, Trish glued to his side and staring up at him like he'd just won Wimbledon.

'Your turn for a round of drinks, Reverend,' said Olly, patting him heavily on the shoulder. 'Maybe get some sambuca chasers while you're up there.'

'I'm going to call it a night,' said Hannah, giving the group a wave.

'Oh really?' said Trish, clearly delighted that she now had Rob to herself. 'Rob, I'll give you a hand with the drinks.'

'You want us to come back with you?' asked Gaynor, throwing Trish a look.

Hannah shook her head and bolted for the door. 'I'll be fine. See you all in the morning.' She hurried out of the bar, then stopped on the pavement and leaned over, resting her hands on her knees as she took some deep, calming breaths.

'Hannah, are you OK?' said a voice. She looked up to find Rob had followed her outside.

'I'm fine,' she said, giving him a smile that she suspected might be a bit manic. 'Just a bit hot in there.'

'Can I walk you back?'

Hannah paused for a moment, processing the question. He looked kind and sincere, like he genuinely didn't want her to walk back alone. But there was also something else; a kind of reluctance, like maybe he didn't want to give her the wrong idea. It made her feel like saying yes would just be another step down the road towards making an idiot of herself.

'I'm fine,' she said. 'I'll be OK on my own.'

Rob nodded and gave her a soft smile. Was it regret, or

relief? Hannah couldn't tell. 'See you tomorrow,' she said, fast-walking up the road until she reached the bottom of the steps. She tucked her skirt into her knickers and ran up them two at a time, pushing herself through the pain until it felt like her lungs would burst.

The others were in the hotel bar when Hannah came in from her swim, a Club Colina bathrobe over her bikini and flip-flops on her feet. They were slumped on a sofa with their shoes kicked off in a heap under the table, a bottle of wine in a bucket in front of them.

'Oh wow, you're still up,' said Jess. 'We thought you'd gone to bed. Grab another glass.'

Hannah took one from the bar and fell onto the same sofa as Trish, kicking her flip-flops onto the pile.

'How long did you swim for?' asked Jess, reaching across to slop some wine into Hannah's glass.

'An hour,' said Hannah. 'Only planned to do fifty lengths, but it was really nice so I kept going.' She'd convinced herself that it was about exercise, but that was a lie. She'd kept her mind occupied by holding imaginary conversations with Graham, her mum, her dad and Luke, but Rob kept creeping into her thoughts. His smile, his arms, the clean, manly smell of him. In the end she started mentally singing every Britney Spears song she knew, which was a lot, and yet still every lyric seemed to be about Rob. *Baby, can't you see I'm calling? A guy like you should wear a warning.*

'You're crazy,' said Jess with a huge yawn. Hannah noted that it was the second time she'd been called that this evening.

'How was the bar after I left?' she asked.

'Fun,' said Gaynor. 'The band were great. We stayed for another hour or so, drank a lot of sambuca, then shared a couple of taxis up the hill with the guys. Olly tried to grope me so I gave him a dead leg.'

'Trish and Rob were all over each other,' said Jess with a sly grin.

Hannah's head snapped up, a swooping, acid feeling in her stomach. 'Really?'

'It wasn't like that,' slurred Trish. 'We were just chatting. And you guys joined in.'

'With what?' asked Hannah before she could stop herself.

'We were ranking the coaches in order of how many women we guessed they'd slept with,' laughed Gaynor. 'We were right to put Aaron at the bottom, bless him.'

'Rob wouldn't give us a number,' added Jess. 'But he was DEFINITELY at the top.'

'I'm not sure he even KNEW the number,' said Gaynor.

'Wow,' said Hannah, the acid feeling pooling into something heavy and viscous in her stomach. 'I didn't realise.'

'Trish still would, though,' teased Gaynor with a grin.

Trish shrugged. 'Yeah, course. I don't want to *marry* him, I'd just be happy to get laid. I haven't had a shag in two years.'

'Really?' Gaynor slopped some more wine into Trish's glass.

'Yep.' Trish covered her mouth as she did a small belch, then drowned it in more wine. 'I'm a thirty-five-year-old divorcee with two kids under ten, which makes me damaged goods.'

'Don't be daft,' said Jess dismissively.

'It's true,' Trish continued. 'Men my age usually want to date twenty-year-olds, so the only offers I get are men over fifty who I don't fancy, or casual hook-ups with total randoms. The whole system is rigged to make women like me feel like shit.'

Jess and Gaynor looked at each other with horrified expressions. 'Why have you never said anything before?' said Jess, leaning over to take Trish's hand.

'Because you'd fucking feel sorry for me,' said Trish, snatching it back. 'With your rich husbands and your fancy holidays. I just want to feel sexy for five fucking minutes, and if that happens to be with a super-fit toyboy tennis coach, I'll definitely take it.' She burst into heaving sobs, then grabbed Hannah's towel and buried her face in it.

'Too much sambuca,' said Gaynor, rolling her eyes at Hannah as Trish continued to wail.

'Come on, it's bedtime,' said Jess, grabbing Trish's handbag and hauling her to her feet as Hannah pushed from behind. Jess pulled a face at the others as she half-carried, half-dragged her towards the lift.

'Happens every time,' said Gaynor, emptying the rest of the bottle into Hannah's glass. 'She's a hot mess.'

'Do you think it might come to anything?' Hannah asked casually, unable to help herself. 'Her and Rob?'

Gaynor shrugged. 'They looked pretty cosy earlier, and he's obviously a total player. But if she's OK with that, I'd be happy for her. Wouldn't you?'

'Sure,' said Hannah, swallowing down a wave of sickness. She wondered what would have happened if she'd let Rob walk her back to the hotel – would he have tried to add her to his tally of women? She'd have turned him down, obviously, but that probably wouldn't have bothered him — it looked like he'd moved on to Trish pretty fast. And even though she definitely didn't want to get involved with anyone, and Rob getting with Trish would entirely solve that problem, somehow it still felt like a kick in the guts.

CHAPTER THIRTEEN

Hannah woke up feeling tired and scratchy, having played her encounters with Rob over in her head and come to the conclusion that he hadn't actually done anything wrong. He'd been charming and fun to chat to, but at no point had he actually made a move on her, or made her feel anything other than the centre of his polite attention.

And that, she now realised, was one of the reasons why she liked him. He was clearly a womaniser, but when they'd chatted in Marbella and in the Luna Lounge last night, he hadn't acted like one. Was that how he got women into bed? Hannah didn't know much about chemistry, but Graham had never made her feel like that.

'We'll be ready in ten minutes,' said Gaynor as Hannah hurried into the hotel breakfast room to find the others. They were all slumped around a table in joggers and sweatshirts, Trish dropping two Berocca tablets into a glass of water, then adding a third for good measure. Hannah smiled, taking comfort in the knowledge that even when her head was full of big questions, these women could be relied on to bring her back down to earth.

Rob was laying out baskets of balls when Hannah got to the courts, but he stopped when he saw her coming down the steps and watched her approach. Being under his gaze made her feel naked, but she did her best to not look away.

He smiled as she stopped in front of him, and Hannah felt that thing again, that crackle of electricity between them that made the back of her neck feel hot.

'Hey,' said Rob. 'Where are the others?'

'Hungover again,' she said lightly, putting on her sunglasses in the hope it might hide how jittery she felt in his company. 'They'll be here in ten minutes.'

Rob grabbed a handful of balls and started to fill his pockets. 'You want to warm up for a bit before they get here?'

'Sure,' said Hannah, hurrying off to the baseline. They hit back and forth for a few minutes, keeping things slow and gentle to allow her muscles to warm up. It gave her a chance to watch the way he moved around the court and marvel at how effortless he made it look. She'd worked with lots of coaches, but he was the first one she'd ever really *noticed*.

'I find you quite challenging to coach,' he told her as they both took a water break. 'There's very little I'd change about your game.'

'Really?' Hannah wondered if he said that to all the girls. 'When did you start playing?'

'I was eight,' said Hannah. It was a long story, and now probably wasn't the time.

'You could have gone all the way, I think,' he said. 'Why didn't you ever pursue it?'

Hannah shrugged and put her water bottle back in her bag. It didn't feel like a chat-up line any more, and she felt bad for dismissing what was clearly a huge compliment. 'I don't know. We weren't that kind of family, I guess.'

'Mmm,' said Rob thoughtfully. 'Well, you're good.'

'Thanks.' Hannah felt the heat rush to her cheeks. 'The others are good too though, right?'

'Sure,' said Rob, looking away. 'But you're in a different league.'

Hannah felt the sweat break out on her neck again, and not just because the day was warming up. Were they still talking about tennis? 'Don't tell Trish that,' she said with an awkward laugh.

Rob looked at her, his brow furrowed. 'What's Trish got to do with it?'

Hannah rummaged through her bag so she didn't have to look at him. 'Oh, I just heard you and she were getting on pretty well last night, that's all.'

Rob gave a weak laugh. 'Her gran lives in Bath, which is where I'm from. We talked about that.'

'It's not a problem or anything,' Hannah said breezily. 'She likes you, I think.' She looked up at him questioningly, her insides writhing with a hundred different emotions.

Rob held her gaze. 'It doesn't matter if she does like me,' he said gently. 'I'm not interested, and besides, hotel guests are off limits. I'd lose my job.'

'Oh,' said Hannah, her eyes widening as she processed this new and unexpected information. 'Right.'

'See, only ten minutes late,' sang Gaynor, hurrying onto the court with the others. Hannah noted that it was actually nearer twenty, but didn't say anything.

'Good work,' said Rob, checking his watch. 'How is everyone feeling today?'

'Not too bad,' said Jess, who actually looked quite sprightly. Gaynor gave him a dazzling grin, clearly her game face, but Trish looked like reheated death. Her skin was pallid and blotchy, and her usually glossy hair was shoved into a bun that looked like a bird's nest.

'Broken,' said Trish. 'But I only have myself to blame.'

'Well, we're all here, which is the main thing,' said Rob. 'Let's get warmed up, shall we?'

Hannah tried to shake off all the confusing thoughts about Rob's rules, and what that signified about whether he did or didn't like her. She'd process that all later, but right now she needed to get her head back in the game.

'Where are we going tonight?' asked Gaynor over lunch.

'I don't have any major plans yet,' said Jess. 'I thought we might want to play it a bit lower key after two big nights out.'

'Bollocks to that,' said Trish, glancing over at Rob and the other coaches. 'It might be years before I get anywhere close to a guy who looks like that. I need to keep up my blowjob practice before I forget how to do it.'

'I can't do blowjobs,' said Gaynor. 'They're not vegan.'

'I'm sorry, what the fuck?' exclaimed Jess.

'Hang on, is that an actual vegan rule?' asked Trish.

'Hi,' said Rob, appearing directly behind Hannah's chair. She resisted the temptation to turn her head, and instead stared intently at her empty lunch plate, wishing her hair wasn't stuck to her sweaty neck.

'Hey, Rob,' said Trish, giving him her most winning smile. 'We were just discussing whether blowjobs are vegan.'

'No, we weren't,' said Gaynor, giving her a glare.

'I just think we should get a third party view,' said Trish. 'Rob, what do you think?'

'Wow, OK,' said Rob, his torso so close to Hannah she could practically feel the heat coming off it. 'Depends how much of a purist you are, I guess. Which one of you is vegan?'

'Gaynor,' said Trish quickly. 'I'll literally eat anything.'

'I think you've made that abundantly clear,' muttered Gaynor.

'Right,' said Rob. 'Well, I'm no expert. Maybe to be safe you should only blow other vegans?'

'I'll pass that suggestion on to my husband,' said Gaynor with a smirk. 'He's partial to a bacon sandwich, so I'm not entirely sure how he'll feel about it.'

'ANYWAY,' said Trish. 'That probably wasn't why you came over.' She looked at him expectantly, and for a moment Hannah wondered if what he said earlier about hotel guests being off limits was true. If it was, Trish clearly either didn't know or didn't care.

'Oh, yeah,' said Rob. 'I've been sent over by my fellow coaches to ask if you fancy joining us for a trip to Marbella this evening.' He sounded a little strained, and Hannah wondered if they'd twisted his arm. Trish, meanwhile, had lit up like a Christmas tree.

'Oh yeah, definitely,' she said, before remembering that there were three other women in her party and it wasn't just her decision. 'What do you guys think?'

'Fine by me,' said Gaynor. 'Although not that bar we were in on Saturday night; there was a guy in there who was a right creep.'

'Bar Solo,' said Rob. 'I'll make sure it's not on the list.'

'How did you know that?' asked Jess, eyeing him curiously.

'Oh,' said Rob, and Hannah could practically hear his inner panic. 'Hannah told me last night, I think. We were talking about where you guys had been.'

How smoothly he lies, thought Hannah. *Just like Graham.*

She checked herself, because Rob was obviously nothing like Graham. She was just brooding because everything felt confusing right now, and another night in Rob's company probably wasn't going to help.

'How are we doing?' said Olly, appearing on the other side of the table directly in Hannah's eyeline. 'Shall I book us a taxi? Nine o'clock in the hotel car park?' She noticed him keeping his voice down and scanning around for anyone listening, so this probably wasn't a plan that Mark the head coach would approve of. Maybe Rob was telling the truth after all.

Jess and Gaynor both nodded, so Hannah shrugged her agreement.

'Great,' said Rob, although his slightly strained tone suggested otherwise. 'Six gentlemen will escort you, including myself.'

'You found five gentlemen?' said Hannah, turning to glance at Rob in wide-eyed innocence. 'Can't the other coaches make it?'

'You're very funny,' said Olly, giving her a wry smile. 'We promise to protect you from unwanted attention.' Hannah hadn't spent much time with Olly, but he had an entitled arrogance about him that she found deeply unappealing.

'Maybe we don't need protecting,' said Trish, looking directly at Rob with a twinkle in her eye.

Seriously? thought Hannah, grudgingly impressed that Trish could pull off that level of playful flirtation. She couldn't see Rob's reaction, but presumably he was enjoying the attention. He was a tennis coach, after all.

'Let's get dressed up,' said Trish excitedly. 'Make a bit of an effort.'

Hannah watched Rob and Olly wander back to the other coaches as Gaynor and Trish started talking about outfits and shoes. Overall, this plan was a good thing, she decided. She could hang out with the group, and if she and Rob did end up chatting she could just be cool and fun and not obsess about something that was never going to happen anyway. She stood up to go to the bathroom, wafting her tennis top in the sticky air and wondering why she was sweating so hard right now.

CHAPTER FOURTEEN

'Look up,' said Jess, gently brushing mascara onto Hannah's lower lashes. 'Why are your lashes so long? It's really unfair.'

'I'm naturally hairy, my mum is Greek,' said Hannah. 'But it means I've got really hairy arms as well, look.'

'I bet bikini waxing absolutely kills,' said Jess, standing back to check out her handiwork. She screwed the mascara wand back into the tube and reached for a red lip liner.

'I've never done it,' said Hannah. 'I shave around the edges to keep it all tidy, but otherwise it's all totally natural.'

'Oh my God,' gasped Jess. 'I heard women like you existed, but I've never met one.'

'Met who?' said Gaynor, strolling into the room to borrow Jess's hairspray. 'My God, Hannah. You look amazing.'

'Hannah doesn't wax down below,' said Jess. 'She's got a full bush going on.'

'No fucking way,' Gaynor exclaimed.

Hannah laughed. 'It's true. Other than a quick tidy if I'm going swimming, it's entirely untouched.'

'Wow,' said Gaynor. 'And look how thick and curly your hair is. Your husband must have needed a machete to hack through that.'

'He never complained,' Hannah shrugged. 'Although he was cheating on me, so maybe that was why.'

'I had all mine lasered off,' said Gaynor.

'What, all of it?' asked Hannah.

'Yeah, years ago,' said Gaynor, spritzing hairspray onto her fringe. 'When Hollywoods were all the rage. Ed loved it, so I spent HOURS having it lasered off. Now I've got a fanny like a nine-year-old girl and I hate it.'

'Doesn't it grow back eventually?' asked Jess.

'Not properly,' said Gaynor glumly. 'Bits of it grow back in little tufts, like a mangy dog. It's easier just to keep it all smooth.'

'Did it hurt?'

'Yeah,' said Gaynor. 'And it took ages and cost a fortune. I could have kept my pubes and had a lovely holiday.'

'Let's take a look at you,' said Jess, giving Hannah's lips a final brush with red lipstick. Hannah stood up and did a twirl. She was wearing a leopard print playsuit borrowed from Gaynor, with silver trainers and huge hoop earrings.

'Ugh, you look gorgeous. That playsuit looks WAY better on you, and you totally have the legs for the whole cute outfit and trainers thing.'

'AND you won't have sore feet at the end of the night,' grumbled Jess. 'It's not fair.'

Hannah beamed, looking at the cool, sexy woman in the full-length mirror and wondering what Graham would think if he could see her now. 'Where's Trish?' she asked.

'Still getting ready,' said Gaynor with a grin. 'She's got Rob in her sights and she's going for full blow-out and battle dress.'

'Are you talking about me?' asked Trish, strutting into the room and giving them a twirl in a fog of perfume and hairspray. She was wearing a black minidress with chiffon bell sleeves and silver strappy sandals, her hair piled up into a messy beehive. With smoky eyes and scarlet lipstick, she looked like a supermodel.

'Holy shit,' said Gaynor. 'You look fantastic.'

'If I can't bag Rob in this, he's either gay or blind,' said Trish.

Don't be jealous, thought Hannah, swallowing down the hot, acid taste in her mouth and trying not to feel frumpy by comparison. *Be cool and fun, remember?* She popped Jess's lipstick and her phone into her pocket and headed back to her room to take a selfie for Sam.

'So, Puerto Banus?' said Olly, climbing into the minibus and sliding the door closed. 'You all scrub up nicely, so they'll let us in the best places.'

'Fine by us,' said Trish, who'd managed to annexe Rob on the back row of seats. Hannah was at the front, now being overpowered by Olly's aftershave.

'Onward, Pedro,' said Olly. 'Take us to the finest bars in Puerto Banus.'

'His name's Ben,' said Hannah, wishing she could hide under the seats.

'Whatever,' said Olly, eyeing Hannah's legs. 'You look a million euros, by the way.'

'Shame I'm not for sale,' muttered Hannah, looking out the window as the minibus made its way down the winding hillside.

'I've never paid yet,' said Olly, like this was some kind of crowning achievement. Hannah turned in her seat to chat to Jess, who was sitting in the row behind, sneaking a glance at Rob at the same time. He was trying to be attentive while Trish jabbered on about how many pins were holding her hair up. As if sensing her eyes on him, he turned his head towards her gaze, hovering on her for a second, a small smile forming on his lips before looking away again. The familiar throb of desire washed over her, and as the miles ticked by she stared out of the window and silently vowed to stay away from Rob tonight. However hard she tried to be cool, the reality was that being in his company made her giddy. So she'd keep him at arm's length, maybe chat to some other people outside the group, and make it really clear to everyone that she was happily single and didn't need attention from him or anyone else. This was her trip, her time, and she didn't want or need a man in her life. And if Trish managed to bag Rob, then that was a great result for everyone. Even in her head, that didn't sound very convincing.

Hannah had been worried that Olly would take them to some noisy sports bar full of drunken stag and hen parties, but the bar he directed Ben the driver to was classy and stylish, with an art deco vibe and leather booths lining the walls around a circular cocktail bar. At the back was a dancefloor with a DJ playing noughties R&B, but at 9.30 p.m. there were only a couple of groups of women dancing. Hannah liked it, and for a moment was willing to forgive Olly for being so obnoxious.

They all ordered drinks at the bar, and Hannah purposely turned away from Rob and tried to relax as she chatted to Aaron and Nick in one of the booths. Neither of them seemed particularly confident around women but they were happy to talk about tennis instead, and after forty minutes of good-natured arguing about the best female player of all time, Hannah had finished her second cocktail and headed to the bar to get a glass of water. She'd discovered it was the only way to ward off a crippling hangover.

'Hi,' said a man waiting at the bar, trying to catch the eye of the barman. 'I'm Matt.'

'Hannah.' She didn't really want to chat to him, but wasn't that what she'd told herself to do this evening? Stay away from Rob, spread her wings a bit, make new friends? Matt wasn't particularly good-looking, but he had kind eyes, so maybe ten minutes in his company would provide a brief but welcome reprieve from thinking about Rob.

'What can I get you?' asked Matt.

'I'm fine,' said Hannah, holding up her empty glass. 'I've only just finished this one, so I was just going to get some water.'

'Water's no fun,' he said with a smile. His accent was generic home counties with the tiniest hint of posh, and he seemed nice enough. Hannah glanced back towards the group – Jess and Gaynor were now dancing to Rihanna with Nick and Chris, Olly and Aaron hovering at the edge of the dancefloor chatting to a couple of women from another group. Trish had Rob pinned into the leather booth she'd just vacated; Hannah could see his gaze searching round the bar as Trish talked at him, and their eyes met just as Matt was handing her what was evidently a gin and tonic. She smiled happily as she took it, not wanting Rob to think she was looking to be rescued.

'Thanks,' she said, refocussing her attention on Matt, who she was going off by the second. Didn't she just tell him she wanted water? 'I need to go and join my friends.'

'Why?' said Matt with a flirty smile. 'You can hang out with them any time, we're just getting started.'

'Wow, this is strong,' said Hannah, taking a sip of the drink.

'They don't bother measuring the gin here,' said Matt. 'Much better value.'

Hannah did a mental calculation while she still could – a glass of Cava while they were getting ready, wine over dinner in the hotel, and two cocktails. Right now her head was swimming happily, but she'd be a right mess if she didn't stop after this one.

'You have gorgeous eyes,' said Matt. 'Please tell me you're single.'

Hannah nodded and forced a smile. 'Very happy that way, though,' she said. 'And no plans to not be single any time soon. I don't want to waste your time.'

'I'm not asking you to marry me,' said Matt with a laugh, his eyes drinking in her body. Not very kind at all, now she thought about it. 'But you're on holiday, we can have a little fun.'

'I'm really not interested,' said Hannah firmly. 'But thank you, I'm flattered.' She wasn't really, but it felt like the kind of thing she should say so he didn't get upset. And now she was annoyed with herself for trying to make a complete stranger feel better about her rejection. She didn't owe him anything – why did women do this?

Matt looked mutinous. 'Well, at least have a drink with me,' he said. 'Then I'll let you go, even though it seems like a massive waste of a beautiful opportunity for us to get very naked and sweaty.'

'Are you OK?' said Rob, appearing at Hannah's side, Trish trailing in his wake and throwing Hannah a dirty look. 'I'm just heading to the bar.'

'I'm fine,' snapped Hannah, annoyed that Rob felt the need to check in on her, particularly with Trish hanging off his arm.

'All right, mate,' said Matt, an edge in his voice. 'Anything we can do for you?'

'No, thanks,' said Rob, clearly forcing himself to sound friendly. 'Just saying hi.'

'Move along then,' said Matt as Rob pushed past towards the bar. 'That your little brother?'

'No,' said Hannah, looking over towards Jess and Gaynor again. The crowd had thickened between the bar and the dancefloor and she couldn't see them any more. She took another gulp of the drink, which really did taste disgusting, then put the glass on the table.

'You not going to finish that?' asked Matt.

Hannah shook her head as she started to edge away. 'Bit strong for me, I'm afraid. I'm going to join my friends, it was really nice to meet you.'

He reached out to take her hand, then lifted it to his lips and kissed it. 'Nice to meet you too, lovely Hannah.' She suppressed a shudder before pulling away and pushing through the crowd, wanting to get as far away from him and everyone else as possible. Her head felt fuzzy and she could feel herself sweating, so she swerved for the door to the street outside, then changed her mind and headed to the toilets in case she was sick. She pushed through the swing doors but there was a queue a mile long, and now the room was starting to spin.

I need air, thought Hannah, wobbling back into the bar and towards the main doors. She felt like she was suffocating, and her head was full of cotton wool – how much had she drunk? The cool air felt blissful, so she leaned against the outside wall away from the smokers and took deep breaths, her eyes closed against the neon glare from the club opposite. The music was too close and too loud.

'You OK?' said a voice. 'I was a bit worried about you.'

Thank God, it's Rob, she thought, but when she opened her eyes it was Matt, not Rob.

'I'm fine,' she said, wondering vaguely why her voice was echoing in her ears and she could see three Matts, all of them fuzzy around the edges. 'Just needed some air.'

'Come with me,' he said, putting his arm tightly around her waist and practically lifting her feet off the ground as he led her away. 'I'll look after you.'

'No,' said Hannah, 'I need to go back.' The street was spinning like she was on a carousel, and now she was in some kind of doorway that smelled of hot bins and Matt was much too close, his face swimming in and out of focus.

'Stop,' she gasped as his hand disappeared up the shorts of her playsuit.

'Come on, we both know this is what you want,' he whispered, his hands groping everywhere and fumbling over the buttons. 'How the fuck do you get into this thing?'

'Don't,' said Hannah, trying to push him away, but her arms felt limp and spongy. He kissed her hard, and she felt the metal taste of blood as his teeth crashed into hers and bit her lip. There was noise and heat and swirling colours as Matt suddenly retreated into the darkness and other hands, softer this time, reached out to touch her.

'Sit her down on the bench,' said a female voice.

'Fuck, she's completely out of it.'

'Where's Rob?'

'Chasing after him.'

'We need to get her back to the hotel. She's hammered.'

'She can't be that hammered, we've barely been here an hour. He must have spiked her drink.'

'Should we call an ambulance?'

'Hannah? Hannah? Can you hear me?'

Hannah half-nodded, wondering why everyone was still talking, then lurched forward and threw up the entire contents of her stomach into a potted palm tree.

'How are you feeling?' asked Gaynor, twisting the top off the second bottle of water and handing it to Hannah.

'Awful,' said Hannah. 'But better than I was.'

'Better out than in, I say.'

'What happened?' Hannah asked.

'We think the guy you were talking to must have spiked your drink. Rob saw him follow you outside and came to check you were OK. He was . . . anyway, Rob lamped him but he ran off.'

'Did he find him?'

Gaynor shook his head. 'No, the fucking arsehole could run like the wind, apparently. Do you want to call the police?'

Hannah shrugged. 'I don't know. All I know is he was called Matt. That might not even be his name.' She clutched her head in her hands. 'I've got such a headache. Do you think I'll be OK?'

'You threw up pretty soon after, but I can take you to the hospital if you're worried.'

Hannah shook her head. 'I feel OK right now, I didn't even drink half of the drink he gave me. Will you take me back to the hotel?'

'I'll stay in your room tonight,' Gaynor said. 'I'll get the others, we'll all go back.'

'No,' said Hannah quickly. 'I don't want to spoil everyone's night. Just you.'

Gaynor nodded as Rob appeared through the door of the bar, his face somewhere unfathomable between fear and anger. 'I'll just let the others know what the plan is,' she said. 'Rob, can you stay with Hannah for a minute?'

Rob nodded and sat down beside her as Gaynor hurried inside. 'How are you feeling?' he asked.

'Awful,' said Hannah. 'I feel like such an idiot.' She turned to look at him, hoping she could find the right words. 'Thank you,' she said. 'I don't know what would have happened if you hadn't come to find me.'

Rob shrugged, looking down at his feet. 'I gave the rest of your drink to the manager, asked him to give it to the police so they can test it. They might want to talk to you tomorrow; I've left your details.'

'I wonder if he's done that kind of thing before,' mused Hannah, thinking of Matt's hands on her body as he tried to kiss her and shuddering. Her lip was swollen and painful, and she could still taste the blood in her mouth.

'I asked in the bar,' said Rob, 'but nobody's ever seen him before, and he paid cash for your drink so they can't trace his card. I chased him down but I couldn't catch him, sorry.'

'You don't have to apologise. You win tonight's hero badge.'

'I still don't like the idea of him getting away with it. Can I take you back to the hotel?'

'Gaynor's taking me back. You guys stay and have a good night.'

Rob opened his mouth like he wanted to say something, then closed it again. 'I think my night is ruined, to be honest, but I'm glad you're OK. I'm really sorry you had to go through that.'

'It was my own fault,' said Hannah, pressing her hand over her mouth and trying not to cry. 'He probably thought I was fair game.'

'No,' said Rob firmly, taking her hands and folding them between his. 'Hey, look at me.' He ducked to catch her eye and gave her a hard, blazing look. 'Whatever happened, whatever was said, it absolutely wasn't your fault. It's important you know that.'

Hannah held his gaze, blinking back the tears that would almost certainly come later, once the shock had subsided. His eyes were full of pain, and he was still holding her cold, shaking hand between his warm, strong ones. Maybe it was trauma or something, but she really, really wanted to kiss him and make the taste of this awful night go away.

'Right, let's go,' said Gaynor, trailed by Jess and Trish and the rest of the tennis coaches. Rob dropped her hands and stood up, nonchalantly brushing down his T-shirt.

'We're all moving on,' said Trish drunkenly. 'Olly says there's another bar down the road that attracts a more discerning clientele.'

'You sure you don't want us to come back with you?' said Jess, glaring at Trish. 'We don't mind.'

Hannah shook her head. 'I'm fine, but thanks.' She glanced at Rob, who was staring at his shoes as Trish edged towards him and hooked her arm through his. Despite her foggy headache she could see they made a gorgeous couple, even though Rob had already shaken Trish off.

Gaynor took her hand and led her to the taxi rank, giving the name of the hotel to the driver and bundling her into the calm, muffled silence of the back seat. 'It's OK,' she whispered, as Hannah buried her face in her shoulder and sobbed her heart out all the way back to the hills.

CHAPTER FIFTEEN

Hannah used the remote control to start the ball machine, sliding it into her pocket and setting her stance in anticipation of the first ball. It punched out of the machine towards her with a satisfying *thunk*, so she *thwocked* it back. It was similar to the model they had at her club in Surrey, so it hadn't taken long to work out.

Thunk. Thwock. Thunk. Thwock. The hopper in the top of the machine held about a hundred balls, so she could keep this up for a while, then collect them all up and start again. She settled into the rhythm of it, emptying her head of Matt and the police and Rob and Trish and Graham and her dad and all the other stuff that had been weighing her down while she rested by the pool all day. Instead she forced every ounce of her concentration onto each yellow ball – on and on, forehand and backhand, until the final ball thunked across the net and the machine was silent.

Hannah had a long drink from the bottle in her bag, then walked to the other end of the court and started to scoop the balls back into the hopper, enjoying the warmth of the setting sun on her back. Tennis was finished for the day, and the courts were deserted. She'd waited for the others to get back and reassured them that she was fine, then headed out to do what she always did in times of stress or anxiety. Just hit balls, then hit more balls.

Rob appeared down the steps and started to say something, but the look on Hannah's face clearly made him change his mind; instead he began kicking over the balls that had drifted onto the next court, so Hannah could corral them back into the machine.

'You OK?' he asked, returning to the net after all the balls had been gathered up.

Hannah nodded, taking another swig from her water bottle. She hadn't expected to see Rob today, and wasn't sure what to make of him being here. 'I feel a lot better.'

'Do you want to talk about it?'

Hannah shook her head emphatically. 'No. I'm happy just to hit balls.'

'We missed you at coaching today.'

Hannah took a deep, shuddering breath. 'Yeah, sorry about that. I needed a bit of space to get my head around everything.'

Rob nodded. 'That's totally understandable.'

'I got bored, though,' said Hannah. 'Turns out you can only read books by the pool for so long, so I thought I'd come over and hit for a while. Is this OK?'

'Of course,' said Rob. 'Would you prefer a human partner? Or are you happy with the ball machine?'

Hannah looked at him intently, weighing him up along with her options. The memory of his hands clasping hers had morphed into Trish clinging on to his arm, the imagined aftermath of which had got more colourful as the day had worn on.

'I'll stick with the ball machine,' she said. 'I like the consistency.'

Rob said nothing for a moment, looking at her with a

concerned expression, his hands on his hips. 'Have you eaten anything today?'

Hannah thought about it for a moment. Some fruit earlier, but that was it. She shook her head.

'Then have pizza with me.'

'Sorry?' she said, not sure she'd heard him properly.

'There's a pizza place I know with a great view, we can walk there in ten minutes.'

'What, now?'

Rob nodded. 'Yeah. We can talk about whatever you like. Or not talk at all, I don't mind.'

Hannah looked at the hopper full of yellow balls and felt a sudden wave of exhaustion. The fruit was hours ago, and she was actually really hungry. She turned to Rob, then shrugged and nodded.

'OK, half and half,' said Rob, dumping the box on the wall between them. 'Mushroom, sweetcorn and pepper for you, actual pizza toppings for me.' Hannah laughed and took the cold bottle of beer from his hand, taking a long swig and soaking up the view across the patchwork valley to the coast. The pink sky was fading into purple, the air warm on her skin and alive with cicadas. For the first time today, she let herself breathe.

'My ex-husband hated all three,' she said. 'Well, technically he was allergic to peppers. So I never cooked with any of them. I guess I'm making up for lost time.'

'Fair enough,' said Rob, folding a slice of pizza in half and taking a bite. 'Did you talk to the police today?'

'Yeah, they sent a man and woman and they asked loads

of questions, but I couldn't remember much, to be honest. They said they might be in touch with you too.'

'That's fine. Do they think they'll find him?'

Hannah shuddered, pushing the memory of Matt's leering face from her mind. She'd been asked to describe him today, and it felt like the image of him was tattooed in her brain. 'Not sure. I got the impression this kind of thing happens a lot. They wanted to know how much I'd had to drink, but at least they didn't ask what I was wearing.'

'Ugh,' said Rob. 'Yeah.' They both ate in silence for a minute, Hannah realising how glad she was of Rob's company. Today there was no pressure to impress him or practise her flirting, she was too exhausted and numb for that. They were just two people eating pizza on a Spanish wall in the evening sun.

'I got a proper bollocking from Mark today,' said Rob.

'Really?' Hannah turned to look at him.

'Yeah. We weren't supposed to be in Marbella. He said that if you guys wanted to go out and get drunk or assaulted or whatever, that's your problem. But we coaches needed to be a very long way away.'

'Wow,' said Hannah, taking a long swig of beer. 'Mark sounds lovely.'

Rob nodded. 'I mean, he's a prick, obviously. But you can kind of see how it looks from his point of view. It's bad publicity for him if people hear that something bad happened to a Club Colina hotel guest, and his coaches were there.'

'Well,' said Hannah, feeling her voice catch in her throat and blinking away tears. 'I'm definitely not sorry you were there.'

'Me neither,' said Rob quietly. 'Sorry, let's talk about something else. What other sports are you good at, apart from tennis?'

Hannah shook her head and smiled. 'I was good at netball at school, because I'm tall. But tennis is the only sport I've ever loved.'

'I was watching you earlier,' said Rob. 'When you were hitting against the machine.'

'For how long?' asked Hannah, giving him a challenging look.

'The whole time, actually. Sorry.' Rob smiled, and Hannah couldn't help but return it. It felt nice to be with Rob like this, still in her tennis gear, no make-up, no stress.

'What was your verdict?' she asked.

'I've spotted a tiny weakness,' said Rob. 'A little bit of under-rotation in your hips that's losing you power in your topspin forehand.'

Hannah nodded. 'Interesting.'

'If you get to training early tomorrow I'll show you.'

'Are you trying to sell me a private lesson?' teased Hannah.

'I couldn't take your money,' he laughed. 'It will take me about five minutes, and then I've got nothing left to teach you.'

You could teach me so many things, thought Hannah, feeling goosebumps break out on her arms. 'Show me now,' she said, putting the beer on the wall and standing up.

'Now? Really?'

She unzipped her bag and pulled out her tennis racquet. 'Sure. Why not?'

'OK,' said Rob, standing in front of her and brushing bits of pizza off his polo shirt. 'Show me your sequence for top-spin forehand, then stop when I tell you.'

Hannah imagined the ball coming towards her, pulling back her right arm and stepping forward on her left leg, her knee turned and her wrist angled to sweep her racquet over the top of the ball at the perfect trajectory.

'Stop there,' said Rob. Hannah froze, her body sideways on.

'OK, look at the angle of your hips,' he said. 'You're not giving yourself room. Give me thirty degrees more.'

Hannah nodded and re-set her stance, running through the sequence several times more. 'Stop,' said Rob again. He walked around her, looking at every angle thoughtfully. 'Something still isn't right.'

'Can I move?' she asked, still with her arm outstretched. Her nerves were jangling, and the smell of him made her giddy. How could anyone focus on tennis when Rob was this close?

'No,' he said. He walked behind her, then reached forward and rested one hand on each hip. Hannah didn't see him coming and gasped as she jumped out of her skin, prompting Rob to back away swiftly.

'Oh fuck, I'm so sorry,' he said.

'No,' said Hannah. 'It's not—'

'I didn't think. After last night, of course you wouldn't—'

'It's not—' Hannah ran out of words, realising that Rob thought the issue was the memory of Matt's hands on her. But how could she tell him that the issue was actually something else entirely? That Rob had awoken something in her that she'd never felt before? That conversation could go one of several ways, and every one of them would leave Hannah looking like a lovesick idiot.

Rob shook his head. 'I'm really sorry, I should have left it until tomorrow. Let's finish our pizza and head back.'

Hannah nodded, still glad that this evening had happened, even though the magic was gone.

CHAPTER SIXTEEN

Rob watched Hannah serve for the match in the final of the mixed doubles tournament, which was scheduled each week as an opportunity for guests to break out of their groups and play with someone different. All the Surrey ladies had made it into the latter rounds, but Hannah had made the final, paired with a seventy-year-old man from Wiltshire called Keith who had two replacement hips. On paper he hadn't seemed very promising, but it turned out that Keith had been playing for sixty years and had a tricksy slice that killed the ball dead. They'd breezed into the final without dropping a set, and Rob was pretty sure this tournament was going to be all over in about three minutes.

He stood on the terrace and watched Hannah follow her serve with a furious rally. Despite him being a thoughtless wanker last night, she'd taken his advice about hip rotation on board and given her topspin forehand some extra punch. Even if you knew nothing about tennis and didn't fancy women, she was spectacular to watch.

He glanced at Jess, Gaynor and Trish on the benches, cheering every point and leaping around when Hannah wrapped up the match with a thundering backhand down the line. Trish had laid her cards on the table on Monday, and he'd gently but emphatically said no, and made it clear that it wasn't just because of his job, but because he wasn't interested. She definitely wasn't his type, although neither was Hannah, at least on paper. And yet.

Hannah finished shaking hands with the other three players, then looked up at him. He gave her an appreciative nod and a round of applause, and was rewarded with a beaming smile that made the breath catch in his chest. She'd consumed his thoughts like no other woman he'd ever met, and the whole incident with Matt had forced him to reflect on what the intensity of this feeling really *meant*. Was the connection between him and Hannah because of what happened? No, he had felt something before that, but Monday had taken it to another level, made him feel protective, somehow. He loved women, treated them well, didn't fuck them around, but none of his relationships up to now had ever felt that *deep*. So what was this all about? Right now it felt like there was only one person who could help him.

Rob hurried through the clubhouse to the car park, pulling his phone and earbuds out of his pocket and scrolling to his dad's number before he changed his mind.

'Hey, Dad, it's me.' Rob started walking laps around the outside of the courts, the sultry heat of the afternoon sun casting long shadows across the ochre walls. He could see Nick and Aaron watering the clay courts furthest from him, the last job of the day once private lessons were wrapped up. But everyone else was celebrating the end of the tournament on the terrace, and the only living things who could hear him were the cicadas in the spiny bushes.

'Hey, son, how's it going?' said Guy. Rob could hear him rattling drawers in the background, suggesting he was in the kitchen.

'Good, just fancied a chat. Is now a good time?' He felt

inexplicably nervous, like he was about to uncover the secrets of the universe.

'Hang on,' said Guy. Rob heard him close more drawers, then move into a different room with a more muffled sound. A chair creaked and he let out an 'oof' of expelled air that all men over sixty seemed to do whenever they stood up or sat down. 'That's better. Everything OK?'

'Yeah,' said Rob. 'Tennis is great, sun's shining.'

'But . . .?' said Guy.

Rob laughed awkwardly, seriously considering just hanging up and going to the nearest bar. 'What makes you think there's a but?'

'Because you're calling me at four thirty on a Wednesday and you haven't asked to speak to your mother.'

'Yeah, OK,' said Rob. Was he actually going to have this conversation? He took a deep breath and closed his eyes. 'I have an, um, weird question for you. About when you met Mum.'

Guy was quiet for a moment. 'OK, that wasn't what I expected you to say. Are you all right?'

'Yeah, I'm fine,' said Rob, feeling like he was on a runaway train. Destination: Awkward. 'Just tell me about when you met Mum.'

'Okaaay,' said Guy. 'That would be May seventh, 1981.'

'Right,' said Rob, swallowing hard. 'Look, here's the thing. You said something in the car on the way to the airport, about being knocked sideways by a woman. And I know this sounds really fucking weird, but I wondered if you could tell me what that feels like.' He was talking too fast, his hands twitching with anxiety and sweat running down his back.

Guy was quiet for a moment, and Rob heard the creak of wood and leather as he leaned back in his office chair. 'Well, that's quite a big question,' said Guy. 'What's this all about, Rob? Have you met someone?'

'I don't know,' said Rob, pressing his hand to his burning forehead.

'You don't know?' said Guy, and Rob could practically hear his dad's bushy eyebrows being raised. 'You're ringing your dad to ask what it feels like to fall in love and you don't know?'

'I . . . it's confusing. I barely know her, but there's . . . something about her. I don't know what it is and it's totally messing with my head.'

'OK, OK,' said Guy soothingly. 'Well, look, maybe I can tell you what it felt like when I met your mother, and you can tell me if any of that seems familiar. How does that sound?'

'Yeah, great,' said Rob quickly. 'Let's do that.'

'Right. Well, then, let's see.' There was another creak of leather, and Rob could imagine his dad leaning back in his chair, his right foot on his left knee, lost in distant memories. 'The day I met your mum. I can't remember what she was doing, but I do remember that once I started looking at her I couldn't stop. And when I wasn't looking at her, I was thinking about her; wondering what she was doing, what she was thinking. And I did completely irrational and stupid things to create opportunities for me to spend time with her.'

'Like what?'

'I found out her lecture schedule and got there early, hanging around in corridors hoping she'd pass by so I could just say hello.'

'This sounds kind of stalker-ish, Dad,' laughed Rob, imagining an early-eighties version of his dad, probably with a New Romantic quiff and drainpipe trousers, pursuing his mother around Durham University like a randy dog. He started to relax, hoping that maybe this feeling wasn't total insanity after all.

'I guess nowadays you'd just find her on the internet and say hello on social media or something,' said Guy. 'But back then you had to be more creative.'

'How did you know it wasn't just a stupid crush?' asked Rob. 'Like, I don't know, teenage hormones or something?'

'Because she wasn't my first turn around the dancefloor,' said Guy. 'I was actually twenty, I'd had plenty of girlfriends by then. But your mother took my breath away. She still does, actually.'

Rob smiled. 'So how did you win her over in the end?'

'I didn't have to,' said Guy. 'I just got her talking, took my time. Let her know that I wasn't going anywhere.'

'I can't do that, though,' said Rob, another wave of anxiety rising in his chest. 'I don't have time. She leaves on Saturday.'

Guy sighed. 'She's a guest, then? Rather than staff?'

'Yeah,' said Rob, his mouth full of sawdust.

'Does any of what I've just said sound familiar?' asked Guy.

'Yeah, kind of,' replied Rob. 'It's definitely different from . . . other women.'

'Well, I'm hardly an expert. But if I had to guess, I'd say it sounds a lot like you've fallen in love.'

'Shit,' muttered Rob, pressing his clammy hands together either side of his nose. 'That's what I was afraid of.'

Guy chuckled. 'Does she know?'

'Fuck, no.'

'Do you think she feels the same way?'

'I don't know. It's hard to tell.'

'Then you need to tell her how you feel.'

Rob gave a manic laugh. 'You make it sound so simple.'

'That's because it is. How does the saying go? "We only regret the chances we don't take." And in the end, what's the worst that can happen?'

I lose my job, thought Rob, but he couldn't tell his dad that.

'Something happened to her a couple of nights ago,' he said, clenching his fists at the memory of seeing her pressed against the wall round the corner from the bar, Matt's hands roaming all over her body. For a fraction of a second he'd thought Hannah was joining in, but then he'd clocked her flailing arms and the way her head was trying to turn away, and a red mist had descended. 'Some guy tried to . . . it's a long story. I wasn't involved, but I was there. I don't want to say the wrong thing if she's feeling vulnerable.'

Guy was quiet again, and Rob could hear the squeak as he twisted the office chair from side to side.

'Well, maybe don't go all in with hearts and flowers, then. Just talk to her, get to know her a bit. Let chemistry do its thing.'

'OK, I will. Thanks, Dad.'

'You're welcome. And Rob?'

'Yeah?'

'I'm really proud of you, you know. It takes a real man to call his dad to ask about love.'

'Yeah, I've been putting it off,' said Rob. 'But you're the only person I know who's ever experienced it that way.'

'Then I'm the luckiest man alive. We're off to Bermuda tomorrow, your mother's currently packing fifteen different bikinis. Maybe see you soon?'

'That would be great. Give her my love.'

'Can I tell her about this conversation?'

Rob laughed. 'Would it make any difference if I asked you not to?'

'Probably not. She has ways of making me talk.'

'Ugh, gross. Have a great holiday.'

'We will. Love you, son.'

'Thanks, Dad. Love you too.'

Rob ended the call and walked back to the terrace, lost in his thoughts, mostly about whether his next move was to spend more time with Hannah or to stay as far away as possible. It was all right for his dad; he'd been a twenty-year-old student with a mullet hairstyle and nothing to lose. How did you tell a woman you'd met less than four days ago that you'd fallen for her? He'd either sound like a really intense weirdo, or a sleazy fuckboy who was wheeling out lines in order to access her knickers. And it was totally, totally against all the rules – those he'd set for himself, and the ones Mark had set for him. Whichever way he looked at it, this whole situation felt doomed from the start.

Rob watched Hannah plough up and down the pool, giving the same focus to the movement of her arms and legs through the water as she did to her tennis. Stroke, turn to breathe. Stroke, turn to breathe. He'd waited until she'd started a new length before he pulled off his shirt and sat on the steps in the shallow end, waiting for her to swim back. The water felt cold, but this was important.

All evening since he'd spoken to his dad he'd been thinking about Hannah, looking for her, wondering what she was doing. He'd gone to every bar on the hill, simultaneously willing her to appear and praying she wouldn't. He'd looked for her on the way back to the hotel, remembering that first night in Marbella when she'd knocked him sideways, figuratively and literally. He'd thought about her on the way back to his room, wondering if she was lying on her bed right now, thinking about him. And then he'd thought of a place where he hadn't looked, and where he was absolutely certain she would be.

She touched the far end of the pool and turned to swim back. Stroke, turn to breathe. Stroke, turn to breathe. Towards the final third of the length she glanced up, making sure she stopped and turned before the steps to avoid beaching herself in the shallows like a whale.

Rob smiled nervously, bare-chested on the steps in waist-deep water, his forearms resting on his knees with his hands clasped between them. She stopped and stood up as she pulled her goggles off, her eyes wide with surprise.

'Hey,' said Rob.

'Hi,' said Hannah breathlessly. 'Are you OK?'

'I'm fine,' he said, trying to keep his voice even and not betray his nerves. 'Just saw you swimming and the water looked nice, so thought I'd join you.'

'Oh,' she said. 'Right.'

'Actually I wanted to talk to you.' Her face looked pale in

the reflection of the pool lights, and he wondered if she was as nervous as he was. 'Can we chat?'

'Um, sure,' said Hannah. 'Do you want to go for a drink or something?'

'No,' said Rob quickly. 'I can't be seen out with you again, even pizza last night was risky. But here is OK, if you don't mind.'

'OK,' said Hannah. 'Maybe we can sit at either end of the steps?' She smiled and raised her eyebrows, and Rob sighed.

'I'm sorry, I sound like such a wanker,' he said, sliding over to one side of the pool and raking his hands through his hair.

Hannah waded over to the same step and sat about two metres from him. 'Is this OK? Or should I move further away?'

'Stop taking the piss,' laughed Rob. 'I just wanted somewhere where we could chat without being overheard, but if anyone saw us it would look perfectly innocent.'

'Well, I think this ticks both boxes,' said Hannah. 'Look, you can see both my hands.' She held them up and waggled them like a chorus girl.

'Stop it,' said Rob, feeling himself relax. 'I just wanted to say something. You don't have to say anything in reply, but I wanted you to know.'

'OK, what is it?' she asked, her voice suddenly unsure. He felt cold, and wondered if she did too. He was too far away to see any goosebumps, and it took everything he had not to edge closer to run his hand down her arm. His mind instantly fast-forwarded to kissing her against the side of the pool, his fingers trailing down her back and her wet body pressed against his. *For fuck's sake, Rob. Focus.*

'I really like you,' he said, feeling a mix of panic and relief as he finally said the words he'd been practising in his head for hours. 'It was kind of an instant thing when we first met, and I can't really explain it. But I can't do anything about it, other than tell you. So that's what I'm doing.'

'I . . .' said Hannah, her eyes wide.

'I wanted to tell you why it's complicated.'

'OK,' she said, raising her eyebrows.

'Firstly, I'd lose my job,' said Rob. 'So that's a whole thing. But actually, I'm just taking a break from women, full stop. I haven't been single for more than about five minutes since I was a teenager. It's not very healthy.'

'No,' she said.

'And also I don't really do relationships. Not proper ones, anyway. My longest one is, like, two months. And you don't really seem like the type for a one-night stand.'

'No, I—'

'So I just wanted you to know. I didn't want you to think I was messing you around. Or just being a dick.'

'Right, can I speak now?' she asked, tilting her head with an amused grin.

'Oh,' said Rob. 'Yeah, of course. Sorry.'

'Thanks.' Hannah took a deep breath. 'I'm not going to pretend I don't fancy you, because I do.'

'Oh, thank God for that,' muttered Rob, shaking his head and laughing, his head down.

'But we're in the same boat,' she said. 'Well, slightly different boats. I've just separated from my husband, literally a few weeks ago.'

'Right,' said Rob, feeling an inexplicable jealousy towards a man he'd never met who'd actually been married to this incredible woman, and somehow fucked it up.

138

'This trip was about taking some time for myself, and a holiday fling is absolutely not on the list. So we're all good.'

Rob smiled with relief, feeling like his insides were melting. 'OK,' he said, blowing his cheeks out. 'I actually feel a lot better for this conversation.'

'Me too,' said Hannah, although she didn't actually look it. 'I mean, even if we were both in a better place,' she continued, 'it doesn't seem like we'd be very well suited, does it?'

'No,' Rob said hesitantly. 'I think we'd want different things. I don't really do relationships, whereas—'

'I don't do holiday flings,' Hannah finished. 'Not exactly a match made in heaven.'

'No,' said Rob. 'Not exactly.'

'Well, that's OK then,' said Hannah. 'Seems like we're both agreed.' She squeezed the water out of her wet hair, and Rob wondered what to say next. They'd laid their cards on the table, but that didn't make it any easier to pull himself away. And whilst he was glad he'd told her how he felt, the idea that nothing was going to happen between them still made him feel a bit empty.

'Talking of being in the same boat, I've had an idea for tomorrow night,' he said, needing to move the conversation on to more positive territories. 'I've mentioned it to the other guys and they're up for it. But I've told them I need to run it past you first, what with everything that happened on Monday. If you say no, we'll bin it off.'

'OK.' Hannah eyed him curiously. 'What is it?'

'A sunset boat trip,' he said. 'Olly knows a guy who owns a boat, he says his name is Manuel but I'm never sure if that's Olly's generic name for anyone Spanish.'

' "Olly knows a guy" makes me nervous,' said Hannah. 'Is the boat seaworthy?'

Rob laughed. 'You think I didn't check? It's a converted fishing boat, this guy does tours all the time, but not normally on a Thursday. Olly puts loads of business his way, so he owes him a favour.'

'Will there be lots of people?' she asked, and he could see how nervous she still was about the idea of being around strange men.

He shook his head. 'Nope. Just the six of us and the four of you. A private charter.'

'Won't you get into trouble if you go out with us again?'

'We'll be more careful this time, go in separate cabs and meet at the marina. Nobody needs to know.'

'OK,' said Hannah. 'I'm game.'

'Great,' Rob said. 'So are we all cool? Can we just play tennis and hang out for a few more days?'

'Yeah,' she said with a smile. 'We can definitely do that.' Neither of them said anything for a moment, so Hannah stood up. 'I might go and get changed.'

'Me too,' said Rob, but he didn't move. 'Can you go first? Just so we're not seen together?'

Hannah rolled her eyes and headed out of the pool, grabbing her robe off a lounger and using the sleeve to briskly rub away a drifting tide of mascara. It was a tiny gesture of self-consciousness, and Rob wished he could tell her that it didn't matter, that even with panda eyes and red goggle marks and hair that fell in lank, wet spirals down her back, she took his breath away.

'See you on court tomorrow,' she said, giving him a half-wave.

'I'll be there,' said Rob. He wondered if she could feel him watching her walk away, but she didn't look back. Something fundamental had shifted between them, and right now he couldn't decide if it made things better or far, far worse.

CHAPTER SEVENTEEN

'You seem a lot happier today,' said Jess to Hannah, both of them sitting on the wooden deck against the railing, sipping ice-cold glasses of Cava. Rob sat opposite on the other side of Nick, and Hannah was glad of her sunglasses so she could turn her face to the evening sun, but also take advantage of the opportunity to shamelessly look at him. The other coaches were all at the other end of the boat, chatting to Manuel as they sailed out of the marina and into open water.

'Yeah, I'm good.' Hannah leaned back on her hands. 'A lot better.' She was wearing a strapless sun dress that faded from hot pink to a pale orange, her feet bare on the warm wood of the deck. She hadn't told the others about the pizza on Tuesday and the conversation between her and Rob in the pool last night, knowing that it would prompt too many questions and put Trish in a mood. There'd been no further mention of Trish's attempts to get Rob into bed, so presumably that had hit a dead end.

'I wanted to say sorry to everyone,' said Trish, waving her empty glass at the assembled group. Rob turned his head to pull a face at Hannah, both of them sensing emotional declarations were incoming. 'I've been a bit of a twat,' she continued.

'No, you haven't,' said Gaynor soothingly, patting her on the shoulder.

'Yes, I have,' Trish said determinedly. 'I said some awful stuff to you guys on Sunday, about your husbands and fancy holidays and stuff. I was pissed.'

'It's fine,' said Jess. 'Forget it,'

'And I haven't been fair to Rob either,' said Trish. Nick grinned and sat up, clearly relishing the spectacle. *Oh God*, thought Hannah. *Where's she going with this?*

'He made it really clear on Sunday that he wasn't interested,' said Trish. 'And the same on Monday. But I kept trying it on anyway, and that wasn't fair.'

'It's fine,' said Rob with a shrug, glancing at Hannah again.

'But at the end of the day, I'm damaged goods.'

'Oh fucking hell, here we go,' muttered Gaynor.

'And Rob, you were lovely and an absolute gentleman, and I probably didn't deserve that. These guys already know that I haven't had a shag in two years, so that was . . .'

'Okaaay,' said Jess, as Nick snorted with laughter. 'I don't think Rob and Nick need to know the details.'

'It's important to share,' said Trish, her lip wobbling. 'It's OK for all of you, you've got perfect lives.'

'I do NOT have a perfect life,' said Gaynor, an edge creeping into her voice. The other women stared at her, so she cleared her throat. 'Ed and I are fine, but he works away a lot and it's definitely not like it used to be. Before the kids.'

'You still love him, though, right?' asked Jess, reaching over to touch her arm. Hannah wondered what Rob was making of this display of female soul-bearing. If Graham was anything to go by, men would rather die in the trenches than have conversations like this.

'Course,' said Gaynor. 'But it's now May, right? And I can

genuinely only think of one time we've had sex this year. Maybe twice, but the other time was barely worth mentioning. I had to finish myself off in the bathroom.'

'Sorry, guys, girl talk,' said Jess, wafting an arm at Rob and Nick, who were both boggle-eyed and speechless. 'Look, it's not just you, mate,' she added to Gaynor, still patting her hand in solidarity. 'Tim and I definitely do it less than we used to. You just have to make the effort, make time for each other every week.'

'Yeah, we tried that,' said Gaynor gloomily. 'Friday night date, no excuses. Until he's tired or I've got my period or the kids are being a nightmare. Then we get out of the habit again.'

'Sorry, but do you guys even know we're here?' asked Nick, turning his palms upwards towards Hannah.

'Yeah, but we don't care,' said Hannah.

'Have you talked to Ed about it?' asked Trish.

'Not really,' said Gaynor. 'I'm worried it's going to open a big old can of worms. Like maybe he doesn't love me, or he's screwing someone else and wants a divorce but doesn't know how to tell me.'

'That's hardly likely,' said Jess. 'What if he assumes you're thinking the same thing?'

Gaynor thought about it for a moment. 'I hadn't really considered that as a possibility.'

'We never do, mate,' said Jess. 'Fuck, it's chats like this that make me wish we all still smoked. You need a pack of Marlboros for a conversation like this.'

'So I haven't had sex in two years,' said Trish, 'and Gaynor is, what, one-and-a-half times this year so far? When was your last time, Jess?'

'Couple of weeks ago,' said Jess glumly. 'The kids were at Tim's mum's for the weekend, we went to a wedding for some guy he works with. It had a free bar so we got wasted, then had a rubbish shag on the sofa when we got home. He did that thing where he held my head while I was going down on him and I gagged so hard I nearly puked. Literally sicked up a Vodka Red Bull in my mouth and had to swallow it again.'

Gaynor and Trish both snorted with laughter. 'Oh my God, I hate it when men do that,' said Trish. 'Like, I've got this, babe. You don't need to STEER.'

'They've definitely forgotten we're here,' said Nick, his shoulders shaking with silent laughter.

'Would you rather they gave verbal instructions?' asked Gaynor. 'I can't be doing with all that "left a bit, down a bit". You're getting a blowjob, not hanging a fucking picture—'

'Is it not enough that we put their dicks in our mouths?' laughed Trish.

'Wait, what?' said Hannah, her face a mask of shock. 'You put it in your MOUTH?'

The others all stared at her in shock. 'Oh my God,' gasped Jess, covering her mouth with her hand. 'I know you grew up in that creepy church, but how could you not know that?'

Hannah grinned. 'I'm just kidding,' she said, then stood up to fill her empty glass, giving Rob a grin as she passed. She knew he was watching her as she walked away, although he was being a lot more subtle about it than Olly, who looked her up and down whilst actually licking his lips. Hannah shuddered as Manuel spotted her empty glass and indicated that he'd be over with another bottle.

'Everyone OK here?' asked Olly, helping Chris and Jonno

dish out cold beers to all the outstretched hands. 'What are we talking about?'

'Nothing much,' said Gaynor quickly. 'Who do we have to thank for all this?'

'It was actually Rob's idea,' said Olly, plonking himself down next to her. 'But it was me who called Manuel. He owes me a favour – I send him all the guests who want boat trips and drugs.'

'I miss the days when we used to take drugs,' Trish said wistfully. 'Jess, how much of the early noughties did we spend absolutely off our faces?'

'Most of it,' said Jess, looking around at the group. 'Gaynor was really into UK Garage, we used to go up to London to these parties. Bodycon dresses and no eyebrows, off our tits on speed so we didn't fall asleep and miss the last train home.'

'I love how she blames it on me,' said Gaynor. 'Her brother was our dealer. Anyway, Olly, we feel very honoured that you'd cash in your favour for us.' She held out her glass for him to clink with his beer bottle. 'Thank you.'

Olly grinned, basking in the glow of Gaynor's attention. Hannah leaned over the railing as the boat sped through the calm water, wondering if Olly would ever learn that not every woman who gave him the time of day also wanted to have sex with him.

'It's a gorgeous boat,' said Rob, appearing beside her and looking out to sea, away from the ugly hotels and apartments along the coast. Manuel was taking them to a spot where they could swim and watch the sun set before having a tapas dinner and heading back. She watched him lean back and turn his face to the sun, his arms taut and the line of soft hair on his stomach glinting gold in the sunlight. She shivered at the thought of stroking her fingers along it; regardless of what they'd agreed last night, he'd still ignited a fire inside her that no amount of swimming, tennis or Cava was going to put out. She wondered if he found them being this close to each other as exquisitely painful as she did.

'This boat is called *Bianca*,' said Manuel, topping up the outstretched glasses. He had a huge moustache that offset the lack of hair on his head, and the wide, flat feet of a man who hadn't worn shoes in decades. 'She belong to my father, he buy her so he could bring the very best marijuana from Morocco.'

'What a family legacy,' said Trish. 'Where is he now?'

'He's in . . . what do you call the place? Where people go to stay when they are old?'

'Prison?' suggested Rob.

Aaron snorted his beer through his nose. 'A retirement home?'

'This is the place,' said Manuel, patting Aaron's shoulder and pointing towards a tiny inlet in the cliffs. 'I will help Felipe now, and then you can swim.'

'I'm definitely going in,' said Aaron, pulling off his T-shirt and bouncing on the balls of his feet as Manuel and Felipe slowed the boat and let out the anchor. Hannah watched Rob, grateful for the anonymity of sunglasses. He looked entirely at peace, a small smile on his lips as he sipped his beer and listened to the others arguing about whether Rafa or Roger was the greatest tennis player of all time. *Serena, obviously.*

'You can swim now,' shouted Manuel a few minutes later. 'We will make you food.'

'Shit, I forgot to bring any other shorts,' said Aaron,

casting around like a pair of swimming shorts might magic-ally appear.

'Me too,' said Nick. 'Just wear those ones, they'll dry off.'

'Or you could dispense with them entirely,' said Trish provocatively. 'We promise not to look.'

Nick caught the challenge in her eyes and grinned, before dropping his shorts and vaulting over the railing with a howl, one hand flailing as the other covered his manhood. Aaron paused for a second, clearly undecided, before following suit, his lily-white backside glowing like a lighthouse. Hannah heard the splash and the whoops and smiled at Rob.

'Unexpectedly, Aaron came out of that better than Nick,' said Trish, leaning over the side of the boat to peer into the crystal clear water below. 'He needed both hands.'

'Trish, he's about fourteen,' said Gaynor. 'You're practic-ally old enough to be his mum.'

'He's twenty-four,' said Jonno. 'And I've seen a picture of his mum. You're way hotter.'

'Jesus,' muttered Trish. 'Is this my life now?'

'You can't say we didn't offer,' said Olly mildly. 'Any one of us could have saved you from all this. But you latched on to Reverend Rob and look how that turned out.'

'Why do you call him that?' asked Hannah.

Olly gave Rob a withering glare. 'Because he thinks he's a better man than the rest of us. Like he operates on a higher plane of virtue.'

'You set a pretty low bar, to be fair,' laughed Rob. Hannah could see he was trying to keep things light and friendly – just a bit of lads' banter, as Olly would say. She was also trying to be charitable to Olly, who had clearly understood the need for her to overwrite the memories of Monday with an evening like this.

'I'll get over it,' said Trish, trying to break the tension by pulling a face at Rob. 'A girl can handle rejection when the man in question is rejecting everyone else too. At least you know it's him and not you.'

Hannah forced a smile, feeling both guilty and relieved that nothing had happened with Rob, and thankful she hadn't told them about last night's conversation.

'Right, come on, ladies,' said Trish, standing up. 'That includes you, Olly.'

'Hannah?' said Jess. 'You coming swimming?'

'I'll be there in a minute,' said Hannah. 'Cramps.' She rubbed her hand over her belly and Jess gave her a pitying look.

'Poor you,' she said. 'Drink more Cava, it will numb the pain.'

'Rob, you coming?' said Jonno.

'Give me a sec,' said Rob. 'I'll just clear up all these glasses.'

'Christ, you're a fucking saint,' said Olly, rolling his eyes as he pulled off his T-shirt and sucked in his abs. Hannah clambered over to the open deck at the front of the boat, watching Rob busy himself with putting empty bottles in a crate so they didn't roll around. Aaron and Nick scrambled up the ladder, no longer bothering to hide their nakedness. Hannah politely looked away, trying not to blush.

'Not swimming?' she asked Rob as he picked his way across the deck to join her.

'In a minute,' he said. 'Right now I'm wondering how Aaron manages to carry that around all day without hurting himself.'

Hannah watched as Aaron did a star jump off the side, his giant cock flapping against his belly like a wet salmon. 'Wow,' she said. 'That's . . . quite a spectacle.'

'And that's in cold water,' laughed Rob. 'In full sail that's going to be a monster.'

Hannah laughed, woefully conscious that her frame of reference was entirely Graham, who definitely hadn't looked like that. 'I can't believe this is all over on Saturday,' she said. 'It's been quite an experience.'

'Don't forget the end-of-week party tomorrow,' he said. 'That's the highlight of the week.'

'Really?'

'No,' laughed Rob. 'It's totally lame. All the guests are forced to hang out together even though they have nothing in common apart from tennis, and we coaches have to smile and tell everyone how much they've improved. Mark says it guarantees repeat bookings for next year.'

'I can't wait,' said Hannah, laughing at Trish, who was attempting some synchronised swimming moves with Gaynor.

'Come in!' shouted Jess, waving at them both.

'We should swim,' said Rob. 'We don't want to be the party poopers.'

'OK,' said Hannah, 'but I wanted to ask you something first.' She'd been thinking about this all day, and it felt like now or never.

Rob looked at her curiously, his head tilted. The setting sun behind his head brought out the copper flecks in his hair. 'What?' he asked.

'Can we stay in touch? After I leave? Just as friends, I mean.'

Rob smiled, a full-beam grin that lit up his face like the sun had gone into reverse. 'Sure. I'll give you my number. Maybe we can play tennis some time.'

Hannah looked at him, feeling a mix of happiness and pain and relief and a million other emotions. 'I'd like that a lot.'

CHAPTER EIGHTEEN

'Here's to us,' said Gaynor, holding up her drink. 'And another brilliant week.'

'It's been amazing,' said Hannah, feeling a combination of sadness that the week was nearly over, but also excitement about the solo road trip she was about to begin. Throw in some confusion and pure unadulterated arousal over Rob, and it was fair to say she was experiencing mixed feelings.

'We need to give our group a new name,' said Jess. 'The Pina Colinas was always us and Carla – she'll feel like we've thrown her out.'

'Carla's expecting twins,' said Trish, slurping the remainder of her cocktail through a straw. 'On top of the two kids she's already got. Realistically, is she ever coming back?'

'Still,' said Jess, 'we should at least consider her feelings.'

Trish pulled a face, like this was an alien concept. 'Fine. What shall we go for?'

Hannah thought about it for a moment. 'It needs to have tennis in it,' she said. 'For me this has been more about the tennis than the booze, not that the booze hasn't been great.' Trish slurped a bit more by way of protest.

'But it should also be about sun,' said Jess. 'Because the tennis here is way different from when we're at home. So something that relates to tennis in the sun.'

'I definitely feel like you're all overthinking this,' said Trish, her face deadpan.

'Well, that's it,' said Gaynor with a huge grin. 'Tennis in the sun. TITS. That's our group name.'

'HA, I love it,' said Jess, clapping her hands together as Trish rolled her eyes. 'We're TITS On Tour. I'll change the name of our WhatsApp group.' She picked up her phone and started tapping intently, as Hannah said the word a few times in her head. She couldn't think of an occasion when she'd said it out loud other than in a bird capacity, although Graham had occasionally observed, during a rare moment of passion, that she had amazing tits. Observation had been a core part of Graham's bedroom modus operandi – *you have nice skin, I love your neck*. Hannah had never found it particularly sexy; perhaps because his tone was more 'man visiting a museum' than 'hot seducer'. Once Hannah had been going down on him and he'd announced that *the view from here is magnificent*, like he'd just unshouldered a backpack to look out over Lake Windermere. Hannah had laughed so hard she nearly choked, which had killed the mood a bit.

'We'll be blue tits if they don't turn the air conditioning down in here,' said Trish, rubbing her goosebumpy arms.

'Do we need more drinks?' asked Gaynor, who hated an empty glass.

'My turn,' said Hannah, leaning forward to gather the empties onto a tray. The past week had taught her that two cocktails gave her a happy buzz, and three was time to call it a night. But since this was their last night, maybe she could stretch to four.

'What's going on over there?' asked Trish, craning her neck.

Hannah turned and spotted Rob and Olly nose-to-nose

at the far end of the bar, deep in conversation. They were both in profile and whilst it didn't look like they were fighting, exactly, there was an intensity to the hand gestures and their facial expressions that suggested hostilities were under way.

'That looks heavy,' said Gaynor.

'Rob looks like he could blow his load at any moment,' murmured Jess.

'If only,' muttered Trish excitedly. 'Hannah, have a listen in while you're at the bar. See what they're arguing about and bring us back the goss.'

Hannah sidled over to the bar with the tray of glasses, positioning herself a few metres away from Rob and Olly with her back to them. She placed her order and listened hard – the conversation was whispered and strained, until Olly said, 'Fuck OFF, Rob,' and things started to escalate. She turned and watched out the corner of her eye, taking in the aggressive posturing and gestures that looked like they might turn physical any moment. Hannah looked around for someone to intervene, but nobody was paying attention – the other coaches were all off schmoozing guests, and Jess, Gaynor and Trish were still on the sofas over by the window, waiting for Hannah to come back. She paused for a second, feeling a little unsteady on her feet from the third cocktail, then held up her hand so the barman knew she'd be back and edged across to where Rob and Olly were engaged in a tense face-off.

'Is everything OK?' she said.

'Oh, here she is, the lovely Hannah,' said Olly with his particular brand of oily condescension. He seemed to think this approach made him appear smooth and charismatic, but

154

it was entirely repellent. 'See, Rob? One of us has magnetic qualities, and it's probably not you.'

'What's this about?' asked Hannah, putting herself firmly between them.

'I'll tell you, shall I?' said Olly before Rob could interrupt. 'I was just telling Rob here that I found you rather attractive – just a passing observation, you know. But Rob seems to have made himself your protector – clearly Monday's unfortunate events have given him a saviour complex.'

'Olly, you're such a fucking . . .' said Rob.

'ANYWAY,' continued Olly, holding his hand inches from Rob's face, 'I reminded Rob that you were your own woman, and if you didn't want to spend quality alone time with me, you'd say so.'

Olly actually made air quotes around 'alone time', and Hannah had to press her lips together to stop herself laughing.

'Sorry, I'm confused,' she said, tilting her head innocently. 'You're interested in "alone time" with me, but you're talking to Rob about it. How does that work?'

'As I said, just a passing observation apropos your attractiveness,' said Olly, licking his lips and moving a bit closer. 'But Prince fucking Charming here seems to think I need to get his permission.'

'You don't need anyone's permission to ask,' said Hannah mildly. 'As long as you agree that my decision is final.' She held his gaze, a veteran of a thousand encounters with difficult country club customers who wanted something from her that she absolutely wasn't prepared to give.

'Of course,' said Olly, his eyes flicking from her face to her chest to her legs and back again. 'So would you be interested? In some quality alone time with yours truly?'

Hannah folded her arms and looked him up and down, wondering if men ever found this as uncomfortable as women did. 'It's a no from me, I'm afraid.'

Olly paused for a second, then pressed his wet lips together and pulled back his shoulders, tossing his head like this outcome couldn't possibly matter less. Hannah glanced at Rob, who was trying not to laugh, then went back to collect her tray of drinks and returned to the table.

'What was all that about?' Trish asked excitedly.

'Nothing,' said Hannah. 'Just Olly being an idiot, as usual.' She glanced back to the bar, gasping softly as Olly shoved Rob in the shoulder. Rob looked over and gave Hannah a long look that clearly signified 'I've had enough', then held up his hands and left the room.

'Hannah?' said Trish, her eyes narrowed. 'What just happened?'

'Nothing,' Hannah said. 'Olly and Rob got into a . . . disagreement.'

'About what?' asked Trish. Her tone was full of suspicion, and Hannah knew she wasn't going to let this go. She reminded herself that these women were her friends, so maybe it was time to be straight with them.

'About me, actually. Olly told Rob he fancied me, and Rob told him to leave me alone.' She looked up at Jess and Gaynor, who were looking between Hannah and Trish with gripped expressions.

'And why would Rob tell him that?' asked Trish. Hannah could feel the barb in every word.

'I . . .' Hannah looked away.

'Oh my God,' said Trish, as realisation finally dawned. 'You and Rob like each other, don't you?'

'Shitting hell,' hissed Gaynor. 'We're definitely going to need more drinks.'

'Hannah?' asked Trish.

She looked at Trish pleadingly. 'Yes. But nothing has happened, I promise.'

'Really?' said Trish, looking a little sickly.

'I totally believe you,' said Jess, ever the peacemaker. 'But why didn't you tell us?'

'There's nothing to tell,' said Hannah. 'I actually met Rob by accident the first night we were here. He was the guy I was talking to outside that bar in Marbella.'

'Fuck,' said Trish. 'How did I not remember that? God, I must have been hammered.'

'And he likes you?' said Gaynor. 'Like, you've actually talked about it?'

'Yes,' said Hannah. 'But he's not into relationships, and I'm not into casual sex, and neither of us is in a great place right now. So we decided to leave it at that.'

'That's actually kind of romantic,' said Jess. 'Where's he gone now?'

'No idea,' Hannah said. 'Back to his room, probably.'

'You should go after him,' said Gaynor. 'We're all heading off tomorrow, and you don't want to leave things like this. It's bad holiday vibes.'

'Really?' Hannah looked around at the three women.

'Totally,' said Jess. 'Go and talk to him, make sure he's OK. Remind him that Olly isn't worth getting fired over.' They all looked at Trish, who wiped her nose with the back of her hand and shook her head briskly, like she was pulling herself together.

'You should have told me he liked you,' she said. 'Stopped me making an idiot of myself.'

'I know,' said Hannah. 'I didn't realise until it was too late. I'm really sorry.'

Trish nodded. 'Best you go and see him then,' she said quietly.

'I don't know his room number,' said Hannah.

Trish gave her a sly smile. 'One-four-two, it's on the first floor. I found out from Aaron on Monday, when I thought I was in with a chance.'

Hannah nodded gratefully. 'I'm just going to check he's OK. I'll be back in a bit, I promise.'

'Sure you will,' said Trish. 'Give him one for me, will you?' She picked up her Cosmopolitan and drained it in one go, then stood up and dusted herself down. 'More drinks?'

Hannah edged her way through the bar towards the exit, ignoring Olly watching her as he chatted to Aaron at the bar. Reception was empty, so she darted through the swing doors as if she was going to the loo, then through the second set of doors and up the stairs to the first floor. There were benefits to wearing trainers and a short dress as party wear – they were quiet and she could move fast.

Rob's corridor was empty, so she hurried down to room 142 and gently knocked. Rob opened the door immediately, his chest bare and a white T-shirt in his hands, like he was just getting changed.

'Shit, what are you doing here?' he whispered.

'I wanted to check you were OK,' she said helplessly.

'You shouldn't be here,' he said, glancing both ways down the corridor. 'Fuck, come in.' He hustled her into the room and closed the door firmly behind her. 'How did you find out my room number?'

'Don't ask. Are you OK?'

'Yeah, I'm fine. Olly was just pushing my buttons, so I got out of there before I punched him.'

'You need to be careful,' said Hannah. 'He's not worth it, and you don't want to lose your job.'

'If someone finds you here I'll definitely lose my job,' laughed Rob.

'I'm sorry, I'll go,' she said. 'I just needed to check on you.' She kept her distance and stayed by the door, even though she could feel the pull towards him. The fact that he was half naked didn't exactly help. What was she even doing here? This was a stupid idea.

'When are you leaving tomorrow?' he asked.

'Oh,' said Hannah, edging further into the room. 'Actually, I'm not. I'm going on a road trip for a couple of weeks.'

'Really?' Rob shook his head in confusion. 'Who with?'

'With myself,' replied Hannah with a smile. 'A solo adventure.'

'What kind of adventure?'

'Not sure yet.' Hannah folded her arms to stop herself reaching out to stroke his bare arm. Could Rob feel this too, or was it just her? 'Bit of hiking, bit of sightseeing.'

'Wow,' said Rob, looking impressed. 'Look, can we meet for a coffee before you go? Tomorrow is my day off.'

Hannah nodded. 'Sure. Why don't you give me your number?' She took a couple of steps towards him as she pulled out her phone, then watched him grab his from the table by the window and come even closer. If she tilted her face to his, surely he would kiss her? The thought of it sent a wave of heat coursing through her body. She looked up at him, seeing his pupils dilate and his lips part just a little. They were alone in his room, right next to his bed, and

Hannah didn't think she had the strength to fight any more. Whatever happened now, she was OK with it.

'Open up,' shouted a male voice, accompanied by a sharp hammering on the door. They both jumped apart like they'd touched an electric fence.

'Oh fuck,' whispered Rob, frantically trying to get his T-shirt back on, but ending up with his head stuck in an armhole. 'That's absolutely the last thing I need.'

'What should I do?' she gasped, trying not to panic. Her reservations over being alone with Rob in his room increased tenfold as the hammering continued. 'Shall I hide in the bathroom?'

'Just stay there, it's fine,' said Rob. He wrestled his T-shirt on and sighed heavily as the hammering started again.

'I'm fucking coming,' he replied, opening the door.

'I'm sure you are,' said Mark with a smirk, looking beyond Rob to Hannah, who tried to look casual but somehow managed to look horribly awkward and guilty, like she'd been caught wanking in church. She swallowed down the sick feeling and countered his lecherous gaze with a hard stare, kicking herself for being so stupid.

'This is not what you think,' said Rob, but Mark wasn't listening.

'My office, nine a.m.,' he snapped. 'And your T-shirt's on back to front.' He stalked off, leaving only Olly standing in the corridor, staring at Hannah and Rob with a look that might once have been triumphant, but now just looked a little sad and empty.

CHAPTER NINETEEN

'I'm going to get fired,' muttered Rob, pulling his T-shirt off and throwing it on the bed. 'I can't believe I'm going to get fired.'

'I'm so sorry,' said Hannah, her hands covering her mouth and her face a mask of horror. 'I shouldn't have come.'

Rob turned to look at her, his expression softening. 'Hey, it's not your fault.'

'I should get back to my room.'

'Look, maybe we're over-reacting. Mark can't fire me for something we absolutely didn't do, it will be fine.'

'I really hope so.' She looked incredibly young and unsure all of a sudden, and Rob realised how unused to dealing with women like her he was – she was older than practically every woman he'd dated, but she was also incredibly naive and he kind of loved her for it. None of his exes would have come anywhere near his room without half a dozen strategies, cover stories and exit plans, it was a rookie move. But he couldn't be mad at Hannah for it – she'd meant well, and right now that counted for a lot.

'I'll see you tomorrow, yeah?' he said, giving her a reassuring smile.

'Sure.' She nodded, pulling herself together. 'Meet me in the café in the square at nine thirty? After you've seen Mark?'

'OK,' said Rob, an acid feeling building in his stomach. Would Mark really believe that nothing had happened between them? They'd never been friends, exactly, but Rob had earned his respect. Although maybe that made everything worse, because now Mark probably thought he'd been mugged off.

'I'm really sorry,' said Hannah. 'I feel awful.'

'No,' he said emphatically. 'I shouldn't have let Olly wind me up; that's what started all this. Do you promise you'll be there tomorrow? You won't drive off and never come back?' He hated how needy he sounded, but the idea of never seeing Hannah again made his chest hurt.

'I promise,' she said, backing towards the door. He wondered if she felt this too, this physical pain of wanting something you absolutely couldn't have, and feeling like it was all slipping away.

'OK.' He took a deep breath and opened the door. 'There's a fire escape at the end of the corridor; if you go down that way you end up in the car park. Less likely to bump into a bunch of idiot schoolboys.' They could talk tomorrow; unravel this mess in the cold light of day.

Hannah nodded and gave him a weak smile. She clearly wasn't a crier, which was a bonus. Rob had a momentary flashback to Nina, squeezing out fake tears in his flat in Bath. That was barely a month ago, but it felt like a lifetime.

'I shouldn't have come, I'm so sorry,' she said again. There was a moment of hesitation, and then Rob instinctively opened his arms and pulled her in for a brief hug. Hannah pressed herself against him for barely a few seconds, then hurried out of the room without looking back. It was about as chaste as hugs got, but Rob realised it was the first time he'd properly touched her. For a moment it felt like he couldn't breathe.

He sat on the bed with his head in his hands, waiting for the pounding in his ears to subside as he processed everything that had happened in the past half-hour. He was pretty sure he could avoid the sack in the morning; Hannah had been fully dressed and Mark had no evidence that anyone had broken any rules. But even if he saved his job, Hannah was still leaving, and the thought sat heavy in his stomach. He wasn't in the right place for a relationship, and clearly neither was she. They'd made a mutual decision to not get involved and he wasn't going to be the one to derail it, even if looking at her made his balls ache. She deserved better than someone like him.

'All right, lover boy,' said a loud voice, as the door was flung open. He'd forgotten to lock it, and now Chris and Jonno were piling into his room. 'Somebody's been playing secret bingo.'

'Leave it, OK?' said Rob.

'What was she like?' asked Chris. 'No wonder you wouldn't let Olly near her, you sneaky fucker.'

Rob stood up and put himself firmly in Chris's face. 'Get out, both of you.'

Jonno shrugged and laughed awkwardly. 'Just a bit of banter, mate.'

'Just fuck off, OK? I've already lost it with Olly this evening, and if you don't both leave my room I will break both your fucking arms.'

Chris held up his hands. 'Whoah, calm down. We're leaving.' They both backed out of the room, giggling nervously. Rob locked the door and stood by the window,

163

clenching his fists and taking deep breaths. He thought about what his parents would say if Mark fired him and he turned up back at home after just a month. The Baxter family didn't do failure. You excelled at everything, you left your imprint on the world. The idea of getting on the Plane of Shame made him want to puke.

And then he thought about Hannah – the feel of her in his arms for all of the three seconds, the smell of her hair, the intense look in her eyes. By this time tomorrow he'd have potentially lost his job and Hannah, and he felt a powerful need to save at least one of them. The question was, which one mattered more?

Another knock, this time soft and tentative. Rob looked through the peephole to see Nick loitering in the corridor. He opened the door to find Aaron was there too, both of them looking worried and sheepish.

'We just wanted to check you were OK, mate,' said Nick, holding out a bottle of beer.

Rob sighed and reached out to take it. 'Come in.'

He opened the doors to the tiny balcony so they could stand outside, leaning on the metal railing as they sipped their beers. It was quiet out here, just the noise of crickets and people laughing as they smoked outside the hotel.

'You all right?' asked Aaron.

'I've been better,' said Rob with a shrug.

'Was Hannah here? Did Mark fire you?'

'Yeah, she was,' said Rob. 'Not sure if I've still got a job. I've got to go to his office in the morning.'

'Are you and her, like, a thing?' asked Nick, looking mildly impressed.

'Nope,' said Rob. 'You probably won't believe me, but I've never laid a finger on her.'

'Fuck, really?' said Aaron.

'I swear to God,' said Rob. 'There's nothing to tell. She was here but nothing happened. We were just talking.'

'Man, that sucks,' said Nick, draining his beer. 'You're into her, though, right?'

Rob thought about how much to tell them; he didn't want to lie, but he didn't want to compromise himself or Hannah either. 'Yeah, I guess. But this isn't the right time or place for either of us.'

'Yeah, totally,' murmured Nick, looking sceptical.

Rob turned to look at them both. 'How did Mark know she was here?'

Aaron shrugged. 'Olly, I guess. I was chatting to him at the bar, then he saw Hannah leave and said something like "Shit, I bet I know where she's gone." Then he left, so I guess he went to find Mark. I should have stopped him, I'm really sorry.'

Rob shook his head. 'Forget it. It's not your fault.'

'I'll be proper gutted if you get fired,' said Nick.

'Me too,' said Aaron. 'You can't leave us with Olly and Chris. They're absolute melts.'

'Out of my hands now,' said Rob with a shrug. 'I've got no idea what Mark is going to do.'

Nick turned to look at him, his expression a mix of regret and admiration. 'Big question though, mate. Is she worth getting fired over?'

Rob thought about it for a minute, weighing up everything that had happened since he arrived in Club Colina. Nothing he'd experienced felt as powerful as meeting

Hannah – tennis was just a sport, coaching was just a job, Spain was just a country.

But Hannah? She was a glimmer of something else; a kind of life that would be made immeasurably better by having her in it. Maybe just as a friend, or maybe something else when they were both ready. Right now it didn't seem to matter, and he wasn't afraid of it. The only thing he was afraid of was never seeing her again.

'Yeah,' said Rob, grinning at them both. 'Never thought I'd say this in a million years, but she might be totally worth it.'

CHAPTER TWENTY

Hannah jogged through the car park and into the hotel with her head down, studiously avoiding the gazes of other guests who'd got wind of some kind of gossip-worthy activity but hadn't quite managed to pin down who was involved. If she could make it back to her room without anyone interrogating her, that would feel like a small win in what had been a hectic evening.

She avoided the lifts and ran up the stairs, exactly as she had barely half an hour ago. But this time she bypassed Rob's floor and carried on up to the third.

'Thank fuck, there you are,' said Gaynor, who was hovering in the corridor outside her room. 'I've been looking for you everywhere.'

'Why?'

'Because . . . shit, let me in.'

Hannah unlocked the door to her room and headed inside, feeling stressed and breathless.

'I wanted to check you were OK,' said Gaynor. 'I saw Chris, he told me Mark caught you and Rob in bed.'

'What?' howled Hannah, covering her face with her hands. 'That's absolutely NOT true. We were just talking – NOTHING happened.'

'Whoah, I believe you,' said Gaynor, holding up her hands.

She took Hannah's arm and led her to the bed. 'Sit down for a minute.'

Hannah sat and took some deep, calming breaths. 'Where are the others?'

'They're down by the pool. After we saw Chris I was sent to find you. Jess was worried.'

Hannah raised her eyebrows. 'What about Trish?'

'Trish was worried too.' She gave Hannah a hard look. 'Come on, Hannah – she's just been told that the guy she's been really into for this whole trip is in bed with her mate. How would you feel?'

'Yeah, OK,' said Hannah, remembering exactly how she'd felt earlier in the week when she thought Rob had turned his attention to Trish. 'I didn't mean for any of this to happen.'

'I believe you,' said Gaynor, giving her a playful punch on the arm. 'But you're in one piece, and it's still our last night, so we need to make the most of it.'

Hannah sighed heavily. 'Yeah, OK. I need a drink.'

Trish ran over as soon as she saw Hannah, her face set to 'brave acceptance'. 'I heard about what happened,' she said breathily, resting her hand on Hannah's arm. 'It's OK, I'm not angry about it.'

'Thanks,' said Hannah, suddenly reminded of her mother's ongoing application for sainthood. 'But it's not true. I've never even kissed Rob, we were both fully dressed when Mark turned up.'

'SEE, I told you Hannah wouldn't,' said Jess. 'She's not the type.'

'Like me, you mean?' snapped Trish. 'Are you saying I'd have shagged him?'

'Well, yes,' said Jess, shaking her head in confusion. 'Wouldn't you?'

'Totally,' said Trish.

'So what happens now?' asked Jess, turning to Hannah. 'Has he been fired?'

Hannah shook her head. 'Not yet. He has to see Mark tomorrow morning.'

'Yikes,' said Trish. 'What do you think Mark will do?'

'I suppose if Rob can't convince him nothing happened, he might get kicked out and have to go back to the UK.'

'And would you go with him?' asked Jess.

Hannah's head snapped up. 'What? No, of course not. I'm off on my road trip. There's absolutely nothing between Rob and me.' She thought about how close they'd been just now, and her stomach did backflips.

'I fancy a swim,' said Gaynor, breaking the tension. 'Who's coming in?' She slipped off her dress and underwear before anyone could answer, then held her nose as she jumped into the pool, gasping as she came up for air.

'You're insane,' laughed Jess, already pulling off her miniskirt.

'It feels lovely,' said Gaynor. She swam to the edge and grabbed the bottle of Cava, pulling off the foil cage and pushing the cork out with her thumbs so it fired off into the darkness. Jess stripped naked and jumped in next to her.

'Shall we?' asked Trish, tilting her chin in a final show of forgiveness. Hannah grinned, kicking off her trainers and yanking off her dress and knickers, then jumped into the water before anyone could pass comment on the dark shadow of her natural pubes. The cool water washed away the heat and stress of the evening, her skin tingling at the memory of how Rob's arms had felt around her, even if it was just for a few seconds. She swam to the edge and sat with her back to the wall of the pool, relishing the strange feeling of freedom that came with not wearing a bikini. Jess, Gaynor and Trish joined her, gasping for breath as they passed the bottle along the row so they could all take a swig.

'Well, this has been quite a week,' said Gaynor.

'I reckon Rob will be fine,' said Trish, clearly trying to be conciliatory. 'He's a really good coach – how are they going to replace him at such short notice?'

'Good point,' said Hannah, happy to cling on to anything right now.

'I'm kind of gutted you didn't shag him, though.' Jess smirked. 'I bet he's got some great coaching skills in the bedroom too.'

Hannah sighed and shook her head, grabbing the bottle and taking a long drink.

'He looks like he'd go hard from the baseline,' said Gaynor.

'Bit of topspin forehand,' added Jess, snorting with laughter. 'Stroke those balls down the line.'

'Bet he has a lovely grip,' added Trish, smiling gamely even though Hannah could see how much it pained her.

'Who wants a go on the slide?' Gaynor suggested.

'What, the kiddie one?' Jess looked over at the blue plastic slide on the side of the pool. 'I'm in.'

'Oh God, this is going to go badly,' said Trish as the two of them swam to the steps and clambered out, their naked skin glowing in the pool lights.

'You'll need to wet it,' called Hannah, but they were too

giggly to hear. Gaynor climbed up the steps, her boobs bouncing merrily.

'I'm going down on my front,' she announced, clambering forward so her chest rested on the slide and her feet were flailing in the air.

'WET THE SLIDE!' shouted Hannah, but it was too late. Gaynor wiggled her way down, screeching in pain as her damp body failed to provide enough lubrication to facilitate a slide, causing her nipples to drag across the plastic like sandpaper. Hannah winced.

'Owww, that hurt,' yelled Gaynor at nobody in particular. 'I should have wet the slide.'

'Jesus,' muttered Trish, watching Gaynor splash water onto the slide so Jess could have a go. 'I love being naked in the water. It makes my tits look really perky.'

'Aren't they always perky?'

'I've fed two kids,' Trish said glumly. 'They're like deflated balloons. Good underwear is my saviour.'

'Couldn't you have a boob job?'

'Yeah, one day. Don't have the money right now, and I'm only thirty-six. I figure if I have them done now they'll need doing again in ten years, but if I wait until I'm forty-five they'll be fine until I'm fifty-five and I won't give a crap about anything below the neck by then.'

'I can tell you've thought this through,' said Hannah, swigging some more Cava. They should have brought a second bottle.

'Haven't you?' asked Trish.

'I can honestly say I've never given it a passing thought.'

'How old are you again?'

'I'm thirty-two.'

'Right, that's why,' said Trish. 'Three or four more years and suddenly you're staring down the barrel of forty. Bits of you start heading south for winter.'

'OK, that's depressing.'

'I've already had my vadge shored up.'

'You've done what?'

'I've had my pelvic floor reconstructed – it was ruined by two nine-pound babies. Lola's sixth birthday party at the trampoline park was the final straw; that place is a river of mum piss.'

'Wow,' said Hannah. 'I had no idea.'

'You wait,' Trish said ominously. 'It's nice to be able to sneeze freely again, that used to be a bit of a minefield. I had to send my fanny a memo, let it know it was coming.'

Hannah snorted with laughter, grabbing the bottle again as Trish leaned in so she could lower her voice. 'Rob really missed out. It's like a Venus flytrap down there these days.'

They both howled with laughter as they finished the bottle between them, shouting out scores as Gaynor and Jess performed increasingly elaborate stunts on the slide.

This is OK, thought Hannah. *I can be this woman; I like her better than the old Hannah. And I'm ready for my next adventure. The question is, where does Rob fit in?*

CHAPTER TWENTY-ONE

Hannah stuffed her clothes into her suitcase, having over-slept after a night of tossing and turning, her mind whirring with conflicting thoughts. She was due to meet Rob in twenty minutes, and she still hadn't decided what she was going to say. Maybe he'd still have a job, and none of this would be relevant. That was the ideal outcome, right? *Right?*

The knock on the door made her jump, and she wondered which one of the other women was hunting for missing hair straighteners. But when she opened the door it was Rob, looking like a man with a lot of stuff on his mind.

'Are you OK?' she gasped. 'I thought we were meeting at half nine?'

'I couldn't wait that long,' said Rob, glancing down the corridor. 'Can I come in?'

'Sure,' said Hannah, hesitating for a second, then opening the door fully. 'Should you even be here?'

'It doesn't matter, I've been fired,' he said, wringing his hands with anxiety. 'I need to pack and hand in my coaching gear, then take the next bus to the airport.'

Hannah covered her mouth with her hand. 'Oh wow, Rob. I'm really sorry. What happened?'

He shrugged helplessly, then plonked himself down on the edge of her bed. 'Mark didn't believe me when I said nothing happened. I explained the whole story, but he wasn't having any of it.'

'Do you want me to try? I can go and talk to him?'

Rob shook his head. 'No, he's made up his mind. He acted like he'd caught me shagging somebody's wife in the dining room, then wiping my dick on the curtains. It was insane.'

Hannah shook her head, her mind boggling at this very vivid description. 'I'm so sorry, it was totally my fault.'

'No,' Rob said emphatically. 'It absolutely wasn't. That's why I talked the woman on reception into giving me your room number – I didn't want you to feel responsible. But I also didn't want to go without saying goodbye.'

Hannah said nothing, her eyes casting around the room as she asked herself the question she'd been pushing around in her head for half the night. *Does this feel like the right thing to do?* She looked at Rob, sitting on the edge of her bed with his hands pressed against his face, and made her decision. 'You don't have to go.'

'What do you mean?' he asked, shaking his head in confusion.

'You can come with me,' she said, taking a step towards him, then changing her mind and folding her arms.

'Come with you where?'

'I'm off on a road trip for a couple of weeks,' she said, keeping her voice clear and strong. 'Thought I'd head up into the mountains, see a bit of Spain. I don't really have a proper plan. You could come with me.'

Rob stared at her, clearly trying to put the words together into something that made sense. 'Are you serious?'

She nodded emphatically. 'I've been thinking about it

all night, what to do if you got fired. Neither of us has anything to go home to, and I'm picking up my hire car in an hour. So you could just throw your stuff in the back with mine.'

Rob laughed, looking at her like she was insane. 'Hannah, I love this idea, but we hardly know each other. What if I wreck your trip?'

'I thought about that too,' said Hannah, who'd spent hours working through the loopholes in her mad plan. 'Let's give it three days, see if we're still getting along. If everything's fine, we'll do three more days. If it's not, I'll drop you off at the nearest bus station and you can head to the airport.'

Rob stared at her intently, and Hannah could see how tempted he was. 'Come on,' she said with a smile. 'It's an adventure. What's the worst that could happen?'

Rob took some deep, calming breaths. 'And just so I'm clear, on what basis would we be doing this? Just as friends, or . . .'

'Definitely just friends,' she said quickly. 'Nothing's changed about our respective situations, so you don't have to worry about that.' This was another decision she'd made in the early hours, not to overcomplicate things between them. Hannah was still on the rebound, and Rob was still a player. But that didn't mean they couldn't have an adventure together.

'So?' she asked. 'What do you think?'

Rob smiled, then breathed out slowly. 'OK,' he replied. 'Why not?'

'Good,' said Hannah happily. 'Then you can start by joining me and the girls for breakfast.'

'Shit, really?' he said. 'Don't you want to tell them about this plan yourself?'

'And spoil the fun they'll get from interrogating you?' said Hannah. 'I don't think so.'

'Oh Jesus,' muttered Rob, following her out of the room.

'So let me get this straight,' said Jess, noisily sucking the dregs of her smoothie through a straw. 'You've been fired, and now you and Hannah are going on a road trip together, but you're not a couple.' They were in the hotel restaurant, rationalising that Rob was their guest and Mark was hardly likely to cause a scene if he spotted them. He couldn't be fired twice, for a start.

'Yet,' muttered Gaynor. Trish said nothing, her arms tightly folded and her expression mutinous. She ran her tongue over her teeth, her lips puckered into a cat's bumhole of disapproval.

'Shush,' said Jess. 'But look, Han . . . are you sure this is a good idea? You're practically strangers. No disrespect, Rob.'

'None taken,' said Rob, catching Hannah's eye and making her smile. Now they'd made the decision she was itching to get away from this place, beautiful as it was.

'I know we don't know each other that well,' said Hannah, looking at each of the women in turn. 'But this trip was all about self-discovery, remember? Those were YOUR words, Gaynor.'

'Yeah,' said Gaynor. 'But I wasn't thinking you'd get your tennis coach fired, then bundle him into a hire car for a road trip around fucking Spain.'

'Obviously I didn't plan this,' said Hannah. 'But it feels like the right thing to do.' Trish raised her eyebrows and

Hannah glared back. 'I'm being adventurous and spontaneous for the first time in my life.'

'Let's leave it there,' said Jess. 'Hannah can do what she likes.'

'Thank you,' said Hannah, relieved. She hoped Rob might be off the hook, but then Trish cleared her throat and fixed her eyes on him.

'And what about you?' she asked, her voice cracking like she was trying not to cry. 'How do we know you're not going to be a total dick?'

Rob turned to face her, holding her gaze. 'Because that isn't who I am,' he said firmly. 'And if this trip isn't working out for Hannah, I'll leave. This was her suggestion, not mine.'

'Hmph,' Trish said grudgingly. 'But will you check in with us, Han? Just to let us know you're OK?'

'I promise,' said Hannah. 'I'll post on the group WhatsApp every day.'

'OK then,' said Trish, nodding at them both like she was bestowing some kind of blessing on behalf of all of them.

'It means a lot,' Hannah added quickly. 'You girls looking out for me. I appreciate it.'

'Well,' said Jess, reaching out to squeeze her hand. 'We're a team now. You're officially one of the Club Colina TITS. Tennis in the sun,' she said as an aside to Rob, in response to his furrowed brow.

'OK, now I'm jealous,' said Rob. 'Can I be one of the TITS?'

'You got fired,' said Gaynor playfully. 'And if you mess with our friend, we'll actually kill you.'

'Noted,' said Rob.

'Right, come on,' said Jess. 'We've got an airport bus to catch.'

Hannah noticed Rob hold back as she hugged them all, clearly not wanting to get in the way of the heartfelt good-byes. She watched them wheel their bags off towards the bus, a mix of excitement and trepidation buzzing through her veins. She didn't move for what felt like ages, just taking a minute to soak up the morning sun and mentally prepare herself for whatever was coming next.

'You OK?' asked Rob, walking up behind her.

'I'm fine,' she said, turning to face him. 'You ready to go?' She scanned his face for traces of doubt, but there was nothing but a reflection of her own eagerness to hit the road.

'Absolutely,' he said. 'Let's get the hell out of here.'

PART THREE

Wild Card

CHAPTER TWENTY-TWO

'So where do you want to go?' Rob relaxed in the passenger seat of Hannah's rental car – a black Seat Ibiza that was now loaded with their luggage. Despite the full tank of petrol, she hadn't moved from the rental centre car park, suddenly paralysed by the reality of her situation. In the past four weeks, she had ended her fourteen-year marriage, agreed to go on a trip to Spain with a group of women she barely knew, gone skinny dipping in a hotel pool, managed to get her tennis coach fired from his job and then impulsively invited him to join her on a road trip across southern Spain. Which was why she was now facing the prospect of two weeks in the company of an incredibly hot man who was strictly off limits – on the basis that she absolutely did not want a rebound fling and he was clearly a serial womaniser. Apparently she was some kind of masochist.

'I don't know,' she said, giving him a feeble smile. 'I'd planned to do some research while I was here, but events kind of took over.'

'I hate it when that happens.' Rob's eyes twinkled. 'Well, this is your trip, so you need to decide. I'm just along for the ride.'

Hannah thought about it for a moment. Her plan had been to travel alone, but having Rob there didn't need to change the destination. Not at first, anyway. 'Then let's go east along the coast for a bit, then up to Granada,' she said decisively. 'It's somewhere I've always wanted to go, and it's only a few hours away.'

Rob nodded. 'Granada it is. Do you want me to find us somewhere to stay while you're driving?'

'That would be great. I was also thinking about doing some hiking for a few days, get up into the mountains. Apparently there are some really nice trails.'

'Sounds perfect. As long as I can do it in trainers, I'm all good.'

She nodded, tapping Granada into the satnav and easing out of the car park – Rob could add the hotel details later. 'Did you manage to say goodbye to the other coaches?'

Rob leaned his elbow on the window ledge so he could rest his head on the heel of his hand as he tapped around on his phone. 'I tracked down Nick and Aaron, who obviously had plenty to say about Mark; I wasn't fussed about the rest of them. What's our accommodation budget?'

'Tight,' said Hannah. 'Nothing fancy. My plan was to find cheap B&Bs or guesthouse-type places where I'd be safe staying on my own. But now you're here, we've got a bit more choice. As long as it's got two beds.' She wasn't sure why she felt the need to clarify, but she didn't want him to think she had any expectations. Or that he could expect anything, either.

'I can chip in my earnings from the last few weeks,' said Rob. 'It's not a lot, but it should keep us out of hostels. Ooh, this Airbnb looks nice,' he added, still tapping on his phone. 'It's got a tennis court and six bedrooms.'

'Yeah, probably a bit over our budget,' laughed Hannah. 'But maybe we can find a local court if we fancy a game. The Spanish love tennis.'

Rob turned his head to look at her curiously. 'Have you spent much time here?'

'Not really.' Hannah could feel the heat creep up her neck. 'I've been here a few times.'

'With your ex-husband?'

'No.' The silence hung heavily in the car.

Rob sighed. 'Look,' he said, putting his phone down on his lap. 'If we're going to make this trip work, we're going to need to get to know each other a bit. That didn't feel like a big question, but I totally understand if there are things you'd rather not talk about.'

He's right, thought Hannah. She needed to be honest with him, and there was no time like the present. 'I'm sorry, I don't mean to be mysterious, it's just I'm not used to talking about my family. I've been here a few times to visit my dad, he lives a couple of hours away from here. North of Malaga, towards Córdoba.'

Rob's eyes widened. 'Shit, really?'

Hannah nodded. 'He and my mum split up when I was fifteen. I don't know all the details of what happened, but he moved to Spain and never came back.'

'Wow, I'm really sorry,' said Rob. 'Do you and he get on?'

'I guess,' said Hannah with a shrug, glad she was focussing on the road ahead and didn't have to look at him. 'We're quite alike in lots of ways. But he's also not exactly parent of the year, so we're still working on it. I come over every few years.'

'Does your mum know?'

Hannah shook her head.

'Would she be upset?'

'It takes very little to upset my mum, so yes.'

'And is your dad due a visit right now? Was that your plan?'

'No,' said Hannah quickly. The answer was 'probably, yes', but Rob being here changed everything. On previous visits Hannah had massively oversold how happy her marriage to Graham was, not wanting her dad to worry that she'd repeated her parents' mistakes. The news that her marriage had fallen apart because of an affair would hit him hard. He'd take it personally, like somehow genetics had played a role in his daughter choosing a man just like her father. Or worse, he'd blame her for being a bad wife to Graham. She'd already had that lecture in stereo from Ruth and her mum, and definitely didn't need to hear it from her dad too.

'OK,' said Rob, raising his eyebrows. 'What else shall we talk about?'

Hannah smiled, appreciating him not pushing too hard against that door. 'Tell me about your family.'

'Hmm,' said Rob thoughtfully. 'My mum and dad have been married for nearly forty years; Dad ran his own business, and Mum was an English teacher. Two sisters, both older, both *very* successful.'

Hannah glanced at him. 'You sound kind of bitter about that.'

Rob shook his head. 'Not bitter, just resigned, I guess. I was never expected to amount to much – I was the dyslexic, left-handed kid who couldn't even manage basic sentences. Primary school was a nightmare, but then Mum started teaching at a private school and they gave me and my sisters a bursary.'

'And that was better?'

'Yeah, I started there when I was seven. Small classes, proper learning support, and it was really big on sport, so that's where I started playing tennis. I still can't write a decent text message, but I can hit a ball.'

'Is that why you never gave me your number?' asked Hannah, giving him a playful nudge with her elbow. 'So you didn't have to write messages?'

'I hate texting,' he said. 'It makes my head hurt. I'm the only twenty-something I know who still picks up the phone to have a conversation.'

'I think that's nice. And you live in Bath, right?' The basic nature of this conversation seemed ridiculous to Hannah, considering they were now essentially on holiday together. But maybe this was OK. Make impulsive decisions first, ask questions later.

'Yeah, I was born there. Mum and Dad have a big old house just north of the city. Two dogs, two cars, nice garden. All very middle class.'

'It sounds lovely,' said Hannah, wondering what Rob would make of her mad family. Probably best to make sure she never found out.

'What about you?' he asked.

'A little town called Westwick, between Woking and Guildford. Born and raised, same as you.'

'Does your mum still live there?'

Hannah nodded. 'With my little brother Luke, he's eighteen. They're still in the same house I grew up in.'

'And how long were you married?'

'Fourteen years.'

Rob's brow furrowed, and she could hear him doing the maths. 'So you were, like . . .?'

'Eighteen.'

'Wow, that's young. Is that like a religion thing? I over-heard Gaynor say something about you going to church.'

'Yeah,' said Hannah. She'd never had this conversation with anyone, and even though she wasn't exactly trying to impress Rob, she didn't want to actively put him off either. 'My family were members of this evangelical church, based in the States. It's how my parents met; they were both members.'

'So where did tennis fit in?'

Hannah was quiet for a moment, gratified that Rob seemed genuinely interested rather than weirded out. The memories of her childhood were hazy in places, and not without pain. But it was also a big part of who she was, and maybe telling this story would help Rob understand her better. 'My mum was having a bad time when I was seven or eight; I didn't understand why at the time, but later I found out it was a lot of miscarriages, depression, that sort of thing. I'd been home-schooled with other church kids until then but Mum couldn't cope, so I started at the local primary school.'

'That must have been weird.'

Hannah laughed awkwardly, her palms turning sweaty on the steering wheel as she raked through the memories. 'Yeah, just a bit. You can imagine how odd I seemed to the other kids. I didn't know anything about TV or films, what the latest thing was. I'd never been given a say in what I wore, and I didn't have any "normal" friends outside the church community. It was a really hard transition, but looking back it was the best thing that could have happened to me.'

'Wow,' said Rob.

'Mum went into hospital for a while, and when it came to

the school holidays, Dad sent me to a sports club while he was at work. I picked up a tennis racquet on the first morning and never put it down.'

Rob smiled hazily, like he remembered how that felt.

'It was the strangest feeling, hitting a ball for the first time. Like I suddenly realised what my right arm was for.'

'What did your mum say about that?'

'She came home from hospital a different person, really. She and Dad made the decision to leave the church, and things were different after that. Less strict, a bit more freedom. Then Luke came along when I was fourteen and she drifted back to the church again, and then the whole thing with Dad kicked off.'

'I'm really sorry. That sounds rough.'

Hannah nodded. 'After Dad left I spent most of my spare time at the tennis club, cleaning the changing rooms in exchange for my subs. I've been ladies' captain since I was twenty-two. Apart from this season, which I've taken off.'

'And where do you work now?'

'At a country club a few miles away from my place. Very exclusive, lots of golfers and rich women who are terrible at tennis. I'm the office manager.'

Rob looked impressed. 'Do you ever coach?'

'Only the kids during school holidays, if I absolutely have to. I hate them all.'

'I love coaching kids,' laughed Rob. 'They're less know-it-all than adults.'

'You haven't met these kids. Absolute monsters.'

'You didn't go to university?'

Hannah shook her head. 'Dad was gone by then and Mum was heavily into the church again. Things were less strict than before, but some rules for women weren't negotiable. Family first, no sex before marriage, no co-habiting, no going off to university and getting wild ideas.'

'So you married . . .'

'Graham. He was part of the community, and we'd been friends since we were children. Sensible, dull, as desperate to escape as I was. He was my first choice because there was no other choice. He's the only man I've ever . . . been with.' Hannah blushed involuntarily, wondering whether Rob was already questioning his choices.

'And what happened, if you don't mind me asking?'

Hannah glanced at him, marvelling at how easy he was to talk to. 'I found out last month he'd got his assistant pregnant. Apparently that wasn't the only affair he'd had.'

'Shit. Not so dull after all.'

'It was a relief, really. A legitimate reason to finally call it a day.'

'Where is he now?'

'Either living with his mother, or with his pregnant girl-friend. I have no idea which. Luckily the house we lived in was mine.'

'Have you changed the locks?'

Hannah laughed. 'No, but my brother is house-sitting right now, so it's fine.'

'So what happens next? When you get back?'

Hannah thought about the question, taking in the land-scape of hotels and apartments and orange groves as she drove the windy coast road, occasionally catching a glimpse of azure-blue water to the south. It was a good question, but life beyond this trip felt hazy. She'd come to Spain to adjust to being alone, and now she was on a road trip with a gorgeous man who she'd only met a week ago. 'I have no idea. Can't think about that right now. What about you? You ever thought about getting married?'

Rob shook his head and laughed. 'Not even close. Don't get me wrong, I love women. Actually, maybe I love women too much.'

'Or maybe you just love too many women,' laughed Hannah, remembering what Trish had said about how many women Rob had slept with. It felt like a void between them, a fundamental difference between her and Rob that could never be bridged. It was hard not to feel disappointed, somehow.

'Only ever one at a time, though,' Rob said quickly. 'And only the kind of women who want the same thing. I don't want you to think I'm a bad person.'

'I'm not judging,' she said, glancing at him. 'What are your plans after this summer?'

Rob cleared his throat. 'I've got a Head Coach job lined up at Bath University, there's a big sports academy there. It's due to start in October, so I was going to do the full season here.'

'So what will you do for the rest of the summer now?'

Rob shrugged. 'Get a job back in the UK, I guess. Do some casual coaching, maybe. I'll work it out.'

'So we're both free birds, living in the moment.'

Rob grinned. 'Looks like it. What would you most like to do right now?'

I'd like to park the car, climb on top of you and kiss you for about an hour, thought Hannah, feeling a blush creep up her neck. *I'd like to be the kind of woman who doesn't get attached, who has holiday flings with gorgeous men, then goes back to her life.*

They navigated a bend and the view opened up ahead of them – a huge blue sky and sparkling water beyond the lemon groves. The temperature gauge on the dashboard told her it was a perfect twenty-three degrees.

'Don't know about you,' said Hannah with a happy sigh, 'but I quite fancy some tennis.'

CHAPTER TWENTY-THREE

'Google says there's a community tennis court in Salobreña,' said Rob, studying his phone. 'It looks like a really nice place, it's got a castle and everything. We could play there, then have a wander round and get some lunch.'

'Sounds great,' said Hannah. 'Let's take a look.'

'Do you realise we've never actually played each other?'

'It's not a fair match,' she said with a fake pout. 'You're much better than me. You'll have to play right-handed.'

'You're still the best female player I've ever coached. And I'm not just blowing smoke so you don't kick me out of the car.' He glanced over at Hannah's legs, brown and inviting in a hot pink tennis skirt, and wondered how on earth he was going to get through the next two weeks. It felt like some kind of endurance challenge; but if she could do it, so could he.

'Turn right here,' he said, checking his phone. 'It says there's a supermarket near the court too, so maybe we can get some food. I've got two bottles of water and some chocolate wafers, but that's it.'

'Not enough to sustain two elite athletes,' said Hannah. 'I'm hoping for an award-winning tapas bar, but I'll settle for a Mercadona.'

She turned the corner and the picture-postcard village of Salobreña appeared on the horizon, with hundreds of whitewashed villas built into the hillside leading up to a red stone castle. Rob was already itching to get out of the car and explore, but some tennis with Hannah felt like a pretty great start to their road trip.

'There,' he said, pointing to the tennis court set back from the road on a patch of scrubland behind a wire fence. 'Looks like there are people using it, though.'

'Let's park and see how long they're going to be,' said Hannah. 'See if we can find some food while we're waiting.'

She pulled into a space on the side of the road and they both climbed out and stretched, neither of them used to being still for any length of time. The coastal breeze felt fresh and inviting, and Rob ambled over to the chain link fence to watch the two men play for a minute. They were good – the one at the far end had a solid forehand and a loose, confident style, and his opponent was fast and powerful.

A noise to his right caught his attention, and he turned to see a scrawny grey dog under a tree. It was tied to a short, frayed rope and was straining to reach him, panting furiously with its front paws flailing in the air.

'Shit,' said Rob, forgetting about the tennis and slowly approaching the dog with his hand outstretched.

'Be careful,' said Hannah, crouching down in the dust next to Rob and tentatively reaching out to stroke the dog's back. It was filthy and smelled terrible, and Rob could feel how dry its tongue was as it licked his hand.

'Is it OK?' whispered Hannah. The dog squirmed with happiness under Rob's gentle attention; he could see some patches of fur were missing from its legs and belly, the skin wrinkled and scabby.

'I don't know,' he said. 'It's definitely thirsty, and that

rope is far too short.' The dog licked the palm of his hand again and pawed at his arm. 'Can you pass me a bottle of water?'

'Who do you think it belongs to?' asked Hannah, rummaging in her bag. Rob looked around, but there was no one other than the two men on the tennis court. He made a bowl with his hands so Hannah could tip some water in; the dog lapped frantically, so Hannah kept pouring until the bottle was empty.

'Look at its ribs,' said Rob, checking round the back end. 'It's a he. Poor thing needs a good bath and a decent meal.'

'*Oye!*' shouted one of the men on the tennis court, running towards them and waving his racquet in time with a barrage of angry Spanish. Rob couldn't understand much of what he was saying, but it was reasonable to assume he was less than happy.

'Is this your dog?' he asked, pulling himself up to his full height and searching for retained scraps from a long-forgotten Grade D GCSE Spanish. '*Tu perro?*'

The man ignored the question and shouted some more Spanish. His friend arrived by his side, and Rob realised that they were teenagers, maybe sixteen or seventeen. They were stocky, but Rob was taller and stronger than both of them. The boy turned to his friend and spat a few more phrases, and Rob caught the word *Inglés*.

'It is his dog,' said the second boy, taking a step closer to Rob but staying beyond arm's reach. 'It's called Pendejo. Leave him alone.'

'He needs food and water,' said Rob firmly. 'And the rope is too short.'

The second boy translated for his friend, who started

yelling and waving his arms around again. 'He says it is none of your business. The dog will not eat, he is *loco*. Crazy.'

'Then let us take him,' Rob said. 'We'll find him a vet or a dog shelter or something. He needs food and proper care.' He glanced at Hannah, who raised her eyebrows. Maybe this was mad, but he couldn't just drive away and leave a dog like that. He'd grown up in a house full of dogs, and this one reminded him a bit of Muffin, the retriever cross he'd shared a bed with as a child.

The second boy translated, but his friend shook his head furiously. 'He says he will fill a bag with rocks and throw Pendejo in the *río* before he gives him to you.'

Rob blew out his cheeks, thinking hard. 'What's your name?' he asked.

'Mario,' said the second man, relaxing a little now he had the upper hand. 'And this is Javier.'

'OK, Mario. Ask your friend if he would like to play tennis.'

'You want to play tennis with Javier?' said Mario with a grin.

'One set. If I lose, we give you one hundred euros so you can buy dog food and medicine. But if I win, we take Pendejo.'

Mario laughed heartily. 'His mother is from Mallorca, her cousin is Rafa Nadal. He will kick your ass all the way to Rafa's house in Manacor.'

'Maybe,' said Rob with a shrug.

'Um, can I speak to you for a moment?' asked Hannah.

Rob turned to look at her, realising with a wave of guilt that in the heat of the conversation he'd forgotten she was there. 'Oh. Yeah, sure.' They walked back towards the car,

Rob casting glances back at the flailing dog as Mario brought Javier up to speed.

'I'm really sorry,' he said desperately. 'I know it's mad, but I can't just leave that dog there. It needs help.'

'I know,' said Hannah quietly. 'Just pretend we're having a fight about it; they'll assume I don't think you can win and am annoyed about you betting our money. It will put them on the back foot when you play.'

Rob's eyes widened in surprise. 'Really? You don't mind?'

'Of course I don't mind,' she said, waving her arms around like she was furious. 'I mean, obviously this wasn't *exactly* how I imagined the first day of my road trip panning out, but we can't just drive away. Get the dog, then we'll take it to the vet and find a shelter or something. Now look angry with me.'

'You're incredible.' Rob thumped his fist on the roof of the car and pointed to the panting dog. 'I'm going to show that little fucker how to play tennis, and then I'm going to buy you an amazing lunch.'

'I'll look forward to it,' said Hannah, giving him a furious glare as she folded her arms and shouted, 'You're an IDIOT!' Rob strode back to the two boys, who both now had a touch of swagger. The dog lay down on the roots of the tree, panting feebly, so Hannah went over to pet him.

'We play doubles,' said Mario with an evil grin. 'Me and Javier against you and your girlfriend.'

Rob shook his head, his lips pressed firmly together. 'That's not an equal match,' he said.

Mario shrugged. 'You have big left arm, like Rafa,' he said, nodding to Rob's tanned bicep. 'So we think maybe you can play, no?' He looked Hannah up and down with a

195

level of disdain only a teenage boy could muster. 'But she is . . . just a woman. So this is more fair for us.'

Rob scowled at him and sighed, then looked at Hannah, wondering how she would react. 'What do you think?' he asked, eyeing her carefully. 'I can lend you my spare racquet.'

'I'm not sure,' she said, chewing her lip and shaking her head.

'Come on,' said Rob pleadingly. 'Please. For Pendejo.'

Hannah took a deep breath and nodded nervously. 'OK. I'll do my best,' she said.

Rob nodded, then went back to the car to get their tennis racquets, leaving Hannah to scowl at the two boys and pet Pendejo.

'You want warm up?' asked Mario, when Rob and Hannah both strolled onto the court. Rob looked at Hannah and raised his eyebrows questioningly.

'No,' said Hannah. 'I'm fine.'

'OK,' shrugged Mario, like he didn't care either way. 'You serve first? I give you choice.'

Hannah nodded and started tucking balls in her tennis skirt.

'You are smart,' said Mario with a grin. 'Get your turn out of the way quickly, then leave it to the men.'

Hannah ignored him and bounced the ball on the baseline for a few moments, then dollied a serve over the net. There was none of her usual power, but it went in. Javier returned it, and they engaged in a long rally, Javier getting increasingly frustrated that Hannah kept returning the ball despite him giving it everything he had. Mario held back for as long as his patience could bear, then dived forward to

196

intercept, purposely avoiding Rob and volleying a ball three metres in front of Hannah. She darted in, scooped it up and dropped it just over the net, taking the first point.

Rob smiled to himself, crossing over with Hannah and returning to the baseline for her next serve, watching the fevered whispering and head-scratching going on between Javier and Mario. He'd coached tennis for the best part of ten years, but these two arrogant little shits were about to receive the most important lesson of their lives.

'You said she could not play!' yelled Mario, slamming his racquet on the net as Hannah spanked another ball past his left ear and into the dust.

'No, I didn't,' said Rob calmly, getting close enough that he could feel Mario's panting breaths and the heat from the angry flush on his neck. 'YOU assumed she couldn't play because she is "just a woman" ' – he made air quotes with his fingers – 'and now maybe you'll be more respectful in future.'

Mario stomped off to confer with Javier, the two of them bickering in rapid Spanish, presumably about whose fault it was that they were now five games to one down, with Rob to serve.

'What do you want to do?' Hannah asked mildly, handing Rob some balls so he could fill his pockets.

'What do you mean?' he asked.

'I mean, do we wrap this up, or do we toy with their bruised egos for a bit longer?'

Rob laughed and glanced at Pendejo under the tree. 'Much as I'm enjoying every minute of this, that dog isn't getting any less hungry.'

'No,' said Hannah, as Pendejo panted at them both. 'Let's finish them off, shall we?'

Fifteen minutes later Rob and Hannah were driving north towards Granada, windows down and mouth-breathing through the stench of a dog who smelled like fishy bin juice. They'd tried putting Pendejo on the back seat but he was having none of it, instead insisting on sitting on Rob's lap with his head out of the window, his tongue hanging out in a giant doggy smile and his ears flapping in the warm breeze.

'I still can't believe how brutal your final shot was,' Rob said gleefully. 'Poor guys didn't stand a chance.'

'Teenage boys are all the same,' said Hannah, wrinkling her nose as Pendejo panted in her face. 'All power, no finesse.'

'Six–one, though. You annihilated them. I'm not sure their pride will ever recover.'

'It was very much a team effort. And you gave them one hundred euros anyway, which wasn't even part of the deal.'

'I know, but I wanted to keep things civil,' said Rob.

'Why didn't you just offer them money for the dog in the first place?'

'It was my Plan B if they actually turned out to be Rafa's distant cousins and we lost the set. But it was way more fun this way.'

'What are we going to do now?' asked Hannah. 'We went looking for some tennis, and now we've got a dog.'

'Yeah, not sure how that happened.' Rob patted the dog's head and recoiled from the smell of his hot breath. 'Let's get us all some food, then check into our Airbnb so we can give him a bath and let him rest for the night. We can find a vet in

198

the morning and get him checked out, then decide what to do next.'

Hannah nodded and gave an exaggerated sigh. 'Best you get back on that phone and find us a pet store.'

The Airbnb that Rob had booked earlier was a ground-floor apartment, located in the centre of Granada down a tiny side street that was approximately six inches wider than their car. Thankfully the key had been left in a lock box so they didn't have to explain the stinky hound to an unsuspecting owner – dog ownership hadn't been mentioned when they'd booked it, and even though Brits were notoriously goofy about their animals, Rob wasn't sure 'we won him in a tennis match' was going to cut it.

While Hannah unloaded their luggage, Rob carried Pendejo through to the shower with a bottle of medicated dog shampoo they'd bought in the pet store, along with a lead and a collar and poo bags and a couple of plastic dog bowls. They'd also picked up a bag of kibble, which Rob had been feeding Pendejo by the handful since they left the store.

'The grey bits are actually white,' said Rob gleefully as he led the dog back into the kitchen. 'Honestly, he was disgusting.' Pendejo shook vigorously, then started doing manic, high-speed laps around the kitchen table, his paws skidding on the tiled floor like Bambi on ice.

'Where's he going to sleep?' asked Hannah, wondering if this was normal dog behaviour, or whether Mario wasn't far off when he'd described the dog as crazy.

'We'll leave him in here tonight,' replied Rob, 'he'll be nice and cool on the tiles. We'll find a vet in the morning.' The dog ran a few more laps, then gave another shake before settling down in the corner with a huge yawn. 'Won't eat, my arse. That dog would eat the whole bag if you gave him half a chance. Javier's lucky we only gave him a kicking on the tennis court.'

Hannah laughed. 'I think Javier is battered enough for one day.'

'Are you sure you're OK with this?' Rob said, touching her briefly on the arm. She flinched and goosebumps appeared, and he kicked himself for forgetting that she was still sensitive about being touched. 'I've gatecrashed your road trip, and now we've got a dog.'

'It's all part of the adventure,' said Hannah. 'And to be honest, a man who will take on Rafa Nadal's cousin's son at tennis in order to save a dog's life is my kind of travel companion.'

'Thank God,' Rob said breathlessly, folding his arms tightly to quell the urge to sweep her up and take her to bed. 'What shall we do now?'

Hannah looked at him with the tiniest beat of indecision, like she knew exactly what he was thinking. 'I need food and Pendejo needs a walk. But first I'm going to have a shower. I've probably got fleas.'

'Same,' said Rob. 'How about we get showered and changed, then take our new friend to get some dinner?'

Hannah smiled, and the visceral desire Rob had for this beautiful, surprising woman felt like a melting warmth in his stomach. How had this all happened so quickly? And more importantly, where the hell was it going to end?

CHAPTER TWENTY-FOUR

Hannah and Rob strolled the streets of Granada in the shadow of the Alhambra, vaguely trying to find a restaurant but actually both just happy to soak up the atmosphere of the city. They didn't bother with a map, instead heading off down alleyways laden with window boxes or up steep flights of steps that looked like they might lead somewhere interesting, Pendejo seeming perfectly happy on his new lead, occasionally wandering off to investigate plants and stray cats and bins. The evening was warm and sultry, and Hannah could have walked for hours.

But eventually they both got hungry, so they followed their noses until they found a tapas bar with pavement seating down a narrow street packed with bustling bars and restaurants. They ordered wine and half a dozen small plates, and Hannah leaned against the cool, stone wall of the bar and relaxed.

'You look happy,' said Rob, feeding Pendejo dog biscuits from his pocket. They both figured that the best thing they could do between now and dropping him off at the shelter was feed him up a bit, and Pendejo definitely wasn't complaining.

'I am,' said Hannah. 'It's been quite a day, but this is perfect.' The wine was cold, the air smelled warm and fragrant, and the street was full of music and bustle and laughter. It reminded her how much she loved Spain, and how happy she'd be to spend more time here. She'd imagined herself roaming these streets alone, but actually having Rob and Pendejo here had been lovely. Rob was easy company and didn't mind slogging up a steep hill at high speed, and Pendejo gave Hannah something to focus on when she felt that fizz of electricity between them. Rob had touched her arm earlier and her knees had practically buckled. He smiled at her, and she tried to ignore the throb of unrequited desire between her legs. *Get used to it*, she told herself. *He's a self-confessed womaniser, and absolutely not what you need right now.*

'What's our plan for tomorrow?' Rob asked. 'Other than finding a vet and a shelter for Pendejo?' He looked and sounded doubtful, and Hannah could see he was already struggling with the prospect of letting Pendejo go. Well, she had good news on that front, at least temporarily.

'We're definitely not going to the vet tomorrow,' she said, taking a sip of her wine.

'Why not?'

'Because it's Sunday, and pretty much everything in Spain closes on a Sunday.'

'Oh shit, I didn't really think about that,' he said, raking his hand through his hair. 'I feel bad, I'm really sorry.'

'Stop apologising,' laughed Hannah. 'I've never had a proper plan for this trip, that was kind of the point. I asked you to come, and now we've got a dog.'

'Maybe the dog will adopt a cat,' said Rob, patting Pendejo's head.

'By the end of the week we'll need a minibus for all our animals,' Hannah giggled. 'Look, why don't we drive up to the Sierra Nevada. I've been looking up hikes, and there's a really nice one about half an hour away from here. Through a gorge along a river; we can see if Pendejo likes to swim.'

'That sounds amazing,' said Rob. 'Do you think he'll be OK?'

'He seems fine,' she said. 'We won't go too far, and if he gets tired we'll turn back, or you can carry him. No hurry.'

Rob smiled at her like she was some kind of miracle; a look she'd never seen on Graham's face in fourteen years of marriage. 'What kind of breed do you think he is?' she asked, glad of the distraction from all these tingly *feelings*.

'Hard to tell.' Rob looked down at Pendejo, who was panting hot breath on his legs. Now the dirt was gone, his ears and the patch over one eye were actually grey, but his back and belly were pure white. 'There's definitely some kind of terrier there, but he's got the same ears and tail as my parents' golden retrievers, just smaller. Have you ever had a dog?'

Hannah shook her head. 'I've always thought of myself as a dog person, but Graham was allergic.' Graham was allergic to a lot of things, including monogamy, apparently. She watched Rob stroke Pendejo's back, prompting the dog to flump sideways into his legs. 'He's already decided you're his person.'

'Whatever that little shit Javier did or didn't feed him,' said Rob, 'I don't think he's been too badly treated.'

'Hey, Pendejo,' said Hannah, as the waitress appeared with a tray of food. The dog panted over and licked Hannah's hand.

'This is a sad name for such a beautiful dog,' said the waitress, bending down to fuss between his ears. She pouted up at Rob from under long eyelashes and a mane of dark hair, giving him a bird's-eye view right down her top. 'What did he do to deserve this?'

Hannah and Rob looked at each other, then at the waitress. 'Why? What's wrong with it?' asked Rob.

'It's a Spanish word for someone who is very stupid or annoying,' said the waitress, scratching behind Pendejo's ears with such blissful vigour that his eyes rolled into the back of his head. 'It's like, maybe like when you call someone . . . asshole.'

'OH!' exclaimed Hannah, pressing her hands over her mouth as Rob started to laugh.

'Right, that makes sense,' he said. 'It totally explains why people were giving me funny looks earlier when I was trying to teach him to give a paw.'

'You give him new name, please,' said the waitress, kissing the dog's wet nose and looking at Rob like she'd happily walk down the aisle and take his name tomorrow. 'He is too beautiful to be a Pendejo.'

'We will,' said Hannah loudly, snapping the waitress out of her lovesick trance. She grabbed her tray and hurried off as Hannah rolled her eyes at Rob.

'So, the dog needs a new name.'

'Apparently so,' said Rob. Hannah noticed how he gave her his full attention, even when faced with the retreating backside of a beautiful Spanish woman in a tight skirt and a push-up bra.

'Maybe we should stick with *Perro*,' said Hannah. 'Or an English version, at least. What about Perry?'

'Like the pear cider,' said Rob enthusiastically. 'My grandparents make it.'

'Really?'

'Yeah. It's a Gloucestershire thing, they live in Stroud.'

Hannah nodded, briefly wondering if there would ever be a time in the future when she'd sit in a Gloucestershire garden drinking pear cider with Rob's grandparents and remember this exact moment. And who would she be, in that imaginary future scenario? The old friend Rob met on holiday, or something else?

'Scrumpy's better, though,' Rob added, rubbing the thin patch of fur between the dog's ears. 'That's how we do it down in Somerset.'

'As a type of cider, or a dog name?'

Rob looked up and smiled. 'Both.'

'Scrumpy,' said Hannah, looking at the dog. He wagged his tail enthusiastically. 'Looks like that's a hit.'

Rob picked Scrumpy up and nuzzled his face into his neck. 'Thanks for being so amazing about this,' he said, reaching out to brush his hand on Hannah's arm. The static on her top made him jump, and they both laughed awkwardly before Rob cleared his throat and put Scrumpy back on the ground. Hannah watched him for a few seconds, wondering if he could also feel the tension in the air, but he was busying himself with topping up their wine. Scrumpy pattered over and clawed at her bare legs, looking for attention, or possibly chorizo, and Hannah squeezed her eyes shut and silently winced so as not to spoil the moment.

'You sure you'll be OK on the sofa bed?' Hannah asked. Rob had just wandered out of the bathroom wearing nothing but a white towel around his waist. It was less revealing than the swimming shorts she'd seen him in before, but felt more intimate, somehow. 'I really don't mind taking it.'

'It's fine,' Rob replied. 'It means I can keep an eye on Scrumpy.'

Hannah nodded, filling a glass with water from the bottle in the fridge. He smelled of citrus shower gel and toothpaste, and it was hard not to stare at his naked torso. She'd used the bathroom first, so she was already in her pyjamas.

'I'll get off to bed then,' she said. 'See you in the morning.'

''Night,' said Rob, giving her a soft smile. She suppressed a shiver and hurried into the bedroom, closing the door behind her and taking deep, calming breaths. *This, for two weeks*, she thought. *What have I done?*

Squeak. Squeak, squeak, squeak. Hannah sat up in bed, brushing the hair from her eyes. *What IS that?* she thought. The squeaking had been on and off for the past hour, and it was driving her crazy. Did this place have mice? If so, they were having a party.

She climbed out of bed and padded across to the door to the lounge, opening it as quietly as possible so as not to disturb Rob. The squeaking was much louder now, and she could see it was coming from the sofa bed. The springs, maybe? Every squeak was accompanied by a small movement in the bedding, like it was bouncing up and down. *Oh good GRIEF*, thought Hannah. *Is Rob MASTURBATING?*

'Scrumpy, get OFF,' whispered Rob, sitting up. Hannah covered her mouth to stop herself laughing, as Scrumpy appeared behind him on the other pillow, happily chewing his back leg like it was a chicken drumstick.

'Are you OK?' she whispered.

'God, sorry,' said Rob. 'Did he wake you up? He's driving me CRAZY.'

'What's he doing?'

'Grooming every square inch of his stupid dog body. He's a proper fidget, and he won't stay on the floor.'

'It was actually the squeaky bed springs that woke me up.'

'Yeah, they're driving me mad too.'

'Why don't we swap? You and Scrumpy take my non-squeaky bed, and I'll sleep in here.'

Rob huffed impatiently and climbed out of bed. 'OR, we could just shut Scrumpy in your room so he can lick his arse all night, and you and I can sleep here.'

Hannah looked at him and blinked. Had he really just suggested that?

'Sorry,' Rob said awkwardly, hoofing Scrumpy off the sofa bed and shooing him into the bedroom. 'Bad idea.'

Hannah lay on the sofa bed, breathing in the smell of Rob on the sheets and trying to ignore the throbbing ache between her legs. Yes, it was a bad idea, and she would almost certainly regret it in the long run. But right now she couldn't think of anything she wanted more.

Club Colina TITS on Tour

Gaynor: Hey Han, how was the first day of your road trip?

Hannah: It was fun! Drove along the coast, won a dog in a tennis match, now in Granada

Jess: You won a DOG? Like a toy dog at the fairground?

Hannah: No, an actual dog. It's a long story.

Trish: Wait, so you and Rob now own a dog? Oh my GOD.

Gaynor: 🐶🤍🐶🤍

CHAPTER TWENTY-FIVE

Hannah had done a decent amount of hiking over the years, mostly alone in the Lake District or on the South Downs while Graham poked around local churches and museums. He claimed to have various weak ligaments and tendons due to ancient rugby injuries, and he always avoided places that might involve pollen. She'd tried several times to persuade him to go to the Alps in the summer, but he didn't like flying much either. Although interestingly he'd managed it on a number of occasions for stag weekends or city breaks with his mother. With hindsight, the issue was possibly less about travelling, and more about travelling with Hannah.

But Graham wasn't here, and Rob was very much up for a day's hiking. They packed water and snacks and food for Scrumpy, then drove half an hour to the town of Monachil where the trail began. It wasn't a difficult hike but it was fun, taking a winding path through a jungly canyon along a river, passing over wobbly hanging bridges and stopping to cool their feet in the river.

'Where's Scrumpy?' asked Hannah, handing Rob a bottle of water from the bag. They'd experimented with letting him off the lead for a few minutes at a time, keeping a close eye on him in case he strayed too far. But he seemed keen to stay close to his new source of food and love, so they let him run free apart from the sections where the path followed the steep canyon wall.

'He's chilling his paws over there,' said Rob, pointing to a large rock in the middle of the babbling river. Hannah leaned forward to watch Scrumpy running back and forth into a large, deep waterhole, his tongue hanging out in a huge doggy grin. She felt a punch of guilt that they were taking him to a shelter tomorrow and wondered if he would understand that this was just a holiday and not real life.

'I feel bad about taking him to a shelter tomorrow,' said Rob.

Hannah smiled. 'I was just thinking the same thing. You and he make a good team.'

'I've been thinking about whether I could ship him home,' he said. 'But I don't officially have a job or anywhere to live, so that's problematic.'

'I don't think it's a very simple or cheap process either,' said Hannah, watching Scrumpy scramble out of the pool, shake himself frantically, then immediately jump back in. 'My friend Sam looked into it after he fell in love with this stray dog in Cyprus. There are loads of vet loopholes to jump through, and I think it takes a while.'

'Months, possibly,' said Rob. 'I looked it up.'

Hannah looked him in the eye. 'Hey,' she said. 'You saved him from a horrible life with Javier, and we'll make sure he ends up somewhere better.'

Rob nodded and gave her a weak smile. 'Just so you know, I'm having a really nice day.'

'Me too,' said Hannah. 'And this trip is all about living in the moment, remember? So let's get in Scrumpy's water hole.'

Rob laughed, his eyes twinkling. 'I don't have my swim shorts.'

She thought momentarily of Nick and Aaron on the boat, and what Rob might look like naked. 'Then you can swim in your underwear, like me.'

He gave her a challenging look, then dropped his backpack and stripped to his black boxer briefs, picking his way through the rocks as Scrumpy jumped around his heels with excitement. Hannah followed suit, glad that she was wearing a robust sports bra and black knickers that were new and covered a decent amount of her backside.

'Are you ready?' she asked, joining him at the edge of the water. She held out her hand and Rob took it, like the two of them holding hands was the most natural thing in the world. He smiled shyly, and for a second it was hard to imagine that this man chewed through women like Scrumpy with last night's chorizo.

'After three,' said Hannah, but Rob didn't wait – he held tight to Hannah's hand and jumped, pulling her into the freezing water. Scrumpy hurled himself in after them, swimming in excited circles as they both whooped and gasped for breath.

'Fuck, that feels amazing,' said Rob, swimming to the edge where he could stand on a ledge in water up to his shoulders.

'It really does,' said Hannah, relishing the feeling of the dust and sweat from the hike being washed away. She swam around for a minute, letting herself adjust to the icy water, then climbed up the slope to sit on a flat, sunny rock.

She could feel Rob's eyes taking in her body and tried not to feel self-conscious about it. She knew she had what was considered a 'good' body – strong and athletic and but still retaining some womanly curves, whatever they were. She'd spent her whole life covering it up, making herself invisible in clothes that were too big or didn't flatter her. She'd never consciously put herself on show this way before, at least not in front of any man who wasn't Graham. Sitting on a sunny rock in wet underwear, Rob breaking his neck to look without it being obvious, made her feel strangely powerful, somehow, like she'd shed her cocoon and could enjoy being a butterfly for a while.

'You look great,' said Rob, as if he was reading her mind. 'Very in the moment, with the rocks and the trees and everything. You should let me take a photo.'

'I don't really do photos,' said Hannah, wrinkling her nose. Scrumpy clambered beside her and shook himself vigorously, showering her with cold water.

'Is that a church hangover? Like, vanity is a sin?'

Hannah glanced at Rob to check he wasn't laughing at her, but he looked genuinely interested. 'It feels self-indulgent, I guess. I took a couple of selfies last week and sent them to Sam; he's the guy who helped me buy clothes for this trip. I felt a bit awkward and guilty about it, which is stupid. I don't have a single social media account.'

'Do you ever swear?' Rob asked.

Hannah laughed. 'What kind of question is that?'

'It's a genuine enquiry. I don't think I've ever heard you swear.'

She wiped the cold water off her face with the palms of her hands. 'The tennis girls thought that was weird too. It wasn't approved behaviour in my family, so I guess I've never got into the habit.'

'So what do you say instead? Like, I'd say "fucking hell, this water's cold" – what's your equivalent?'

Hannah thought about it. 'I'd probably say "wow", or "oh my goodness". Although, admittedly, sometimes that doesn't quite capture the scale of my emotion.' She laughed, thinking about how lost for words she'd been when Rob had soaked her in beer the first night they met.

'You should try it,' he said, giving her another challenging look. 'Swearing. It's quite invigorating.'

Hannah shook her head, enjoying his playful mood. 'So I hear.'

'Come on. You're in the arse end of Spain, and nobody's listening. Scream "fuck" as loud as you can.'

Hannah laughed. 'I can't. I'll lose my ticket for the second coming.' A ghost of a smile flickered on Rob's lips, and she wondered if he was thinking that he'd quite like a front row seat for her second coming.

'Yeah, but it might be worth it,' he shrugged.

'Fine. Fuck,' said Hannah quietly, enjoying the frisson of sinfulness that would, as a child, have earned her a very heavy talking-to from her mother about keeping the devil at bay, followed by a soul-cleansing trip to prayer group.

'Nope, sorry, not loud enough,' said Rob, boosting himself up onto a ledge at the edge of the waterhole and leaning back on his elbows in the sun. He had broad shoulders and a hard, athletic body that sent Hannah's sinful thinking in all kinds of colourful directions.

'FUCK,' she shouted, tilting her head to the sky and holding her arms aloft like she was praising the heavens. Scrumpy clambered out of the water and joined her on the flat rock, shaking furiously.

'Come on, one more time,' laughed Rob. 'Give it everything you've got.'

'FUUUUUUCK,' yelled Hannah, listening to her voice echoing off the canyon walls. 'SHIIIIIT. WAAAAAAANK. BASTAAAAAARD.'

She turned in triumph to face Rob, just as a group of pensioners walked past with hiking poles and map pouches hanging around their necks. They all studiously looked the other way, tutting and chuntering under their breath.

'Let it all out, dear,' whispered an elderly woman at the back of the group with a conspiratorial grin. 'Whatever you've been through, leave it all right here in this canyon.'

Hannah smiled and nodded, wishing she could stop her for a proper chat. But the group had already moved on, so the woman waved her stick in farewell and hurried to catch up.

'Better?' asked Rob with a grin.

'So much better,' said Hannah. 'Let's have lunch.'

Club Colina TITS on Tour
Hannah: Went for a hike today, it was amazing
Gaynor: Because of the amazing outdoor sex you had with Rob?
Hannah: NO. But I did shout FUCK really loudly in a canyon
Gaynor: WOOOAHHHH FUCK
Hannah: I KNOW
Trish: FUUUCCCK YES Hannah!
Jess: SO PROUD OF YOU HAN

CHAPTER TWENTY-SIX

'I want to take Scrumpy home,' said Rob, holding tightly to his lead on the patch of scrubland at the side of the vet surgery. For fifty euros they'd learned that he was a little underweight, but otherwise young and strong, probably no more than two years old. He'd had vaccinations and tablets for fleas and worms, and they now had some special shampoo for the scaly patches on his skin. They also had the number for a local grooming parlour, where they would cut his claws and clean his teeth and ears, and the details of a local dog shelter about ten kilometres to the north of Granada.

'OK,' said Hannah, wondering if there was somewhere near here that would provide them both with a decent coffee. The vet was on a scruffy retail park, sandwiched between a supermarket and a furniture store, but there was no café in sight. 'Where will he go in the meantime? It could be months before he's got his passport to travel, so what happens between now and then?'

'I have no idea,' Rob said gloomily. 'I was thinking we could go to the shelter the vet mentioned; maybe we can pay them to keep him until we can ship him home.'

'Let's go there next,' Hannah suggested. 'Have you got any other options?'

'Maybe,' said Rob. 'I've got a list of about ten, none of them very good.'

'What's your ideal scenario?'

Rob hesitated, then swallowed hard. 'Somebody who lives here. Somebody we know who would care for Scrumpy until he's ready to travel. Take him to vet appointments, get his jabs, look after him like he was their own.'

Hannah raised an eyebrow as Rob looked away shiftily. 'So when you said you had no idea, you actually meant you want to ask my dad to take him,' she said, folding her arms.

'Not necessarily. I'm thinking he might know someone,' Rob said quickly. 'He's part of the ex-pat community – how long has he lived here?'

'Seventeen years, nearly.' *Almost all of Luke's life*, she thought, trying not to feel bitter about it.

'Exactly,' said Rob. 'He'll have friends who love dogs; maybe he can help us find someone.' He was talking too fast, and Hannah realised how desperate he was.

'Look. My family . . . it's complicated.' She raked her hands through her hair, wondering how to explain. She didn't understand most of it, so what chance did Rob have?

'I know,' he said. 'Actually, that's not true, obviously. But I'm not asking you to turn up on his doorstep and beg; I just wondered if you could give him a call.'

'It's not that easy,' said Hannah. 'If he knows I'm in Spain, he'll wonder why I haven't gone to see him.'

'And why haven't you?' Rob asked.

Hannah sighed again, more heavily this time. 'Because of you, basically. He doesn't know that my husband and I have split up. I can't just turn up with a different guy and expect him not to ask questions. My family doesn't do separation or divorce, and he won't believe we're just friends any more than Mark did.'

Rob's brow furrowed. 'Wait, but isn't he divorced from your mum?'

'Yeah, and his punishment was to move to Spain permanently. It was a huge drama that broke up our family.'

Rob pressed his lips together thoughtfully, absently stroking Scrumpy's head until the dog licked his face and snapped him out of his reverie. 'And he was good mates with your ex? What was his name again?'

'Graham. And no, they didn't know each other. They never met, actually.'

'Wait, what?' said Rob, his eyebrows now off the scale. 'You were married for fourteen years and your husband and dad never met?'

'No,' said Hannah. 'It's not that weird, if you think about it. Our families knew each other when Graham and I were young, but he was a spotty little kid that nobody noticed. Dad was gone by the time I was fifteen, so he didn't come to our wedding.'

'And you never brought Graham here to visit?'

'No. He didn't like flying, and he's allergic to everything. I got back in touch with Dad about ten years ago, and I've visited him three times since then. Graham knew, obviously, but I always told my mum I was on a work training course and came in winter so I didn't get a tan.'

'Christ,' said Rob. 'Your family is really quite messed up.'

'You have no idea.' Sometimes Hannah wondered what family therapy might be like with her estranged, ex-religious cult parents, her cheating husband and her closeted little brother. What therapist in their right mind would take that on?

'I'm still confused, though,' said Rob. 'Why can't I meet your dad?'

'It's hard to explain.' Hannah briefly considered all her options and decided that honesty was probably the way forward. 'I always told Dad things were great between me and Graham, because it made him happy. He messed things up with my mum, and he didn't want me to repeat his mistakes.'

'Right,' said Rob. 'So him finding out you're knocking around Spain with a random tennis coach after your husband cheated on you wouldn't be ideal.'

'No. He'd be REALLY upset.'

Rob nodded thoughtfully. 'Yeah, OK.'

'Let's keep thinking,' said Hannah. 'And in the meantime we'll go to the shelter and see what it's like. No pressure, and we definitely won't leave Scrumpy there today.'

Rob grinned. 'You're pretty cool, you know that?'

'Yeah, I know,' said Hannah, waving her hand dismissively. 'Come on, we'll call them now.'

'Here is where the dogs sleep,' said the man, gesturing to a concrete pen with a chain-link gate. The hard floor was scrubbed clean and smelled of bleach, but there was no bed or blanket, just metal water and food bowls and a rubber mat, presumably for the dog to sleep on. It looked like a prison cell, and Hannah was glad they'd left Scrumpy tied up in the shade outside so he didn't have to see it.

'We can look after your dog,' the man said with a reassuring smile. 'You pay for him to stay here, we do all paperwork and vets, then we send him home.' He showed them the day pen, where fifty or so dogs of all shapes and sizes and colours were hurling themselves at the fence, panting and barking and begging for attention while a young woman silently picked up poo with a shovel and bucket behind them. Hannah reminded herself that these dogs had been rescued from worse situations; that this man and his team of staff did amazing work. The place was clean and the dogs were clearly well fed and cared for, but it was still the saddest place she'd ever been. She glanced at Rob, who looked haunted.

'Thank you,' said Hannah, resting her hand on Rob's arm. 'We'll talk about it, then let you know.' Rob nodded at the man and hurried outside, his face pale.

'Are you OK?' she asked, as Rob untied Scrumpy's lead and picked him up, burying his face in his furry neck. The dog's tail wagged furiously as he licked Rob's face and tried to work out where all the other doggie smells had come from.

'I've really fucked up, Hannah,' Rob sobbed. 'I should never have taken Scrumpy off Javier; I should have left him where he was. It's not fair to give him an amazing few days then put him somewhere like this.'

'It's OK,' she said soothingly, stroking Rob's arm. 'We're not going to leave him here.'

Rob looked up at her. 'What other choice do we have?'

Hannah smiled and stroked Scrumpy's soft head. 'We're going to go and see my dad.'

Rob's eyes widened, then he put Scrumpy on the passenger seat and pulled Hannah into a hug so tight he lifted her off the ground. 'Fuck,' he said, pulling away so he could look at her. 'You're incredible.'

'Oh,' she gasped, taken aback by the force of his response.

She looked into his eyes and there was something deep and unfathomable; a look that pooled in her stomach like hot chocolate on a snowy day. He looked like he wanted to kiss her, and in that moment she absolutely wouldn't have pushed him away. She half-closed her eyes, but he'd already let go and was backing away.

'Sorry.' Rob tucked his hands under his armpits. 'Got a bit carried away.'

'It's fine,' laughed Hannah, trying to look like she was totally cool with this whole situation. 'I'll grab us both a coffee, then we'll talk about it.'

Rob turned his attention back to Scrumpy, so Hannah grabbed her bag and headed into the tiny village café along the street from the shelter. She ordered two café con leches and waited, her foot tapping anxiously as she tried to get a handle on things. Kissing Rob was a very bad idea, because that would only lead to one place, and then she'd just be another summer notch on Rob's bedpost. But maybe that was OK? Lots of people had holiday flings, and none of them died of heartbreak. But Rob was different. She liked him; in fact, she REALLY liked him. Enough to invite him on her road trip, despite knowing that she'd already half-fallen for him and it would probably end in tears.

Don't get hurt, she told herself. *You're not emotionally strong enough, not yet.* She'd give herself some space until later in the year, then maybe ease herself into dating with men who scored low for potential heartbreak. Like learning to ride a bike with training wheels.

Forget about Rob as a potential boyfriend, she muttered to herself, taking deep breaths in time with the hissing of the coffee machine. *He's not right for you.* But Rob was also

219

funny, he was kind and he was good company. He could be part of her adventure without being in her bed. Couldn't he?

The thought of Rob in and out of her bed made her anxious, so she pushed it aside for a moment to deal with a more immediate problem – what was she going to tell her dad?

CHAPTER TWENTY-SEVEN

'Dad's a two-hour drive away,' said Hannah, as they made their way up a rocky path through an orange grove. The woman in the café had sent them that way when Hannah asked if there was a nice place to walk a dog; apparently it ended at a ruined castle with a beautiful view across the Andalusian hills. 'But I need to sort a few things out before I call him.'

'Like what?' asked Rob, nudging Scrumpy away from some discarded food wrappers at the edge of the path.

'I need to decide how much I'm going to tell him about Graham. Like, shall I be completely honest, or leave out some of the details?'

'Can we choose the option that's most likely to make him fall in love with my dog?'

'Well, you're a whole other problem. If Graham and I were still blissfully happy, why would I be travelling around Spain with you? It doesn't add up.'

Rob smiled playfully. 'Why ARE you travelling around Spain with me, again?'

Hannah shrugged, unable to help returning his smile. 'I have no idea. It was a moment of madness. I was probably still drunk from the night before.'

'Sounds about right,' laughed Rob. They were both quiet for a moment, Hannah pushing various options around in her mind and coming up with nothing that wasn't riddled with loopholes.

'Wait, I've got an idea,' said Rob, waving his arms for added drama. 'If your dad has never met Graham, I could *pretend* to be him.'

Hannah rolled her eyes at him. 'You of all people could probably pull that off. And actually, I don't think Dad's ever seen a photo of him.'

'Ah, of course. No photos in your family. Which means I could definitely be Graham.'

She let out a bark of laughter. 'You definitely couldn't.'

Rob gasped and pressed his hand to his chest, pretending to be offended. 'Why not?'

She looked at Rob, all tanned and gorgeous and out-doorsy, and imagined Graham standing next to him, probably eyeing everything suspiciously and mumbling about pollen. 'Because the two of you are *completely* different. My dad would be on your case in minutes.'

'OK, but let's just say I *could* pull it off,' said Rob, holding open a gate so Hannah could pass through. 'What would I be like?'

Hannah shook her head, deciding to play along because Rob was so clearly enjoying himself. 'Hypothetically, right?'

'Of course,' said Rob. 'I'm just trying to work out why you married him, because to be honest he sounds kind of lame.'

Hannah thought about it for a moment. 'He wasn't lame, he was safe. And at the time, safe was what I needed.'

'And what about now?'

Hannah shrugged. 'I grew up, found my own strength. Graham, not so much.'

'Did you ever love him?'

Hannah stopped walking and gave him an intense look. 'Sorry,' he said awkwardly, burying his hands in his pockets. 'You don't have to answer that.'

'No,' said Hannah. 'It's fine. I just don't think anyone has ever asked me that before.'

'It's quite a personal question, to be fair.'

'Hmm,' she said thoughtfully. 'Looking back, I don't think love was involved on either side. We had nothing in common, other than wanting to escape from our families and never go to church again. So we did each other a favour, then stayed together because neither of us had any other option.'

Rob nodded. 'At least you didn't have kids, so that's something.'

Hannah was quiet for a moment, wondering how this fun conversation had suddenly strayed into such tricky territory. 'I can't have kids. We did try, but it turned out that's not an option for me.'

Rob blew out his cheeks. 'Shit. I'm really sorry, Hannah. I shouldn't have said that.'

'I'm OK about it, actually,' she said. 'I only realised recently that I don't have any real desire to have children. I just wanted something at the time that belonged to me. Something that wasn't Graham.'

'I don't want kids either,' Rob said cheerfully. 'Never have.'

'How come?'

Rob shrugged. 'I was the black sheep of a perfect family. There's no way I could ever give my kids what my mum and dad gave me, so I'd rather just have an amazing life and be a really cool uncle.'

'I'm going to call you in ten years,' Hannah said. 'I bet you've got a beautiful wife and two cute kids.' She forced herself to play along, but inside her stomach felt like ice. Where would she be in ten years? Would she and Rob even remember each other?

'You're wrong, and I'd put a bet on it,' he said. 'But sadly I don't have money to gamble.'

Hannah pulled a face at him, trying to get the conversation back on track. 'So going back to your original question, if you did pretend to be Graham, you'd be a solicitor from Guildford.'

'OK, that's a very bad start.'

'Exactly. The whole thing is a disaster waiting to happen.'

'Like, a cool solicitor who fights for the underdog in court?'

'No, a deeply uncool solicitor who specialises in mortgage conveyancing, wills and probate.'

'Right. But at least I'd be good at tennis.'

'Ah, another small problem there. Graham has never picked up a racquet in his life, nor has he ever watched his wife win a tournament.'

'OK,' said Rob, holding up his hands. 'Can I just say that Graham sounds like a prick.'

Hannah smiled. 'I was fine with it,' she said. 'Tennis was my thing, and I was very happy for him not to be involved.'

'So not a tennis player, then,' said Rob. 'Cricket? I'm not bad at that.'

'No. Rugby. But to watch rather than play these days.'

'I hate rugby. Can't risk messing up this pretty face.'

Hannah laughed. 'See? Even more reasons why this is a terrible idea.'

'Graham loves dogs though, right?'

'As mentioned previously, Graham is allergic to dogs. So him desperately wanting to adopt a Spanish mutt would be very much out of character.'

'Right, but does your DAD know he's allergic to dogs?'

Hannah thought about it. 'No, I don't think he does, actually.'

'Right, so we're reinventing Graham. He's tall and extremely good-looking and loves dogs. And his gorgeous wife, obviously. He absolutely worships her.'

'I should hope so,' said Hannah with a grin.

'But there's no way we can make him love tennis.'

'Absolutely not. He definitely hates tennis. I'm afraid that can't be fixed.'

'Shit,' said Rob. 'What else does your dad know about him?'

Hannah thought about it for a moment. 'Surprisingly little, actually. I never talked about him much. Law degree, small practice in Guildford, rugby, cooking. And obviously Graham had the same evangelical upbringing as me, so he never swears.'

'Ah, fucking bollocks,' said Rob, crouching down to pat Scrumpy. 'Help me out here, Scrumps. I'm screwed.'

Scrumpy panted happily and licked his face. Hannah watched them together, back to worrying about how she was going to explain the absence of Graham, and the presence of a really hot tennis coach. She imagined for a moment what it might be like if Rob WAS her husband; her dad would love him, particularly if he thought this was the man who'd made his daughter happy for the past fourteen years. She wouldn't have to explain about Graham's affair, and it would only be for a few days. And if Rob messed it up, she'd be in no worse a position than she was now.

'Oh my God,' said Rob, snapping her out of her trance. 'You're actually thinking about doing this, aren't you?'

'No,' she said quickly. 'OK, maybe a bit.'

'I could totally pull it off,' he said fervently. 'And if your dad thinks I'm Graham, he's much more likely to fall in love with my dog.'

Hannah opened her mouth, then closed it again. In the grand scheme of things, was it any more insane than any other idea she'd had in the past few weeks?

'Dad, it's Hannah.' She chewed the end of her little finger nervously, remembering her conversation with Luke a month ago, when he'd done the same. A family trait, apparently.

'Oh, what a lovely surprise,' he said. His voice boomed around the car, the rich baritone of a man who'd once been one of the most powerful orators in their church until he'd lost his faith and his way. 'It's been a little while. How are you?'

'I'm good. How are you?'

'Oh, I'm fine. Keeping busy, you know. You sound like you're driving.'

'I am. Actually, I'm in Spain.' Hannah paused, trying to read his silence. 'I've been here playing tennis, and now I'm having a road trip.'

'Oh,' her dad said in surprise. 'How lovely. Can you come and visit?'

'I was hoping you wouldn't mind, just for a couple of days. We're only two hours away right now.'

'We? Is Luke with you?'

There was a pause, where Hannah let the lie take shape in the back of her throat. 'No, he couldn't come. Graham's here.' She winced, an acidic feeling lining her stomach like a duvet of guilt.

'Really? Graham is with you? That's wonderful. When can you get here? I'll make up the spare room.'

Hannah paused, having not previously considered that her dad only had two bedrooms. She glanced at Rob, who gave her a helpless grimace. Scrumpy was snuggled into his chest, the seatbelt securing both of them like they'd never spent a moment apart. Hannah looked at the grinning, happy dog, and swallowed her reservations. 'We can be there for dinner?'

'Perfect. I'll look forward to it.'

'Me too, Dad. See you in a bit.' She pressed the button on the steering wheel to end the call, watching the road with a determined expression.

'Are you OK?' Rob asked.

'Three days,' she replied. 'You've got three days to convince him to either look after your dog, or find someone who will. We're leaving on Thursday so we can get this road trip back on course.'

'OK,' said Rob, nodding frantically. 'I can definitely do this.'

'There's no way he'll believe you're Graham. I'm going to have to tell him the truth.'

'Wait, what?' Rob looked horrified. 'You can't do that.'

'Why not?' Hannah said. 'I have to.'

'No, you can't. If you tell him about Graham, he'll be focussing on that rather than falling in love with my dog.'

Hannah was quiet for a moment, chewing her lip. This was the stupidest idea ever, but Rob was right. The alternative definitely wasn't going to help Scrumpy. 'Our dog,' she said quietly.

'What?'

'Our dog,' she repeated. 'If we're married, Scrumpy is our dog. We found him on the street in Granada a few days ago, and he followed us home.'

Rob grinned. 'So you're going to let me do this?'

'Yes,' said Hannah, pushing aside a million reservations. 'But only because it will help Scrumpy, and it's only for three days. And because you're probably arrogant enough to pull it off.'

'Right,' said Rob determinedly. 'I'm going to absolutely fucking smash this.'

'No swearing. The minute you swear, it's game over.'

'Ah, shit. OK, I can do this.' He sat upright and cleared his throat. 'Goodness, what a complex and interesting challenge.'

'OK, now you sound like you're constipated.'

'And I'm a solicitor, right? I don't know anything about solicitors.'

'Yes, but you can probably dodge that. Just say you're on holiday and don't want to talk about work.'

'Is he going to ask me loads of questions about the church? Get all nostalgic for the old days?'

'No, we never talk about that. Also you need to be thirty-two.'

'But I'm only twenty-eight.'

'I know. You need to appear older.'

'How do I do that?'

'I have no idea. Talk about pensions and car finance?'

'Christ,' said Rob, taking deep breaths. 'Will he want you to play tennis with him?'

'Probably,' said Hannah. 'We usually do when I go to visit. There's a British woman called Joyce in his village, she's got a court. She's got three adult sons who visit a lot; we've made up a four with one of them before.'

'Brilliant,' said Rob. 'What am I going to do while you play tennis in the sunshine with your dad and Joyce's hot sons?'

'Look after our dog,' Hannah said. 'Make friends with the neighbours, focus on your assignment. Cook us food – Graham's a really good cook, when he can be bothered. You can cook, right?'

'Of course,' said Rob, but Hannah could hear the uncertainty in his voice.

'Just be dull. You don't have to be the centre of attention all the time.'

'I'm a tennis coach, Hannah,' he said with a grin. 'That's literally why we do it.'

'You think I don't know that?' she countered. 'You're all the same. But surely even you can be boring for three days?'

'I could try, I suppose.'

'We don't have to do this, you know,' she reminded him.

Rob nuzzled his face into Scrumpy's neck, suddenly serious. 'No, I want to. It's the best thing for Scrumpy.'

Hannah nodded. 'Why don't you call a dog groomer? If

we're going to make my dad fall in love with our dog, he needs to look like he's just strolled off the catwalk.'

'Dogwalk,' said Rob happily, pulling out his phone. 'I'm on it.' Scrumpy yawned lavishly and snuggled deeper into his chest, like he already knew that he was on his way home.

CHAPTER TWENTY-EIGHT

Hannah parked up outside a small, well-kept terrace of houses with red-tiled roofs, and felt a flutter of anxiety as she spotted Rob taking a deep breath and wiping his sweaty hands on his shorts. Her dad lived in the end house, in the middle section of a small hillside community of homes that grew progressively larger the higher up the hill you lived – they'd passed a couple of two-storey apartment blocks lower down, and you could see glimpses of villas with turrets and towers further up the road. A leathery old man wearing nothing but faded shorts and sandals wandered past, everything about him screaming 'British ex-pat'. His white chest hair covered an impressive set of man-boobs, and he was carrying a striped towel that suggested he was off to the community pool.

'You ready?' asked Hannah, eyeing Rob as she turned off the engine. Scrumpy immediately woke up from his nap and turned in excited circles, his claws digging into Rob's legs.

'Fuck,' said Rob. 'That hurt.'

'No swearing,' said Hannah. 'Are you sure you're up to this? It's not too late for us to come clean. It might still be OK.' In truth she could no longer foresee any scenario where this wasn't going to be a complete disaster, but it was too late to turn round and drive back to Granada now.

Rob shook his head as he took off his seatbelt. 'I'll be

fine.' The front door of the house opened, so Rob gave her a nervous grin as they both climbed out of the car.

'Hi,' said Rob. 'It's so great to finally meet you, Mr . . .' he trailed off, and Hannah realised that she'd never told him her maiden name. He looked mildly panicked, like this was something Graham would obviously know.

'It's fine, just call me Barnaby,' said Hannah's father, shaking his hand warmly.

Rob glanced back at Hannah, who had also failed to mention that her dad was called Barnaby. She gave him the tiniest shrug and turned to greet her dad.

'Hello, love,' he said, pulling her into a long hug. She let herself relax for a moment, genuinely glad to see him even if the circumstances were complicated. They'd worked hard to rebuild their relationship over the past decade, and it was still very much a work in progress. But he was still her dad, even though they looked nothing alike – Hannah's olive skin, brown eyes and wild curls were all from her mum's side of the family. Her dad was blue-eyed and fair, with tanned skin from seventeen years in the sun. He was wearing a blue polo shirt and grey canvas shorts, a pair of sunglasses propped on his head and old, faded flip-flops on his feet. Other than a further inch or so lost on his hairline, he looked exactly the same as he had three years ago.

'Well,' said Barnaby, giving them a beaming smile as he stepped back to look at them both. 'I can't tell you how glad I am to finally meet you, Graham. How long have you been married now?'

'Fourteen years,' said Rob, taking Hannah's hand and showcasing a level of affection that Graham had never managed, even in the early days. Rob's hand felt warm and strong, and it actually hurt to let go.

'Well, that's lovely,' said Barnaby, looking delighted. 'And who's this?' Scrumpy was watching them from the front seat, his tail thumping wildly.

'This is Scrumpy,' said Hannah quickly. 'We picked him up on our travels, I hope you don't mind dogs.'

'Not at all,' said Barnaby, fussing Scrumpy's head and getting a barrage of licks in return. 'He seems like a very good boy.'

Rob beamed, looking like a proud parent. 'He's had a vet check and a trip to the grooming parlour, and he's house-trained.'

'Well, in that case he's very welcome,' said Barnaby, as Scrumpy turned onto his back and offered up his white belly for scritches. 'What happens to him when you two go back to the UK?'

'Not entirely sure, we haven't quite worked all the details out yet,' said Rob. Hannah watched Scrumpy soaking up the attention, and silently prayed that he wouldn't suddenly decide to sink his fangs into Barnaby's arm or sick up the slice of watermelon he'd eaten earlier.

'He's a very lucky dog, aren't you?' Barnaby scratched behind Scrumpy's ears as the dog's eyes rolled back into his head with bliss. 'I thought you were allergic to dogs, Graham? I'm sure Hannah told me that once.'

Oops, thought Hannah, taking a moment to inspect her fingernails.

'I used to be, but it's got better,' said Rob, quickly rallying. 'Still can't do cats though. Or rabbits. Or llamas.'

'Goodness,' said Barnaby. 'Llamas, eh?'

Rob went back to the car to get their bags, leaving Hannah to wonder if they were going to make it through the next three hours, never mind the next three days.

'So, how long are you staying for?' asked Barnaby. They were relaxing on the camping chairs on the paved terrace at the back of Barnaby's house, with an open bottle of white wine and a few plates of tapas. The evening was warm and still, and Hannah could totally understand why people chose to give up the unpredictability of the British spring weather and live like this instead.

'Until Thursday, if that's OK with you,' said Rob. Hannah watched him for a moment, the patio lights catching the flecks of blonde in his hair, then casting a glow across the brown skin of his strong thighs. Instinctively she held out her hand and he took it, not even looking at her. It felt like the most natural thing in the world, even though she couldn't say what music he listened to, what his middle name was or whether he cried at soppy movies.

And yes, obviously this was just pretending for her dad's benefit, but it didn't feel like it. She wondered what Rob would do if she stroked her thumbnail along the palm of his hand; whether she'd see the goosebumps on his arms or hear his breath catch. She didn't know any special moves to turn a man on, but she instinctively knew that Rob would respond. She watched him out of the corner of her eye as he shifted in his seat and crossed his legs the other way, so she couldn't see his groin. The idea that just holding his hand was enough was actually kind of thrilling.

'Anything's fine by me,' said Barnaby. 'I'm just happy

you're here. Shall we see if Joyce fancies some tennis tomorrow?'

'Sounds great,' said Hannah, giving Rob's hand a consolatory squeeze. Scrumpy mooched over from napping on the cool grass and flumped down on Rob's foot, like he was making sure his owner couldn't run away.

'Do you play, Graham?' asked Barnaby. 'I know Hannah said it wasn't your thing, but I thought perhaps she'd changed your mind over the years.'

'No,' said Hannah quickly, trying not to crush his fingers.

'Not really,' said Rob, as Hannah whipped her head round to glare at him. 'I mean, I HAVE played a few times. I can hold a racquet, but I'm not very good.'

'Well, that's definitely a good start,' said Barnaby happily. 'You and Hannah can take on me and Joyce, if you like. We'll be gentle with you. And when we get back, maybe you can make dinner. I'm not much of a cook and Hannah told me you're quite the chef.'

Hannah pressed her lips together as Rob smiled and nodded, busying himself with his glass of wine so he didn't have to look at her.

'Why would you do that?' whispered Hannah. They were standing at the end of the bed in Barnaby's spare room, Scrumpy already sprawled out on his back on Hannah's pillow. She'd used the en-suite bathroom to change into her pyjamas, and was now violently rubbing moisturiser into her face like she was trying to sand the top layer off.

Rob smiled guiltily. 'Are you actually angry, or just pretending?'

'Of course I'm not *angry*,' said Hannah, hanging her towel over a chair. 'I just can't work out why you'd put yourself in a position where you have to pretend to be bad at tennis, when you could have just not played at all.'

'I don't know,' Rob shrugged. 'I panicked.' He opened his bag and pulled out some clean boxer shorts and a T-shirt, presumably to sleep in; Hannah was confident that Scrumpy would create a canine barrier between them in the bed, but she was still glad that Rob was planning to wear actual clothes.

'No, you didn't,' she laughed. 'You just couldn't stand the thought of us playing without you.'

'OK, fine.' Rob grinned, turning his palms upwards. 'I've got massive FOMO, and I'd rather pretend to be shit than not play at all.'

Hannah rolled her eyes and shook her head. 'What do you think of my dad?' They could still hear him moving around in the kitchen, but she whispered anyway.

'He seems great,' said Rob. 'It's hard to imagine him being, like, a crazy preacher.' He half-closed the bathroom door so he could get changed behind it, and Hannah resisted the urge to check out his reflection in the mirror above the sink opposite.

'He was never crazy,' Hannah said. 'Just . . . devout. And it was a long time ago.'

'What does he worship now?' Rob asked.

'Peace and quiet, I think,' said Hannah. 'Trees and flowers. He calls himself a Humanist, which is all about kindness and compassion, having a meaningful life.'

'Sounds like my kind of religion. Do you think he's happy?'

Hannah shrugged. 'I think so. I know the situation with Luke bothers him. I might talk to him about it tomorrow.'

'Don't spoil his good mood,' said Rob quickly, appearing in his boxers and a very fitted T-shirt. He looked entirely delicious, and Hannah suddenly felt quite warm. 'I need his kindness and compassion to extend to being Scrumpy's temporary guardian.'

'Well, best you don't mess up then,' she said playfully. 'Accidentally reveal your tennis skills, or start boring him to death with details of your llama allergy.'

'Yeah, sorry about that,' Rob mumbled. 'Not sure where that came from.'

'Peru, probably,' laughed Hannah, gently rolling Scrumpy into the middle of the bed so she could hop under the sheet.

'You're very funny,' said Rob.

'Also, can you actually cook?'

'Sure,' said Rob, but Hannah could hear the slight wobble in his voice. 'Everyone can cook, right?'

'I'm not talking about beans on toast,' said Hannah. 'Graham is, like, a proper cook, when he feels like it. He's been to classes to learn all those fancy Ottolenghi recipes so he can impress his boring friends. I've told Dad about that, so he's going to be expecting something amazing.'

'I'll be fine,' said Rob. 'Just take him for a walk or something, give me a couple of hours to sort things out.'

'OK,' she said. 'It'll be a good opportunity to talk to him about Luke. Have a family chat.' She surreptitiously watched Rob clean his teeth and ruffle his hair around, imagining for the hundredth time what it might be like if they were a couple. Admittedly some of those imaginings had been naked and horizontal, but the majority had been about whether there was any future for two people as different as they were. Whatever feelings she had for him didn't change who they both were, and she definitely wasn't ready to risk that kind of pain so soon after Graham.

'Is this OK?' asked Rob, climbing into bed next to her, Scrumpy occupying the no-man's land between them. 'I can sleep on the sofa if you like.'

'Then my dad will think we've had a fight,' she said. She lay rigid under the sheet, her nerves jangling at how close he was. It occurred to her that she was thirty-two years old and this was the first time she'd ever shared a bed with anyone but Graham. How many beds had Rob shared? Could he even remember?

'You OK?' he whispered.

'Yeah, I'm good,' she said. 'Pretty tired.'

'Mmm. Me too.'

'Night, then.'

There was a tiny pause, like Rob was about to say something, then changed his mind. 'Night,' he said, then turned onto his side so he was facing her, his body curved around Scrumpy's sleeping form.

Hannah lay awake long after Rob had fallen asleep, thinking about how sometimes this felt like an adventure, and other times it felt like a tangled mess. She wished she could ask the TITS ladies for advice, but she'd already messaged them once today to say she and Rob had been hiking again. No mention of the visit to her dad's; it was too complicated to explain, and she could imagine the reaction to the news that Rob was pretending to be her husband and they were sharing her dad's spare bed. Sometimes it was best to keep your stupidest ideas to yourself.

CHAPTER TWENTY-NINE

'Please don't apologise,' said Joyce as Rob shanked the ball into the net for the umpteenth time. She hadn't changed a bit since Hannah had last seen her three years ago – still a large, well-groomed woman in her sixties with a huge smile and a killer backhand. Personally Hannah thought Rob was over-egging it, hacking the ball around the court like he was clearing a jungle path with a machete. Then every now and then he'd accidentally stroke a forehand across the net with effortless style and leave everyone a bit speechless.

'Perhaps we should take that as a sign to call it a day,' said Barnaby calmly. 'I'll go and get the balls.' He put his racquet by the fence and headed off into the surrounding scrubland with Scrumpy on his heels, bounding towards one of the dozen or so yellow balls Rob had fired into the sun.

'I'll go and help,' mumbled Rob, hurrying off after him so it was just Hannah and Joyce left on the court.

'I'm so sorry,' Hannah said. 'He's a little inconsistent.'

'That's rather an understatement,' Joyce said with a smile. She had a posh English accent that reeked of old money, with added gravelly undertones from decades of heavy smoking. Usually cigarettes, but Hannah had once seen her puffing on a cigar and her dad had mentioned that she occasionally enjoyed a pipe. Her traditional Spanish villa was huge and beautiful from a distance, half a mile further up the hill from Barnaby, behind electric gates. But close up it was all crumbling plaster and cracked tiles. The tennis court was immaculate, however.

'Forgive me for being blunt, but Graham is nothing like I expected,' said Joyce, fishing a pack of Camels from her pocket and lighting one with a red plastic lighter.

'Oh,' said Hannah, instantly wary. Her father seemed entirely oblivious, but Joyce was a wily old bird and didn't miss a trick. 'In what way?'

'He doesn't look like a solicitor,' she said, watching Rob pick up three tennis balls and juggle with them for Scrumpy's entertainment.

Hannah laughed nervously. 'What do solicitors look like?'

'I don't know,' mused Joyce, unleashing a hacking cough. 'But not like that. He's positively yummy.'

'I suppose he is,' replied Hannah, fussing with the strings on her racquet so Joyce wouldn't see her blush.

'Definitely not the kind of man you'd expect to find in church.'

'I guess not. I got lucky, I suppose.'

'Hmm,' said Joyce, watching Hannah carefully. 'Maybe you both got lucky. You seem very much still in love, even after all these years.'

'Yes,' said Hannah, desperate to change the subject. 'How are your sons doing?'

'They're splendid,' Joyce said with a beaming smile. 'Dominic is here tomorrow, actually. We're having a little tennis tournament on Friday, just some people from the village. Will you still be here?'

'Sadly no,' said Hannah. 'We're heading off on Thursday.'

'That's a crying shame, although possibly more for you

rather than Graham. Poor chap; he seems so co-ordinated on land, but on a tennis court he's almost comical.'

'I think he was feeling the pressure,' said Hannah. 'He needs more practice.'

'Well, you're both welcome to use the court any time.'

'Thank you. Which one is Dominic? Is he your eldest?'

'He is,' nodded Joyce, carefully grinding her cigarette end with her tennis shoe so she didn't start a local wildfire. 'I don't think you've ever met him, actually. He's thirty-five, works in something called "wealth management", which I think is just helping rich people avoid taxes.'

'Sounds lucrative,' said Hannah with a smile.

'It is. Extraordinary that he's still single, really, but he keeps telling me he still has wild oats to sow. He's got two Maseratis and is quite the ladykiller, by all accounts.'

'I'm sorry we won't get to meet him,' lied Hannah, thinking that Dominic sounded dreadful.

'Don't be silly,' said Joyce dramatically. 'You can come over for dinner tomorrow evening. He and Graham will have lots in common.'

Hannah laughed breathlessly, wondering what on earth Joyce had worked out about Rob. 'Like what?'

'Well, I don't know,' said Joyce, wafting her away. 'Finance, law. It's all the same, isn't it?'

Later that afternoon, having left Rob in possession of Barnaby's kitchen, Hannah and her dad put water bottles in a backpack and hiked up the road to the old village at the top of the hill; it was a tough climb and they said little on the way up, dodging scooters and cars on the narrow lanes. Eventually they reached the village square and headed down a scrubby path to the left of the church that brought them out to a lookout point. It was easy to miss it if you didn't know it was there, but well worth hunting for because it opened out onto a breathtaking view of countless hilltop villages.

They sat on a low bench against the church wall, sipping water and getting their breath back. 'I can see why you'd want to live here,' she said, taking in the rolling patchwork of yellow, green and umber that made up the vast landscape of southern Spain.

'I never wanted to live here,' Barnaby said quietly.

'What do you mean?' she asked, turning to look at him.

'How was Luke's eighteenth birthday?'

'Umm, OK, I guess,' said Hannah, confused by the sudden change of subject. Luke's eighteenth had actually been a stilted family dinner with Graham and her mother, which Luke had escaped the minute the food was cleared away, no doubt to meet Dan.

'That's good,' said Barnaby breathlessly, his eyes brimming with tears. 'Eighteen is a good age.'

'Dad, you're being weird,' said Hannah with an awkward laugh. 'Can we talk about this?'

Barnaby sighed heavily and patted her hand. His were large and leathery with callouses on his palms from years of keeping his house standing. He'd worked as an accountant when Hannah was a child, mostly for small businesses run by other members of the church. He'd done well enough to buy a house here and set up a successful practice in Spain until he'd retired a few years ago. Now he played tennis, grew tomatoes and pottered around the house doing maintenance jobs. It clearly wasn't a bad life, but Hannah wondered if he was lonely.

'Have you and your mother ever talked about what happened?'

Hannah shrugged, suddenly feeling nervous. 'Not really. I've tried a few times, but she always refuses to talk about it. All I know is that you cheated on her, then moved to Spain. Isn't that about the size of it?'

'Yes, in its most simple form,' said Barnaby, his voice wavering a little. 'It wasn't an easy decision to move here, but it was a necessary one.'

'Necessary? In what way?'

Barnaby gave her hand a small squeeze. 'I did have an affair – it was a moment of weakness that I profoundly regret.' He swallowed and looked down at their clasped hands, and Hannah could feel the weight of his shame.

'Your mother and I were having some . . . difficulties,' he continued. 'We both parted company with the church after she was ill, but when Luke was born she drifted back. Perhaps that was my fault and I wasn't supportive enough, but I was working long hours, trying to keep our heads above water.'

'I remember,' said Hannah. At least, she remembered him not being around much after Luke was born, but actually she hadn't been around much either. She was fourteen, in the grip of puberty and teenage angst. The house was always full of church people cooing and praying over the baby, so if she wasn't at school she was doing homework in the library or at the club playing tennis.

'I didn't realise how deeply your mother had become part of that community again until I made a stupid mistake, and she turned to the church leaders for counsel.'

'I don't remember any of this,' said Hannah.

243

'Why would you?' said her dad with a soft smile. 'You were a teenager with your own interests. We kept it all as far away from you as we could. And of course Luke was just a baby.'

'So what happened?'

'I'd broken ties with the church by then,' he said. 'And after my . . . indiscretion, the leaders turned on me. They convinced your mother that you and Luke would be forever shamed by your association with me; that any contact would make you unclean.' He turned and looked at her, his eyes willing her to understand. 'They persuaded her to take you both to America.'

Hannah gasped, her ears suddenly feeling like they were full of water. 'America? Are you serious?'

Barnaby nodded. 'The church had a community there, in some big compound in Arizona. Not any more, obviously – it was disbanded some years later and the leaders charged with all kinds of awful things. I think some of them are still in prison.'

'Mum was going to take us there?' said Hannah. 'To live?'

'Yes,' said Barnaby sadly. 'It was all arranged. I fought harder than I've ever fought for anything to change her mind; I knew it would be a terrible decision for both of you. But the church had its hooks in deep.'

Hannah shook her head. 'So why didn't we go?'

Barnaby clasped his hands. 'Because I did a deal. I offered to leave the country instead, and never contact either of you again. Which I've stuck to, mostly. You, of course, were old and stubborn enough to make your own decisions.'

Hannah stared at him with her mouth open, trying to process the magnitude of what her dad was telling her. 'But why am I only finding this out now? Why didn't you tell me before?'

'I've been waiting for Luke to turn eighteen. I have no idea if your mother is still involved with those people, but they can't touch Luke now he's an adult. So I've fulfilled my side of the bargain.'

Hannah waved her hands like she was swatting flies. 'I don't . . . I can't . . . are you saying you gave up seventeen years as our dad to protect us?'

'Yes,' he said quietly, his head bowed.

Hannah clamped her hand over her mouth and let out a sob.

'Please don't blame your mother,' he said quickly. 'They were terrible people, and she was vulnerable. I wasn't a good husband and my behaviour drove her straight into their arms.'

'What happened to the woman?' asked Hannah, wiping the tears from her face.

'What woman?' said Barnaby.

'The woman you had an affair with.'

'Ah,' said Barnaby, leaning forward and looking down at his feet. 'Well, that was all part of the problem, and why the church reacted the way they did.' He turned his face to Hannah's and gave her a weak smile. 'It wasn't a woman, Hannah. It was a man.'

'Oh,' gasped Hannah, the final pieces of the story falling into place. 'Why didn't you tell me before?'

'It was a long time ago,' he said. 'He was a mistake, and that situation was . . . a one-off. I thought it was what I wanted, but it wasn't. I've made better choices since. All women, incidentally.'

Hannah clasped his hands in hers, wondering if she should tell him about his gay son. But it wasn't her news to tell, and he and Luke would have a chance to talk eventually. 'I'm glad,' she said, suddenly making the connection from this morning. 'Are you and Joyce . . .?'

Barnaby smiled shyly. 'We are, for some years now, but nothing formal. Her sons don't know, so perhaps you might not mention it. You can tell Graham, of course.'

Hannah nodded. 'Everyone deserves to be happy. And don't beat yourself up about what happened. We all make bad decisions, sometimes.'

Barnaby looked at her shrewdly. 'And what bad decisions have you made, exactly?'

Hannah wafted him away, feeling her neck go red. 'Oh, you know. Nothing specific.'

Barnaby tilted his head to one side. 'Hannah, I know we haven't seen each other much over the years, but you're still my daughter. And I've never been a gambling man, but I would bet every last euro in my bank account that the man you came to my house with yesterday is not your husband.'

Hannah rubbed her face, then stood up and took in the landscape, feeling like her world was wobbling precariously on its axis. But she was also pretty sure that there would be a soft landing; that in view of everything that had happened, her dad wouldn't let her down.

'How did you know?'

'Just instinct,' said Barnaby with a soft smile. 'And neither of you is wearing a wedding ring.'

Hannah gasped, then looked at the tell-tale bare skin on the fourth finger of her left hand. 'We didn't think of that,' she said. 'It was all a bit of a rush, to be honest.'

Barnaby nodded like somehow he understood. 'So what happened?'

'Graham and I split up,' said Hannah with a huge sigh.

'Oh darling, I'm so sorry.' Barnaby stood up to join her and squeezed her arm. 'How did that come about?'

Hannah shrugged. 'I found out he was having an affair. Not his first, by all accounts, but this one is pregnant.'

'Good grief, I'm so sorry.'

'To be honest, Dad, I wasn't that upset,' she continued. 'It wasn't a great marriage, and we're better off apart.'

Barnaby nodded thoughtfully. 'Well, perhaps it's for the best, then. But why didn't you just tell me? Rather than this ridiculous charade?'

'Because I didn't want to upset you,' she said quickly. 'And . . . Rob wanted to get into your good books.'

'Who's Rob?'

'The man currently cooking dinner in your kitchen.'

'Oh, I see. But if he's not your husband, who IS he? And why is he trying to get into my good books?'

Hannah smiled and shook her head. 'Come on, let's go back,' she said. 'I'll introduce you properly, and let him explain.'

CHAPTER THIRTY

'Hi. Can you help me?' squeaked Rob, his hands twitching frantically as he hopped from foot to foot. The woman was platinum blonde, tanned and slim and probably in her mid-thirties, kneeling in her front garden to snip dead leaves from some kind of yellow shrub. In another life she'd have been right up his street, but now really wasn't the time for that train of thought.

'Are you OK?' she asked, squinting at the sun as she turned to look at him. 'You look kind of stressed.' The accent was neither Spanish nor British – maybe Swedish, or Dutch? Not that it mattered right now; she could be a KGB sniper and Rob would still worship her if she could help him out of this mess.

'I'm the opposite of OK,' he said, pressing his fingertips into his temples. 'I tried to make dinner and it's all gone to shit, and I really need my friend's dad . . . I mean my wife's dad, to like me. Can you help? I'm desperate.'

The woman stood up and put her hands on her hips, her eyebrows raised. *Shit*, thought Rob. *She's totally gorgeous.* 'Your friend's dad, or your wife's?' she asked, a curl of amusement on her lips.

'My wife's,' said Rob. 'It's complicated. Look, I've made a horrible mess and if I don't sort it out he won't fall in love with my dog.'

'There's a dog too?' asked the woman, shaking her head in surprise. 'This just gets better.'

Rob took a deep breath and fixed her with his most needy, puppy dog expression. 'I'm glad you're enjoying this, but please. I need help.'

'OK,' she said. 'Show me the horrible mess. I'm Clara, who are you?'

'Rob,' said Rob, then shook his head in frustration, wishing he wasn't so shit at this whole deception business. 'But my friends call me Graham.'

'Why would they do that?' asked the woman, her brow furrowed. 'Rob is a much sexier name than Graham.'

Rob smiled awkwardly, studiously ignoring her pert backside in skin-tight caramel hotpants and a matching crop top, both so close to her natural skin colour that she looked pretty much naked. Why couldn't Barnaby's neighbour have been a friendly grandma? He was in enough trouble without being caught checking out the super-hot woman next door. What if Hannah came back early and found them together in her dad's kitchen?

'Are we going, or not?' asked the woman, giving him a knowing smile that suggested she was familiar with men being entirely cross-eyed and befuddled in her company. Rob nodded and hurried into the kitchen, failing to restrain Scrumpy before he bounded over to greet the visitor. Clara completely ignored him, which made Rob re-evaluate how attractive she actually was. She surveyed the carnage with her mouth hanging open, taking in the chaos of smoking pots piled in the sink and half-open packets of food littering the counter. 'Holy shit,' she said. 'What happened?'

'I tried to cook something to impress my . . . wife's father.

But I can't actually cook, and they'll be back soon and all I've got is chaos for a starter and a shitshow for the main course.'

'Fuck,' said Clara. 'This is bad. How is this so bad?'

'I just got flustered,' said Rob, raking his hand through his hair. 'But even worse, my wife has just messaged to say they'll be back in forty minutes.'

'Wow,' said Clara, shaking her head. Her hair was long and soft and moved like a curtain in the breeze, and Rob momentarily wondered what it smelled like. 'You're in big trouble,' she added.

'I know,' said Rob, snapping himself out of his impure thoughts. If he was ever going to be good enough for Hannah, he needed to stop thinking like a player ALL THE FUCKING TIME and endeavour to deserve her. 'I've got time to clear up, but not to make any actual food. I was hoping you might save me.'

'In what way?' laughed Clara with a shrug. 'I can't cook either. I've lived off green vegetables and coffee for the past two decades.'

Rob rubbed his hands across his face like he was trying to wake up from a bad dream. Clearly it was too much to hope that the hot neighbour was also Nigella Lawson. 'I don't know,' he said. 'I guess I thought you might have a magic wand.'

'Wait, I have an idea,' said Clara, holding up her hands. Her eyes were blue and huge, like a Disney princess. 'There is a tapas bar up in the village, I can call them now. Maybe you can clear up all this shit, and I can scooter up there and grab some things that you can put in the oven? You could say you made them.'

Rob could have kissed her, but that wouldn't be remotely helpful. 'You'd do that? Really?'

'Sure. Do I get an invite to dinner?'

'Absolutely not,' laughed Rob. 'I don't think my wife would understand.'

Clara laughed too, showing perfect white teeth. 'Neither would my husband, now I think about it,' she mused. 'Fine, Rob-also-known-as-Graham, I will save your dinner and your marriage and your dog, even though there are many other things I'd rather do for you right now. For three people, yes?'

'Yes.' Rob nodded, feeling like a huge weight had already been lifted.

'Give me fifty euros, and we'll be all fixed in thirty minutes.'

Rob rummaged in the pocket of his shorts and pulled out some crumpled notes. 'Thank you, Clara.'

'Hmm,' said Clara, rolling her eyes. 'Lucky for you you're so handsome. Clean this place up, I'll be back soon.'

'Hey, Rob,' said Hannah, strolling into the kitchen. Rob was casually slicing bread like a man who'd spent all afternoon cooking up an authentic Spanish dinner. The kitchen was spotless, all the spoiled food bagged and squashed into Clara's bins. The smell of chorizo and tortilla and herby prawns and patatas bravas wafted from the oven, where they were happily keeping warm under Scrumpy's watchful eye.

'My name's Graham,' said Rob, giving Hannah a 'babe, are you MAD?' glance of sympathy.

'It's fine,' said Hannah. 'Dad knows you're not Graham.'

'It's nice to meet you, Rob,' said Barnaby. He leaned over

251

the counter and held out his hand, so Rob shook it warily. He had a sneaky feeling that dinner might not be the focal point of this evening after all. Scrumpy nudged his leg with his nose, like a wet splodge of comfort and reassurance.

'So where does this young man fit into your story?' asked Barnaby.

Hannah sighed heavily. 'We met at Club Colina last week. I was on a tennis holiday with some girlfriends.'

'Ah, so you ARE a tennis player,' said Barnaby with grin.

'Actually, I'm a coach,' said Rob with a guilty smile.

Barnaby clapped his hands together like he'd had some kind of revelation. 'Well, that explains your very bizarre performance this morning. So what is this, exactly? A holiday romance?'

Hannah glanced at Rob, then blushed and rubbed the space on her finger where her wedding band had previously been. Rob had seen her do it before when she was nervous, and in that moment he realised how head-over-heels crazy about her he was.

'No,' he said, even though it gave him a stomach ache to say it. 'We're just friends.'

'Really?' said Barnaby, his expression incredulous.

'Really,' said Rob firmly. 'Neither of us is in the right place for a relationship right now.'

'Fine, if you say so,' said Barnaby, not looking entirely convinced. 'Hannah said you wanted to get into my good books. Why?'

Hannah nodded at Rob, so he took a deep breath.

'Because of Scrumpy,' he said, lifting the dog into his arms. 'I want to ship him home, but it's going to take time. I need to find someone to look after him in the meantime.

Hannah and I took him to a shelter but it wasn't the right place for him.'

'Wait. You want me to look after your dog?'

Rob nodded. 'For at least a few weeks, it could be a bit longer.' Scrumpy wagged his tail and panted happily, as if he was trying to put on a good show. 'Or if you can't, I thought you might have a friend who would be open to helping. I was going to ask you after dinner.'

'I see,' said Barnaby, folding his arms.

'We thought you might be more inclined to do that for Hannah's husband than some random she'd just met.' Rob tried not to sound too desperate.

Barnaby rubbed his chin thoughtfully. 'Well, I don't see why he can't stay here. He seems to be a lovely dog. And if we time it right, perhaps he can travel home with me.'

Hannah looked up. 'You're coming back to the UK?'

'Yes,' said Barnaby with a firm nod. 'I've completed my mission, and now it's time for me to come home.'

Rob said nothing, wondering what the mission was. He briefly considered the possibility that Barnaby might be secret service, then dismissed it as too many James Bond films.

'You're moving back to Westwick?' asked Hannah, glancing at Rob and adding, 'I'll explain everything later.'

Barnaby laughed. 'Well, perhaps not quite that close to home. But close enough that I can get to know my children again, build some kind of retirement plan. I love Spain, but home will always be where you and Luke are.'

'Wow,' said Hannah, pressing her hand over her mouth. 'I don't know what to say.'

There was a prolonged moment of silence as everyone

processed all this new information, but Rob decided to break it before things got too heavy. 'Should we tell Joyce before we go there tomorrow?' he asked. 'About me not being Graham?'

Barnaby thought about it for a moment. 'I'll tell her when we get there,' he said. 'Her son is going to be there too, I forget his name.'

'Dominic,' said Hannah.

'That's the one. He's rather full of himself, I'm afraid. But Joyce is a wonderful cook, so let's just have a lovely final evening before you go.'

Hannah nodded and smiled, and Rob could see that she looked much happier for finally being honest with her dad. Whatever they'd talked about on their walk, it had clearly been important.

'And talking of wonderful cooks,' said Barnaby cheerfully. 'Let's see what Rob here has rustled up for dinner.'

Rob blushed, feeling like he had no choice but to come clean. 'Ah,' he said. 'Well, actually, if we're doing the honesty thing, I had some help.'

'What kind of help?' asked Hannah, immediately suspicious.

'I'm not really much of a cook,' he mumbled. 'And I got in a bit of a mess. But one of your neighbours helped me out.'

'Which one?' asked Barnaby.

'Clara,' said Rob casually, thinking he could style this out.

'Oh, lucky you,' laughed Barnaby. 'She used to be a Danish beauty queen; now she's some kind of fitness celebrity. She's got about half a million disciples on Instagram, or whatever they're called.'

'Followers,' said Hannah, fixing Rob with a penetrating stare. 'She sounds lovely.'

Rob held her gaze and smiled softly, gratified that Hannah was a tiny bit nettled, and hoping his expression conveyed the depth of how he felt about her and definitely didn't feel about Clara. 'She didn't even pat Scrumpy when she came into the house,' he said. 'Not a dog person, apparently.'

Hannah laughed, her face softening. 'Oh dear,' she said. 'Never mind.'

Barnaby nodded at Rob. 'I'll make up the sofa bed in the lounge after dinner. Now you two aren't pretending to be happily married, you can have a bed each.'

Rob glanced at Hannah, wondering if she was feeling the same wave of disappointment. Obviously sharing a bed with Scrumpy fidgeting between them hadn't been very comfortable, but he'd still enjoyed the strange intimacy of it. Mostly, he just liked being wherever Hannah was.

'So what else have you done to get into my good books?' asked Barnaby, pulling a bottle of wine out of the fridge and grabbing three glasses off the shelf.

'Oh, nothing much,' said Rob. 'Although . . .' He hesitated, wondering if he was about to cross a line. Barnaby seemed pretty easy-going, but everyone had their limits.

'What?' asked Hannah, her eyes narrowing.

Rob blew out his cheeks. 'You know this morning when Scrumpy was licking your feet and you thought that was really adorable?'

'Mmm,' said Barnaby, his forehead wrinkled in confusion.

'I smeared a bit of fish pâté on your flip-flops.'

Hannah snorted her wine down her chin as Barnaby started to laugh. 'You didn't,' she said.

'I did,' said Rob. 'I'm really sorry. The clock was ticking and I was getting a bit desperate.' On cue, Scrumpy rubbed himself against Barnaby's legs, as if to say, 'Look how cute I am.'

'Well, it succeeded,' said Barnaby, scratching between Scrumpy's ears. 'I'm happy to be his guardian for however long it takes.'

'Thanks, Dad,' said Hannah.

'But honestly,' he said, giving both of them a stern look. 'You could have just asked.'

'I was planning to,' said Rob with a helpless smile. 'I was just laying the groundwork so you definitely wouldn't say no.'

Barnaby gave them both an indulgent smile. 'Rob, I've barely seen Hannah in seventeen years. I can't think of anything I'd say no to, if it really mattered to her.'

Rob looked between them as Hannah started to sob, then moved into her dad's open arms. Rob turned away, wondering what on earth had happened on their walk. Hannah would no doubt tell him later, but for now he had a fancy dinner to serve.

CHAPTER THIRTY-ONE

'I think you should talk to Luke,' said Hannah to her dad the following evening. 'I can organise it.' She glanced around the table under the overgrown pergola at the back of Joyce's house. Rob was over by the lemon tree with Scrumpy and Joyce's son Dominic, who was smoking furiously and kept throwing appreciative glances in her direction. It made her wish she'd put a longer skirt on, or maybe a Victorian nightgown that covered her from the neck down. Joyce was in the kitchen, noisily loading the dishwasher.

'I'd like to,' Barnaby said nervously. 'He must be so angry with me.'

'He's furious,' said Hannah. 'But he needs to understand what happened, and why. He'll give you ten minutes to explain if I ask him to.'

'I don't want him to be upset with your mother instead,' said Barnaby, twisting his wine glass anxiously. 'It wasn't her fault.'

'Why don't you ALL talk?' she suggested. 'Clear the air a bit. As far as I know, Mum has never been open about what happened, or met anyone new. We might want to consider the possibility that she's also been carrying this burden for seventeen years.'

'I suppose she has,' said Barnaby. 'There isn't a day goes by when I don't wish I'd done things differently.'

'But you didn't,' said Hannah. 'Bad decisions were made all round, and everyone's spent too long living with the consequences. Let me speak to Luke tomorrow, see if he'll consider coming out here to see you.'

Barnaby nodded. 'OK. But not your mother. I'm not ready for Elena yet.'

'No,' said Hannah. 'But I shouldn't worry. Mum doesn't really go further than Camberley on a good day, I don't think she's going to be rushing to get on a plane to Spain.'

'It's a lot for Luke to take in,' said Barnaby. 'The whole America thing, the decisions I made, his dad having been with . . . a man. Do you think he'll even begin to understand?'

Hannah smiled softly, realising for the first time how alike her dad and Luke were. The same anxiety about what others thought of them, the same selflessness at the expense of their own happiness. 'He'll understand just fine, Dad. He's a good person.'

'I miss him,' said Barnaby, tears welling up in his eyes. 'It seems odd that the last time I saw him he was just a baby. I've thought so many times about reaching out to him, or asking you to help. But those church people . . . it's hard to explain the power they had. I didn't want to take the risk.'

Hannah nodded, not really knowing what to say.

'I've kept an eye on them,' Barnaby said quietly. 'Online, I mean. Read all the news about the break-up of the church in America, followed the trials and the convictions. I even set up a fake Facebook profile so I could join a church group in Guildford. I was trying to work out how many were left, if any of the old names were still there. People who could bring your mother and Luke back into the fold if I made contact. They're still around.'

'What happened to Christian forgiveness? Is that not their thing?'

Barnaby gave a hollow laugh. 'No. Vengeance is much more their style.'

'You make them sound like some kind of crime syndicate.'

'It took me a while to see it, but you're not a million miles off. There are some wonderful churches who do amazing work around the world, but that one was about power and money. They took years of my life, and they almost took my family.'

They sat in silence for a moment, listening to the cicadas. 'Mum's different now. Still devout, but just normal church.'

Barnaby nodded, patting Hannah's hand that was resting on the table. 'That's good.'

'Should I go and help Joyce, do you think?' asked Hannah as the sound of plates clattering came from inside.

'No, she'll be having a cigar and a whisky, which she prefers to do alone.'

'Have you told her about coming back to the UK yet?'

Barnaby shook his head. 'No, I was saving that detail for after dinner. I wonder if you and Rob could head back on your own later? Give me a chance to break the news?'

Hannah nodded, thinking about going back to another night of Rob on the sofa bed and her in the bedroom. Even though they'd only slept together once, last night's bed without him and Scrumpy had felt vast and empty. Today Barnaby had joined them for a hike to an old monastery, so she and Rob hadn't spent any time alone together at all. Obviously that was for the best under the circumstances, but it still felt like she was being punished for something.

'I wonder how that conversation is going?' mused Barnaby, looking over at Rob and Dominic. 'Interestingly, Joyce knows he's not your husband, but Dominic doesn't.'

'Really?' said Hannah, raising her eyebrows. 'Why didn't she tell him?'

'She said Dominic would make a big fuss and interrogate you both for his own entertainment. He's not one for letting things go, apparently, and since you won't see him again after tonight, it was easier to leave things as they were.'

'Fair enough,' muttered Hannah, taking advantage of the opportunity to watch Rob. He'd swapped his usual tennis shorts for red canvas ones, paired with a white polo shirt and the black and white Vans he'd been wearing the first night they met. He looked, by any standards, incredibly hot.

'I think we should talk about Rob, don't you?'

'There's nothing to talk about,' whispered Hannah, feeling like she'd been caught out. A flutter of anxiety bloomed in her stomach.

'It's none of my business, of course, but I'm struggling to believe the whole "just friends" thing.' Barnaby made air quotes with his fingers and raised his eyebrows.

'It's true.' Hannah looked him straight in the eye. 'Nothing's happened.'

'Right, but that's not the same as "just friends", is it? You'd have to be blind or stupid not to see how mad he is about you.'

Hannah blushed. 'I don't think . . .'

'Trust me,' said Barnaby, giving her a knowing look. 'He's

absolutely smitten. And unless I've entirely misread this situation, it's very clear you feel the same way.'

Hannah sighed. 'It's complicated.'

Barnaby tilted his head and raised his eyebrows in question.

Hannah glanced around to make sure nobody could hear their conversation. 'The thing is, I only split up with Graham a month ago. It's too soon to go into another relationship, I need to get my head around the one I've just left.'

'That's fair enough.'

'And Rob's lovely, and yes I DO like him,' said Hannah. 'But he's also a self-confessed womaniser. He's twenty-eight, and he's never been in a relationship for more than a few weeks.'

'Goodness, lucky Rob,' mused Barnaby. 'Has he tried to add you to his summer scorecard?'

'No. He's taking some time out too, and he knows I'm not his type anyway.'

'Hmm,' said Barnaby. 'So why is he here with you, and not coaching at Club Colina?'

Hannah sighed again. 'Because I went to his room to check he was OK after he got into a fight with another coach, and having any kind of involvement with guests wasn't allowed, so he got fired.'

'My word,' said Barnaby, looking amused. 'A lover AND a fighter.'

'I've made it sound more dramatic than it was,' muttered Hannah, wondering where they'd be if that hadn't happened. She'd be on her road trip alone – no Rob, no Scrumpy, definitely not having this conversation with her dad.

'So in summary, he's the right person at the wrong time.'

'I'm not actually sure he's the right person,' said Hannah, her thoughts confused and jumbled. 'But it's definitely the wrong time.'

'Hannah, people change. They grow up. I'm nothing like the man I was in my twenties.'

'I suppose.'

'That young man could be carving a trail through Spain's bars and nightclubs right now, picking up a different woman every night. But instead he's chosen to go on an adventure with you. What does that tell you?'

'I don't know, Dad. I'm no good at this. I've never played this game.' She felt momentarily overwhelmed, like all these feelings were too much to carry.

'I know, darling,' he said soothingly. 'But it's not difficult. Trust your judgement, and listen to your heart. It's all any of us can do.'

'I don't want to get hurt,' said Hannah, blinking away the tears. 'I'm not sure I'm strong enough.'

'Ah, I don't think that's true,' said Barnaby. 'You walked out on a marriage that didn't feel right, something I never had the strength to do. And you made contact with me ten years ago, without ever asking anyone's permission. You have your mother's beauty and your grandmother's determination.'

Hannah gave him a weak smile. 'If you say so.'

'So what would you prefer?' asked Barnaby, fixing her with a penetrating stare. 'To sit on the edge of life and feel nothing? Or throw yourself onto the dancefloor and see where the night takes you? In the end we only regret the chances we don't take.'

Hannah glanced over at Rob, his hands buried deep in his

262

pockets as Dominic droned on. She took in his broad back, the hair that was starting to curl at his neck and needed a cut, the strong, tanned calf muscles. *Will he know I'm looking at him?* she thought. *Can he feel it? If he looks in the next ten seconds, then maybe that's a sign.*

Rob turned and caught her eye, then smiled, and Hannah was irretrievably lost.

CHAPTER THIRTY-TWO

'How long have you two been married?' asked Dominic, grinding his cigarette out on the trunk of the lemon tree and draining his glass of wine. He reminded Rob of Olly – the same sloppy manner and lazy drawl, the same alpha male tendency to take up too much room, whether it was physical space or just hogging the conversation. He had the same square jaw too, but Dominic's was permanently on the move, accompanied by a sniff that suggested a robust coke habit. He'd disappeared for a few minutes after Joyce's incredible paella and returned with shiny bug eyes and restless hands that repeatedly raked through his floppy hair. He could only have been mid-thirties, Rob guessed, but everything about him suggested an impending midlife crisis. Rob actively hated him on sight, but Joyce was lovely so he was playing nicely. For now, anyway.

'Fourteen years,' said Rob, noting how Dominic was shamelessly checking out Hannah's legs as she chatted to her dad at the table. Rob desperately wanted to go back and join them, but the conversation looked quite intense and he didn't want to interrupt.

'Fuck, how old were you when you got married?' asked Dominic, dragging his attention back to Rob. 'Twelve?'

'I was eighteen,' said Rob through gritted teeth. 'We both were.'

'Proper Romeo and Juliet shit,' sneered Dominic. 'Teenage lovers,' he added, in case Rob was too stupid to understand the literary reference. 'You did well.'

Rob gave him a thin smile, imagining locking Dominic in a windowless room with Olly and leaving them to bore each other to death.

'No, you know what I mean,' Dominic continued, warming to his topic. 'Some women totally give up when they get married, right? Get a ring on their finger and it's all greasy hair and no make-up. They leave the bridal suite in a pair of fucking leggings and it's game over.'

'Well, I wouldn't know,' said Rob.

'Meanwhile, if I may say so, your wife is a total fucking knockout.'

'You may NOT say so, actually,' said Rob, giving Dominic a look that would melt a polar ice cap.

'Well, I just did,' blustered Dominic, wiping his nose with the back of his hand and shuffling nervously. 'But well done for keeping her on her toes.'

'I've never kept Hannah anywhere,' said Rob mildly, wondering what it might be like to drag this idiot round the garden by his scrotum. 'She's very much her own woman.'

'I hear she's quite handy on the tennis court too.'

Rob nodded and smiled. 'She's a great player.'

Dominic snorted out a laugh. 'Meanwhile I hear that YOU play like your arms and legs are in traction.'

Rob shook his head, refusing to give Dominic the satisfaction of seeing him get riled. 'Well, I guess that makes me lucky to have Hannah as my partner.'

'Shame you're not here for the tournament on Friday,' said Dominic, lighting another cigarette. 'I'm playing with your dad's neighbour Clara, who is an absolute ride but also dogshit at tennis. Might have been up for a little wager.'

Rob narrowed his eyes. 'What kind of wager?'

'A gentlemen's bet between professionals,' said Dominic, blowing smoke in Rob's face. 'Put a bit of money on which couple does better. Make the whole tedious business a bit more interesting.'

Rob shrugged. 'Sadly we're leaving tomorrow. Also I'm not a gambling man.'

'Ah yes, I forgot,' sneered Dominic. 'What was that cult you grew up in?'

'It was a church, actually.'

Dominic leaned over to refill his glass from the bottle he'd propped in the branches of the lemon tree, not bothering to offer Rob any even though his glass was empty. 'All churches are fucking cults.'

'If you say so.' Honestly, this guy was the worst. How could he possibly share DNA with Joyce, who was so funny and charming? Maybe she'd found Dominic in a forest, being raised by feral pigs.

'What kind of legal work do you do, anyway?' asked Dominic, eyeing Rob beadily.

Rob kept his face deadpan, wondering if Hannah had any plans to rescue him. 'I'll tell you what, can we not talk about work? I'm on holiday.'

'What else is there?' said Dominic loudly. 'I've already told you about my job and my cars, and I'm definitely not allowed to talk about how much I'd like a go on your wife. What's left? Your dog?'

Rob moved a little closer and saw Dominic flinch, like he was fully expecting a punch in the face. Scrumpy scrambled from his position by the tree and parked himself by his master's side, his furry superhero sidekick. 'Could you excuse me for a minute?'

'Sure,' said Dominic, already pulling out his phone to find more interesting conversation, or probably call his dealer.

Rob walked back to the table and stood beside Hannah, just as Joyce appeared with a cloth to wipe the now-empty table. Hannah tilted her head up to smile at him, setting off the butterflies in his stomach again. Maybe he was still hungry.

'Are you sure we can't help?' he asked. Joyce wafted him away, so Rob turned to Hannah and lowered his voice. 'Can we talk for a sec?' He nodded his head towards the overgrown terrace by the kitchen door.

'Sure,' said Hannah, standing up and following him. Scrumpy trotted behind them and took the opportunity to give the rubbish bag another sniff. 'Is everything OK?'

'Yeah, I'm fine. Dominic, however, is a sexist prick who's being incredibly disrespectful to my beautiful wife.'

Hannah laughed. 'I gathered that much over dinner. AND he keeps looking at my legs.'

Rob seethed. 'He's a coked-up, entitled little shit. He needs putting back in his box.'

'Well, that's easy,' shrugged Hannah. 'Since he still thinks you're Graham, you could take him on at tennis.'

Rob grinned. 'Wait, are you thinking of staying for the tennis tournament? Doesn't that mess with your plans?'

'Not really,' she shrugged. 'It's only one extra day, and it would be nice to spend more time with Dad. We can leave straight afterwards.'

Rob exhaled, wondering whether there were other women on the planet who were this relaxed and easy-going, or if Hannah was a one-off. 'Excellent,' he said. 'This is going to be fun.'

'You're going to be nice about it, right? I know Dominic is awful, but Joyce is my dad's friend.'

'Of course,' said Rob happily. 'I'm always nice.'

'And when I say friend, I mean . . . girlfriend,' said Hannah, giving him a significant look. 'Dad told me yesterday.'

'Yes, I got that the first time,' said Rob, wondering how on earth Hannah hadn't noticed when they'd played tennis together two days ago. It had been plain as day to Rob that Barnaby and Joyce were a couple, and he'd assumed it was such old news to Hannah that she hadn't bothered to mention it.

'Talking of which, we need to head home,' said Hannah, as Joyce settled down at the table with Barnaby and lit a cigarette. 'Dad needs to talk to Joyce about his plans to go back to the UK.'

'Fine,' said Rob. 'I'm ready whenever you are.' He looked around for Scrumpy, and spotted him disappearing round the side of the house, several prawn shells poking out of his jaws like pink fangs.

'I'm off to meet some friends,' announced Dominic loudly. 'Thank you for dinner, Mummy.' He kissed Joyce on both cheeks and waved at the others.

'Nice to meet you,' said Rob affably. 'We might be here for the tournament on Friday after all, so maybe we'll see you then.'

'I'll look forward to it,' said Dominic through gritted teeth. 'Don't forget about my offer of a little wager.'

'I won't,' said Rob, giving Joyce a hug. 'Thank you for a wonderful dinner.'

'It was lovely to meet you,' said Joyce. 'And DO stay for Friday. I think it will be a very valuable learning experience for Dominic.' She smiled conspiratorially as she hugged Hannah and waved them both off, Scrumpy trotting at their heels.

'Are you going to tell me about this wager?' asked Hannah, once they were a little way down the hill.

'It was nothing,' said Rob. 'Dominic tried to get me to make a bet on which one of us would do better in the tournament, but I turned him down.'

'Good,' said Hannah with a smile. 'I don't approve of gambling.'

'Even when it gets us a lovely dog?' teased Rob, bending down to fuss between Scrumpy's ears. 'Look at his little face.'

'Well, that was a special case,' said Hannah. 'But you should only bet money if you're prepared to lose.'

'I think Dominic would happily take my wife in lieu of cash,' said Rob.

'Ugh,' said Hannah. 'She's definitely not for sale.'

'I should hope not,' said Rob, putting his arm around her in what he hoped was a casual, friendly fashion. 'What were you and your dad talking about?'

Hannah hesitated, then gently extracted herself from his arm and looked away. 'Luke, mostly.'

'Right.' He waited for her to elaborate, but she said nothing. 'Anything else?'

Hannah stopped and turned to look at him, then took a deep breath. The air was cool on his skin, and he could see goosebumps forming on her arms. 'He wanted to know what the deal was between you and me.'

'And what did you say?' Rob felt his voice crack as his heart started to pound in his chest. Was this going to be the moment when everything changed?

'I said I liked you,' said Hannah. 'But you already knew that. And then I said that I didn't think I was ready for a relationship, and that you weren't either.'

'And what did he say to that?' asked Rob, feeling a bit sick.

'He said you only regret the chances you don't take.'

'Holy shit,' said Rob with a gasp.

'What?'

'My dad said exactly the same thing.'

'What? When?'

'I rang him. The day after the whole thing in Puerto Banus.'

'You told your dad about that?'

'No, of course not.' Rob paused, realising that he now had to tell her about what he'd said to his dad. But Hannah had been honest with him, so the least he could do was return the favour, however much like a lovesick wanker he sounded. 'He and my mum are, like, actual couple goals. It was love at first sight over forty years ago and they're still all over each other.'

Hannah smiled. 'That's nice.'

'Anyway, I rang Dad to ask what that felt like. To meet someone and feel like you'd been knocked sideways.' He glanced at Hannah to see if she was laughing, but she wasn't.

'Really? You asked him that?'

'Yeah,' replied Rob with a nervous laugh.

'What did he say?'

'Same as your dad. You only regret the chances you don't take.'

'Wow,' said Hannah. 'Maybe they're on to something.'

'It's just . . .' Rob rubbed his face, casting around for the right words. 'Look, Hannah. You know I've never done a proper relationship before, and I really don't want to mess this up. Not with you.'

'What does that mean? That you're happy for it to be someone else?'

'No. Yes. Shit, I don't know.' The desire in Rob's stomach turned to acid panic as he desperately tried to keep a hold on the conversation. 'Look, I'm not explaining this very well.'

'It's fine,' said Hannah. 'I totally agree that I'm not the right person to be your commitment experiment. You need someone who can pick herself up if things don't work out, and I'm not sure I'm ready for that yet.'

'But—' said Rob, looking at her desperately.

'So let's just accept that the timing isn't right for either of us, and enjoy the rest of this trip.' She didn't sound annoyed and the words all made sense, but her jaw was clenched with something that looked like pain.

'OK, but what about what our dads said? About regret . . . and chances . . . and stuff.'

'Maybe that's not about us having a relationship,' said Hannah. 'We both already took a chance on this trip together. Are you regretting that?'

'Definitely not,' said Rob, wondering why life couldn't be more like the films, where he'd sweep Hannah into his arms, snog her face off, then they'd both live happily ever after.

'Me neither,' said Hannah. 'So let's make the most of it,

and not make things any more complicated than they need to be.'

Rob nodded and smiled weakly, thinking about the empty sofa bed at the bottom of the hill. That had made things less complicated, and in lots of ways everything between him and Hannah was great. So why had this conversation left him feeling so empty?

CHAPTER THIRTY-THREE

Hannah called Luke early Thursday morning, and was gratified that he agreed to a lunchtime video chat with his dad on the basis of very little information, but absolute trust in his big sister. So she and Rob walked Scrumpy up to the tapas restaurant in the village, figuring they'd make themselves scarce for an hour, then check in with Luke to make sure he was OK.

'How do you think it will go?' asked Rob, spooning patatas bravas onto their plates.

'I think it will be fine,' said Hannah, topping up both their glasses from the jug of white sangria. 'Unlike me, Luke has a level head.'

'What does that mean?' asked Rob playfully. 'Are you saying your little brother wouldn't go off on a road trip with a random he'd only met the week before, adopt a dog and create a fake partner to deceive his father?'

'That sounds really bad, when you put it like that,' laughed Hannah. 'I didn't realise I was that much of a rebel.'

'It's one of the many things I like about you,' said Rob, making Hannah wish she had the confidence to ask him to give her the full list. 'What else have you discovered about yourself?'

'What, since I split up with Graham?' Hannah thought about it for a moment. 'Hmm. I've definitely discovered that

I like nice clothes. And that female friendships are important to me. I've never really done the whole gal pal thing.'

Rob nodded thoughtfully, and Hannah marvelled for the twentieth time how easy he was to talk to. She'd expected someone like him to get bored, or to look at his phone all the time, but he never did.

'Have you stayed in touch with your tennis crew?' he asked. 'Are they up to date on all your rebel activity?'

Hannah shook her head and smiled. 'I send them a message every day, as promised. But I've left out quite a lot of information – they know about Scrumpy, but not that we're at my dad's. They think you and I are hiking around Andalusia.'

'You can tell them about tennis this afternoon, though.' Joyce and Dominic were out for the day, and Barnaby had some errands to run in Córdoba, so Hannah and Rob were planning to take advantage of the chance to play some tennis on Joyce's court. It would be their first time playing against each other properly, and Hannah couldn't wait.

'Yeah, remind me to take a picture of us on court, so I can send it to them.'

'Are they still OK about us travelling together?'

'They seem to be finding it quite entertaining.' Hannah smiled at the memory of Gaynor's WhatsApp from yesterday, asking if the heat of Hannah's unrequited lust had set fire to southern Spain yet. It hadn't quite, but despite her best efforts to dampen things down during their walk home last night, she could still feel the electricity between them.

'There must be questions about the sleeping arrangements, I imagine.'

Hannah blushed. 'There have been a few. How's the sofa bed?'

'Uncomfortable,' said Rob. 'Some of the springs have gone.'

Hannah nodded, the air suddenly heavy with tension.

'I guess your dad doesn't believe in sharing a bed if we're not married,' said Rob, picking up a prawn from the bowl of *Gambas al Ajillo*. He held it out to Hannah, and she instinctively leaned forward so he could put it in her mouth, her lips briefly brushing his fingers. Rob cleared his throat, then wiped his hands on his napkin and took another slug of sangria.

'I don't think it's a moral thing,' said Hannah, wondering why this terrace was suddenly so hot. 'I think he felt he was doing us both a favour.'

Rob nodded and held out the last prawn. 'Well, I liked it better the other way.'

Hannah leaned forward again, wondering if he could actually see her heart beating out of her chest. What would he do if she took one of his fingers in her mouth? Was that even a sexy thing? It felt like it might be, but there was an equal chance he might be weirded out, so probably best not to risk it. 'So did I,' she said, wondering why her voice was suddenly so weak and husky.

Hannah practically bit Rob's finger off as her phone rang, Luke's name lighting up the screen. She looked at Rob, who nodded. 'Go and talk to him,' he said. 'I'll get the bill.'

'Luke?' said Hannah, hurrying out into the village square, out of earshot of the restaurant diners. 'Are you OK?'

'Yeah, I'm fine,' said Luke, his face filling the screen of Hannah's phone. 'Dad and I talked for, like, an hour. My mind's a bit blown, if I'm honest.'

'Yeah, I know,' said Hannah, feeling a wave of relief that Luke was OK and everything was finally out in the open.

'People make podcasts about this kind of shit.' Luke half-smiled, and she swallowed the urge to tell him off for swearing or mention that he could do with a haircut.

'I know,' she said. 'But we've only heard Dad's side of the story, not that I think he'd lie. It's easy enough to check with Mum.'

'I'm going round this evening, and I've got a day off tomorrow so we can talk it through properly. I've got SO many questions.'

'Be gentle with her, Luke. It was difficult for her too.'

'But why didn't she let Dad know when she'd properly left the church? It was years ago; he could have got back in touch with me then.'

'I don't know,' sighed Hannah. 'Maybe she was scared about the church people finding out; Dad said they're still around.' She shrugged helplessly, wishing she was there to have this conversation in person. 'Or maybe she decided it was just easier for him to stay away.'

'Easier for her, you mean,' huffed Luke. 'I've grown up hating my dad for no reason. That doesn't seem fair.'

'Well, let's wait until we've talked to Mum,' said Hannah, conscious of how pious and sensible she sounded. In truth she was as upset as Luke about the years they'd lost, but there was no use kicking off about that now.

'When are you back? We should probably see her together.'

'Not for at least another week.' Hannah thought about getting back on the road with Rob tomorrow, and where that might take them. 'But I think we should involve Dad, too. There's a lot of stuff that we need to get straight.'

'I don't think I can get Mum on a video call, especially with Dad. She thinks everything is being recorded by the Russians.'

Hannah laughed softly. 'Did he tell you he was planning to come back to the UK?'

'Yeah. But that could be ages.'

'Well, come over to Spain, then. Take a few days off work and spend some time with him. We can arrange a conversation between him and Mum later.'

'Maybe,' mumbled Luke. 'I could do that in a few weeks, or something.' He fell silent for a moment, chewing purposefully on his little finger. 'He told me about the guy . . . and the woman he's with now.'

'Joyce,' said Hannah with a smile. 'You'd like her. Did you tell him about Dan?'

'No,' Luke replied. 'Felt like that was quite a lot of information for one day. And anyway, I reckon I should come out to Mum first.'

Hannah nodded. 'Do you want me to be there?'

'No, I'm just going to tell her tonight.' Luke folded his arms and set his jaw in a way that reminded Hannah of their dad. 'If she doesn't like it, that's her problem. I don't think our family should be keeping secrets any more.'

'Me neither,' said Hannah. 'I'm here if you need me, OK? And I'll come back sooner if you want me to.'

'Thanks,' said Luke. 'But I'm fine. Quite enjoying having your place to myself, actually. I'll give you a call in a couple of days.'

'OK,' said Hannah, relieved that this first hurdle had been crossed and Luke was dealing with it well. 'I should probably go and check on Dad.' *And Rob*, she thought, but she didn't want to make this conversation any more complicated than it needed to be.

'We haven't talked about you,' said Luke. 'How's your trip been? Met anyone cool?'

'I've made some new friends,' she said breezily, glad she didn't have to try to explain any kind of relationship with Rob, because there wasn't one. The conversation yesterday had helped her feel confident that they were doing the right thing, but being hand-fed prawns had put her in a sweaty, breathless spin again. One way or another, she needed to resolve the situation between them before she spontaneously combusted.

Hannah was already in bed by the time Rob emerged from the en-suite bathroom, his hair damp from the shower and wearing nothing but a pair of shorts. It was hotter tonight than it had been since Hannah had arrived in Spain, and her plan was to strip naked and lie on top of the bedding as soon as he'd gone to bed. Scrumpy sat up from his position on the tiles by the bathroom door, poised and panting to follow Rob to whichever bed he was sleeping in.

'Can I stay here?' asked Rob, like that question hadn't been hanging over them since lunch. Hannah nodded, unable to trust herself to say anything sensible, and scooted over so Rob had plenty of room to wriggle under the sheet. Scrumpy stayed on the cold floor and without him, the gap between them suddenly felt like a canyon of wanting.

'Goodnight,' said Hannah, her voice sounding like air being squeaked from a balloon.

'Sleep well,' said Rob, turning on his side with his back

facing her as Hannah turned off the light. She lay in total stillness for a while, marvelling at Rob's ability to fall asleep so quickly. For her, turning off the light was an invitation for her mind to fill with a million different thoughts and doubts and anxieties, like they'd been waiting patiently for darkness to fall so they could start a party in her brain.

She moved her legs to find a cooler bit of the sheet, listening to Rob's slow, steady breaths, overlaid with the gentle hum of the crickets outside the open window. The mosquito mesh theoretically kept the bugs out, but Hannah knew she'd be covered in bites by morning. She thought about their tennis match this afternoon, alone on Joyce's court for the first time. They'd both played hard and been fiercely competitive, like they were using it as an outlet for all their unrequited passion. Over dinner Barnaby had wanted to talk about his conversation with Luke, and the glances she'd shared with Rob had felt strained and awkward, like both of them had food on their face but neither of them wanted to be the first to mention it. A big, sexy elephant in the room.

Hannah's brain started to play out an imagined scenario between her and Rob, mostly involving him pressing her up against the wall of the tapas restaurant and kissing her hard. The thought made her breathless, so she slowly and carefully slid her hand into her pyjama shorts and dipped a finger into the wetness between her legs. She obviously knew about women getting hot and wet for a man, but it had never really happened with Graham – he couldn't light a barbecue, never mind a fire in Hannah's knickers.

But Rob had kindled something that had been lying dormant for a very long time, since the confused teen years when Hannah had silently touched herself at night, her eyes screwed shut and her head full of muddled thoughts about lust and sin. She had no idea what was going to happen at the end of this road trip, or whether she'd ever see Rob again. But either way she'd lifted the lid on some kind of well of female desire, and she had no intention of screwing it back on again. There was a lot of lost time to make up, after all.

She removed her hand before she lost herself in the moment and woke Rob up, then turned on her side to face him, pulling her knees into her chest. The glow of the full moon through the window cast silvery shadows across the hard muscles of his shoulders and the bumps of his spine. There was a tiny mole on the back of his neck, just below his hairline, and a pink scar across one shoulder blade. Hannah reached out to brush her finger along it, then changed her mind and withdrew her hand – that definitely wasn't going to help the pulsing heat between her legs. But the compulsion to touch him was too strong, so instead she covered the scar with the flat of her palm, resting her whole hand against him as softly as she possibly could whilst still maintaining contact. His skin was smooth and warm, and for a moment she closed her eyes and breathed in and out, just needing a few seconds of human connection before she would absolutely, definitely take her hand away.

'Don't stop,' whispered Rob. Hannah gasped and guiltily buried her hand under her pillow as Rob turned over to face her.

'Hi,' he said with a gentle smile.

'Hi,' said Hannah, hoping he couldn't see her blush.

'That felt nice.'

'I'm sorry,' said Hannah, her mouth feeling like it was full of dust. 'I thought you were asleep.'

'I was,' said Rob, his voice gravelly and full of sleep, 'until you started touching me up.'

Hannah smiled. 'I'm not sure that qualifies.'

'Did you want to talk?' he asked, raising his eyebrows.

'No, it's fine,' said Hannah. 'I think we said all the important stuff yesterday.'

'Right,' said Rob, huffing out a short breath. 'Did you want to get naked instead?'

Hannah laughed, feeling her heart start to pound in her chest. 'Yes, but I'm not sure that's helpful.'

'I wasn't aiming to be helpful,' said Rob, the smile sliding from 'playful' to 'seductive'.

Hannah narrowed her eyes. 'Just out of interest,' she asked, 'have you ever had a woman say no to you?'

Rob's brow furrowed. 'Hmm, good question. I'd need some time to think about it.'

Hannah shook her head. 'You're quite special, you know that?'

'Thank you,' said Rob with a grin. The moment stretched awkwardly between them, and suddenly the gap of white sheet really wasn't very big at all.

'Look,' Rob whispered. 'Maybe now is a good time to remind you that I really like you. Like; a lot.'

'You've said,' smiled Hannah, as a million butterflies started a rave in her belly.

'And just because I haven't had a proper relationship before, doesn't mean I don't ever want one, or that I can't be the person you need. So maybe, if we were invoking the wisdom of ABBA, you could take a chance on me.'

'Right,' said Hannah, wondering what he was actually asking. A minute ago he was asleep, and now they were talking about ABBA.

'I can't promise not to fuck up,' he continued. 'But I CAN promise to try my absolute best.'

Hannah looked at him intently, processing his words and mentally bundling all her reservations into a huge ball and stuffing them under the bed. 'Kiss me,' she whispered.

'Really?' said Rob, his eyes wide.

'Yes,' said Hannah, wondering if her heart might beat out of her chest and splatter all over the duvet. 'I don't care what happens tomorrow or next week or next month, I just want you to kiss me. Do it now, before I change my mind.'

Rob reached over to cup her face, his hand hot and insistent and his eyes never leaving hers. She lifted the sheet to move towards him, her nerves jangling as she anticipated the heat of his lips, his body pressed against hers, and all the things that might happen after that. But before she had the chance to move, Scrumpy bounded onto the bed and wiggled himself firmly between them, his tail wagging frantically as he licked both their faces. He barked happily, and a sliver of light appeared under the door as Barnaby turned on his bedroom light.

'Bleurgh,' said Hannah, batting the dog away. He turned several circles and flumped on the bed between them, before twisting onto his back and offering his belly up for a scratch.

'I guess that's told us,' laughed Rob.

'Clearly quite enough for one night,' said Hannah.

Rob reached over and took her hand, creating a bridge over Scrumpy's belly. 'Well, there's always tomorrow,' he said with a sleepy grin.

'That's true,' said Hannah, lying back on the pillow as the heat of Rob's fingers flowed through her chest into her stomach, then finally came to rest between her legs. She thought about her fourteen years of marriage to Graham, and how nothing – NOTHING – he had ever done in the vicinity of her body had felt as powerfully erotic as having her hand held by this man. The fire inside her burned, and the promise of what might lie ahead tomorrow kept her awake long after Rob had fallen asleep again.

PART FOUR

Love Match

CHAPTER THIRTY-FOUR

'That was painful,' said Hannah. 'I want you to know that that was painful, so that I can remind you again later how painful it was.' They were standing at the edge of Joyce's terrace, a short distance away from the small group intently watching the doubles match currently in progress. It was Joyce and Oscar, another one of her British ex-pat neighbours, against Dominic and Clara the Danish beauty queen, who was deeply average at tennis but seemed to have attracted a crowd of onlookers anyway, all of whom seemed entirely transfixed by her one-shouldered white tennis dress, conker-brown skin, swinging ponytail and endless legs. There was no sign of Clara's husband Eddie, who owned a huge shipping company and apparently spent most of the year in Copenhagen.

'I'm sorry,' said Rob. 'I'm playing as badly as I can without it being obvious, but we needed to get to the final.' Hannah noticed how he kept his eyes fixed on hers, determined not to let them drift to Clara even for a second.

'Why?' said Hannah, putting her hands on her hips and pressing her lips together. She could see the sheen of sweat on his skin and vaguely wondered how many more years she might have to wait before she was allowed to see him naked, or even kiss him without being attacked by a jealous dog. Wars had been fought and won in a shorter time than this courtship.

'Why what?' he asked.

'Why is it SO important to you that you win?' She couldn't help but smile, so he knew she wasn't really annoyed. If she was honest, she was just keeping up this conversation as an excuse to look at him.

'What, today?' asked Rob, furrowing his brow. 'Or generally?'

'Both,' she said. 'Are you always this competitive?'

Rob grinned. 'No. OK, yes. We're still in the final, though.'

'I know,' said Hannah. 'Despite you holding that racquet like it's a golf club.'

'It's because you're such a great player,' said Rob with a hopeful grin. 'Even though I'm pretending to be shit, we still won the semi.'

'Don't start piling on the flattery,' said Hannah, poking him in the shoulder. 'It's just less painful if I get to the ball before you do.'

'I appreciate it,' Rob said. 'Look, I come from a really competitive family. Like, everyone's a high achiever. But I've only ever been good at tennis, so it's hard not to want to win.'

'I get that,' said Hannah gently. 'But this is a friendly competition in my dad's village. And yes, Dominic is awful—' There was a polite round of applause, and they both glanced over to the court. The couples were shaking hands over the net, the match apparently over. '—but we don't need any more drama, and neither does my dad. We *could* just lose gracefully.'

'Fine,' said Rob. 'Understood.'

'Everything's on track,' shouted Dominic, strolling over to join them. He was wearing baggy white shorts and a pink Ralph Lauren polo shirt that still had creases from the packet. 'Clara and I are joining you in the final,' he continued, leering at Hannah.

'Graham, can you help me with a tray of drinks?' asked Clara sweetly.

'I'll help,' said Hannah, not wanting to be left alone with Dominic or let Rob be annexed by Miss Superhot Denmark. She headed over to the drinks table and started to load glasses onto a tray. Clara reluctantly followed, but not before Hannah had spotted her throwing a lustful look in Rob's direction.

'Christ,' muttered Dominic. 'The things I could do to those two. Preferably both at once.' Hannah glanced at Clara and raised her eyebrows. Apparently Dominic didn't care that they could both still hear him.

'Can I remind you that Hannah is my wife?' said Rob through gritted teeth. Hannah smiled, enjoying how well Rob was continuing to play the role of protective husband.

'You don't need to remind me, it's a source of constant pain,' grumbled Dominic, licking his lips. 'I'd argue that Clara's more classically beautiful, but Hannah is WAY hotter. Not that I wouldn't fuck them both, obviously.'

'I'm sorry?' said Hannah, appearing behind him with a jug of white sangria in each hand. 'What did you just say?' Clara joined her with the tray of glasses, giving Dominic a glare of such intensity that he actually recoiled.

'Sorry,' blustered Dominic. 'Just a bit of banter, you know.'

Rob opened his mouth to speak, then closed it again when he saw Hannah's expression, which she hoped communicated that she'd very much got this situation under control.

'Right,' she said. 'Because from where I was standing it sounded really quite offensive.'

'I'll be back in a minute,' muttered Clara, hurrying back to the table on the terrace to dump the tray, then gently taking the jugs out of Hannah's hands before she threw them both in Dominic's face.

'It was just a passing observation,' Dominic said smoothly. 'I forgot that complimenting women isn't allowed these days.'

Hannah glared at him through narrowed eyes, hoping he could feel the loathing seeping from every pore. 'Graham mentioned that you might be interested in a wager,' she said lightly. 'On the final match.'

'I was,' said Dominic. 'But your husband told me he wasn't a gambling man.'

'He's not,' said Hannah. 'But I'm the one asking, not him.' She glanced at Rob, who raised his eyebrows imperceptibly.

'I don't think this is a good idea,' said Clara quickly, putting her hand on Dominic's arm. 'Hannah is a much better player than me.'

'It's fine, you've got ME on your team,' said Dominic, patting Clara's hand. 'Whereas Hannah is stuck with this useless fuckwit.' Rob clenched his fists, and Hannah gave her head a tiny shake. *Leave it*, she silently told him. *I've got this.*

Hannah tossed her hair and turned back to Dominic. 'So what are you thinking? A hundred euros?'

Dominic roared with laughter. 'That's not a wager, that's a barmaid tip. I was thinking more like a grand per couple, winner takes all.'

'Wow,' said Rob, glancing between the two of them. 'That's a bit punchy.'

'Worried your lovely wife can't carry you all the way to

the end?' asked Dominic. 'Perhaps she needs a husband with a little more strength than you.'

'Let's make it two grand, shall we?' said Hannah, folding her arms.

'Well,' said Dominic, giving her a lascivious smile. 'I seem to have woken the tiger, and it turns out she's quite hungry.'

'Dominic, stop this,' snapped Clara. 'You're embarrassing yourself.'

'Clara, this isn't about you, or Graham,' said Dominic rudely, making Hannah wonder what the exact nature of their relationship was. 'You two are just making up the numbers. This is all about me and Hannah.'

'Fine, three thousand euros,' said Hannah, holding out her hand for Dominic to shake. He took it, and Hannah silently prayed that Rob didn't fall over and break an ankle.

'Done,' said Dominic triumphantly. 'I hope you're good for it.'

'Of course,' said Hannah. Rob glanced at her, as if he was wondering where in her tennis outfit she'd tucked three grand he didn't know about.

'Is everything OK?' asked Barnaby, appearing at their side and casting concerned glances at all of them. 'We're all getting a bit thirsty over there.'

'Sorry,' said Hannah, returning to the table to grab the jugs of sangria. 'We're just coming.'

'Can I speak to you for a minute?' asked Rob.

'I'll take those,' said Barnaby tactfully, extracting the jugs from Hannah's hands. He followed Clara over to the table as Dominic gave Hannah a wink and headed into the shade of the lemon trees to light a cigarette.

'What?' said Hannah.

'Come with me,' said Rob, taking Hannah's hand and leading her into Joyce's house.

'Where are we going?' she asked.

Rob said nothing, hurrying through the kitchen and into the front hall. He opened the door to the downstairs bathroom and turned to pull her in, but she stopped in the doorway and held on to the frame.

'Why are you trying to lock me in a bathroom?'

'Because I really need to kiss you. Right now. Please.'

Hannah laughed nervously. 'Why now, specifically?'

'I mean, I've been needing to kiss you all day,' said Rob, sliding his hands around her waist and making her feel like she couldn't breathe. 'Actually for the past two weeks. But that was quite a performance, and now I'm all hot and bothered.'

'You're no better than Dominic,' laughed Hannah, peeling his arms away and holding firmly to the doorframe. 'But the answer is no. I'm not sharing our first kiss in Joyce's bathroom. Someone hasn't flushed the loo, for a start.' She nodded at the floating turd in the toilet, and Rob let go.

'Fine, this was a bad idea,' he said. 'But just to be clear, I will always be better than Dominic. At everything.'

'I'm very glad to hear it,' she smiled. 'Now can we go and win this match?' She could feel the flush of heat through her chest and wished she could tell him how much she wanted him. But they also deserved better than this, and within a few hours they'd have said their heartfelt goodbyes to Barnaby and Scrumpy and be on their own again. She wanted the moment to be right, and they could wait a bit longer.

'OK,' said Rob. 'Let's get this done and then find

somewhere to celebrate.' He gave her a look that she felt in the pit of her stomach. If you could win a match on pure lust, right now she felt like she could take on both the Williams sisters at once.

'What the fuck is this shit?' hissed Dominic as they changed ends at five games to four. 'How come you suddenly know which end of a racquet is which?'

'It's just taken me a while to get warmed up,' shrugged Rob. 'And there's three grand on the line, so it's absolutely in my interests to dig deep.'

'This is a fucking scam,' said Dominic. 'You've totally played me.'

'No,' said Rob firmly. 'This was never about me, remember? Clara and I are just making up the numbers, this is all about you and Hannah.'

'Until YOU suddenly discovered you could hit a ball,' spat Dominic.

'Well, that's your fault for thinking you could win this match all on your own, isn't it?' Rob gave Dominic a broad grin, then strode off to join Hannah on the baseline.

'Are you going to get into a fight?' she asked.

'Nothing to do with me,' he said. 'This is your wager.'

'Shall we finish him off, or take it to a tie break?'

'Let's finish him off,' said Rob. 'We've got other places to be.'

Hannah nodded and readied herself to receive Dominic's thumping serve, rejecting the easy return to Clara's feet in favour of inviting Dominic into a furious rally until Rob could quietly drop the ball over the net. Each point of the final game played out the same way – Rob staying out of the way so Hannah could cover the court, only stepping in to keep the ball in play or finish it off. Fury was making Dominic sloppy and erratic, and five minutes later it was all over.

'You've completely screwed me over,' hissed Dominic, squeezing Rob's hand at the net. Rob forced a smile and Hannah could see him trying not to wince at the attempt to crush his knuckles.

'Don't be such a baby,' said Clara, rolling her eyes at Hannah. 'They beat us fair and square.'

'We'll be leaving in half an hour,' said Hannah coldly. 'Let me know if you'd like my bank details, or if you'd rather pay in cash.'

'I'll pay cash,' muttered Dominic. 'Luckily it's the kind of money I'd blow on a night out.'

'Well done you,' said Hannah witheringly, silently apologising to the local drug dealers for doing them out of a lucrative weekend.

'I'll get it now,' said Dominic, turning to Clara. 'I'll pop down to your place in an hour, yeah?'

'I don't think so,' said Clara, inspecting her manicure. 'I have other plans.'

'What, today?' he asked, a flush creeping up his neck. 'Or more generally?'

'Generally,' said Clara, tossing her ponytail breezily. 'I've reconsidered what I want out of life, and I'm afraid you're not it.'

Dominic pursed his lips and breathed through his nose for a moment, then stalked furiously back towards the house.

'Thanks for the game,' said Hannah, holding her hand out for Clara to shake.

'You play very well,' said Clara. 'It is good for men like

Dominic to realise they cannot have everything they want.' She turned and smiled at Rob. 'That is why Joyce didn't tell him that you are actually Rob the tennis coach.'

'But you knew?' asked Hannah, entirely delighted.

Clara shrugged. 'Of course. Joyce wanted you both to teach her son a little humility, but I don't think she intended it to cost him three thousand euros. You may want to leave before she finds out.'

'Come on,' said Rob, putting his arm around Hannah. 'Let's collect your winnings, then say our goodbyes to your dad and Scrumpy. We've got a road trip to go on.' He grinned and headed over to join the group by the drinks table.

'How is it possible for two people to be so happy together?' said Clara to Hannah wistfully. 'What's your secret?'

Hannah wondered what Clara would say if she told her that she and Rob had never even kissed. 'No secret,' she said, watching him shake her dad's hand and kiss Joyce on both cheeks. 'We just like each other a lot. Since the first day we met.'

'Wow,' said Clara. 'I think I might be pregnant.'

Hannah watched her dad slap Rob on the back, and wondered fleetingly if this was what love felt like. Because if so, she was all in.

CHAPTER THIRTY-FIVE

'So,' said Hannah, as Rob turned east at the junction onto the main road that would take them back towards the Sierra Nevada. 'Just us.'

'Just us,' said Rob, and she could hear the excitement and anticipation in his voice. 'I'll miss Scrumpy, though.'

'He's in the best hands,' she said.

'I really appreciate how cool you've been about all this,' said Rob. He glanced at Hannah and smiled, and she felt her insides start to melt. She needed to get on her phone and book somewhere for them to stay tonight, but she'd left it in her tennis bag so it would have to wait until they stopped somewhere. Would it seem forward if she booked somewhere with just one bed? As far as she was concerned, she and Rob were definitely going to happen, and there was no point wasting any more time worrying about whether he was the great love of her life. She wasn't getting any younger, and two weeks of unrequited desire was now manifesting as a permanent ache in her groin, like a vaginal headache.

'So what's the plan for your winnings?' Rob asked.

'That's a good question,' she said. 'I haven't really thought about it.'

'I can't believe he paid you three grand in cash, like he was fucking Pablo Escobar or something.'

'At least it was all in twenties,' said Hannah. 'So I'm not the woman trying to break a hundred-euro note for two sandwiches and a Coke.'

'Can't you pay it into the bank?'

'Which one?' said Hannah. 'I don't have a Spanish bank account. I'll just use some of it for food and hotels and stuff, then take the rest home and exchange it.'

'You could have asked your dad to put it in his account for you,' Rob mused.

'What, and tell him we gambled three grand we didn't have on a tennis match against his girlfriend's son?' said Hannah. 'He'd think you'd corrupted me.'

'Whoah, it was all your idea,' said Rob gleefully.

'Yeah, well. Dominic deserved it,' muttered Hannah, thinking of the things she'd overheard him saying earlier. 'He was vile. I can't believe Clara was sleeping with him.'

'Some women like that kind of thing,' Rob shrugged. 'Rich guys who fuck and run, no strings.'

'Is that what you do?' asked Hannah, her eyebrows raised. 'Fuck and run?' She hadn't meant the question to sound accusatory, but Rob's face fell.

'No,' he said quietly. 'I've never done that.'

'I'm sorry,' she said. 'I didn't mean it to sound that way. I'm still trying swear words on for size.'

'Also I'm definitely not rich,' said Rob with a small smile.

'Well, I'm feeling quite rich right now,' Hannah said. 'What would you do with this money, if you were me?'

'Hmm,' said Rob, pondering the question as he watched the road. 'I think I'd probably split it into three. Put a thousand into the rest of this trip, so we can stay in nice places, then I'd give a thousand to your dad to cover all of Scrumpy's food and vet bills and travel and stuff. But I'm going to pay that, obviously.'

'Fair enough. What about the other third?'

'If it was me, I'd give it to that dog shelter in Granada,' he said quietly.

Hannah looked at him and smiled, feeling like she'd struck gold. 'That's a great idea. I'll do an online donation when I'm back in the UK. So where shall we go now?'

'I'm saying nothing,' said Rob. 'I've already derailed your trip once, so everything from now on is entirely your choice.'

Hannah thought for a moment. 'Then let's go back to the mountains,' she said. 'Do a few more days hiking, stay in a nice hotel. Just the two of us.' She gave him a significant look and reached over to take his hand, realising that within a matter of hours they would very likely be having sex. The thought filled her with a combination of desire and terror, like a strange fizzing in her belly. What if she wasn't any good? What if fourteen years of Graham had made her sexually incompatible with any other man? What if she just lay there like a plank of wood, not knowing what to do? What if Rob's penis was massive, or tiny? Graham's had seemed like a perfectly normal size – bigger than Michelangelo's David, but smaller than that picture of Orlando Bloom on a paddle board. The only other real one she'd seen belonged to Aaron, and she suspected he might not be within the boundaries of normal.

'You know there's no pressure, right?' said Rob, seeing the uncertainty on her face. 'For us to . . . you know.'

'I know,' she said, squeezing his hand.

'I don't want you to feel—' said Rob, but he was cut short

as his phone rang through the hands-free speakers, making them both jump. 'Shit, that's my mum.'

'You should answer it,' said Hannah. 'It might be important.'

Rob's finger hovered over the button on the steering wheel. 'No, it's fine,' he said. 'She's probably just letting me know they're back from Bermuda. I can call her back later.'

'Rob,' said Hannah, giving him a look. He sighed and rolled his eyes, then answered the call. 'Hey, Mum,' he said.

'Hello, darling,' said a loud, posh woman's voice. 'Is everything OK?'

'Yeah, I'm fine,' Rob said nervously. 'I'm just driving. Where are you?'

'Well, that's the thing. We're at Club Colina – we just flew over to surprise you, but they've told us at the desk that you don't work here any more.'

'Ah,' said Rob, pulling an *oh shit* face at Hannah. 'Right. We should probably talk about that.'

'Well, quite. Where are you?'

'I'm a couple of hours away. I'm with a friend.'

'Oh, how lovely. Is this the woman your father told me about?'

Hannah raised her eyebrows at Rob.

'Um, yeah,' said Rob, clearing his throat. 'It is, actually. Her name's Hannah, and you're on speakerphone.'

'Hello, Hannah,' said Rob's mum cheerfully. 'We'd love to see you both, and we're only here for a few days. Is there any chance you could come back?'

Rob looked helplessly at Hannah, who shrugged and twirled her finger to indicate 'turn around'.

'OK, we'll be back in a couple of hours,' said Rob. 'Are you staying at the hotel?'

'Your father's just sorting that out now. Shall I ask him to book you an extra room? Or two rooms?'

He looked at Hannah, who smiled shyly and held up a single finger. 'One room is fine. Thanks, Mum.'

'All right, we'll see you later. Sounds like we have a lot to talk about.'

'Hmm,' said Rob, looking like he'd rather be horse-whipped. 'See you later. Love you.'

He ended the call before his mum could offer declarations of love in return, and blew out his cheeks. 'I'm really sorry,' he said. 'I totally understand if you want to drop me off at the hotel and do your own thing.'

Hannah smiled, rationalising that a few days of tennis, swimming and those lovely big Club Colina beds might be pretty nice, actually. And meeting Rob's parents might be fun too. 'It's fine,' she said. 'Let's just take a couple of days to relax. We can play some tennis, you can hang out with your mum and dad, and then we'll head off again. We've still got time.'

'Do you mind if I drive slowly? I'm not sure I'm ready to face a lecture from Mum and Dad about getting fired.'

'Right, but that wasn't your fault,' said Hannah. 'Do you think they'll be angry?'

Rob gave a hollow laugh. 'Oh, they won't be angry. They'll be disappointed, which is SO much worse.'

'Ugh,' said Hannah. 'I know how that feels. Pray you never meet my mum, she's QUEEN of "I'm not angry, just disappointed".' She made quote marks in the air with her fingers, and thought about eighteen years of mother–daughter conversations. *We've talked about this, Hannah. It's not your turn to*

300

speak right now. Your yia-yia would be so sad to hear what people in the church are saying.

'I'd actually really like to meet your mum one day. It seems only fair, since you're about to meet mine.'

'Hmm,' said Hannah, picturing the interrogation Rob would get about his family, his career prospects and the role the Lord played in his life. 'Is yours a fervently religious and permanently angry Greek mama who kept a massive secret from her children for the best part of two decades?'

'Well, no,' said Rob, pulling a face. 'Maybe I'll let you sort that out first.'

Hannah looked out of the window as Rob made a U-turn in a dusty lay-by, swapping the view of the mountains for rolling hills and the tiniest sliver of azure-blue sea on the horizon. Very little about this trip so far had been what she'd imagined, but she was here, with Rob, and regardless of which direction they were going in, it still felt like the right place to be.

CHAPTER THIRTY-SIX

'Ready?' said Rob, taking Hannah's hand as they walked through the hotel towards the pool. They'd left their bags in the car, not sure whether they'd be staying in the main hotel or one of the fancy little annexes scattered around the grounds.

'I'm ready,' said Hannah, giving him a smile that made his heart skip a beat. He knew she was also thinking about later, when they'd finally be alone in their hotel room. The anticipation was delicious, but also absolute torture.

He spotted his parents before they saw him, occupying a couple of sun loungers by the pool, both tanned from their trip to Bermuda and soaking up the golden hour before the clock struck gin o'clock and they could acceptably move on to the next phase of the evening. His mother looked up as he approached and shielded her eyes with her hand, before breaking into a huge grin and leaping up to pull him into a hug.

'Hey, Mum,' laughed Rob, prising himself from Kate's grip so he could hug his dad. 'This is Hannah.' He looked at his parents side-by-side and wondered what Hannah made of them. His dad looked handsome and well put-together in navy shorts and a white polo shirt with two-tone deck shoes, a Panama hat casually tossed on the nearby table. But his mum had gone all out in a bright green bikini that had been artfully covered up with some kind of semi-transparent, ethnic print

302

wrap, paired with bejewelled sandals and a huge white sun hat, and finished with a selection of jangly bangles around her elegant wrists. It was a statement poolside outfit, and Rob knew that his mother's choice of clothes was never accidental.

'Hello, Hannah,' said Kate with a warm smile, giving her a much gentler embrace. 'How lovely to meet you. I'm Kate.'

'And I'm Guy,' said Rob's dad, joining his wife and giving Hannah his most dazzling smile. If Hannah was taken aback by their slightly intense parent energy and display of high-end dentistry, she didn't show it.

Rob pondered the performance for a moment, then realised that this was the first time he'd ever introduced a woman to his parents, which was ironic considering that, on this occasion, Hannah wasn't technically his girlfriend. But his mum had clearly decided that they might be meeting 'the one', so they'd both made the effort to look casually glamorous. It was kind of sweet, if a little terrifying.

'It's lovely to meet you both,' said Hannah. 'Rob's told me a lot about you.'

'Your dad will help with your bags, Rob,' said Kate, wafting Rob away. 'Leave Hannah here with me so we can get to know each other a bit.'

Rob nodded, knowing he was now surplus to requirements and Hannah was about to get the Kate Baxter third degree. He wondered what Hannah would say about the nature of their relationship, and how well his mother would take the crushing news that they weren't exactly love's young dream. He gave Hannah an apologetic smile and turned to lead his dad back to the car park, but not before his mother called him back.

'Oh, just so you both know,' she said. 'They were a bit short of rooms.'

'What does that mean?' asked Rob.

'All they had left was the room next to ours,' said Kate with a pained expression. 'So I'm afraid you're both in there.'

Rob glanced at Hannah – her face was unreadable, and he wondered if this whole situation was about to test her reserves of patience and goodwill. Was there some kind of cosmic intervention to stop him and Hannah getting naked in the same time zone? So far the celibacy gods had sent him a scruffy dog and two sets of parents on the other side of paper-thin walls. What next? A flood? A plague of locusts? A yeast infection? Lesser men might have thrown in the towel by now, but Rob had come too far to give up on Hannah now.

'So,' said Guy, his voice intoned with several tonnes of significance. 'Is that the girl who knocked you sideways?'

'She's a woman,' said Rob. 'She's thirty-two.' He lowered his head and picked up his pace through reception, hoping he wouldn't bump into Mark or any of the other coaches.

'Of course,' said Guy, rolling his eyes as he hurried to keep up with his son. 'She's certainly a beauty.'

'She's smart and a brilliant tennis player too,' said Rob, feeling slightly affronted on Hannah's behalf. His dad was old school, where women were decorative first and anything else was a bonus. At some point he was going to have to tell him the truth about his relationship with Hannah, or lack thereof, but the idea of explaining how he'd failed to sweep her off her feet felt kind of mortifying.

'Hmm, sure,' said Guy vaguely. 'And worth quitting your job for, I take it?'

Rob stopped and turned to face his dad, pressing the

button to open the boot of their dusty car. 'I didn't quit. I was fired.'

Guy's abundant eyebrows shot up. 'And how did you manage that?'

Rob sighed heavily and sat on the edge of the boot, raking his hands through his hair. 'Because my boss Mark found Hannah in my room. We weren't doing anything, but he decided it was against his bullshit rules about not shagging the guests.'

'Right.' Guy gave Rob a penetrating look. 'So you got fired for fraternising with a guest, even though you weren't technically fraternising at the time?'

'Pretty much,' said Rob. 'And actually, we're still not fraternising.' He wasn't entirely sure what fraternising meant, but decided to go with it.

'Really?' said his dad incredulously. 'You've spent two weeks in the company of a woman who looks like that, and kept your hands to yourself?'

'Yep,' said Rob, wondering if he qualified for some kind of medal. 'It's not great timing for either of us right now.'

Guy raised his eyebrows. 'Mmm, timing. What a passion-killer.'

'Leave it, Dad,' said Rob, suddenly exhausted. 'It's complicated.'

'Fine, I'll keep my questions simple,' said Guy, hefting Rob's rucksack out of the car and dumping it on the tarmac. 'Do you like her?'

'Yes,' muttered Rob.

'And does she like you? To the best of your knowledge?'

Rob dropped his eyes. 'Yeah.'

'Good start. Are you both single?'

'Yes, but . . .'

'Excellent. So what's your problem?'

Rob thought about it for a second. 'Hannah's not my usual type.'

'What do you mean? She's a knockout.'

'No, I don't mean how she looks. She's . . . different. Like, she's got this whole weird upbringing, and she's just split up with her husband. Only ever been with one guy, very wary of getting hurt.'

'Ah,' said Guy. 'I see.'

'And I don't know if I'm ready to commit. I've never tried it, no idea if I've got what it takes.'

'So you don't want to hurt her either.'

'Definitely not.'

'And why is that?' asked Guy, giving his son a penetrating stare.

'What do you mean?' asked Rob, wondering where his dad was going with this.

'It's a simple question,' Guy said mildly. 'Why don't you want to hurt her?'

Rob shrugged. 'Because I don't like to hurt ANY woman, if I can help it. I always establish what the deal is up front.'

'Good for you. Sensible.'

'And even though Hannah seems OK with a fling, no pressure or whatever, I'm not sure that's true.'

'Right, so you've talked about that.'

'Kind of, I guess. She said she didn't care what happened next week or next month, and we almost . . . kissed, but a dog got in the way. It's a long story.'

'So you've established the deal, like with every other woman. So what's holding you back?'

'I don't know,' said Rob, his brow furrowed and the beginnings of a headache forming behind his eyes. 'This just feels different, somehow. I don't want to fuck it up.'

Guy flumped down on the tailgate beside his son, making the car bounce and creak on its rear axle. 'Is it possible – and bear with me here, because I'm about to put a big, scary idea out into the universe – that you've fallen in love for the first time in your irresponsible playboy life?'

Rob turned to look at his dad with a soft smile. 'Yeah. Maybe.'

'Because if you have, you need to go and tell that girl right now. Before she talks herself out of you altogether.'

Rob nodded, trying to imagine the conversation in his head. He probably should have done it properly when they were talking in bed last night, if he was entirely honest, instead of spouting some old crap about ABBA and hoping it would all just happen naturally.

'I've got one more question,' said Guy, 'then I'll hand you over to your mother for further interrogation. If you were a betting man, would you put money on the possibility of Hannah being the one?'

Rob contemplated it for a moment, thoughts of their imagined life together playing through his head like one of those wholesome, happy-ever-after Netflix movies his sisters watched at Christmas, and he also secretly loved. It made him feel warm inside and inexplicably happy. 'Yeah,' he said. 'I think I would.'

Guy put his arm around Rob's shoulders. 'Well, in that case, it was totally worth getting fired. But promise me you will do everything possible not to fuck this up.'

'Yeah, OK. Thanks, Dad.' They gathered up the bags and

locked the car, then headed back towards the hotel. 'What's your plan while you're here?'

'We didn't really have one.' Guy shrugged. 'We thought you'd be coaching all day, but your mother will be delighted to spend more time with you. Let's all have a nice few days together, get to know Hannah a bit, then we can talk about what's next. We'll pick up the bill.'

'I'm coming home in the next couple of weeks,' said Rob, walking into the air-conditioned cool of reception. 'So I'll find some summer work in Bath, if I can stay with you guys. And I've still got the job lined up in October.'

'Rob?' said a voice. Rob's heart sank as Mark wandered into view from the direction of the lifts, his white polo shirt glowing against his conker-brown arms. *Seriously*, thought Rob. *If he doesn't have a sunbed for an all-over tan, he must have the whitest torso in Spain.*

'Hey, Mark.'

'What are you doing here?'

'Checking in as a guest for a few days,' said Rob, forcing a smile. 'This is my dad, Guy.'

Mark thrust out his hand. 'Pleased to meet you. I'm Mark, I run the coaching operation here.'

'I've heard a lot about you,' said Guy, and Rob stifled the urge to laugh.

There was a brief and deeply awkward silence, then Mark cleared his throat. 'Look, I was going to call you tomorrow, actually. Can you spare ten minutes for a chat in my office?' He rubbed his jaw awkwardly. 'No problem if you can't, obviously.'

Rob considered his options, most of which involved inflicting ritual humiliation and moderate pain. 'Sure,' he replied with a casual shrug. 'I'll just help my dad drop these off in my room.' Mark nodded at them both and strode off, his calf muscles gleaming in the soft lights.

'He's going to offer you your job back, isn't he?' said Guy with a knowing smile.

'Yeah,' said Rob. 'I reckon he is.'

'What are you going to do?'

'Not sure. I'll find out what he wants first, then speak to Hannah. But I'll make him suffer either way, obviously.'

'That's my boy.'

'Look, Rob,' said Mark, his foot jiggling nervously despite his best efforts to sound nonchalant. 'About last Saturday. I might have been a little hasty.'

'A little?' said Rob, his eyebrows making a break for the heavens.

'Yes, a little,' said Mark tersely. 'Tensions were running high, things got a bit heated.'

Rob nodded and folded his arms. 'Right. And this sudden change of heart has been prompted by . . . what, exactly?'

Mark turned his palms upwards. *Here it comes*, thought Rob. 'We got another coach over to take your place, but to be honest he's not a patch on you.'

What a surprise, thought Rob. Any coach available to drop everything and up sticks to Club Colina in May was guaranteed to be shit. 'Right. So what are you asking, exactly?'

Mark sighed heavily. 'I'm asking you to come back for the rest of the season.'

Rob said nothing for a moment, eyeing Mark carefully. 'I'm not sure that's going to work, to be honest.'

'Why not?'

'Because Hannah is going to be staying in the hotel for the next few days.'

'And she's your girlfriend?' sneered Mark, like he'd been right all along.

'No, she's not my girlfriend. But she wasn't my girlfriend a week ago either, and somehow that didn't seem to matter.'

'Olly told me she was gay,' said Mark. 'That true?'

'I'm pretty sure that's none of your business,' said Rob, wondering if that was Olly's attempt to make amends for the problems he'd caused. They stared each other down for a moment, both knowing full well that Rob held all the cards here.

'Right, well. The offer's there, if you want it. I'm not going to beg, obviously.'

'I need to speak to Hannah first. It changes our plans.'

'Fine,' said Mark, standing up and putting his sunglasses back on his head. 'Just let me know by tonight. If you're up for it, I'll send the other coach home tomorrow, and you can pick up with the new group on Sunday.'

Rob nodded, wondering what Hannah would say. It was a chance to get his summer back on track, but it would also mean the end of their road trip together. It felt like their relationship had been teetering on the edge of something new and exciting for the past few days, and the thought of saying goodbye made him feel sick.

CHAPTER THIRTY-SEVEN

'Well, this is lovely,' said Kate, coming back from the bar with two gin and tonics and giving Hannah a warm smile. 'So nice for us to have a chance to get to know each other.'

Hannah forced a smile in return, wondering what Kate would make of her and Rob's slightly unconventional situation. She was also struggling to reconcile a woman who looked as young and fresh as Kate being Rob's mum – only some crepey skin on her chest when she leaned over gave any indication that this was a woman who was pushing sixty, possibly older.

'So, you and Rob make a beautiful couple,' said Kate happily.

'Oh,' said Hannah. 'Thanks.' What else was she supposed to say? *We're not actually a couple and we've never kissed each other, but we were definitely planning to have sex later, before you called.* However open-minded Kate was – and it was reasonable to assume she was considerably more liberal than Hannah's own mother – it still sounded stupid. And the last thing Hannah wanted was to have to *explain*. She sipped her drink, feeling tired and scratchy, but also rationalising that even if they were in the room next door to Kate and Guy, she and Rob would still be alone together, dog-free in a big bed with a whole night ahead of them. They'd just have to be slow and silent, which might actually be kind of amazing.

She shivered at the thought of it, even though the air felt warm and sticky.

'Oh, here's Guy,' said Kate, looking as relieved as Hannah was. 'Where's Rob?'

'He'll be along in a minute,' said Guy. 'We bumped into Mark, who runs the tennis coaching. I think he might be offering Rob his old job back.'

Hannah raised her eyebrows, wondering how that was going to pan out. Hopefully Rob wouldn't lose his temper this time.

'I said I'd show Hannah to their room,' said Guy. 'I've just dropped your bags off, but I'm afraid it's not quite what we'd hoped.'

'What do you mean?' asked Hannah.

'It's not just the room next door, it's an adjoining room,' said Guy apologetically, rubbing his face in a way that reminded her of Rob. 'So it shares our bathroom, and it's got bunk beds.'

'It's got bunk beds,' said Hannah, not sure whether to laugh or cry as Rob hurried in, his face anxious. The tiny room was accessible from the main corridor, but also from a door in Guy and Kate's much bigger room, which they had to use to access the bathroom. 'Actual bunk beds.'

'I'm sorry,' Rob mumbled. 'We can see if we can find something else.'

'No, it's fine,' said Hannah, rummaging in her bag for a bikini and a T-shirt dress. 'There isn't anywhere else, and it's just somewhere to sleep, right?' She fixed him with a challenging stare until he looked away. 'I'm going for a swim, it's fine.' She took her clothes into the bathroom and closed the door behind her.

This situation isn't Rob's fault, she reminded herself, looking at her tired reflection in the huge mirror. *Don't take it out on him*. If she was honest, she'd pinned all her hopes for today on letting Rob take her to bed – no, taking Rob to bed herself – and now that opportunity was gone. The frustration at their situation manifested like a pain in her stomach, weighing down on top of two weeks of intense desire.

'Can we talk?' said Rob from the other side of the door.

'I can hear you,' said Hannah softly, pulling off her tennis skirt.

'I just spoke to Mark,' said Rob. 'He said . . .'

'Is the room OK for you both?' said a high, female voice – Kate had turned up. Hannah pulled on her bikini as fast as possible, then threw the dress on top.

'It's fine, Mum,' said Rob. 'Hannah and I were just talking. Can you . . .?'

'Very narrow beds,' said Kate. 'Especially considering children aren't allowed to stay in this hotel. I suppose it's good for a group on a budget, though, and people who play tennis are usually quite thin.'

'I'm ready,' said Hannah, opening the bathroom door. 'Just off for a swim.' She stuffed her bra and knickers into her bag and grabbed her goggles.

'Oh, good idea,' said Kate. 'Lovely way to freshen up after a long drive.'

Hannah swam lengths of the pool, feeling like a million lifetimes had passed since she'd last swum here. When was that? Ten days ago? In lots of ways it felt like everything had changed between her and Rob, but at the same time nothing had changed at all, really. She'd convinced herself that everything was OK, but he was still a commitment-phobic playboy and she was still one-man Hannah. She was so lost in her thoughts she forgot to look up for the shallow end until she collided into Rob, who was back in the exact spot he'd occupied last time.

'Sorry,' she spluttered. 'Didn't see you there.'

'It's OK,' laughed Rob, wiping the water off his face. 'It looked a bit like angry swimming, so I just wanted to check you were OK.'

'Not angry, just disappointed,' said Hannah with a smile.

'Ouch,' said Rob.

Hannah took a deep breath, then sat on the steps beside him. 'It's lovely for you that your mum and dad are here, but the bunk beds weren't entirely what I had in mind for tonight, that's all. But it's not your fault, and I'm fine about it.'

'I'm really, really sorry,' said Rob. 'It wasn't what I had in mind either. Not by a very long way.' He reached out to touch her arm, and Hannah wondered if he was finally going to kiss her. But she could see Kate and Guy spectating from their pool loungers, gin and tonics in hand, and pulled away.

'Do you fancy a drink?' Rob asked, peering over her shoulder towards the doors to the bar. 'Mum and Dad have opened a bar tab, so we should probably make the most of that.'

'I've already had one,' said Hannah, wishing more than anything that it was just the two of them again. It felt like there was so much to say, and so many feelings to express, and the constant presence of other people felt stifling. Maybe gin was the answer. 'But I'll happily have another.'

'Who IS that guy?' asked Rob, squinting at a figure standing by the door.

'What guy?' Hannah twisted to look in the direction of Rob's gaze.

'The one over there, staring at you.'

Hannah narrowed her eyes, taking in the tall, thin man with floppy brown hair, looking crumpled and sweaty in torn jeans, a faded black T-shirt and bare feet. She marvelled for a moment at how much he looked like her brother Luke, then realised with a jolt of shock that it WAS Luke.

'Luke?' she shouted.

'Oh, thank God, it is you,' said Luke, turning back to shout through the door. 'Dan, I've found her.'

'Is that your brother?' asked Rob, as Guy and Kate leaned forward to see what was going on.

'And his boyfriend,' said Hannah, hurrying up the steps and yanking her dress over her wet head. An acid feeling of panic bubbled in her stomach, like today was spiralling even further out of control.

'Hey,' said Luke, glancing at Rob curiously as he climbed out of the pool and grabbed a towel.

'What are you doing here?' Hannah asked urgently.

'I didn't know where else to go,' said Luke. 'I've been trying to get hold of you all day.'

'Wait, what?' said Hannah. 'Is everything OK?'

'Yeah, we're all good,' said Luke, holding up the palms of his hands to calm her, and checking out Rob again. 'But you haven't been answering your phone.'

Hannah covered her mouth with her hand, remembering

putting her phone in her tennis bag last night, so everything was packed and ready for them to leave straight after the tournament. Rob's phone had been hooked up to the hands-free in the car, and so much had happened she hadn't thought to check if she had any messages or missed calls. 'Why didn't you tell me you were coming?'

'It was a spur-of-the-moment thing – we just decided to come late last night and jumped on a flight this morning. And when we couldn't get hold of you, we came here, thinking someone might know where you'd gone, like maybe you told one of the tennis coaches or whatever.'

'I didn't tell anyone,' she said.

'Yeah, I know that now. So we booked some rooms and thought we'd try you again tomorrow.'

'You and Dan can share a room, Luke,' she said impatiently. 'You don't have to hide that you're a couple; half the staff here are gay. Hi, Dan.'

'Hi,' mumbled Dan, looking like he'd been strong-armed into gatecrashing a party when he'd much rather have been at home watching *Buffy the Vampire Slayer*.

'We ARE sharing a room,' replied Luke, rolling his eyes.

'Then who's the other one for?' asked Hannah, the panic bubble expanding to fill her chest.

'Mum's here.'

'What? Are you kidding?'

'No. She wanted to come so we could all speak to Dad together, we had this whole big heart-to-heart thing last night. But that's not . . . oh shit.'

'Hannah!' sang Elena, appearing through the doors to the hotel in a black maxi-dress with white sleeves and a pair of enormous Jackie O sunglasses, like an orca at a Greek funeral. She shifted to avoid a pool lounger and for a minute Hannah was blinded by the late-afternoon sun, but then another figure appeared in Elena's wake, and the shadow was unmistakeable.

'Graham?' gasped Hannah, grabbing hold of Luke's arm so she didn't pass out.

'Shit, really?' said Rob with a nervous laugh.

'Ah, fuck,' muttered Luke. Guy and Kate took in the whole scene like they had Centre Court seats at Wimbledon, but had no idea who the players were or who was winning.

'Another gin?' muttered Guy.

'Only if you're getting it,' Kate replied. 'I'm not moving an inch.'

'I can probably wait,' said Guy mildly, leaning back in his pool lounger and folding his arms. Hannah waited for any sign that this was a nightmare and she'd wake up soon, but no. This whole scenario was actually happening.

'Excuse us for a second,' she said to nobody in particular, grabbing Graham by the arm and marching him to the far end of the pool, out of earshot. Hannah clocked Elena joining Luke and Dan by the next set of pool loungers along from Guy and Kate. Even the dark glasses couldn't hide the disapproving glances she was throwing in Rob's direction as he re-joined his parents and towelled off. Hannah wondered with a sick feeling of despair what he must think of her and her mad family, but there was nothing she could do about that right now.

'What are you doing here?' she hissed at Graham, angling him so his back was facing the avid spectators.

'I wanted to talk to you,' he said softly, turning his palms up like he was the only reasonable person in their current

317

postcode. His face was pink from the heat and he'd done the top button up on his purple polo shirt, which made his blotchy neck look like a German sausage. Hannah forced herself not to look at Rob, whose thighs were still glistening from the pool, the tanned muscles of his arms rippling as he pulled on a T-shirt.

'About what? We've said everything there is to say.'

'I felt like we should chat again,' said Graham, 'and since Elena was coming over, I thought I would come too. It was an impulse decision.' He puffed his chest out with pride, like being impulsive was a new skill he'd just learned. *Aside from that time you impulsively ejaculated inside Lucy and left her carrying your baby*, thought Hannah. 'She didn't want to travel alone,' he added, giving her his most caring smile.

'She wasn't alone,' said Hannah. 'Luke and Dan are here.'

'Well,' said Graham, raising his eyebrows significantly. 'That bit of news was a shock, along with everything else. I thought she could do with the moral support.'

Hannah narrowed her eyes. 'Why moral support, Graham, and not just support? What's morality got to do with it?'

Graham blushed. 'I didn't mean—'

Hannah shook her head dismissively. 'Forget it. Now isn't the time.'

'You're twisting my words,' Graham spluttered.

Hannah put her hands on her hips and held her ground. 'And you're interfering in my family business.'

'They're my family too.' His voice became whiny and wheedling, and Hannah briefly wondered how Lucy felt about being left pregnant and alone in the UK while the father of her unborn child dashed across Europe to plead with his estranged wife.

'No, they're not,' she said firmly. 'Not any more. You've got a new one on the way, remember?'

'Look, this isn't about them,' said Graham, clearly realising that the clock was ticking on Hannah's patience. 'It's about us.'

'What about us?' asked Hannah, glancing over Graham's shoulder. Rob was sitting on the tiled terrace next to his dad's sun lounger, his arms resting on his knees and his hands clasped. He had sunglasses on so Hannah couldn't see him watching, but she knew she and Graham were firmly in his gaze. Elena, meanwhile, had removed her giant sunglasses and was still casting radioactive glances at Rob and his parents. Luke and Dan had disappeared, no doubt ordering drinks at the bar and staying away from all the drama.

'I just think us splitting up was a bit hasty,' said Graham.

'You got another woman pregnant, Graham,' Hannah said with a hollow laugh. 'I'm guessing that was pretty hasty too.'

'Don't be vulgar,' he snapped, his neck deepening to the colour of a boiled ham. 'I made a mistake, I admit, but it doesn't change how I feel about you. I've had time to reflect.'

'And what about Lucy? Where does she fit in? And the baby?'

'They don't,' said Graham. 'I'll support the child financially, obviously, but Lucy and I are never going to make it work as a couple. She's nothing compared to you.' His lip wobbled, and Hannah could see that an emotional outpouring wasn't far away.

'You're revolting,' she spat, wondering how she could ever have thought staying with Graham was better than literally any alternative. 'You can't just pick women up and then throw them away when things get messy.' She thought briefly of Rob, and how she'd assumed he was that kind of man. But actually he was nothing like Graham. Nothing at all.

'Don't say that,' said Graham, tears rolling down his face. 'I love you, Hannah. I'm nothing without you.' He put out his arms and tried to pull her into a hug, but Hannah wriggled free. Graham sobbed and grabbed her arm, desperate not to let her go.

'Don't,' she said, wrestling her arm away. 'This isn't going to happen, Graham. You need to leave.'

'Is everything OK?' asked Rob, appearing suddenly at Hannah's side, his chest heaving like he'd sprinted from the other side of the pool.

'Who are you?' asked Graham, taking in the rippling arms and broad shoulders. 'This is a private conversation.'

Oh shit, thought Hannah, trying internal swearing for the first time. There'd never been a better time, frankly.

'I'm a friend of Hannah's,' said Rob, very obviously giving Graham the once-over. She could only imagine what he'd make of this pale, paunchy, red-faced man.

'Well, I'm her husband,' snarked Graham.

'Ex-husband,' hissed Hannah through gritted teeth. She looked at her feet and silently cursed Rob for getting involved. Although in fairness to him, she could see why he'd be reluctant to sit on a pool lounger and watch Graham yank her around.

'Right, so what is this, exactly?' demanded Graham, glaring at Hannah, and then Rob. 'Have you met someone else already?'

'How DARE you ask me that question,' shouted Hannah, waving her hands in her face like she was fighting off a swarm of bees. 'YOU of all people.'

'That's not fair. I've come all this way . . .'

'NO,' said Hannah. 'I'm done with this conversation, I'm not talking about this any more.' She turned to Rob and met his gaze. 'What did Mark want?'

'Sorry, but who's Mark?' interrupted Graham. 'Whoever you are, can you go away? I'm having a private conversation with my wife.'

'Hannah, darling,' said a loud voice, as Elena wafted into view. She'd clearly been on the fringe of this drama long enough and needed to get involved, particularly now Rob had joined the party and added a new layer of intrigue.

'Mum,' said Hannah breathlessly. 'Can we talk later?'

'You look wonderful,' said Elena, patting her daughter on the arm. 'The Mediterranean sun agrees with you, you should spend more time with your family in Crete.'

'Yeah, sure,' said Hannah. 'But right now I need to . . .'

'Luke is here too,' Elena said, stepping to one side to make room for Luke and a mutinous-looking Dan, both clutching bottles of beer behind her. 'He's brought his friend Dan.'

'I know, Mum, I saw him ten minutes ago.' Hannah could hear the strain and exhaustion in her own voice, but she couldn't let this go. 'And Dan's his boyfriend, not his friend.'

'Well, it's all the same,' said Elena airily, as Luke gave Hannah a glare and a shake of his head.

'No, it isn't,' said Hannah. 'It's not the same at all.'

'I don't think now is the right time to talk about this,' said Graham.

'Shut UP, Graham,' said Hannah. 'This has nothing to do with you, and you're just as bad as Mum.'

'It's fine,' Luke mumbled.

'NO,' shouted Hannah, holding her hands up. 'None of this is fine. I can't deal with all this SHIT. ANY. MORE.'

Elena gasped and clamped her hands over her mouth. 'Hannah,' she shrieked. 'What's happened to you? Why are you talking like this?'

'I've fucking had enough,' said Hannah, tears spilling over. 'This trip was supposed to be about ME, taking some time for MYSELF, and I CANNOT FUCKING DEAL with ALL. YOUR. SHIT.'

Everyone stared at her, not knowing what to do. Graham moved first, reaching out to touch her arm, but she snatched it away.

'Luke,' she said softly, turning to her brother. 'I'm really glad you're going to see Dad, but I can't come with you right now. Mum, go with Luke and talk things through as a family; it's long overdue. Rob will give you his address.' Everyone turned to look at Rob, who cleared his throat awkwardly. Graham's eyes narrowed to tiny slits.

'Graham,' Hannah continued, 'please go home to Lucy. You've got a baby on the way and that's a huge deal whether you like it or not. Our marriage is over, and that's my final decision. You're wasting your time trying to talk me out of it.' Graham stared mutinously at his shoes as Hannah turned to Rob.

'Rob, I'm sorry, but I need some space right now. Hang out with your mum and dad, sort out everything with Mark, but I'm taking some time out on my own.' He gave her a look of such calm and understanding, for a moment she felt like she'd been hollowed out.

'OK,' he said with a firm nod. 'I'll put your bag back in your car.'

'Thank you,' said Hannah, breathing out slowly as she addressed the whole group. 'I'm sorry to leave like this, but I've been on a crazy journey for the past month, and I just need some time to process it all.'

'But . . .' said Elena, glancing at Graham. 'Don't you think . . .?'

'No,' said Luke firmly, putting his hand on his mother's arm. 'We can go and see Dad tomorrow, we don't need Hannah there. Let her do whatever she needs to.'

'I'll call you in a few days,' said Hannah, leaning forward to kiss her mum and her brother on both cheeks. She touched Graham briefly on the shoulder, but he wouldn't even look at her, so she gave Luke a helpless glance before heading through the hotel to the car park. She waited by the car, taking deep breaths until Rob appeared with her bag.

'Are you OK?' he asked, putting it in the boot and handing her the keys.

Hannah nodded, her arms wrapped around herself in a way that probably looked defensive to Rob, but was actually more about physically holding it together. 'I'm sorry to run away like this. It's not you, I promise. I just need some time out.'

'That's OK,' he said. 'I understand. Are you coming back?'

Hannah looked at him and swallowed, her eyes tracing his face in the hope of committing it to memory. 'I'll say goodbye before I go,' she said. 'What did Mark say?'

'He's offered me my job back,' said Rob. 'I guess I should probably take it.'

Hannah nodded. 'That's good news. And yeah, you should.'

They stared at each other for a moment, the air heavy

with unsaid things. Rob looked away first, and Hannah knew it was time to go.

'You know where I am,' he said, reaching out to squeeze her hand. In another version of this story she would have fallen into Rob's arms and kissed him, but that wasn't how their story was supposed to end. Hannah had been hiding from that truth all week, but she knew it now.

'I do,' she said. 'Enjoy the time with your parents.' She slid into the driver's seat and started the car, then lowered the window. 'It's been a really fun week,' she said.

Rob smiled and nodded. 'Yeah,' he said. 'It's been amazing.'

'I'll see you soon,' said Hannah, pressing her lips together as she drove away. The tears were already rolling down her face before she reached the exit to the car park, and when she looked in her rear-view mirror Rob was still there.

CHAPTER THIRTY-EIGHT

Hannah sat on the dry, brittle grass that formed a natural step at the base of the mountain, trying to imagine what this would look like covered in snow. The pylons of the ski lift stretched away into the distance, the metal chairs presumably stored somewhere for the winter. Dry, stony paths down the hillside showed her where the pistes would usually be, scattered with metal arrows and striped poles that she guessed had some kind of job during the ski season, but in summer just made the hillside look like a busy road junction. Hannah had never been skiing before, so she had no useful point of reference.

She turned to look the other way, but the view was no better. Huge machines covered with tarpaulins were parked next to a long plastic tunnel that stretched from the lift station to the car park, like the kind of structure Sainsbury's used to store shopping trolleys. Presumably when the owner of her B&B said 'the Sierra Nevada ski resort is beautiful for walking in summer', she hadn't meant this particular bit that looked like a B&Q delivery yard.

Her eyes followed the line of the ski lift up into the distant peaks, trying to gauge how far it was. A mile to the top, maybe? Half an hour of hard uphill walking if she followed the dusty path that ran parallel to the pylons. Her trainers would be fine, and she had plenty of water in her rucksack.

She could see the scars of other paths at the top that would bring her back via a different route – presumably they all ended up back here eventually. Pity her legs felt like lead.

Get it together, she chided herself. She'd made the decision to leave Rob at Club Colina three days ago, and it had definitely felt like the right thing to do. So why was her head still full of him? Why had she spent pretty much every minute since she'd left reliving every conversation, every glance, every moment spent in his company? It felt like everything had conspired against them from the beginning, and the universe had offered up precisely zero signs that they were meant to be together.

And yet. There was still this *feeling*, this hot, tangled weight in her chest whenever she thought about the way Rob had looked at her as she drove away. She'd felt it when he held her hand at her dad's house, even though that was just pretend, and she'd felt it in bed when she put her hand on his warm back and they'd nearly kissed. That definitely wasn't pretend, was it? It was hard to pick apart the real moments from the fake ones, or at least what had been fake for Rob. For her it had felt like they'd ALL been real, albeit weighed down by doubt and uncertainty. She'd gone out of her way to avoid getting hurt, and yet here she was on the side of an ugly mountain in Spain feeling nothing but pain.

She'd walked countless miles in the past two days, through scrubby forests and shadeless vineyards and sweltering canyons and tiny villages, pushing up hills like her heavy heart could be healed by burning thighs and a sweaty back. But it just dulled the feeling into something more like sadness. Hannah didn't really do sadness; she'd never been one to wallow in self-pity. Which was a miracle, really, considering her mother hadn't smiled for the best part of two decades.

She unzipped the front pocket of her rucksack and pulled out Rob's note, which she'd found in her bag when she checked into her B&B late on Friday night. It had obviously been scribbled in a hurry when he collected her stuff from their room, with each letter slanted so far forward it looked like it was tumbling into the next one like a row of dominoes. A left-handed thing, presumably.

I'm sorry this hasn't worked out and I hope your trip gets better now. Thanks for letting me tag along. Rob x

It was hardly Shakespeare, but Hannah could feel the pain and sadness there too. She'd analysed the words for hours, trying to work out if the first sentence meant he was sorry the trip hadn't worked out, or whether he was referring to things between them. A comma would have helped, but just because Rob hadn't included one didn't mean it wasn't there in spirit. He was dyslexic and in a hurry, right?

But there were other things that he could have written that were notably not there. *I'll miss you. I wish you weren't leaving. I'll be here when you get back. I don't want this to be the last time I ever put a note in your bag, and I want us to trust ourselves and the power of the universe that we can make this work.* Hannah snorted with hollow laughter at her desperate need for a Disney ending and stuffed the note back in her rucksack, feeling the rough fuzz of the tennis ball against the tips of her fingers. She pulled it out and looked at the smiley face Rob had drawn on it in the same scribbled biro. Huge wide eyes with long lashes, a round nose like a clown, and a huge half-moon of a smile, with the words 'HAVE A BALL' written in capital letters underneath. It was kind of adorable; a reminder that

327

even in a moment of sadness, he could still be the playful, cute Rob she'd been drawn to in the first place.

She pulled out her phone and opened WhatsApp. Rob had an account; she could see from the annoyingly upbeat *Hey There! I am using WhatsApp* in her contacts list. But they'd never exchanged a message so it was just a blank page with a timecode at the top. *Last seen today at 03:42.* What was he doing looking at his phone at that time? Couldn't sleep? Or just got in from a night with some other woman? For a second the pain in her chest felt like a knife, then subsided to a dull ache again. This wasn't the first time she'd looked at the tiny timecode since she'd left on Friday, which definitely wasn't healthy behaviour. She should delete his number really, so she couldn't look at it any more. He still had hers, so he knew how to get in touch. Surely even he could write a text message if the occasion really called for it?

She hadn't spoken to anyone for two whole days, she realised. Other than the couple who ran her B&B, who didn't speak much English, and a young woman in a local supermarket who'd asked her if she'd wanted a bag for her pathetic selection of cheese and meat and bread and wine. In Spanish at first, because presumably Hannah's olive skin and dark hair made her look like a local. But then the woman had clocked Hannah's UK bank card and switched to English, to which Hannah had nodded and smiled in thanks, so actually that didn't even count as a conversation.

Hannah logged out of Rob's page and scrolled through her WhatsApp chats. A message from Luke, saying they'd arrived at Dad's and all was fine, and that he'd call her in a day or two. Nothing from her mother – she'd still be angry and judgemental about her storming off. Nothing from Graham either; she had no idea if he'd gone home or was still dragging his emotional baggage around Spain. Her dad had sent a message two days ago saying *Luke, Dan and Elena here, Scrumpy fine, hope you're OK.* Clearly Luke had filled him in on the Club Colina drama, so she'd replied with *All good, sorry I'm not there but this is your show now.* He was probably still reeling from a visit from his ex-wife, a son he hadn't seen in seventeen years, and his son's largely mute-but-extremely-fit boyfriend.

Who else could she talk to? Sam? She'd never burdened him with the heavy stuff, and she'd have to fill him in on all the background to the situation with Graham, which felt too exhausting. Hannah had never cultivated strong friendships; she'd always been happier alone. Until the trip to Club Colina, anyway – drink-spiking incident aside, that had been one of the best weeks of her life.

I need you guys, she typed into the TITS On Tour WhatsApp group. *Got myself in a bit of a mess, anyone around for some poolside therapy?*

A minute went by before Jess replied. *I can talk now? Just out of yoga.*

Me too, added Trish. *Am in Waitrose car park but nothing frozen.*

Don't you dare fucking start without me, typed Gaynor. *I'm in a meeting will tell them it's a family emergency give me 5 mins.*

Hannah smiled and turned her face to the sun while she waited, taking slow breaths and trying to get her thoughts in order. What did she want from them, exactly? She waited for the ringtone that invited her to a video call, then smiled for the first time in days at their collection of beaming faces.

'Where are you?' asked Jess, scanning the backdrop of blue sky and rocky grass behind Hannah for clues. 'Is Rob there?'

'No, it's just me. I'm on a hiking trail in the Sierra Nevada. I'm actually in the ski resort right now.' She turned her phone around and gave them a full 360 of the car park and the pylons.

'Looks like Woking,' said Trish.

'Why are you alone on a mountain, like Maria in *The Sound of Music*?' asked Gaynor. 'Where's Captain Von Rob?'

Hannah took a deep breath. 'He's with his parents, back at Club Colina. Hopefully not beating the shit out of Graham.'

'Wait, what?' said Jess, as the three women looked at her in wide-eyed horror. 'Graham's there?'

'Yeah,' said Hannah. 'Well, he was. He turned up on Friday with my mum. And my brother.'

'Holy shit!' squealed Gaynor. 'What the fuck happened?'

'That's why I'm currently alone in the mountains,' Hannah said. 'It all got a bit much. I haven't told you about seeing my dad yet.'

Trish squinted in confusion. 'Your dad? Wait, I didn't even know you had a dad.'

Hannah shrugged. 'Yeah. It's a long story.'

Jess laughed. 'Mate, we only left you, what, nine days ago? And now both your parents are in Spain, and your brother, and your ex-husband. And you still haven't told us about what happened with Rob.'

'You forgot my brother's boyfriend,' said Hannah.

'Fuck, this has gone full *EastEnders*,' said Gaynor. 'Isn't your brother about twelve?'

'He's eighteen,' laughed Hannah, already feeling the tension

330

in her shoulders start to ease. She should have called these guys days ago.

'Hang on, did you say Rob's parents were there too?' asked Trish.

Hannah nodded and rolled her eyes. 'They turned up a couple of hours before my family. We had no idea any of them were coming, so the whole thing was . . . a lot.'

'Jesus Christ,' muttered Jess.

'He's yet to make an appearance, but it's still early days.' Hannah rubbed her eyes with her left hand, realising what an absolute circus her life was right now. She was exhausted, but even saying this stuff out loud made her feel infinitely better.

'So what do they all want?' asked Gaynor, popping the tab on a can of Diet Coke on her desk and slurping it down.

'Lots of things,' said Hannah with a sigh. 'It's complicated. But before this all kicked off Rob and I were in an OK place, and now we're not.'

'An OK, horizontal place?' asked Gaynor, complete with eyebrow theatre.

'No,' said Hannah. 'Just a good place. We were working things through, deciding if we wanted to take the plunge.'

'I can't believe you spent a whole week with Rob and there was no plunging,' said Gaynor. 'Trish would have been like "plunge me now" within the first hour.'

'I would NOT,' said Trish, outraged. She was quiet for a moment, then smiled. 'Yeah, OK. Maybe I would.'

'Han, forgive me for being blunt,' interrupted Jess. 'But if you two spent a whole week together and still couldn't decide you were a thing, is it possible it's just not meant to be a thing?'

Hannah nodded sadly. 'I know. You're right, but I'm finding it really hard to let go. Because, you know, for a minute there I thought maybe it was going to work out.'

'Tell me about it,' muttered Trish. 'It's all fucking golden until they say "it's just not what I'm looking for right now" or some other bullshit.' The words felt like salt being rubbed into the open wound of Hannah's heart, and she had to blink frantically to stop herself crying. She hardly ever cried, but right now she felt like a leaky tap. What was wrong with her?

'So what are you going to do now?' asked Jess.

'I don't know,' Hannah said. 'Mark's given Rob his old job back, so he'll be staying in Spain for the rest of the season. I couldn't handle all the family drama so I've run away.'

'Don't blame you,' said Jess. 'Sometimes you need a bit of space. Like, when Tim is working away I sometimes book a babysitter for a couple of hours, then just go and sit in the car at the McDonald's drive-thru and eat a bacon double cheeseburger while I watch *Real Housewives* on my phone.'

'You're fucking joking,' laughed Gaynor.

'Nope,' said Jess. 'Did it last week while he was at a conference in Birmingham.'

Hannah cleared her throat. 'Guys, I need your help. What should I do?'

Gaynor shook her head. 'Mate, you can't stay in Spain for ever, wandering the mountains like a fucking goat. It's not safe on your own, for a start.' Jess and Trish both nodded in agreement, their expressions full of concern. 'You either need to go back to Club Colina and sort stuff out with Rob, or come home.'

'I'm not ready to go back,' said Hannah quickly. 'I need

some space for a bit. And Jess is right; I really don't think Rob and I are going to work out.'

'Well then, you know what to do,' said Trish. 'We'll be here, we can help you find the right person whenever you're ready.'

Hannah nodded, thinking about how nice it would be to sleep in her own bed. She wasn't due back at work for another two weeks, so she could give the house a belated spring clean, clear out the rest of Graham's stuff. Maybe do some work on the garden. Actually, a bacon double cheeseburger and some *Real Housewives* wouldn't go amiss either. Graham thought it was mindless trash TV and insisted he was allergic to bacon, even though he'd eaten about eight of his mother's pigs in blankets last Christmas and lived to tell the tale.

The other women said nothing, watching her carefully.

'OK,' she said. 'I'm coming home.'

Jess and Trish both smiled in relief as Gaynor clapped her hands. 'Good decision. I'll book a ladies' doubles court for Thursday night, get you back where you belong, kicking all our arses.'

'I'll be there,' said Hannah, waving at them all before ending the call. Up to now she hadn't thought about going back to Surrey early, but now it felt like the right place to get her head in order and properly process everything that had happened. She and Luke and her mum could talk about the whole situation with her dad and make a fresh start as a family. She could get back to work, throw herself into the summer plan with Sam at her side to keep her sane. She could get over Rob and get on with her life.

Hannah stood up and stretched her tired limbs, then

hoisted her rucksack onto her back. She took a deep breath, then pulled her phone out of her pocket and deleted Rob's number before she changed her mind. Her hand shook a little and her heart started to race, so she opened and closed her fists and took deep breaths until she felt calmer. One final glance at the vista of mountains under a cloudless blue sky, then she picked her way down the slope towards the car.

CHAPTER THIRTY-NINE

'You all right, Reverend?' sneered Olly, punching him in the shoulder. 'Glad to be back? Missing your girlfriend? What was her name again?'

'Fuck off, Olly,' Rob muttered. 'You're incredibly boring. You know that, right?'

Olly grinned. 'Yeah, but at least I don't have to suck Mark's dick to keep my job.'

'You're pathetic,' said Rob. 'Just leave me alone.'

Olly barked out a laugh, then swaggered off to annoy someone else. It was lunch break from coaching, and Rob had taken himself away from the group to sit on his own by the bar on the terrace. He turned his back and hunched over his phone so he didn't have to make eye contact with Shauna, an incredibly fit woman who was part of a group of eight women from Glasgow. She'd been flirting shamelessly with him since their first session two days ago, and at some point between now and the end-of-week party on Friday he was going to have to make his lack of interest extremely clear because she definitely couldn't take a hint.

He stared at Hannah's WhatsApp page, wondering if he should break the seal and write something. Her profile picture had disappeared for some reason, which made him feel a bit sad. It was the only picture he had of Hannah, other than a photo of her and Keith holding the Club Colina tournament cup from two weeks ago, which was pinned on the noticeboard in the clubhouse under a printed header saying 'This season's winners'. He'd almost written her a message a couple of nights ago, when he couldn't sleep and found himself staring at her smiling face at nearly four in the morning. Then her timestamp had said she'd last seen her WhatsApp at midnight, but now the time was gone too. Maybe she'd changed her settings so he couldn't stalk her?

'Rob?' said a soft, male voice that definitely didn't sound like Olly. Rob turned to find Luke standing a metre away, his arms wrapped round his skinny body. Dan shuffled awkwardly a little further away, his fists buried deep in the pockets of his pastel green shorts.

'Hey, Luke,' said Rob, standing up to greet him. 'I didn't realise you were still here.'

'Got back from Dad's this morning,' said Luke. 'We thought we'd stay for a couple more days before heading home, make a proper trip of it. Can we catch up for a beer later?'

'Course,' said Rob. Luke had less of his mother's colouring than Hannah – he looked like a skinnier version of Barnaby. But the tilt of his chin, the way he held himself upright and made eye contact – that was just like his sister.

'Where's good for you?' said Luke. 'We don't have any plans this evening.'

'Let's go to the Luna Lounge,' said Rob, spotting Olly across the terrace, breaking his neck to see who Rob was talking to. 'It's a nice bar just down the hill; it will be pretty quiet on a Tuesday.'

'OK,' said Luke. 'What time?'

'Six?' said Rob. 'I've got a private lesson at four, so I'll be done by five.' It was the second of four private lessons Shauna had booked for this week, because apparently her lust for Rob had no price tag.

Luke nodded and smiled softly. 'See you then.' He mooched off towards the hotel with Dan in tow; Rob watched them lean their heads together to chat as they walked, then Luke briefly reached out to squeeze Dan's hand as they laughed together. It made Rob's heart hurt watching them like that, and he realised that a beer with Luke later was the closest he was going to get to Hannah until she got in touch to say goodbye.

'Where's your mum?' asked Rob, half-expecting Luke and Dan to still be trailing Elena and Graham, along with a whole host of other family members they'd picked up along the way. Maybe a long-lost sister or a weird cousin.

'She came with us to see Dad, then got a taxi to the airport,' said Luke, taking a sip of his beer.

'How did the family reunion go?' Rob asked.

Luke shrugged. 'It was OK. Pretty intense, but we talked about lots of stuff. There was a lot of crying and hugging.'

'Well, that's a good start. Any big drama?'

Luke sighed. 'Loads, but nothing we didn't already know. Mostly stuff they should have talked about at the time, really. Dad said sorry for the affair about a thousand times, and Mum apologised for not being stronger when the church leaders moved in on her. The whole situation was really fucked up.' Rob nodded but said nothing, giving Luke the space to keep talking.

'I'd always assumed she was angry about what Dad did,' Luke continued. 'But actually I think she was just kind of sad. Under different circumstances I think they probably would have just split up like a normal couple, and we'd have spent time with both of them.'

'Yeah,' said Rob. 'Are you glad that it's all out in the open now?'

'Definitely,' said Luke. 'I'm not angry with Dad any more, anyway. He properly messed up, but he's paid for that ten times over.'

'And how was it for you, Dan?' asked Rob, pointing his bottle in Dan's direction.

'Mental,' muttered Dan. 'Like, Jeremy Kyle-level mental.'

Rob laughed. 'What about Graham? What happened to him?'

'He didn't come,' said Luke. 'Stayed here for one night, kicked off about being allergic to the bedsheets, then flew home the next morning.'

'Have you heard from Hannah?' Rob asked, unable to keep it in any longer.

'Yeah, she messaged me yesterday,' said Luke. 'She's OK.'

Rob breathed out slowly, glad that Hannah was alive and well even if it wasn't him she wanted to speak to.

'Look,' said Luke, leaning forward and resting his forearms on the table. 'I don't want to stick my nose in or anything, but what happened with you guys?'

Rob shrugged and peered into his beer bottle. 'What did your dad say?'

'Not much,' Luke replied. 'He just asked where you and Hannah were, and I told him about her having a meltdown at the hotel. He said something about how she did the right thing taking the chance, even if it didn't pay off.'

'Yeah,' said Rob, draining his beer and waving at the barman for three more. 'That makes sense.'

'So what's the deal? Are you and Han, like, a thing?'

'No,' said Rob. 'We could have been, I think, but the timing wasn't right. For either of us.'

'Why not?' Luke's eyes had a wide-eyed innocence, and for a moment Rob wished he could be eighteen again. Maybe he'd do things differently second time round.

'She's not ready for another relationship after Graham, and definitely not the type for a holiday fling.'

'And what about you?'

'I've only ever done holiday flings, and am not nearly adult enough for a relationship.'

Luke laughed. 'What are you, like, thirty?'

'I'm twenty-eight.'

'Right,' said Luke, and Rob caught the mocking tone in his voice.

'It's not that I don't want to,' said Rob, 'and obviously Hannah is great. I'm just not sure I've got what it takes, and I don't want to hurt her.'

'Sorry, but that's bollocks,' said Luke, and Rob caught a waft of Hannah's fiery spirit.

'What?'

'It's bollocks. I know I'm biased or whatever, but my sister is AMAZING.'

'I know that,' Rob said softly.

'She pretty much helped Mum raise me, and made sure it was a normal life rather than the crazy shit she had to deal with. She lasted fourteen years married to Graham, who is a boring fuckhead, she's brilliant at her job, and, I don't know, the best female tennis player in Surrey or something.'

'I know that too,' said Rob, even more softly.

'Like, she commits to EVERYTHING and never lets

anyone down. Why wouldn't you make the effort for someone like that? She's an entirely fucking kickass human being.'

Rob nodded, feeling his heart start to pound in his chest. 'I know you're right,' he said, picking anxiously at the label on his beer bottle. 'But what if SHE'S not ready for someone like me?'

Luke shook his head and rolled his eyes. 'Seriously, Rob. Are you really that stupid? Like, she worried about you so much she got you fired. She invited you on her road trip, despite you clearly being an untrustworthy fuckboy. She completely changed her plans for your fucking DOG.'

Rob laughed nervously. 'How did you know about all that?'

'Dad told us the whole story. About how you messed up dinner and roped in Clara and everything. And we met Joyce, she was cool.'

'Yeah, we liked Joyce too,' said Rob.

'Although she said something about Hannah screwing her son over for three thousand euros which Dad didn't know anything about.'

'Hmm,' said Rob, shrugging like he didn't have a clue. 'Not sure what that's about. How's Scrumpy?'

'He's amazing,' said Luke. 'Follows Dad everywhere.' He paused for a second then turned to Dan, his eyes wide. 'That feels weird. Saying "Dad" like this whole situation is completely normal.' Dan replied with a smile of such love and warmth, and the connection between them made Rob want to cry. Why could other people do this, even two guys who were practically kids, but not him?

'He emailed me all Scrumpy's notes from the vet visit,' he said. 'I should be able to send him home in a month or so.

My mum and dad will take him as soon as your dad's had enough.'

'I think Dad will be fine,' said Luke with a smile. 'Anyway, you've changed the subject. What are you going to do about Hannah?'

Rob shrugged and sighed heavily, trying to organise his thoughts. 'Talk to her, I guess. Tell her how I feel and hope she hasn't given up on me. Although . . .'

'Although what?' asked Luke.

Rob pulled out his phone and opened his WhatsApp. 'I've never messaged your sister, I'm not very good with texts,' he said awkwardly. 'But I could see on WhatsApp when she'd last been online, and her photo. But now both the time thing and the photo have gone.' He turned the phone to show Luke and Dan, who both leaned over to inspect the screen.

'She's deleted you,' mumbled Dan.

'What?' asked Rob, his eyes wide.

Dan shrugged. 'She's deleted you. That's what it looks like on WhatsApp when someone deletes your number.'

'Oh wow,' said Rob, the disappointment twanging around in his stomach like a ball of elastic bands. 'She said she'd say goodbye before she went back to the UK, so I'm hoping she might come back here.' He could hear the pathetic, last-ditch hope in his voice, but now wasn't the time to pretend everything was fine.

Luke shook his head. 'Mate, I'm sorry. She flew back to the UK last night, she called me from the airport.'

Rob half-laughed, then rubbed his hands across his face and raked them through his hair, pushing the heels of his palms into his eye sockets. He thought back to the day in the canyon, when Hannah had leaned back on the rock in her underwear and screamed swear words at the sky. How she'd taken the whole Scrumpy thing in her stride, how she'd placed that warm, soft hand on his back. He'd been scared to fall in love, but now he realised that ship had long sailed and taken Hannah with it.

'I've really fucked this up, haven't I?' he mumbled to no one in particular.

'Yup,' said Dan, draining his beer.

'Nah,' said Luke. 'It's not your fault. If Hannah's deleted your number and gone back to the UK without saying goodbye, it's because she'd made a decision. She doesn't do impulsive stuff. Not when it's important, anyway.'

'Yeah, I noticed,' said Rob, thinking about how she'd invited him on her road trip. That was impulsive, wasn't it? But maybe not important, after all. 'So what do I do now?'

'Only one thing you can do,' said Luke. 'Same as what we told Graham. Respect her decision and leave her be.'

'But—' Rob frantically searched for loopholes in that plan, but came up with nothing. 'Ah, fuck,' he sighed, wondering how he could have had something so amazing and screwed it up quite so badly.

CHAPTER FORTY

'I think we've done it,' said Sam triumphantly, then looked a little deflated when Hannah didn't respond with whoops and cheers. She'd been back at the country club for two weeks, and so far had said very little about what had happened on her trip, beyond the usual small talk about weather and flight delays and the odd story of fun nights out. The weight she'd been dragging around since she'd left Spain was getting lighter and more manageable, but it had been replaced by the stress of juggling the shift rota for the looming summer holidays.

'Good work,' she said. 'How did you manage it?'

'Overtime for both of us, a few of the casuals from last year, a couple of newbies.'

'And I'm not coaching any tennis, right?' asked Hannah.

'Nope,' said Sam with a grin. 'The sessions are all booked up, but we can manage with the coaches we've got. Unless anyone gets sick or falls under a bus.'

'Bubble-wrap them all,' said Hannah with a half-smile. 'I'm not doing it.'

'Hello?' said a snippy female voice. 'Are you going to leave me standing here much longer?'

Hannah and Sam both turned from the rota on the screen to see a woman tapping her manicure on the edge of the desk, swishing her immaculate curtain of blonde hair like a

343

pony swatting flies. Hannah knew her as Sophia Carmichael, wife of Jack Carmichael – they'd been members of the country club since just after Hannah started working there and had three spoiled, obnoxious sons.

'Sorry,' said Hannah. 'What can I do for you?'

'I need to book my three boys onto summer holiday tennis,' said Sophia, wrapping her hair round her fist and securing it into a bun with a hairband. 'Felix is nine and Archie and Albert are seven. I'm actually in a hurry, so can you just make a note and I'll fill out any forms later?' She artfully pulled out a few strands around her face, then checked her reflection in the glass cabinet of golf trophies.

'Oh,' said Hannah. 'We don't actually have any spaces left for tennis this summer. They were all booked up weeks ago.' She braced herself for incoming fury, already wishing she and Sam hadn't agreed to work their Friday off. Janice had asked for the favour because she'd been to a funeral in London this morning; she was due back any minute, but it almost certainly wasn't going to be soon enough.

Sophia's mouth fell open, revealing two rows of perfect white teeth. 'What?' she said, her eyes widening in panic. 'That's not possible. I need to book them all in now. I can't look after them for the whole holidays.'

You gave birth to them, thought Hannah, who saw Sophia here all the time so she clearly didn't have a job. 'We're completely booked up,' she said with her best conciliatory smile. 'We do send an email to all our members telling them to book early. But I can put you on the waiting list for any cancellations?'

The woman's eyes narrowed. 'That's completely unacceptable,' she spat. 'This is a private country club, not Woking

344

fucking Leisure Centre.' She pointed a finger in Hannah's face. 'You make as many spaces available as your members need. That's what we pay for.'

'I don't think . . .' said Sam, putting his hand on the counter.

'I'm not interested in what you think,' said the woman, giving Sam a top-to-toe look and clearly deciding she didn't much like what she saw. 'I'm not moving until all three names are on your list, and I'm really happy to talk to the manager if that's what it takes.'

'I AM the manager,' said Hannah through gritted teeth.

'Is everything OK?' said Janice, taking in the scene as she came down the stairs. 'Mrs Carmichael? Can I help?'

'I'm trying to book my three boys in for summer tennis,' said Sophia. 'But Hannah here –' she squinted at Hannah's name badge, even though Hannah knew full well that Sophia knew her name, '– isn't being very helpful.'

'Right,' said Janice. 'Do we not have any spaces, Hannah?'

'No,' said Hannah. 'We're at full capacity.'

'Then make MORE capacity,' said Sophia icily, then turned to Janice. 'My nanny has left, it's an absolute nightmare.'

'Oh,' said Janice with a sympathetic head tilt. 'I'm so sorry.'

'She's a lying bitch,' muttered Sophia. 'Made some fake accusation about Jack touching her up. Like he'd ever do anything like that.'

I bet he would, thought Hannah, who'd been on the receiving end of plenty of winks and leers from Jack Carmichael, and once a hand brushing her backside as he passed her on the stairs leading down to the spa. She couldn't prove it wasn't accidental and decided at the time it wasn't worth making a fuss about.

'I'm sure we can sort things out, Mrs Carmichael,' said Janice. 'Leave it with me, I'll drop you an email to confirm.'

'Thank you,' said Sophia, giving Hannah a fuck-you glare as she stalked out of reception towards the car park.

'Hannah, come and see me when you've got a minute,' said Janice, heading into the back office and closing the door behind her. Hannah sighed and rolled her eyes at Sam, who shook his head.

'You in danger, girl,' he said, doing his best Whoopi Goldberg impression.

'I honestly don't care,' said Hannah. 'That rota took for ever; I'm not sure why we bother.'

'Well,' said Sam. 'That's a very big question. Because you've been totally miserable ever since you got back from Spain, and if you ask me it feels a bit like your heart's no longer in this job.' She gave him a sharp look, and he held up his hands. 'I'm just saying.'

Hannah looked at him for a moment, then let out a heavy sigh. 'No, you're right. I just . . . I don't know. This place feels like part of my old life, I guess. And a month off kind of made me want a new one. I feel like I'm going backwards.'

Sam nodded sagely. 'I get that. But the minute you moonwalk into that office, Janice is going to tell you you're on the coaching team for this summer.'

'Oh God,' breathed Hannah.

'So if you're looking for a new life, now would be a good time to quit.'

Hannah laughed. 'That all sounds great, Sam, but I don't know what the new life looks like yet. I can't just quit my job.'

'Why not? You might not know what you want yet, but

you clearly know what you DON'T want. So deal with that, and work the rest out another day.'

'Really?' said Hannah. 'Even if that meant I abandoned you to Sophia Carmichael and her handsy husband?'

'Even if,' said Sam. 'That's how much I love you.'

Hannah smiled, feeling suddenly calm and focussed. 'OK, I'm going in.'

'Don't be afraid to throw caution to the wind,' said Sam, flourishing a hand in the air. 'I've always got your back.'

'Thanks, Sam. You're the best.'

'So, I guess you'll be leaving us,' said Janice.

'Sorry?' said Hannah, feeling like all the breath had been sucked from her lungs. 'Are you firing me?'

Janice smiled. 'Of course not. But I've known you for a long time, Hannah, and it's very obvious to me and everyone else that you're not happy.'

'No,' said Hannah, lowering herself into one of the office chairs. 'I'm not.'

'Also I'm about to ask you to coach kids' tennis this summer, including the evil Carmichael boys, and I figured that might be the final straw.'

Hannah laughed. 'It is. I'm sorry. I promised before I went away that I wouldn't do this, and I feel terrible.'

'Oh, don't worry about that,' said Janice, waving her arm dismissively. 'Life happens, and I know you wouldn't leave me without a good reason.'

'I do have a good reason,' said Hannah. 'At least, I think it's a good reason.'

'Hmm,' said Janice. 'You don't have to tell me, obviously.

I just need to know that nothing bad happened here, or we did something wrong.'

'It's nothing to do with you,' said Hannah. 'I've loved working here. But it's been ten years, and I think I need a change.'

Janice nodded. 'So. When do you want to go?'

'What are my options?' Hannah felt like things were suddenly moving incredibly fast, although if she was honest this decision had only been one obnoxious customer away from being made since the day she got back from Spain.

'How about you finish your shift today, then don't come back?'

'Really?'

'If you like. My daughter loved covering your job while you were away, and she definitely doesn't want to go back to working in hotels. We can offer Sam a promotion to your role, he's earned it. And then Steph can join the team full-time, if you think that would work. We'll find another casual coach to make up the shortfall, and then we're all good.'

'I'm sure it would work,' said Hannah. 'Steph did a great job while I was away, and that's brilliant news for Sam.'

'I expect he'll miss you,' said Janice kindly. 'I know I will.'

'I'll miss all of you,' said Hannah. 'But I definitely need a change.'

'Yes, I think you do. Where are you going to go?'

'I'm not sure. It depends.'

'On what?' Janice smiled knowingly. 'Or is it a who?'

Hannah shook her head emphatically. 'This change isn't about anyone else. It's all for me.' *It is*, she thought. *Rob isn't the destination, he's just a lesson learned along the way.*

'Well, that's exactly how it should be. Good for you.'

Janice stood up and opened her arms and Hannah moved in for a hug.

'Thank you,' said Hannah, leaning into Janice's shoulder as she felt the weight pressing on her shoulders lift just a little.

'So, now you've quit your job and scored me an epic promotion,' said Sam, sloshing more wine into Hannah's glass from the bottle in the ice bucket on the table, 'are you finally going to tell me what happened in Spain?'

Hannah shrugged, looking around at the busy bar. She and Graham used to come in here sometimes, on the rare occasions they had something to celebrate. The last time had been her thirtieth birthday, after a tense dinner at the gastropub next door where Graham had kicked off because the waiter didn't write down the details of his various allergies. Graham hated waiters who didn't write stuff down; in his opinion people with memories that good should work for MI6. Hannah had pointed out that maybe the waiter DID work for MI6, and being a waiter was his undercover mission. Graham had asked her why she always needed the final word and the evening had pretty much gone downhill from there.

'Nothing much to tell,' she said now. 'Played tennis, met a guy, went on a road trip with him for a week, nothing happened.'

'Shit, that's intense. You got a picture? I need to get a look at Mr Nothing Happened.'

Hannah picked up her phone and opened up the Club Colina website, taking her time so Sam didn't realise it was a shortcut on her homepage. Rob's picture appeared on the coaches' page, along with a couple of paragraphs of blurb about his various sporting and coaching achievements. He was wearing his white Club Colina tennis shirt and blue shorts, his tanned biceps glowing in the sunshine and his sunglasses propped on his head.

'Here,' she said, handing Sam the phone.

'Holy fucking Mary mother of Jesus,' said Sam. 'He looks like the love child of all the Hemsworths.'

'I know,' said Hannah with a grin.

'You went on a road trip with a Hemsworth for a week, and nothing happened?'

'Oh, loads happened on the road trip, but not between Rob and me.'

'No kissing? Quick hand job? Cheeky finger?'

'Nope,' said Hannah, feeling her face flush. 'We nearly kissed at one point, but Scrumpy got in the way.'

'You chose cider over THAT?'

Hannah laughed. 'No, Scrumpy is a dog Rob rescued on our travels.'

'Shit, he's a Hemsworth who rescues dogs? I think I might be in love.'

Hannah smiled but said nothing.

'So no kissing. Not even a lingering snog when you said goodbye?' Sam zoomed in on the photo, taking in every square inch of Rob's tanned thighs.

Hannah looked away guiltily, feeling like she was no longer entirely in control of this conversation.

'You did say goodbye, right?' asked Sam, ducking his head to catch her eye.

She shook her head guiltily. 'No. I just left. Spent a few days hiking on my own, then got a plane home feeling awful.'

'Wow,' said Sam, holding up the palms of his hands. 'So when did you last talk to him?'

'The Friday before I left, when I told him, his family and my family to fuck off.'

Sam boggled at her, his mouth hanging open. 'OK, I feel like I've missed several episodes of this soap opera.'

'I've made it sound more dramatic than it was.' The phrase rang a bell even as she said the words – had she said them to her dad on Joyce's terrace, or on the hill, when she was telling him about the night she'd gone to Rob's room and inadvertently got him fired? That night had been a turning point for Hannah; a moment of spontaneous madness when she'd decided to invite Rob on her road trip. It had felt empowering and exciting at the time, and she wondered if she'd ever have that feeling again.

'Right, but you definitely can't leave things like that.'

'Why not?' said Hannah, pushing the pain in her chest down into her abdomen. 'I'll probably never see him again.'

'Because you were OBVIOUSLY crazy about each other,' said Jess, appearing at the table with Trish and Gaynor and dumping another bottle of wine and three glasses on the table.

'What are you all doing here?' asked Hannah, her mind reeling.

'Sam messaged me before you left work,' replied Jess. 'Told us to get down here because you'd quit your job and were having some kind of emotional crisis.'

'Wait, how do you know Sam?' said Hannah, looking at them all in confusion.

'I rang the country club and tracked him down when we got back from Spain, told him how much I loved your new look. He's taking me shopping next Friday.'

351

'And me the following Friday,' said Gaynor. 'He has a great future ahead of him, making the women of Woking look fabulous.'

'I've got no money so I'll just borrow all their clothes,' added Trish. 'So what's the deal here?'

'Sam's trying to persuade me that things aren't done with Rob.'

'He's right,' said Jess, shuffling everyone along the bench seat so she could squeeze in. 'You're just scared of how you feel about him, and that makes it easier to run away.'

'But you all told me to come home,' Hannah protested.

'I know,' said Jess. 'Because you needed some perspective to work through how you felt. But that was two weeks ago, and you're clearly still bonkers about him.'

Hannah sighed heavily. 'Maybe, I don't know. It all feels like such a mess; I don't really have the right words.'

'Fine, explain it in tennis terms,' said Gaynor with a grin.

Hannah laughed and looked up at the four of them. In some ways she'd known all of them for years, but had only really opened up to their friendship in the past couple of months. And yet every one of them had dropped everything to be in this bar and make sure she was OK. The thought made her want to cry.

'OK, I'll try,' she said, furrowing her brow thoughtfully. 'It's like, neither of us was mentally ready for the match, our heads weren't in the right place. And then things got disrupted – I don't know – distractions from the crowd, a dog invading the court, whatever. So we never really found our flow, and then in the end the match was called off. Rain stopped play.'

'I have literally no idea what you're talking about,' said Sam.

'Right,' said Jess, nodding along. 'But what you've described is just a temporary interruption. Play can resume at any time.'

Hannah shook her head. 'I'm not sure we're meant to finish this match.'

'See, here's the thing about tennis,' said Gaynor, laying her palms flat on the table. 'If you miss a serve, what happens?'

'What do you mean?'

Gaynor smiled patiently. 'What happens if your first serve hits the net?'

'I don't . . . I mean, you get a second serve, obviously.'

'Exactly,' said Gaynor. 'It's one of the only sports that gives you a second try if you fuck up the first time round.'

Hannah looked at them all. 'So what does that mean?'

'It means the match isn't over,' said Jess softly. 'You've got a second serve.'

'Right,' said Hannah. 'And how does that play out, exactly?'

'You get the first flight back to Spain and resume play. You can't just leave things like this.'

'Really?'

'Yes, Hannah,' said Gaynor. 'Maybe Rob is your second serve, and maybe he isn't. But if you don't play on, you'll never know.'

'She's right,' said Trish. 'Much as it pains me to admit it, you're walking away from a match you can absolutely win.'

'Are we still labouring this awful tennis metaphor?' asked Sam.

'Yes,' said Gaynor. 'And I'm the umpire, so pipe the fuck down.' She turned to Hannah and sloshed more wine in her glass. 'You've quit your job, so go and see him, have the big conversation, agree if this thing between you is or isn't happening. Then you can stop wallowing and get on with your life either way.'

'Or alternatively,' added Sam. 'Tell him you love him, then let me style your huge white Hemsworth wedding.'

'So what are you saying?' asked Hannah. 'That I should just fly out there and see him?'

'I'm already on the EasyJet website,' said Jess, tapping frantically at her phone. 'Shit, nothing from Gatwick to Malaga until four p.m. tomorrow. The flights in the morning are all full.'

'Saturday's his day off,' said Hannah. 'He could have gone off somewhere by then. This isn't going to work, guys.'

'You could message him?' said Trish. 'Tell him you're coming?'

Hannah sighed. 'I deleted his number. I was staring at it feeling sad all the time, so I got rid of it.'

'Christ, you've got it bad,' muttered Trish. 'Maybe you could call Club Colina? Ask reception to get a message to him?'

'Yeah,' said Hannah. 'I guess I could leave a message and tell him to ring me?'

'No,' said Jess. 'You need to go over there. This is too big a conversation to have on the phone.'

Hannah thought for a minute, weighing up all the options, then nodded. 'OK.'

'Wait, are you really going to do this?' asked Sam incredulously.

'Yes,' said Hannah, nodding emphatically. 'I've spent my entire life overthinking everything, so I'm going to be spontaneous.'

'Okaaay,' said Sam, looking doubtful.

'No, it's fine,' said Hannah, feeling the blood start to flow in her veins for the first time in weeks. 'I've done it four times in my life so far – kicking Graham out, agreeing to go on a tennis holiday, asking Rob on my road trip, and quitting my job. I don't regret any of those decisions, so I'm going for a fifth.'

'Got one,' said Jess triumphantly. 'EasyJet from Bristol. Leaves at nine thirty tomorrow morning, so you'll be there by lunchtime.'

'Nothing earlier?' said Hannah. 'No six a.m. flights?' Having embraced this idea, she was now itching to go and draw a line under this thing one way or the other.

'Not in this half of the country,' said Jess. 'I can check Ryanair from Stansted?'

'Christ, she's not that desperate,' muttered Gaynor. 'No man is worth Ryanair from Stansted.'

'OK,' said Hannah. 'At least we'll get the afternoon and evening together, then I can come back on Sunday, or maybe go and see Dad for a bit. Depending on how things go.'

'You sure you want to do this?' said Jess, her finger hovering over her phone.

'I don't know,' said Hannah, suddenly unsure. 'Do I?'

'It comes to a hundred and seventy quid, one way. Another fifty quid if you want a cabin bag.'

'That much, for one way?'

'Yeah,' shrugged Jess. 'But it's tomorrow, and there's only one seat left.'

Hannah swallowed and took a deep breath. 'OK,' she said, looking round at the others. 'Should I do this?'

'Hell yeah,' said Sam. 'You could be banging a fake Hemsworth in less than eighteen hours.'

Hannah looked at Trish, who nodded and smiled, despite looking a little sick. 'Go for it,' she said firmly. 'This match definitely isn't over.'

'Gaynor?'

'Absolutely,' said Gaynor, topping up everyone's glass. 'Second serve, mate. Gotta be done.'

CHAPTER FORTY-ONE

When Rob woke up in the early hours of Saturday morning it was still dark outside. He stared at the shadows on the ceiling for a while, then reached over to check the watch his parents had given him for his twenty-first birthday. Three thirty. He'd been asleep for four hours, and apparently that was all he was getting.

Like every day for the past few weeks, Rob had fallen asleep thinking about Hannah, and woken up still thinking about her like no time had passed at all. It felt like a gnawing pain in his stomach that wouldn't go away; a yearning he hadn't felt since he was a kid and spent all of Christmas Eve praying that Santa would bring him a Buzz Lightyear toy.

He rolled over onto his side and picked out the glowing white of his tennis shoes by the door, next to his tennis bag. This room was much bigger and nicer than the one on the first floor he'd started out in, and he wondered if that was Mark's doing. His old room was now occupied by an American coach called Amy who was working exclusively with a couple of up-and-coming future tennis stars from Croatia. She was in her late twenties and single and had been flirting with Rob all week. Yesterday she'd asked him on a date and he'd briefly considered it, just for the opportunity to stop thinking about Hannah for five minutes. In fact five minutes was probably ambitious, considering how long it was

357

since he'd last had sex. He thought about when that was – Nina, the night before he left for Spain. Two months ago, which was probably the longest he'd gone without getting laid since he was fifteen years old.

He picked up his phone and opened WhatsApp. Still no photo or timestamp for Hannah, although obviously she wasn't putting his number back into her phone unless he told her what it was. He scrolled to his browser and the page for Upton Country Club, which had a smiling photo of Hannah standing behind a desk with a small team of reception and admin staff. Her outfit was frumpy and her hair was longer and didn't suit her. He remembered Trish saying she'd had some kind of glow-up before their trip, but it was hard to reconcile this woman with the gorgeous, sexy Hannah he knew.

The only other photos he'd found during his various snooping sessions were on the website for her tennis club, where she seemed to have won every cup going in the previous season. These photos felt more familiar; Hannah's hair held back by a sun visor or a hairband, and endless legs that could never, ever look frumpy in tennis gear. She had no Facebook or Instagram pages, but he already knew that. He was all out of stalking options, and he also hadn't forgotten what Luke had said about leaving her be.

Rob sighed, feeling twitchy and unsettled. He switched back to WhatsApp, scrolling through the endless messages from women he'd dated over the past couple of years. A gallery of twenty- and thirty-somethings, mostly slim and pretty and natural-looking, although he wasn't hung up on any particular hair or skin colour. There were so many Sophies in his phone he'd had to give them descriptive surnames. Sophie Boat Party. Sophie Wimbledon. Sophie Ricks Sister.

As he scrolled the names they all started to blend into one, and it made him flush with shame to realise that he could barely remember some of these women, even when he read their messages. Jas, a two-night hook-up from a trip to Ibiza with some old school mates. *That was fun, I'm going back to Toronto tomorrow but I'll let you know when I'm next in the UK.* He could remember what she looked like, but not where they went or what they did beyond having a lot of sex. Niamh, a drop-dead gorgeous primary school teacher from Dublin who'd been in Bath for a hen weekend. *You're cute and a great fuck. Thanks for a fun night.* Was she the screamer, or was that Siobhan, the other Irish girl he'd hooked up with not long after? He'd had to ask both of them to write their names in his phone because he couldn't spell them.

And then most recently of the women before Hannah, a message from Nina sent a couple of hours after she'd stormed out of his flat, read while he was waiting in the departure lounge at the airport.

I'm not going to say sorry for getting emotional – when you have feelings for someone you have to tell them, even if your timing is shit. Have fun in Spain.

He thought again about what Luke had said, about how Hannah had made her decision and he had to respect that. It had been over three weeks; maybe she'd stopped thinking about him by now. Or maybe she'd stopped thinking about him the minute she'd left Spain. She'd deleted his number, which was pretty clear in its intention. It was pretty fucking arrogant of him to assume she was pining as hard as he was. He wished he could call his dad, but their chats about

359

Hannah hadn't been much use either. *You've done the right thing, son. Give her space, and if it's meant to be, she'll come back to you.* It felt like some kind of inspirational Instagram quote – uplifting on paper, absolutely bloody useless in practice.

The knock on the door made him jump – who the hell was that at 4 a.m.? He pulled on a T-shirt over his boxers, very much hoping it wasn't a drunk Olly looking for trouble. They'd done their best to keep their distance since Rob had returned to the Club, knowing that Mark was watching their every move and would fire them both in a heartbeat if there was any aggro. He peered through the peephole but there was nobody there, so he opened the door.

'Hey,' said Amy, sliding into the doorway. She was wearing tiny white denim shorts that barely covered her backside, paired with an oversized pink shirt that had fallen off one tanned shoulder. No bra, bare feet. In fact, not very much outfit at all. Her long, tousled hair was all on one side, dirty blonde at the roots and white at the tips. She leaned against the doorway, and Rob couldn't tell if it was all part of the sexy look, or just that she was so pissed she couldn't hold herself upright.

'Amy, it's four in the morning,' said Rob, raking his hand through his hair. 'What do you want?'

'I want what all drunk girls want at four in the morning,' said Amy with a seductive smile. Rob was pretty sure that was a line from a movie, but he couldn't think which one, and now didn't seem like a good time to ask. 'I want you,' she added breathily, taking a step forward and sliding her warm hand under his T-shirt and around his waist.

'Amy, I . . .' said Rob.

'Ssh,' whispered Amy, pressing her hips against his and tilting her head until her lips were just a few inches from his. She smelled of wine and pure, unadulterated lust, which made his head swim. 'Just do what feels right.'

Rob looked at her for a long moment, feeling that familiar stirring in his shorts. *What feels right, in this moment, right now?* he thought, then reached out and wove his fingers into her other hand.

CHAPTER FORTY-TWO

Hannah waited impatiently by the departure gate window at Bristol Airport, watching a tiny drama play out on the tarmac outside. A man in a high-vis jacket was gesticulating wildly at the set of steps currently a few inches from the exit door at the front of the plane, whilst other men in high-vis jackets were rubbing their jaws thoughtfully as they tried to come up with a way to fill this particular void.

The inbound flight had arrived ten minutes ago, but clearly nobody was getting off until the steps and the plane had come together in aviation matrimony, even though you could easily step over the gap. Obviously that would be a health and safety nightmare, but Hannah wasn't worried about that right now. If nobody was getting off the plane, she wasn't getting on, which made Rob feel further away with every passing minute.

The stress of it all was starting to make her arms itch, and she wondered for the hundredth time if Rob had got the message she'd left with the receptionist at Club Colina last night. *Don't go anywhere tomorrow. I'll be there by lunch. We need to talk.* She'd made the woman write it down and read it back to her, then promise to take it up to Rob's room immediately – Hannah had even given her his room number. But she had no way of knowing if he'd received it – wouldn't he have texted if he had? Just a basic *Got your note, I'll be here.* Or even *Don't come, I'm spending the weekend on a yacht with Megan Fox.*

Finally the steps made contact with the plane, and the passengers started to disembark. She watched them mooch across the tarmac and through the door to the inbound corridor on the other side of the glass wall, looking moodily up at the grey sky and bracing against the sideways wind. One by one they all filed up the stairs and past the waiting outbound passengers, all sporting that grumpy look of tired, post-holiday blues. Even that handsome guy in the blue hoodie who looked a bit like . . . Rob.

That's actually Rob, thought Hannah with a gasp, pushing through the crowd to reach the glass wall. Her heart was pounding in her ears and nothing about this situation made sense, but the fact remained that Rob had just got off the plane she was about to get on. He walked within a few feet of her, but even though a woman glanced her way when she hammered on the glass wall, Rob didn't notice. She could see he was wearing giant headphones and felt a frisson of panic as he disappeared from view, presumably heading towards passport control and baggage reclaim. If she couldn't track him down before he left the terminal, there was no way of knowing where he might be headed next.

Hannah shouldered her backpack and pushed through the crowd once again to the passenger help desk, which was manned by a woman with an on-brand orange face and the tightest ponytail Hannah had ever seen.

'I need to get back to Arrivals,' she gasped. The woman's name tag said 'Fay'.

'Sorry?' said Fay. 'Can I help?' Her accent was pure West Country.

'I'm not getting on this plane, I've changed my mind. I need to get back to Arrivals to meet someone who's just got off it.'

Fay sighed with her whole body and shook her head slowly, like her day had just taken a distinct turn for the worse. 'Right.'

Hannah jigged around desperately. 'I was going to fly to Spain to tell a man I love him. But I've just watched him get off the plane that's just arrived.'

'Right,' said Fay again, glancing at her screen like she wasn't giving Hannah her full attention. Hannah wondered if she was frantically looking for the panic button.

'But he didn't see me from the other side of the glass, so now I need to get to the Arrivals area before he leaves the airport.'

'OK,' said Fay doubtfully. 'Why can't you just call him?'

'Because I don't have his number.'

Fay's eyebrows shot up. 'You're going to Spain to tell a man you love him, but you don't have his number?'

'I deleted it. It's a long story. Look, can I go back the way I came? Please?'

Faye shook her head and rolled her eyes. 'You can't just go wherever you like in an airport, my love, there are security measures. It's not like in the movies. Honestly, that little kid in *Love Actually* properly drives me mad. Little bastard would get tasered if he pulled that shit here.'

'Right, great,' said Hannah, forcing a smile so as not to antagonise Fay, even though she'd happily taser her all the way to the border with Devon. 'So how do I get out of here?'

'You need an escort. It's a proper pain in the arse, to be fair. Usually it's for people who swan in after the gate has closed. Once they've stopped screaming at us, we get them escorted back so they can buy another ticket, or go home.'

'Great, perfect,' said Hannah. 'Can we do that?'

'Most of the time they lose track of time in Duty Free,' said Fay, lowering her voice and leaning forward like she was sharing secret airport intel. 'Or they've had one pint too many in the pub. Don't realise some of the gates are, like, a fifteen-minute walk from Departures. Well, you'd know that. You've just walked here.'

'I know, and now I really, really need to walk back. Or run, ideally. Before he leaves the airport.'

'Aww, my love, I'm not being funny, but this is Bristol Airport on a Saturday in June. It's like the last days of Rome down there, he'll be lucky if he's out before dark. God help him if he's got checked baggage. That's probably halfway to Glasgow by now.'

'I don't know if he's got luggage or not, but I'd rather not risk it.'

Fay smiled and reached over the counter to pat Hannah's arm; her acrylic nails were at least an inch long and had been painted like a sunset. 'Is he worth it, do you reckon?' she whispered conspiratorially. 'You could be on a Spanish beach in time for your lunch. All-you-can-eat paella and a jug of sangria, absolutely lush.'

'He's definitely worth it,' said Hannah, hoping Fay could see the desperation in her eyes. 'Please.'

'Well, in that case, I'll call you one of the Ground Handlers to escort you back, shall I? It might take a while, so I'd grab a seat and pop a bit of make-up on if I were you.'

Hannah laughed nervously. 'Do I really look that bad?'

'You look bloody amazing, love,' said Fay. 'But this is like one of those scenes from a chick flick, isn't it? You might as well go all in.'

'Rob,' said Hannah softly, reaching out to touch his arm as he walked past the metal barrier. Despite one of the most stressful airport walks of her life, accompanied by the world's slowest and most talkative man, she'd made it back to Arrivals. She'd spent the past ten minutes watching the flow of people coming through the doors, the worry that he'd already left the terminal giving her stomach cramps. But now he was here, and it made her want to cry with relief.

Rob jumped and did a double take, then yanked off his headphones and shook his head in confusion. 'Hannah. What are you doing here?'

Hannah shrugged and smiled. 'Waiting for you.'

'But . . . I didn't tell anyone I was coming. How did you know?'

'I was at the gate. I watched you get off the plane.'

'What were you doing at the gate?' gasped Rob. 'Where were you going?'

'To Malaga, to see you.'

Rob's jaw dropped open in surprise. 'Really? That's insane. I was coming here to see you.'

Hannah took in the whole of him, finally giving in to the reality of how much she'd missed him. He looked as breathless and blown away as she felt – surely this was all a good thing? That he'd flown back to see her?

'Were you really?' she asked, wanting to check that she hadn't got this all wrong and he'd come back for a family funeral or something.

'Yeah. I quit Club Colina. Well, not technically because

Mark was still asleep when I left for the airport. But I'm going to email him later and quit.'

'You're quitting? How come?'

Rob shrugged off his rucksack and put it on the floor next to his suitcase and tennis bag, then gave Hannah a penetrating look. 'Shit, I can't believe this.' He took a couple of deep breaths. 'It didn't feel right. You being here and me being there. I feel like I've lost an arm or something, and I can't stop thinking about you. And that makes me think that maybe we should stop being dicks and tell each other how we feel.'

Hannah smiled, wondering how long he'd spent working on that little speech. 'You've never even kissed me,' she said, reaching out to take his hand.

'Can I kiss you now?' he asked, his eyes wide as he softly wove his fingers into hers.

'No, I'm sorry,' she said. 'I'm not kissing you for the first time outside WHSmith in Bristol Airport.' She was buying herself time, trying to control the cage of butterflies in her stomach. Everything felt like it was moving too fast and she wanted to remember every moment.

'Why not?' said Rob, taking her other hand and running his thumb across the back of it in a way that made her knees feel like they were made of sponge. 'Airports are romantic.'

'Still no,' laughed Hannah. 'But we should probably book another flight back to Spain.'

'Why?' asked Rob. 'I've quit my job.'

'I thought we'd just established that you haven't actually quit your job. Technically this could be a day trip to England.'

'I suppose.'

367

'But I HAVE quit mine.'

'Whoah, really?'

Hannah nodded happily. 'Yeah. I've been there ten years and need to do something different.'

'So what's your plan?' They were still holding hands, their fingers clasped together like that's where they'd always belonged.

'Take the rest of the summer off, think about what I want to do next. Luke and Dan want to properly rent my place, so I don't need to make any big decisions right now.'

'And what if I told you I'm crazy about you and want us to be together?' said Rob quickly. 'Would that make any difference to your plans?' His eyes were full of love and hope, and Hannah couldn't believe she'd nearly let this man slip through her fingers.

'Yes,' she said, nodding furiously. 'That was what I was coming to talk to you about. Whether you and I could give things a go, and maybe I could stay in Spain until the end of the season. Hang out with you, spend some time with my dad and Scrumpy, see how things pan out.'

'And what if I'd said no?' said Rob, smiling playfully.

'Then I'd have headed off somewhere else,' said Hannah emphatically. 'This decision is mostly about me, Rob; I don't want you to think I'm dropping everything just for you. But I also think maybe there could be an us, if we really want it. ARE you saying no?'

'Are you fucking kidding me?' Rob laughed. 'I've just flown back at the crack of dawn so I could tell you in person that I love you. I just wish I'd done it weeks ago.'

'I left a message with the hotel last night,' said Hannah, her brow furrowed, pushing aside the fact that Rob had just told her he loved her. It felt too huge to process right now. 'I told them to take it to Room one-four-two, but clearly you didn't get it.'

'I've moved rooms,' Rob said quickly. 'I think there's another coach in there now.'

'Weird,' said Hannah. 'The message had your name on it, you'd have thought he'd have passed it on.'

Rob gave a manic laugh, looking vaguely flustered. 'So what do we do now?'

Hannah smiled and shrugged. 'Book two seats back to Spain on the next flight, I guess.'

'Christ, that's going to be expensive,' said Rob.

Hannah shrugged. 'Yeah, but I've still got that money we won playing tennis. The bit we never spent staying in amazing places.'

'Yeah, sorry about that,' said Rob with a grin, leaning in hopefully for a kiss. Hannah pulled away, eternally conscious of the bustle and crowds of people around them. Nobody was looking at them, but it still felt too public for their first kiss. She let go of one hand and led him to a bench by the window, where Rob sat with his arm around her while she scrolled through Skyscanner. She could feel his fingers in her hair and his warm breath on her neck, and resisted the temptation to turn her face to his. He felt so close, and he couldn't fail to notice the goosebumps on her arms.

'Here,' she said. 'Ryanair at three thirty. Wow, that's expensive.'

'How much?' asked Rob.

'Never mind,' said Hannah, silently clocking how much luggage Rob had. 'Let's do it anyway.'

'OK,' said Rob mildly. 'You're in charge of this plan, apparently.'

Hannah grinned. 'In which case, can you get me a coffee while I book two seats?'

Rob bounded to his feet and headed off to the café, leaving Hannah to complete their booking and process everything that had just happened. She'd envisaged various scenarios for their conversation today, but none of them had involved declarations of love in Bristol Airport. The ache in her chest had been replaced by some kind of fizzing anticipation, like suddenly the fog had lifted and the world seemed full of possibility again.

'Flat white,' said Rob, appearing in front of her ten minutes later. 'Are we all booked?'

Hannah nodded, standing up to take the drink. 'Yep. Check-in opens in four hours.'

'What are we going to do until then?' said Rob.

Hannah instantly knew what she wanted, and wondered if this might be one spontaneous decision too many. She'd quit her job and booked a flight to Spain in the space of two days – but didn't all good things come in threes?

'When you decided to get on that plane this morning,' she said, taking his hands and pulling him down onto the bench beside her, 'how did you imagine today panning out?'

'I don't know,' said Rob. 'I was going to go to my parents' place today to dump my stuff, then drive down to Surrey to find you tomorrow. I planned to start with your tennis club, but I hadn't got much further than that, really.'

'But we're both here.'

'Yeah. We are.' He gave her that smile again, the one that she felt in the deepest, darkest part of her.

'Gaynor said something to me yesterday,' Hannah said quietly, shuffling along the bench so she was a little closer. 'About how one of the great things about tennis is that if you mess up your first serve, you get another go.'

'That's incredibly profound and romantic,' said Rob, sliding his hand around her neck, his thumb tucking a stray curl behind her ear. 'Seriously, Hannah,' he whispered. 'You really are going to have to let me kiss you.'

'Fine,' breathed Hannah, her voice catching in her throat. 'You can kiss me.'

'What, now? Right here? Outside WHSmith?'

'You win. I can't wait any longer,' whispered Hannah with a slow smile, tilting her head and closing her eyes as the last remaining gap between them finally closed.

CHAPTER FORTY-THREE

Rob waited by the boxy sofas and the fake plants in the hotel reception, watching as Hannah had an intense, whispered conversation with the woman behind the desk. He would probably have made up something about a flight delay, but Hannah wasn't big on elaborate lies. Although she presumably wasn't going with 'Look, I've just kissed that guy over there for the first time and now we'd really like to spend four hours naked in your hotel.'

He fidgeted with the straps on his rucksack, his nerves jangling with breathless anticipation. He'd been thinking about this moment for weeks, wondering whether it would ever actually happen, or whether he and Hannah just weren't the right match. Women in his life had been a revolving door, but he couldn't remember any pre-sex build-up feeling as momentous as this. Plenty of fun times, sure. A few encounters that really got him going, absolutely. But this? This felt pivotal, somehow, like the beginning of something new and different and meaningful.

He thought about Amy last night, and how the old Rob might have behaved in that situation. But instead of being a temptation, Amy turning up at his room had been a catalyst for this decision; a realisation that he didn't want superficial, two-dimensional relationships any more. The sex probably would have been great, but it would just have been a temporary high, a momentary feeding of a beast that could no longer be satisfied by women like Amy. So, he'd taken her hand and walked her back to the first floor, telling her firmly but kindly that he absolutely wasn't interested and she needed to go to bed. Then he'd run back to his room, locked the door and packed his bags, then called a taxi to the airport. Had Amy received the message from Hannah that was meant for him? Possibly. And if so, had that prompted her to launch a seduction mission before the competition arrived? Probably. And people said men played games.

'You OK?' asked Hannah, coming back from reception with a key card in her hand.

'Definitely,' said Rob. 'Are we all sorted?' His palms felt clammy and he was suddenly a bundle of disconnected limbs trying to pick up his luggage without tripping over a coffee table. *What's wrong with me?* he thought. In a previous life he'd been a practised seducer, and now he was Rob the Awkward Virgin.

'Yep,' said Hannah, waving the key card. 'Are you coming?' He could hear the nervous tremor in her voice and resisted the temptation to say 'I certainly hope so' like the comedy legend he was. So instead he just smiled and nodded and followed her to the lift.

'I keep expecting one of our family to appear,' Hannah said breathlessly as they silently ascended to the fifth floor. 'Or Scrumpy.'

'Maybe the fire alarm will go off,' he laughed, playing along to break the tension. 'Or, I don't know, a plague of locusts or something.'

Hannah laughed, a full-body expression of relief and happiness that they were here together, and nothing was getting in their way this time. Rob knew how she felt.

The room was small and clean, like all airport hotels, and they both made a meal of quietly putting their bags by the bed and using the bathroom to delay the inevitable. Rob thanked the heavens that he'd had a shower before leaving Spain this morning, although another one definitely wouldn't go amiss at some point. Maybe later, with Hannah.

They met by the hotel window, drinking each other in, both waiting for the other to make the next move. In the end it was Hannah who broke first, leaning in to kiss him gently as she cupped her hands around his face, sliding them up behind his ears and raking her nails through his hair. Kissing Hannah felt so natural, like two sets of lips that fitted together perfectly. How had he wasted so much time NOT kissing her, when they could have been doing it for hours, every day?

'God, you're beautiful,' he breathed.

Hannah pulled away. 'I don't think anyone's ever told me that before.'

'Seriously? How is that possible?'

'Well, you know a lot of that story.'

Rob wove his fingers into hers. 'Come here,' he said, leading her to the edge of the bed. 'Are you OK?'

'Yes. No,' said Hannah with a nervous laugh. 'I'm kind of new to all this.'

'So am I, at least at this level of intensity,' said Rob, leaning over to envelop her hands in his. 'The only thing I know is that I haven't been able to stop thinking about you since you threatened me with a pair of killer heels, so we should probably do something about that.'

'They weren't killer heels,' laughed Hannah. 'And I definitely didn't threaten you.' She stood up and looked at him for a moment, then straddled his lap so she was facing him with her arms wrapped around his neck.

'Just one question,' Rob whispered, too curious not to ask. 'I get that you've only ever slept with one man, but how many have you kissed?'

'Also just one,' breathed Hannah, her lips making a trail from his collarbone to his ear. 'And now it's two.'

'Man, you're good at it,' he said with a smile, pulling her into a deeper kiss. He knew she could feel the hardness of him through his jeans – the people in the room below could probably feel it through the floor, like a gathering storm cloud above their heads. Other women he'd been with would have their clothes off by now, spreadeagled on the bed and begging him to bang them into next week. But Hannah wasn't like that, and he knew he couldn't rush her, much as he was desperate to feel her naked body against his. He slid his hand under the hem of her sweatshirt and trailed his fingers across the bare skin to her ribs, feeling the tiniest flinch as her body tensed.

'Do you want me to stop?' he said.

'No, it feels good,' she said. 'I'm sorry.'

Rob pulled back and looked at her. 'Hey. You don't ever have to apologise. If four hours of kissing you is all I'm allowed, I'll take it.'

Hannah smiled and relaxed a little. 'I think we both know that four hours of kissing would kill us both.' She shifted a little on his lap. It was exquisite, but also agony.

Rob pulled her in tighter to his body, deepening the kiss and letting his hands stroke her neck and back. He could feel her hips grinding into his and the pounding of her heart as his hand gently brushed against her breasts. His other hand drifted over the curve of her hips to her backside, then he quickly pulled it back.

'It's OK,' she whispered into his ear. 'I don't want you to stop.'

'Are you sure?' said Rob, his breath coming in short gasps. 'I don't want you to feel like . . .'

'It's OK,' said Hannah, standing up and taking a step back. She gave him a soft smile, then with one motion crossed her arms over the hem of her sweatshirt and lifted it over her head, along with the T-shirt underneath. She kicked off her trainers and socks and stepped out of her denim skirt, then stood in front of him in just a pale pink bra and matching lace knickers.

'Holy shit,' said Rob, drinking in every inch of her.

'Your turn,' said Hannah nervously.

Rob wrestled off his clothes, managing to get down to his white boxers without falling sideways or trapping anything important in the zip. They both stared at each other, their chests heaving, until their bodies crashed together in a breathless frenzy of hands and lips and limbs tumbling across the bed.

'I don't have any condoms,' gasped Rob into Hannah's neck, trailing his fingers up her spine. 'I hadn't expected this to happen quite so soon and it felt weird to mention it in the airport.'

Hannah smiled and leaned over the side of the bed to rummage in her bag for a small box. 'I bought some. Figured if I was just going to turn up in Spain I should probably be prepared.' She climbed back onto the bed and straddled him again, and for a moment he wished he could freeze time and remember every detail of this moment – the glow of her skin, the smell of her hair, the panting rise and fall of her chest, the feeling of blood and adrenaline racing through his veins. They had hours ahead of them; acres of time to explore and discover each other, and that was just the beginning.

Rob took the box from her hand, his brain scrambled as he tried to balance his urgent desire with his need to not fuck this up. He paused for a moment, his lips parting as she unhooked her bra and tossed it on the floor.

'Rob, I'm absolutely sure,' she whispered, reading his mind as she lay back on the pillows and threw her arms above her head. Every nerve in Rob's body caught fire as the final piece of their jigsaw slid effortlessly into place.

EPILOGUE

September

'Is everyone ready?' asked Barnaby, twisting round in the driving seat of the people carrier and grinning broadly. Hannah and Rob were in the first row of seats, Scrumpy wedged between them so he could see out of the front wind-screen through the gap. Hannah wasn't expecting to make it to the bottom of the hill before he'd scrambled into the front passenger seat like the canine diva he was.

'We're ready,' said Luke, piping up from the rear row of seats. 'Woo,' said Dan with his usual deadpan, but Hannah knew he was happy to be there. It was a ten-day road trip and Barnaby was picking up the entire bill, so being stuck in a rental Citroën Berlingo with his boyfriend's family and a flatulent dog was probably a price worth paying.

'Where to first?' asked Hannah, reaching over to scratch between Scrumpy's ears. Barnaby had planned this road trip like a military operation, and had turned down all Hannah's offers of assistance. So instead she'd stayed busy helping him sell off his belongings and arranging transport of his remaining stuff back to the UK. The boxes had been collected yesterday and would be waiting in Barnaby's rented flat in Guildford when they got back.

She glanced at Rob's profile as he looked out of the window, wondering how he was feeling about leaving. The past three months had been a dream summer for both of them – she'd stayed with her dad in the week, then on Fridays drove back to Club Colina to meet Rob, then hung out with him until Sunday morning when he went back to work and she went back to Barnaby and Scrumpy. She and Rob had spent every Saturday doing something different – road trips, boat trips, picnics, hikes in the hills. In three months she'd banked more happy memories than she'd managed in fourteen years of marriage, and right now it felt like they were just getting started.

'Madrid first,' said Barnaby. 'Then San Sebastian before we cross the border into France. Do a night or two somewhere in the Loire Valley before we push on to Calais.'

'How long are we staying in each place?' asked Luke.

'No idea,' said Barnaby happily. 'Let's decide that as we go along. We've got ten days, so we'll see how things go.'

'That's a good plan,' said Rob, reaching out to take Hannah's hand and giving her a smile that still made her insides turn to mush.

'Excited about your new job, Rob?' asked Barnaby.

'Yeah,' he replied. 'I start first of October, so it gives me time to get Scrumpy settled into my parents' place.'

'Are you and Hannah going to live there too?'

'Just for a few weeks until my old flat is free for us to rent,' said Rob. 'Mum and Dad own that too, so that's really easy. But we can stay in their guest annexe in the meantime.'

'Fancy,' muttered Luke, pulling a face.

'And what about you, Han?' asked Barnaby. 'Any job interviews lined up?'

'Two, both at the end of next week,' said Hannah. 'Bath has loads of country clubs and spa hotels, so I'm not worried.

Rob's parents have offered to dog-sit Scrumpy while we're both at work.'

'Ooh, I meant to tell you,' said Luke. 'I saw Graham the other day. Pushing a *pram*.'

'Yeah,' said Hannah. 'Mum messaged to say they'd had the baby a few weeks ago.'

'A boy,' said Luke. 'Apparently they've called him Xander.'

'Xander?' said Hannah, twisting round in her seat so fast she nearly gave herself whiplash. 'Graham has a child called Xander Chandler?'

'Nope,' said Luke with a smirk. 'Lucy wouldn't let him take Graham's name, I'm not sure she trusts him to stick around long enough. So it's Xander Pearson or something. Apparently she's told him that once they're married she'll change it to Pearson-Chandler.'

'I'm sure Graham is thrilled,' Hannah said drily.

'His mum is spitting feathers, apparently. Also, Lucy's saying she's not interested in Xander being baptised, so that's absolutely kicked off.'

Rob twisted round and smiled at Dan. 'This whole family is really fucking weird,' he said in a stage whisper. 'We may have to form a support group.'

'Definitely,' said Dan, rolling his eyes.

'No swearing in the car, please,' said Barnaby.

'Oh no, it's fine,' said Hannah. 'I swear all the time now. Rob taught me.'

'Rob TAUGHT you?' exclaimed Barnaby, as Luke hooted with laughter. 'How does that work?'

Hannah grinned. 'Wind the window down.'

Barnaby glanced at her suspiciously.

'Go on,' nodded Hannah. 'Wind it down.'

Barnaby sighed and pushed the button to wind down the window, letting in a blast of warm air. 'Now what?'

'Lean your head out, and shout SHIT as loud as you can,' said Hannah, raising her voice against the buffeting wind.

'I'm not doing that,' said Barnaby firmly.

'Come on, it's cathartic,' said Hannah. 'It's about leaving all your shit here in Spain, rather than carrying it with you back to the UK.'

'And that's what happened to you, is it?'

'Yep. I left Graham and Lucy and all my bad decisions in a canyon near Granada.' She turned and gave Rob a soft smile. 'It just took me a while to realise what I'd found instead.'

'Same,' said Rob.

'Fuck's sake, get a room, you two,' muttered Luke. 'Seriously, I might vom.'

'Right,' said Barnaby, gripping the steering wheel. 'How does it go?'

'Shit,' said Hannah. 'Really loud.'

'Or fuck,' Luke chipped in.

'Shit,' said Barnaby, popping his head out of the window for a second, like he was tossing the word out like an apple core.

'Yeah, you need to go a LOT louder, and add some feeling,' said Rob, holding Scrumpy back before he crawled through the gap and clambered over Barnaby so he could stick his head out too.

'SHIIIIT,' shouted Barnaby. 'SHIT SHITTY SHIT.'

'All those years of being embarrassed by my dad that I've missed out on?' said Luke to Dan. 'Totally making up for it right now.'

'Anything else?' said Hannah. 'You might as well let it all out.'

'COCK,' shouted Barnaby. 'COCK AND FANNY.'

Luke gave Dan a meaningful look. 'See? Still bisexual.'

Barnaby closed the window again, plunging the car into silence.

'How was that?' asked Luke.

'Good,' said Barnaby, taking a deep breath. 'Great, actually. Or fucking great, even. Let's go home.'

Hannah turned to Rob, who gave her that smile again, stroking his thumb across the back of her hand in a way that make her wriggle uncomfortably in her seat. 'You ready?' he asked.

'I'm ready,' she said emphatically. 'Definitely.'

She watched the arid landscape fly by for a few minutes, thinking about how far she'd come in the past five months. Her life with Graham felt like ancient history, and now she had a new adventure to look forward to. With Rob, who was on a journey too. Not every game in their match had played out perfectly, but there was no question they made a good team.

Final set, everything to play for, thought Hannah, wondering idly if the hotel her dad had booked in Madrid had a tennis court.

Acknowledgements

I went on my first girls' tennis holiday to Spain in 2014, and never looked back. So my biggest thanks go to my TITS ladies – Carol, Erica, Maggie, Sue A, Sue B, Tamsyn and Vicky – for providing the inspiration and impetus to turn all those cocktails and matches and fun times into a story. All the tennis holiday tales and characters in this book are entirely fictional, apart from the bit with the late-night skinny-dipping and the nipple injury on a pool slide. Thanks, Tam, for letting me tell that story; we definitely should have wet the slide.

Huge thanks to Pip for continuing to be my biggest supporter and champion, and for that incredible road trip in Andalusia that provided so much inspiration for this book, even though we didn't know it at the time. Thanks also to my friend Nigel Scott for explaining how you go backwards through Bristol Airport, to my ex-Army brother Jon for giving so much thought to the best way to frame a metaphor featuring exploding grenades, and to the team at BrandPointZero for feeding me Haribos on my tired and grumpy days.

I'd also like to thank the team at Headline – my brilliant editor, Bea Grabowska, production controller, Rhys Callaghan, publicist, Felicia Hu, copy editor, Sarah Bance, proofreader, Jill Cole and cover designer, Versha Jones. And of course my agent, Caroline Sheldon, who continues to be the publishing mentor of dreams.

And finally, a heartfelt thank you to everyone who has bought one of my other books, left nice reviews, sent me lovely tweets or Insta messages, asked for a preview or a signed copy, supported me via their indie bookshop (with special thanks to Alex at Bert's Books in Swindon, you are an absolute legend), asked me to do an Instagram Live, borrowed one of my books from a library or just generally been kind and generous and supportive. It makes a huge difference on the good days, and on the bad days it's what gets me out of bed. You are the best people.

**Discover more utterly irresistible
novels from Heidi Stephens . . .**

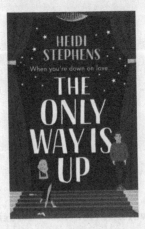

Twenty-five years in showbiz is a good run, right? Because after tonight, when her small (read: huge) wardrobe malfunction was broadcast to the nation's living rooms, Daisy's time in the spotlight might be over.

It's all about damage control now, and Daisy needs an escape route. Fast. Especially when her sporting hero boyfriend publicly announces their engagement – the one she hasn't actually agreed to tell the world about.

All she needs is space from prying eyes and time for the press to get bored and move on. But the only place she can run to at such short notice is the Cotswolds cottage she used to own with her ex-husband. Not ideal, but at least it's in the middle of nowhere and close to her teenage daughter.

Seems like a perfect plan, apart from the person selling stories to the tabloids about her and Tom, the local headmaster.

But that's just a rumour, right?

Available to order

Emily Wilkinson has lost everything. Literally. In a hair-straightener fire. Oh, and her boyfriend (and boss) has announced he's going back to his wife. So, she needs a new job, a new plan, and somewhere to live that isn't her childhood bedroom.

Charles Hunter is looking for a live-in PA to help run Bowford Manor and Emily thinks she's the perfect fit. Well, she's spent ten years propping up demanding men, so she can definitely handle some tricky characters – like Charles's eldest son and heir, who's got plans for the estate that might raise a few eyebrows.

No one's mentioned Jamie though. The stable hand – and youngest Hunter. Dashing, of course, but totally unsuitable. And Emily's not about to make that mistake again.

Definitely not. No, really.

Available to order

ACCENT

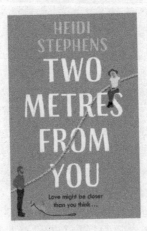

HEIDI
STEPHENS

TWO
METRES
FROM
YOU

Love might be closer
than you think . . .

Gemma isn't sure what upsets her more. The fact she
just caught her boyfriend cheating, or that he did it on
her *brand-new* Heal's cushions.

All she knows is she needs to put as many miles between
her and Fraser as humanly possible. So, when her
best friend suggests a restorative few days in the
West Country, it seems like the perfect solution.

That is, until the country enters a national lockdown
that leaves her stranded. All she has for company is
her dog, Mabel. And the mysterious (and handsome!)
stranger living at the bottom of her garden . . .

Available to order

ACCENT